Oaken

REBELLION

First edition. April 30, 2025.

Copyright © 2025 R.P. Wollbaum.

ISBN: 978-1989210215

Written by R.P. Wollbaum.

Rebellion

R.P. Wollbaum

Chapter One

There was a small bump as the landing craft touched down and the silence was overwhelming as the engines spun down. After a few seconds, the silence was broken by the sound of hydraulics, as the loading ramps along both sides of the craft came down, followed by the sound of running boots on the ramps, as his troops exited the craft.

The commander stood and slowly walked to the nearest exit, making sure his communications links and video transmitter were operating properly, then calmly walked down the ramp to join his command.

"Video and Audio links confirmed," came over the head phones embedded in his helmet, as the commander took in the scene before him.

They had landed on the outskirts of the small community which was located in a small valley, which had gently sloping hills cleared to the tops of the hills two thousand paces away where the tree line started. The fields were bare as the harvest had been completed and the view was unrestricted to the tree line. Nothing moved other than his command who were forming up in groups of one hundred. Their highly polished black ceramic armour shining brightly in the sun. All of them had one pace long batons that would emit a high voltage, low amperage shock when contact was made to human flesh. For this deployment each man had also been issued with a pistol and they had twenty longer range lasers. The mistake of the last punishment raid would not be repeated by his command.

The inhabitants of the settlement were loosely gathered, watching quietly. The leaders had decided to make an example of this group. Individuals would be selected for immediate execution, the leaders of the settlement and any trouble makers would be sent to the capital for a trial and televised executions.

A slow mournful sound could be heard in the distance. It became louder and was recognized as a song being sung by many voices, male and female, in an unfamiliar language. The sound seemed to be coming from all around them as it echoed around the valley. Almost immediately, the people of the settlement scattered to their homes.

'So much the better,' the commander thought. 'It will be much easier to round them up that way.'

He was about to order his men to break up into groups of ten and start rounding the people up, when one of his men pointed to the far hill side. A large silver coloured object was slowly emerging from the tree line. It was three hundred paces wide and looked to be one hundred paces deep.

"Orbiter, what is that object coming out of the trees?" the commander said to his mother ship twenty thousand feet in the air above him.

"Nothing on the scanners sir," came the reply. "We can see it on your monitors, but nothing is showing on the scanners."

As the object came closer, it was soon revealed that it was not one object but five and as they came closer still, the five became fifty. When it was within three hundred paces it was revealed to be fifty blocks of individual silver figures, ten wide and ten deep. Each figure in the block had a pole a pace tall, with a shiny silver object perched on top. A small red flag was attached to one of these poles in each group. A small group of ten came five paces in front of the whole group and stopped. In the centre of this group were two larger poles which held large cloth banners that flew out in the light breeze. They were one pace by two paces. The one on the left, had blue yellow and red vertical stripping with a large black bird, wings out stretched on one side and a snarling large brown animal, fangs exposed on the other side. In the centre was a large red leaf. The other banner had blue white and red stripes with a doubled headed large black bird in the centre. The figures stood in silence.

Then the villagers returned. All of them, young and old. They lined up in a similar formation. The eldest, youngest and mothers with children strapped to their backs, had two pace long wooden poles in hand, and were arranged in the back. In the centre, were tall young and strong men with the same poles, but with a pace long silver axe with spike on top of the pole. To each side of them were another hundred in a square. These had large wooden hammers alternating with others that had two pace long and three finger widths wide silver objects which were held in both hands. On the outsides of them were ranged another block of a hundred with two pace long poles with one pace long leaf shaped shiny objects. These were also armed with solid semi curved rectangular devices held in the left arm, not unlike the smaller versions of the same his men had. These, the front two lines locked into place, so that they covered the entire line.

Then the villagers began to sing the same song that had come from the hillside, but in a different, somewhat familiar language. Two banners sprang up in the rear. The first was the same blue yellow red as the group on the hill. The second was blue, with a large red x centred on a large white x which ran the whole length corner to corner of the banner. Intersecting the x's was a large red on white cross that ran the full length and height of the banner.

"Well if they think five thousand peasants armed with sticks scare God's Holy Warriors they are mistaken," the commander said loudly. "We will deal with these in front of us first, then those on the hill. We will show what we do to those who choose not to follow Gods words and defy the Holy Church by taking up arms against us. No quarter! Form up!"

As his men formed into the solid block formation with shields overlapped that they used in these situations, the group before them began to beat out a rhythm with their sticks. On the ground or against shield. Thump, thump thump. Thump. It sounded similar to a four legged animal walking and they began to sing a song to the rhythm in the common lounge.

"A young Cossack, far from home, stood in the line one thousand strong. His legs were trembling, he wanted to run. The enemy came one thousand deep, one thousand wide against the two lines so thin."

Then the beat picked up a notch. Thump, thump, thump. They started the next verse and a trembling could be felt under his feet and a rumble was in the air. The commander looked behind him and saw the figures descending from the hill. They were coming faster than a man could walk and the song picked up its pace again and the figures coming down the hill came faster. Still all in a line, now with a cloud of dust behind them.

"Front two ranks hold!" the commander yelled out. "Rear ranks about face! Prepare to repel!"

His men had barely formed the new formation and locked shields when the song sped up again and the front two ranks of those approaching came faster yet putting distance between themselves and those following. Both groups merging their lines together so that they were knee to knee. The rear group spaced their ten lines five paces apart. Then as the song was almost to fast to follow and the words were being screamed instead of sung, the commander saw the tails and mains flying in the wind and saw it was men mounted on horses. The first two rows rose in their stirrups almost as one and hefted two paces long objects with reverse double curves on them and pulled long thin sticks placed on a string with one hand to their ears while the other arm held the curved stick at arm's length from their bodies. Then as one, they released the thin stick which flew at high speed towards his men. Then again and again so that three sticks were in the air at one time. The first came crashing in on his men, piercing the ceramic armour and felling most of the first and second ranks. The men that were lucky enough to catch the sticks on their shields had the shield driven back into their chests and the sticks went through the shields anyway and still penetrated the armour.

Then the first two lines of horses split left and right, still shooting the missiles and the lines behind were revealed. The long poles levelled and pointing at those still standing. Then his rear was hit. First came the men in the centre with the long axe headed poles which descended and pulled down or lifted his men's shields. The groups on the right and left darted in and smashed the hammers and stabbed with the long silver hand held objects. The hammers smashed into pieces the armour and the silver hand objects took off heads and arms and legs. The ones with the shields and long poles stabbed his men and crashed head long into his flanks buckling them. The silver leaf shaped objects entered his men's chests with armour shattering all around them. Then the horse riders hit them and it was all over. Some of his men tried to run, but were run down and speared from horse back or shot by arrows. Others were ridden down by other horsemen who had lost their poles and heads and blood were sprayed into the air as the riders swept the same long silver objects at them from horseback that the ones on the ground were using to such good effect.

His core of warriors fought hard around him, but it was hopeless. All that were left now were he and his core of ten warriors. All were bloody and wounded, some barely able to stand. Now the fighting stopped as a bugle sounded a call. Silently the villager's retreated back out of range from his pistols as his men finally had time to draw them. The sun disappeared into shadow as they were ringed by horse riders, long silver tipped poles levelled at their chests. A single rider rode out of the circle to within five paces of them. One of his men shot the man with his pistol, but the laser blast just shimmered on the man doing no damage. The man laughed.

He was young, maybe twenty five and had blond hair and blue almost grey eyes.

"You fuck with the friends of the eagles and the bears and you fuck with the eagles and the bears," the young man said quietly. "No quarter, you told your men. No quarter will be given."

He raised his right hand in the air and twirled the wrist. Immediately each of the eleven men were pierced by five arrows.

Within an hour, the settlement was empty, as another five thousand joined the first and the riders, now fifteen thousand strong, with their horses and herd animals departed for the next settlement.

The silence in the room was overwhelming as the lights came back up. The large monitor dominating the room at the front was still showing an overhead shot of the destroyed settlement. Bodies still laying amidst their shattered armour. Destroyed homes, stables and granaries in piles of rubble. All of the men in the room were still absorbing the live video that had been recorded from the security teams helmets as the attack unfolded. Hearing the grunts and screams of the men as they were wounded or killed. The pleads for their lives that went unheeded. Then the video and commentary of the follow-up teams as they described the scene and the wounds. The dead animals, some butchered, most not.

"My Lord Emir," a man in a dark turban and black robes said. "What they did not take, they destroyed. There is nothing usable in either settlement. A new contingent of settlers will be here for resettlement in the two communities in time for the planting season. Home world has assured us of that. But they will need to be fully supplied. Housing, food, herd animals, seed, implements. All were destroyed or taken."

"Well at least they will not have to clear the land," the Emir said. "How will this effect the supplies for the rest of the planet?"

"The effects will be marginal," another man in a dark business suit said. "It will retard our plans to expand factory and mine output by another two years."

"Have the projections and the reports sent immediately," the Emir said. "That goes for all of you. Home World is expecting a detailed report and analysis as soon as possible."

The Emir let that sink in for a few moments as the men reflected on how this would effect their bonuses and chances of promotion.

"Your Eminence," the Emir said to the tall thin black dressed man across the table from him. "What do we know of this young terrorist?'

The man rose and nodded, then moved to the front of the room and the video screen came alive with an identification file complete with a photo was displayed.

"Demetri Bekenbaum, twenty five. Born on planet, the second generation of his family to be so. His people were among the first arrivals from Home World."

The screen shifted to a live action shot of men in security uniforms roughing up a settlement. Ending with the rape of a young woman and the killing of her and her husband and a young girl.

"The team over stepped their orders," the dark suited man said. "They were only to go in and arrest the leaders on charges of hypocrisy. Demetri was found hiding with a few other children in the corn fields a few days later. He was six at the time. He and the others were transported to Home World, where they were placed into an academy and trained for their eventual specialties and reintegration back here. None of them were suited to God's work, as can be expected. Demetri showed promise as a military candidate and did well in the training and tactics area. However he also scored high on administrative and agriculture and was given his preference as to assignment as is the norm for those who placed high. He chose agriculture."

"While his methods were unconventional, the results were much higher than expected. Crop returns were well above average as were the tax returns. Soon all of the first colonies were deferring to his methods, with a result in a twenty percent increase in revenues from the region and a decrease in demands for supplies and equipment by approximately forty five percent."

"A power plant had been ordered, paid for and was in production. Orders for on World and off world consumer goods had increased thirty percent. Ten students had been sent to Home World to be trained as teachers, medical and veterinary doctors. Twenty more had just returned from on world technical training as mechanical repair specialists and robotic manufacture specialists. A factory to build farm equipment and automated equipment was set up and the first models undergoing field tests, which appeared to be successful."

"So let me get this straight," the Emir said. "Less than five years after he returns on world, not only his settlement, but five others, are not only self-sufficient, but on the verge of substantially increasing the self-sufficiency of the whole planet? Now, in less than six months, he is labelled as a terrorist? Something is very very wrong here."

"The regions overseer suspected some wrong doing and sent in some investigators," a man at the end of the table said. "He noted a lack of respect from the inhabitants and suspected the inhabitants were not strictly adhering to doctrine. A forensic audit was ordered by my department and the Holy Church notified."

"Well?" The Emir asked. The man scrolled furiously through his displays, until he came to the report which he flashed onto the large screen at the front of the room.

"It would appear that nothing was amiss," the now concerned man said. "Tax revenue was submitted on time and in full. In fact the returns are more thorough and complete than any others on the planet. We seem to have closed the investigation My Lord and are completely satisfied. We were intending on interviewing Bekenbaum on how we could implement his techniques on other settlements."

The Emir shifted his now angry gaze to the Bishop standing uncomfortably by the monitor.

"The Holy Church sent in the local Imam to investigate certain allegations," the man said. "He noted a disrespectful attitude from the residents and fined them for that disrespect. A subsequent investigation showed no improvement, if anything the reverse and he doubled the fine and again the next month. On the next monthly visit he was met by verbal and aggressive assault and he called in an enforcement team. This team was roughed up and sent away. At that point, the Holy Church sent in a detachment of Holy Warriors who were beaten and sent away. We then had no choice but to arrest and punish."

"Put your monthly and yearly tithes for that and the other settlements on the screen," the Emir said.

"So once again we see the same thing," the Emir said. "Your tithes have increased roughly thirty percent in the last five years. They are paid on time and in full."

"That is correct My Lord," the bishop said.

"Put the names of the overseer, the Imam and the head of the districts Holy Warriors and security teams on screen," the Emir said.

The names flashed up and the room collectively took a deep breath. All of them had the same last name.

"You fools!" the Emir exploded out of his chair and pointed a finger at the Bishop. "Get those three idiots here tomorrow morning!"

Then he turned to the man on his right.

"Have that overseer arrested immediately! Get somebody down to the other three settlements and try to calm things down. See if we can get a hold of this Bekenbaum. We need to calm all this down right now before it spreads. Blood has been shed on both sides. Hopefully Home World will let us handle this on our own."

"I am afraid I will be unable to bring my people in My Lord," the Bishop said. "They were all killed in the last fight."

"Oh shit!" the Emir said. "Now it's all out of our hands. The Holy Church will take control of this now. God help us all."

"My Lord," a messenger said from the doorway. "Patrol are saying the other three settlements are completely empty and destroyed My Lord."

The Emir turned to the Bishop who had now turned pale.

"You have done this," the Emir said, his voice barely over a whisper. "I will take no responsibility at all for any of this. You and your people have brought this all on our heads and ruined everything we have been trying to build here. May God forgive you for what we are about to receive, for I never will."

"Oh no Cardinal, your people started this mess, you can finish it," the Emir said. "You people made it a religious matter, not we. We were completely happy with those groups. We had no trouble with them, in fact the exact opposite. They have broken none of our laws and as far as the civilian authorities are concerned, they were acting in self-defence. No warning was given by your people nor were any formal charges ever laid against them. They had previously paid the fines levied on them in full. The Sultan is very displeased and intends on bringing the matter up at the next Home World conference."

A month later, ten thousand Holy Warriors had been sent to 'handle' the situation of two months prior. They had spent the month overflying the area in ever widening circles, trying to find the missing settlers and being frustrated at every turn. Now they were asking him to supply his security forces to augment their own.

"I still do not understand how better than thirty thousand people and herd animals can completely disappear," the cardinal said.

"There are no communications, no drive signatures, no electrical impulses, nothing. The Ayatollah is not happy."

"Again, not my problem," the Emir said. "Until they break our laws my hands are tied. I did not make the rules. It was the Holy Church that demanded and received complete authority over matters deemed by the Holy Church to be in their realm, which they have in this matter."

"I personally feel all this has been overblown," the Cardinal said. "If they would just talk with us we would come up with a compromise. Of course this Bekenbaum and the other leaders and ring leaders would have to be burned to set an example."

"So, your people screw up," the Emir said. "Exceed their authority and break your own laws and these people have to be punished for it?"

"Exactly," the Cardinal said. "We cannot have the appearance of the Church being weak."

"You better hope those people stay lost and not want to retaliate and escalate this," the Emir said. "The Holy Church could find itself in a very bad position if it does. Now get back to work and leave me to mine."

'I hope that young man and his people stay lost,' the Emir thought after the Cardinal had left. 'I really don't know how we can stop them if they really get mad.'

Chapter Two

The six young people were sitting around the small campfire they had set up away from the main group of their people. The people were spread as far as six miles behind. The next day they would break out of the trees and into the wide prairie lands beyond. The animals needed the fodder that the virgin grass would provide. Once they entered the prairie proper, all the five groups would be able to stay closer together and they would stop and rest for a while.

"Have the groups been told?" Demetri asked.

"Yes," one of the men around the fire said. "I still don't see why you can't represent your group."

"No, I will only advise at this point," Demetri said. "I have enough to do just with that. We have discussed all of this."

"Yes," a tall black haired girl said. "I thought you were all talk and had dreams in your eyes back at Home World, but you called it right."

"I wish it had been otherwise," Demetri said. "The civil authorities had no problem with us. Just that shit overseer upset he couldn't steal from us and the government anymore. They would have caught him soon had he not talked his brother into that Church nonsense. Even that would have blown over but for their heavy handedness."

All six had been together on Home World. All of them victims of overzealous Church officials excesses. Demetri had been the best of them, in fact he was in the top twenty of the whole school. He tutored them all, so that all of them were in the top fifty. As a reward for his standing and his tutoring efforts, the officials had given him much freedom, which he took advantage of by wandering farther and farther from the school compound.

One day on his explorations of the countryside he had stumbled on an ancient grave yard. It was dominated by a large statue of a horse. Then further along were single grave stones arranged in pairs. All had unfamiliar writing on them. All had a depiction of a leaf in the centre of a bear on the right and a bird on the left. Some of the birds had two heads, but most only one. There were numbers on each and the numbers seemed to decrease as he went along. The next time he had a free day, he took a video with him and took pictures of each. When he returned that evening, he uploaded the pictures to his computer and set it to search for a translation of the inscriptions on the stones.

Demetri thought no more of it as his studies once more took hold. The Holy Church had taken an interest in him now and he had less free time as the added work of religious studies took up much of his time. After several weeks, on the advice of one of the monks he took some time off. Once again, he found himself drawn to the ancient grave yard. He explored further and three hundred paces away from the grave yard, he found, by tripping over it, a concrete foundation. Then he found more and while trees had grown up and into it, a complete concrete structure. The day was drawing to a close and he had a long way to walk to get back to his skimmer, so he left that for a later exploration. Vowing to return the next day, he spent a restless night, thinking of what he had seen.

He was gone right after morning prayers, the sun barely up and was exploring the building an hour later. It was fairly large and had a concrete floor, which had been reinforced with steel. Even after centuries, it still held, but was crumbling in places. He found an entrance with what appeared to have been a steel door. The rusted remnants still hanging in places. This led to a concrete stairwell going down and Demetri followed it to another floor. This one was empty but for tree roots hanging from the roof. He went down two more floors, each was the same, empty and dark, but each floor was in better shape than the next. He finally came to the bottom, six floors beneath the others. The door to this one was mostly intact. It took some time to force it open and he found another door behind this one and it would not budge. Now his interest was really peaked. He vowed to return, determined to see behind that door.

The next week was a blur and he needed no urging to take time off and was gone, again right after morning prayers. This time he brought a bag of tools and lubricants and headed directly to the bottom floor and its stubborn door. After an hour of hard work, he was able to remove the damaged locking mechanism and by then the lubrication had worked its magic and the door was noisily forced open enough for him to squeeze his way inside.

Inside, he found mostly intact desks, rows of them and other rooms, one of which had several raised table like benches and chairs, much like the ones found in his lecture halls at school. There was what appeared to be a large type of monitor on the wall facing the benches and what appeared to be primitive computers all around the room. Exploring further, Demetri found another smaller room which still had some of the panelling intact and another larger desk with what looked like a portable computer. Behind what had once been a panelled wall, was a large steel door with dials on it. Twirling the dials, they crumbled in his hands and he saw locking mechanisms behind them. It was a matter of moments for him to figure out how to slide the locks away and the steel door swung open to reveal a smaller room with shelves ranged along the back and the sides. On these shelves were ranged row on row of files, but the contents crumbled to dust and fragments as soon as he touched them.

Then he found a shelf with many little plastic devices that had what appeared to be an electrical contact port on one end. Carefully taking one out, Demetri walked back to the portable computer and saw that the device would fit into it. He took the little device back and placed it back into the box he had found it in. On the back wall, he found plastic sealed boxes, opening one, he found it filled with what looked to him something called books. Each had a number on it. Demetri gingerly picked one out of the box and found that it did not crumble and that it had similar writing on it that he had found on the grave stones. Putting that book back, he found the one with the earliest number on it and after taking it out, he resealed the box.

Now he took a closer look at the little plastic devices and saw that the shelves were numbered. Once again, he took the earliest of the disks. Walking back to the outer room, he picked up the portable computer and placed it with the other items in the bag that contained his tools and left.

His days were spent at his studies and the first night he checked the first enquiry he sent for the deciphering of the grave stones and found he had answers. The stones were inscribed in not one, but three languages. Something called Russian, German and English. English was the closest one to the standard language they all spoke. As he expected, they depicted the names of the long dead. Not expected was that all the names had the same last name. Bekenbaum, his name.

Now he had to find out what this was about! He video scanned several pages of the book he had found and had the decryption program work out a translation protocol for him. Then he tore apart the portable computer. It was a matter of hours before he was able to find a suitable power supply to work on it and jury rig it. It took more time to get the disc like memory to work and once he did, the attached monitor came alive and after an eternity, the computer came alive. He explored the operating system. It was archaic and not very efficient or complex. Inserting the small plastic device, he found that it was a memory device and that it contained data files in another noncomplex format. It was a matter a few hours, before he had transferred all the data from the computer and the storage device to his personal portable device and was having the files deciphered.

As his computer worked on that, he went back to the vid scans and started to read its translation. The book was written in German and was a history of the man listed on the oldest head stone in the grave yard. He had just finished the last page, when the computer let him know it had finished with the small storage device. It held the same material as in the hard copy book, so further scanning would not be necessary. The more he read, the more he wanted to read. This was of a much earlier time. A time before computers, before electricity or mag drives. When the prime means of transportation was by horse or on foot. Where much of life revolved around the cycles of the year and the harvest of food. It was a violent time of strife and fighting.

There was something else he found. The last names of his six companions. Vonhoadle, Rosenthal, Stewart, Anderson, Chimilovitch, Hood, Makarov. How this group had come together and been molded into a team. A team that had inspired and motivated a generation of their pears to accomplish great deeds. He learned something else and his religious studies faltered and he was no longer considered to be a candidate for the Holy Church.

It was a matter of weeks, before he retrieved all of the books and storage devices. After installing all of the data on his personal device, Demetri carefully packed it all away and had it shipped to his world for storage for his return. He learned many things from his readings. Now his studies went to animal husbandry, farming methods and land management. He also spent more time on military organization and tactics. One by one, he began feeling out his companions and steering them in a certain direction. He transmitted nothing to them electronically about these matters. Only discussing them in person and out of doors. Once they had returned home, each to his own settlement, they began to implement Demetri's ideas and to slowly bring first their relatives and then slowly others into what they had learned of their past.

In five years they were ready. Now all the planning and training was being put to good use.

In three days, the whole party was camped along both sides of a slow moving shallow river. The five settlements had held their elections and Demetri was standing in front of the thirty elected leaders, one for every thousand in their group. It was no surprise to him that his five school mates had been elected the leaders of the five settlements.

"Welcome," Demetri said. "You have just finished your first step in the process of being free. Now I will tell you what you will need to do to prepare you and your families for what we are about to face. We must conserve as many of our herd animals as possible. The herds need to grow. This should not be a problem. There is much wild game out here, there is one particular large herd animal that will provide most of our needs. We must waste nothing. We need to build shelters, clothing, bathing soaps, lubrications, ropes. Horses will be at a premium and need to be increased. Skills will need to be learned, metal of any kind must not be lost. Weaving, wood working and blacksmithing will be important. Edible herbs, bulbs, berries and grasses are in abundance and will have to be harvested and conserved. The doctors and pharmacists will let us know what they require and these supplies must and will be gathered. Bows and lances, saddles and tack will have to be manufactured and many, many arrows.

"Ours will be a mobile society. This will be hard at first, but will become normal soon. Everyone over the age of ten will be trained in the martial arts. Any able bodied will be trained extensively in weapons use and tactics. All will be required in the defence of our people. No and I mean no, electronic communication can or will be permitted. Our very survival depends on it. If we don't use it,

they can't find us. They will not think to look for us out here and if
they fly over, they will see what they expect to see, herds of nomadic
animals. They won't even come down to look.

"Questions?"

There were none and they agreed to meet in this same spot the
next year. The leadership group broke off to go their separate ways
while the six old classmates stayed behind.

"I will be coming to each of your groups," Demetri said. "I will
stay two months with each group. Then move to the next. I will
be evaluating your progress and helping with the training of your
troops."

"This is well and good," Chimilovitch said. "You have the best
skills and training, it should be so. But you are also the last of your
name. You are to valuable to loose and there is much danger for a
single man alone. Bears, large cats and wolves. No we cannot permit
it."

"Aye it is true," Vonhoadle said. "But it is also true that we need
him to train and evaluate our progress. I think an escort for him is
needed."

"Then it is we, his Home Settlement, that shall provide this
escort," Makarov said. "It is only right."

The other four agreed and started to discuss the number of
escorts required. Demetri let them debate for a while, then stood to
make a comment.

"It will be ten," he said. "Just like our basic unit configuration.
But not just any ten. They must be between eighteen and twenty one.
They must have their own weapons and supplies. They must have
four capable horses each, I don't care how they obtain them."

This was readily agreed upon and promises made to supply him
with the best.

"One last thing," Demetri said. "They will compete for it. It will
not be given to them. They must prove their worth with lance and

sword and bow. I will choose, none other. They will serve me for two rotations. Then they may leave, if they wish, or they may stay. One last thing. Each settlement will provide me with ten, chosen the same way, the last day I am with that settlement."

This also was agreed upon and the group left.

Each morning as the sun came over the horizon, found Demetri in a small level patch of ground beside the river bank. His shirt would be off, his trousers rolled up to be just below the knees. He would then begin the slow intricate moves he had learned from one of the ancient recording devices left by the old ones. All in the camp knew he did them, no one understood why and more than a few of the males shook their heads and smiled as they walked by. Some of the young boys had started to copy him, but had been mocked by their older brethren and all but a few stopped doing it. The younger women especially saw the rippling muscles as he performed and dreamed.

After an hour, Demetri would dip the towel he carried into the river, ring it out and wipe down his body, removing the sweat that had accumulated there. Then he would walk back to his small tent and after stoking his fire, cook himself a breakfast. Finishing, he once again went to the river bank and washed his dishes, packing them back into his tent after he had finished. At that point, he would go to the horse herd. His horses knew his routine and came to him without being called. He would brush down each of his now eight horses and select the one he would use for the days training. Today, he chose a five year old stallion that was showing much promise and put him through a series of slow intricate movements. Again he received more than a few smiles and winks were exchanged between other riders putting their horses through training.

Then he would pick up lance and bow. Slinging his pace and a half long slightly curved sword and its scabbard to hang across his back, hilt over his left shoulder. He hung a quiver of ten arrows in front of his right leg and once again began a slow walking progress through the arrow targets. Then again through the lance and sword targets after he had retrieved his arrows. Now he would begin a set of strange maneuvers with sword and bow. He would pass slowly down the row of targets and drop to the side of the horse, firing the bow under the horses neck, then flip backwards on the saddle and fire to the rear, flipping once again to the front of the saddle and hanging the bow on it, he would draw the sword and advance on a sword target, taking a slow swing at the first, then flopping back to lay on the saddle as he came to the second. After just passing it, he would come upright and swing backhanded at the neck of the dummy. Then he would drop the sword so it fell on the ground and would advance a few paces, turn the horse around and walk back to the sword, where he would hook his left leg around the saddle horn and drop down to pick the sword up from the ground. Only a few of the young boys who watched, saw how he had never once used his reins to control the horse. Usually after this, Demetri would take the chosen horse for a ride before turning him loose to join the herd. Today he did not.

Demetri walked the stallion to where his admiring group of boys stood. They were all the same ones that tried to mimic his personal training each morning.

"In a few days I will be leaving," Demetri said. "I will need someone to look out for and work my remaining horses. It will be one of you. Go to your parents and ask for permission. Then come back here with your ponies and I will select the best one of you."

The five boys, all about ten, sprinted to their parents tents and all were back with their ponies saddled within half an hour. Mothers and sisters following them, soon to be joined by fathers and a few others.

Demetri had them go through a series of his morning exercise moves, then one by one had them, do the horse exercises and the bow, lance and sword drills he performed each morning. After they had finished, but before Demetri could make his choice known, one of the group of young men who had come by to watch spoke up.

"Big deal, they can hit something walking," he said. "I'd like them to try that with me at full speed."

"Really?" Demetri said. He turned and pointed to the youngest and smallest of his little group. "Get your practice sword and go to that end of the line."

"You big mouth, get yours and go to the other end," he said to the teenager. Demetri handed the reins of his horse to the father of one of the youngsters and walked down to where his young lad was nervously waiting.

"Get down," he said. "Make sure your saddle is on properly and the cinch is tight. You can do this. Your muscles know what needs to be done. So does the pony. Concentrate, don't look at his sword, look at his eyes, he will strike where he looks. Don't try to parry the blow, he is to strong for you. Duck under, then whack him a good one across the back after he passes. Then I want you to spin your pony around and hit him again. This time hard on the leg, by the knee. It should be over then."

Demetri patted the lad on the shoulder and walked back to the centre of the line. The older lad had a group of his fellows gathered around him and they were all laughing and making comments about how the young fellow and his pony would be laying in the dust. Demetri raised his hand and made a fist. Both riders watched the hand, the teenager barely able to control his horse, which was prancing in a circle. Demetri brought his hand sharply down and both riders spurred to a gallop, the teenager whooping loudly. The riders met almost at the middle and the teenager swept his sword at the youngsters head. The boy's mother could not stop the small scream she made. The young lad flopped onto his back and the sword passed over him, in a flash he was back up and whacked the teenager hard across the back, the wooden sword making an audible smack as it hit. Then something else happened at the same time. The young lads pony sank its teeth into the teenagers horses flank and kicked a rear leg to catch the bigger horse under the jaw as they passed.

The youngsters pony sank back on its rear legs, stopping and pivoting almost in one motion and the youngster was at the attack almost before the teenager had turned round. The pony had its head down and was charging hard, lips and ears peeled back and mouth open for another bite. The teenagers horse tried to shie away and the young man lost his sword as he tried to gain control of the animal, just in time to receive a hard knock on his right leg from the youngsters wooden sword. The horse reared and the teenager found himself on the ground and his horse running away. Now the youngster spun his pony around again and spurred back down the line, flopping to one side, he deftly picked up the fallen sword from the ground and flipped back into the saddle. The pony came back to a walk and the youngster turned him back to the teenager, now sitting up, rubbing his knee. The youngster tossed the teenagers sword back to him and rode back to his fellows and parents yelling at the top of his lungs in triumph as he did so.

Demetri kept his eyes on the defeated teenagers companions and as he had expected, one of them exploded in rage and spurred his horse at the youngster, drawing a real, not a practice sword as he did so.

Demetri walked to the centre and placed himself into the charging horses path. The teenager levelled his sword at Demetri's chest and kept coming to the shock of the onlookers, more than a few of the women present crying out in alarm. Demetri assumed the sideways position he used at practice, both knees slightly bent hands and arms loose and before him, fingers spread open. He made no move to avoid horse or rider and as they swept down on him at full gallop, the enraged teenager swept his sword up over his head and moved his horse to the side as the sword came down aimed at Demetri's head. Then in a motion almost to fast to see, Demetri swept his right hand forward, knocking the sword away and grabbing the wrist it held, at the same time he pivoted, sweeping his right leg forward and catching the horse behind its left front knee. In one smooth motion, almost in slow motion horse and rider came crashing to the ground and Demetri stepped agilely away. The teenager's sword in his hand.

Demetri jammed the sword point first beside the young man's head as the horse staggered to it feet.

"Anger will defeat you faster than arrogance," he said in a low voice to the young man laying at his feet. "And you have an overabundance of both. You and your buddy there will report to me after supper."

Demetri then walked over to the other teenager who was still sitting on the ground holding his knee. Demetri took the leg and examined the knee.

"You'll live," he said. "Get up, gather you horse and walk it off before it gets stiff."

Demetri then walked over to where the youngster was. The young fellow was surrounded by his buddies and beaming parents, none of who noticed Demetri walk up to them.

"Well, young fellow, well done," Demetri said. "What is your name?"

"Alex sir," the youngster said. "Alex Nagy."

"Well Maser Alex Nagy, you have the job then," Demetri said. "If your parents allow it and only if you continue the chores your parents give you to do."

The young lad looked to his parents who smiled and nodded.

"Good then," Demetri said. "You start right now. Unsaddle and cool down your pony and Barney here. Find me after."

The young lad surrounded by his admiring friends left and Demetri turned to the boy's parents.

"He is the smallest and the youngest, but has the biggest heart," Demetri said. "I was going to pick him anyway. The four mares I am leaving are in foal. I have arranged to have them bred once the foals are weaned with Jacob's stallion. Thank you for this Mr. and Mrs. Nagy."

After the evening meals had been complete, the two young men came to Demetri's camp and stood while he tended to his fire and a pot of water on it. He left them standing until the water was ready, then he added some tea leaves to the pot and bade them to sit. He pored each of them a cup and handed each a small slice of bread. While they drank and ate, he asked them of their families and their horses. Once they had finished the tea, he pored once more and got down to business.

"I had much promise for the both of you," Demetri said. "Now I am not so sure." He pointed to the first boy.

"You had the faster and stronger horse, more and better training, yet you lost. You had an unarmed man standing on the ground. Yet you lost."

"Had this been real, both of you would be dead. If the first cut would not have broken your back, the second would have severed your leg. In any case, you were unhorsed, had no weapon and your horse had galloped away. You, you just would have been dead, I would have stabbed that sword into your neck not the ground."

"You both assumed because your horses were bigger stronger and faster and that you were the same, you would win. You forgot, that kid has been almost constantly in the saddle for five years, with the same horse. It is natural for him. You grew up with skimmers and horses were just a hobby. He had the advantage of you and you did not even know it. The younger ones will be even better, they can ride before they can walk."

"Both of you are going to have to work very hard to make my ten. My ten will be with me for a year at least. They need to be tough and they need to be smart. They will be used to train those in the settlements we come to and the ten that come from each. They will be MY ten! They come from my home. What they do reflects on me personally. I need to trust them more than I trust myself. I need them to protect me and my animals from anything at any time. I need them to keep me from doing stupid things. What I don't need, is more displays like todays. You dishonoured me, your families and your settlement. You have three days to get your shit together, or you will be left behind. Go now and think on these things."

The next morning, Demetri was joined by three women, two late teens and a thirtyish woman. The gang of ten children had been joined by thirty more and as Demetri started his movements he saw Alex and the other ten helping the new comers and smiled, as the older women tried to mimic the movements. The older woman had a grace and fluidity that soon had her making the initial movements easily. Demetri took her aside after.

"Go see Jimmy," he said. "He has copies of the vids that show how to do this. You do know what I am doing here?"

"Yes," she said. "You are training your mind and body in the movements you will need to fight with hand and sword. They are not unlike the movements we use in our dances. The girls will pick this up fast I think."

"I can't take you with me Hanna," Demetri said. "You have two young children and a husband and household to look after. But if you would not mind. I would like you to start training any who wish it. Much like Alex has done with the younger children already. Once you become familiar and more proficient, move to spears and swords. Then move to horseback. Once this starts for real, we will need you women and old timers to look after the camps."

"Unlike others in the camp, my family and I have been listening," Hanna said. "Already we have eight horses, ten cows and fifteen sheep. My sisters and I are learning to spin wool and horse hair. We have trained the children to look for roots and herbs. We are learning how to smoke meat and milk mares and cows. Our husbands work at making better arrows, one of them has a smith showing him how to work metal. Another to make shields and leather armour. All of us practice with the bow, sword and spear. I only hope the others will learn. I fear once we enter the prairie proper we are going to need those skills."

Chapter Three

D emetri spent the next three days walking through the camp, his head on a swivel. He observed everything and everyone. By the time the three days were up, he had pretty much made up his mind who the ten who would be his companions would be. The competition would just be a formality. He thought.

One hundred young men and women turned out. He put them through their paces and noted down the results of the tests. There was more than one surprise. Some who practiced well, failed miserably under pressure, others who practiced poorly performed well above expectations. Now would come the final test.

"Now is the final test," he told them. "Each of you will collect your four horses. Saddle one to ride. Pack one with what you will be bringing with you. The other two you shall trail with halters. You will have lance, bow, ten arrows and your sword and armour. You will meet me at the edge of the camp in half an hour ready to go."

Demetri collected his four horses, electing to ride one of his mares and to use the stallion as a pack animal. When the gaggle arrived, Demetri said nothing. He mounted his mare, took his horses to hand and started off at a brisk trot. In half a mile he changed to a canter. After an hour, he brought another unburdened mare up close and deftly swung over to her, not breaking stride. An hour later he did it again. An hour later, he slowed to a walk and slid to the ground walking beside the horses. After ten minutes he stopped, shifting the pack to the first mare he had ridden bare back, he put the saddle on Barney along with his weapons, except for the sword on his back and started walking again. While he could tell from the groans and odd complaint that he still had people following him, at no time did he speak or even look at them.

Making sure he had Barney's reins firmly in his gasp, he sprang up onto the first mare he had ridden and took off at a trot once again. A number of audible groans could be heard from behind him as the candidates hurriedly swung up on mounts and matched his pace.

He made a slow circle and by the time he reached the point where he swung up on Barney's back, they were in sight of the smoke coming from the camps cook fires. Now he brought his trailing horses up, deftly tied their reins together and let them hang free across their necks, then increased speed to a canter. His other horses spread out in a line abreast behind him as they had been taught and when Demetri was within four hundred paces of the camp, he came to a full gallop, pulling his bow out as he did so. At three hundred paces, he drew an arrow and started firing at man sized targets that had been set up. His quiver empty and three arrows still in the air, he placed the bow back on its saddle hook and brought the lance from its scabbard behind his leg. At fifty paces he levelled it at a target. Spearing it in the chest he let the target pull the lance from his hand, swept the sword from his back, cut the next with a back hand sweep to the head and had it level for the next which he took in the chest. Then he put Barney through a much faster version of the exercises he had done slowly, spinning and kicking at targets while he himself swung his sword. Then he slowly walked to the other end of the target range and collected his animals.

Only twenty of the candidates had made it to the end. Eleven of those with all of their horses. One of them had a horse that fell right at the end blown and dying. That left his ten. Six male and four female.

"You ten are my ten," he said with no fanfare. "We leave in the morning. Pack everything you will need for a week. The pace will be the same as todays."

Then he left them to look after his mounts, rubbing them down. After which in true horse fashion they promptly rolled on their backs and sides covering themselves in dirt and grass. Handing them to Alex finally.

"Have them ready at day break Alex," Demetri said and he went to bed.

His pack saddle was packed, his saddle, bedroll tide to the cantle ready. His weapons stacked and ready. He had two quivers of twenty arrows, one of which was attached to his saddle, the other packed away in the pack saddle. A spare lance was tied to it as well, the other beside his bow and sword. His shirt and jacket were laying across his saddle, his trouser legs were rolled up below his knees and the first grey of day was breaking out as he started his movements. He was midway through, when Alex and the other children arrived. There were fifty of them now. Five more young women joined belatedly. Demetri acknowledged no one and continued. The sun was peaking its leading edge over the horizon and he stopped, put on his shirt and jacket, pulled on his battered wide brim hat and threw the pack saddle on a mare. Then he saddled Barney and as the sun fully broke clear of the horizon he rose into the saddle and without a word or a look back, trotted out of the encampment.

A rapid clatter of hooves at the gallop that slowed to a trot beside him announced another rider. It was Alex on his pony.

"I had them ready for you at day break like you asked my lord," Alex said.

"Yes, thank you Alex," Demetri said. "I am not your or anyone else's lord Alex. You take good care of my horses Alex. Work hard at your studies and your horse and arms training. I will see you in a year and a half. If you keep going the way you are, in eight years you might be one of my eagles."

"Oh yes sir!" Alex said. "Your mares shall breed good foals and I will make sure they meet Jacobs stallion like you asked. I have also made a deal to stud your old stallion with several other mares. You get half the foals produced sir. Oh and my lord, I will be ready to try out for your eagles by the time you get back. I am small for my age and this is my sister's pony. My pop needed my good horse and my other three are to young yet to ride, but they will be ready when you return, as will I my lord."

Now Alex dropped back and turned around headed back to camp.

"I told you Alex," Demetri said. "I am no lord."

"Whatever you say my lord," Alex shouted back over his shoulder as the other ten galloped past him.

At that point, Demetri nudged Barney to a canter until he heard his ten behind him, then opened up to a gallop for half an hour. The only change in the routine from the day before was the direction of travel and every hour, they stopped and switched saddles, then walked for ten minutes, before rising again to a gallop. Just past midday, they came to a small stream with a clearing, the spot Demetri had chosen to stop for the day.

"Pick one horse to stay close," Demetri said. "Hobble the others and turn them loose. Once you have taken care of the horses, set up your camp. Then report to me."

Like the others, Demetri unsaddled pack and saddle horse, hobbled three, Barney among them and turning them loose. He kept his chosen mare on a long lead and took her to the stream to water. After he found a good spot with a lot of good grass around it and staked the long lead down, leaving her to graze. Only after that, did he take his small pot to the river after collecting enough firewood to start a fire. He filled the pot and gathered a number of rocks to make a fire ring, then started a small fire and set the pot to boil.

He had just finished his cup of tea and laid back, his hat blocking the sun, when the sound of boots coming his way announced the ten approaching. He sat up and watched them gather in a semi- circle across from him.

"This is how we will travel each day," Demetri said. "Today we travelled as far as a skimmer could go from camp and make it back before the batteries went dead and we did it in about three quarters of the time. In a week, we will be traveling twice as far. Your horses want to do it, but are in no shaped for it now. But they are in better shape than you are.

"Tomorrow, three of you will ride ahead. One in the front and two, three hundred paces to each side. You will keep each other insight at all times and I do not want to see you or catch up to you until you have found us a suitable camp spot. Leave your chosen pack animal with us. If you spot any danger, one of you rides back to warn us. You will leave an hour before the rest of us. We will trade off this job every day. Rotate your animals every day as to the one you start to ride and which will carry the pack.

"When we stop like this for the night, we always keep one horse close in case we have to run, or fight. Rotate that horse as well. We will have three guards out at all times. That means day and night. One will guard the horses, one will ride perimeter of the camp and one tends the fire. You will trade off every four hours.

"After we stop for the day, we will do like today. Look out for our horses first, then an hour for yourselves. Then we will train until the sun starts to go down. At that time we will eat and go to bed. As the sun breaks the horizon we will be in the saddle and on the move."

He let them think about that for a while.

"The others are training to fight in groups, on foot and horseback. They will be Bears. They are our claws and fangs. They will fight our battles. Eagles will be our eyes and ears. Without accurate information, we are blind and dumb and we lose. Eagles need to be agile and silent. Quick and smart. Fight only when necessary and always quick and efficient, ready to run. Eagles will fight from ambush or to their own advantage. A nibble here, a nibble there. The Bears stand and fight, but the Eagles slash and scurry. Together, we will win battles.

"Right now, you are not Eagles or Bears. If you survive the next year and a half, you might be. The rest of today is yours. Set up your guard and scout rotations. It has been a long two days. Get some rest."

For me too, Demetri thought as the ten walked away.

Halfway through the night and a half hour before they would change guard, Demetri slunk out of camp. He positioned himself at the edge of the horse herd and settled down. An hour after the guard had changed. He began to stalk the guard. The horse almost stepped on him as it passed, then Demetri sprang up and roughly pulled the guard off the saddle to thump hard on the ground and the horse skittered away.

"Now you are dead," Demetri said. "My friends are closing in around your camp and my other friends are about to steal your horses. Your camp has no warning and every one will die, because you were not alert. Your job is first to watch, then to yell a warning, then to fight. Keep that in mind. We are not the only ones out here and they will want our horses, weapons and women. Remember that."

As silently as he had arrived, he left. He did the same thing to the camp perimeter guard and the camp guard.

The next day after their midday break, Demetri had them gather around again.

"Last night you all died," he said. "You were not vigilant. How many of you saw that bear today or the wolf pack?"

"You must learn to work as a team, with each other and your horses," Demetri continued. "The horses have better noses and ears than you do. Your eyes detect movement better than theirs and your mind works faster. Look and listen. Your horses and other prey animals around us will give warning when something is not right. Those wolves may stalk us for a few days. If they keep it up, we will have to do something about it."

"Now, who can tell me why I train as I do every morning?"

"Alex told me it is to train the mind and the body to work together," the one who Alex had dumped on the ground at the trial said.

"Very good trooper, you get a cookie," Demetri said. "When we find some cookies and if I remember. Yes, we train slow and as precisely as we can. This trains the muscles in the movements they will need and the brain what to do. Well that and for some reason the girls like to watch me with my shirt off. Just like we train with heavy wooden swords and shields. When the time comes for the real thing, we react fast and don't hold back."

"All of you candidates have had rudimentary weapons and horsemanship training," Demetri continued. "Now I will teach you how to kill fast and efficient, as quietly as possible. In all weathers, in all terrain and all situations. You will learn to rule the night."

"We will start with what I do every morning. Once you are good enough, we will start with weapons, then on horseback. At first the girls will be better than you. You lads have been trained for heavy lifting. Your muscles are geared for that. The girls are not. At the end, you will have greater strength and stamina than they will, but they will be faster and more agile."

"My name is..." the young man started, but Demetri held up his hand to silence him.

"You have not earned the right to a name yet candidate," Demetri said. "You all will be addressed as candidate by me and you will address me as sir. Now line up and follow my movements as best as you can. Do try not to fall all over the place candidates, will you? The horses might get embarrassed."

Two weeks later and they were training with him every morning. They were riding twice as far, faster than when they had first started. Muscles, man and horse were firming up, horse and man were working as a team. The candidates were able to spot possible danger and ambush sites, for there were hiding spots even on the prairie. At that days end, the scouts reported a herd of buffalo not far away. That was good, as they were running short of meat and a hunt was planned for the next day. They downed two of the massive animals and dragged the car-cases back to their camp, where they started the long butchering process.

It took two days to quarter and skin the animals, scrape the meat and fat off of the hides. Fires were set up to smoke as much meat as they could and they feasted the first day on the most tender parts. A constant guard was kept for wolves and other scavengers that might be drawn to the smell of fresh meat.

"Sir, we have eyes on us," a female candidate said the next evening.

"Yes I know," Demetri said. "They have been watching us for two days now. How many, do you think?"

"There are five on this side of the river and five on the other," she said.

"There are ten in that draw over there and another ten behind that hill," Demetri said. "Good job, I didn't spot the five on this side of the river. Keep your bow and quiver handy and your sword loose. Are the others aware?"

"Yes sir. Kind of hard to miss them. They smell awfully bad."

"Yes they do at that candidate," Demetri said with a smile. "Time for dinner I think."

The camp settled down to their usual dinner routine and as the sun went down Demetri heard them coming.

"You know, if you would have asked, we are willing to share," Demetri said. "We have to much for ourselves. You can have the rest."

"Ya well, I think we will take it all," a voice said. "The meat, the horses and the women."

"Well that is not very friendly of you," Demetri said, standing up.

"Just what exactly are you planning on doing to stop us?" the voice said. "Ten kids, four of them women and one fairy."

Now they came into view. All of them male. Dressed in a variety of skins and furs. All of them armed with heavy clubs or fire sharpened long poles. All of them had long unkempt and unwashed hair and beards.

Demetri and his ten rose and formed a circle around the fire, facing outwards and presenting their sides to the oncoming group. All of them balancing their weight on bended knees.

"Well come and take it if you can," Demetri said quietly. Not one of them reaching for a weapon. "As I said, we are willing to share, the meat, nothing else."

"No, I think we will take it all," the leader of the group said. "Get 'em boys!"

With a roar, the twenty five rushed the small group. In a flash, swords were drawn and arrows were flying, putting three down before they got halfway to the group. Soon blood and limbs were flying as swords made contact with flesh. Screams of wounded and dying men filled the evening air as with elegant and efficient movements, swords parried blows and cut off heads and arms. Usually both. Arms first. It was soon over. Five were running and twenty lay on the ground in widening pools of blood.

"Shit now we are going to have to move," Demetri said. "I'm not staying here with all this fresh meat and blood around. Saddle up, we'll get down wind about an hour. Keep a sharp lookout for any others that may be about. I missed that last five. Anybody hurt?"

"Just them," one of the ten said.

The only sounds in the full moon lit landscape were the hooves of the horses striking the ground. Demetri kept them down to fast walk. Even though the moon lit the landscape brightly, there were still many shadows and it would be easy for a horse to step in a hole and break its leg. They came to a small depression that would shelter them from the wind and the sight of their fire from view and Demetri called a halt, ordering all the horses to be ground tethered close by and to keep saddles on.

Once a fire was burning and everyone gathered around watching it and the pot of water boiling on it, Demetri looked at each face. Their bodies were there but their minds were not. Sighing to himself, he rose to one knee and removed his hat holding it in his left hand. He took his right hand and touched his forehead, then the left shoulder, then the right.

"In the name of the Father, the Son and the Holy Spirit," he said. There were more than a few gasps heard from the ten. "Heavenly Father, I thank you for allowing my troopers and I to live tonight. I thank you for allowing no harm to my troopers. I ask you to hold them blameless for the taking of your children's lives, as it was I who trained them to do so. The fault is all mine. I ask you to heal their confused minds and ease the pain they are feeling tonight."

Demetri made the same gesture and sat down, placing his hat back on, looked at the ten again.

"They would have killed all the men and right now they would be enjoying the women," he said. "Then they would have killed them too. I apologize to you that I did not spot the other five men. That could have been enough to do us all in."

"You killed five before I swung my sword," one girl said.

"And your sister killed three before I drew mine," Demetri said nodding to the girl with the bow. "To bad we lost the arrows, but I couldn't spare the time to retrieve them."

The girl held up three blood stained arrows.

"Thank you for rectifying my oversight," Demetri said. "Now you understand what I have been talking about. How the brain and the body react as they have been trained."

"It was like time slowed down," one candidate said. "I could see where his blow was going and I moved. My sword was like it was alive, it struck where it wanted to go."

"They are used to fighting people like themselves," Demetri said. "They outnumbered us, had us surrounded and thought we were young and weak. Not all our fights will be as easy. We were better armed and better trained. We come up against Holy Warriors, things will be much different."

"Speaking of that sir," one of the young men said.

"Ah yes," Demetri said nodding his head. "My blasphemy. Don't tell me that you haven't seen others do that gesture, maybe even your parents? We were doing that long before the Holy Church came to this planet. They don't teach you all in school you know. They only teach you what they want you to learn."

"It's not that sir," the young man said. "It's just that, I, we, all thought you hated God and his teachings."

"Don't believe everything you hear," Demetri said smiling. "Just because I hate the Holy Church and all they have done to us and others, does not mean I do not believe. Now I know it will be hard, it was for me the first time I had to kill a man, but try and get some sleep. Tomorrow we ride hard and we ride until we reach the next camp. We need to let them know about these bad people out here."

Chapter Four

They were spotted by the youngsters guarding the herds as they came into sight of the encampment as the sun was going down to the east over the horizon. They slowed to a walk from a canter at two hundred paces from the camp and formed up in a column of two lines, pack and spare horses trailing to the sides of them. Demetri rode at the front centred between the leading two candidates. Once they had done that, a commotion broke out as shouts of welcome came from voices and people began to gather to greet them. Then the sweat stained dust on horse and rider could be seen and the dark stains, almost covering the whole right arm that showed through the dust. The crowd quieted as they came closer and saw the grim looks on dried blood covered faces.

They rode up the centre aisle of the camp until they came to the wide centre space and they stopped and wearily dismounted. Helping hands rushed forward to take horses, but not until the candidates and Demetri had removed their weapons from the horses.

The leader of the camp rushed forward and hugged Demetri, then held him at arm's length and looked him in the eyes.

"What the hell happened out there?" he asked.

"Why have you no guards posted or scouts out?" Demetri asked. "We ran into a group of nasty fellows yesterday."

"They usually stay far away and leave us alone," the leader said. "They are not a problem."

"They aren't anymore," the girl with the bow said. "They made the mistake of attacking us."

"How many of them?" the leader asked.

"Only twenty five," the girl said. "No big deal."

40

"Twenty five! They never gather in that big a group," the leader said. "You defeated them? Four girls and six boys?"

"We had a good teacher," one of the young men said. "He only killed five and let us kill the rest."

"Do you mind kind sir," Demetri said. "My troopers and I have had a long day and night before. Could we perhaps have a chance to clean up and maybe some hot food that we haven't cooked ourselves?"

"Of course of course," the leader said. "Come. My good people! Make our gallant friends welcome!"

"You're with me brother," a voice said from behind before the man grabbed Demetri and hugged him close. He dragged Demetri to a large tent not far away and Demetri was once again hugged by his friends wife.

"Well Demetri, spill the beans then," he said.

"For God's sake Alphonso, let the man at least wash up and sit down first won't you," Alphonso's wife said.

"But of course Greta, how rude of me," he said.

"Not much to tell," Demetri said as he took off his blood stained shirt and began to wash the dust and blood off his face and arms. "I tried to be nice and they decided not to be. They came at us. Wooden clubs and spears against steel and arrows. No contest. The kids did well. For their first fight. Better than we did on ours."

"Ya, but we had more troops and nobody but us noticed the mistakes," Alphonso said.

"You better start making mounted patrols," Demetri said. "Ok, I am sure the council is waiting. Let's get this over with so I can catch up and get some sleep."

Demetri related the attack to the council a short time later.

"There is likely more like them out there," he said. "You were lucky they didn't hit you before this. Make sure those kids keep a sharp look out. You should also have mounted patrols out, no less than ten troopers strong. I would find their camp, surround it and make them an offer first. Then wipe them out if they refuse it. If they are all males, I would just wipe them out. That bunch we ran into were only interested in horses and women."

"Who are they I wonder?" one of the council asked.

"Most likely criminals on the run," Demetri said. "They are hard characters make no bones about it. They only obey one law. The strongest wins. We must and will show them who is the strongest. Send riders to the other camps and warn them. Once these people get wind of what we have, they will start to try and take it away from us. We must show them that this a big mistake. Now are you ready for me? Your month starts tomorrow. Make the best of it. Have my ten at Alphonso's tent at dawn."

As the sun came up, all eleven were doing their morning warm ups. Before the hour was up, they had a large audience, mostly of young adults. The boldest of the males making comments about the four females and the masculinity of the males.

"There always was something odd about that settlement," one of the boldest said. "Look at their leader. How could it be any different? He was probably hiding behind his mommies skirts when our fathers took on the Holy Warriors to save his settlements asses for them."

Demetri carried on with his routine and gave a hard look at one of his ten who faltered and made to turn around.

"Oh yes, must not disturb our dance lesson," the big mouth said. "Come on boys, I've had enough of this crap"

The crowd dispersed after that comment, leaving the ten to finish in peace. Demetri had the ten sit down in a circle after they had finished.

"We do not win if we sink to their level," he said. "We know what we are capable of. We do not need to show off, or defend ourselves by the likes of him."

"But sir," the girl with the bow said. "He disrespected you and by disrespecting you, he disrespects us."

"Oh poo," Demetri said. "And you were any different? If I got in a fight every time somebody said something stupid I would be fighting all the time and have no time for other things. Like training young hot heads how to give respect to receive it."

"Point taken," she said looking down. "The candidate asks forgiveness for her words and previous disrespect sir."

"Yes yes," Demetri said. "Now, I expect my troopers to use the knowledge they have acquired to watch the perspective candidates we will meet and evaluate in the next month. A trooper does not acknowledge the existence of a prospective candidate, let alone speak to them. A trooper is always respectful of the supposed skills of a prospective candidate. A trooper with no status is always respectful and acknowledges those who have earned the bear, no matter the rank. A trooper is always respectful to elders and those of lower status. Except for prospective candidates, who of course do not exist to us. A trooper is always helpful and treat with honour the children who looks up to the trooper as his idol. As the children are our future. A trooper always treats everyone with the respect that the trooper wishes to receive from others. Except of course...."

"For perspective candidates, who do not exist," the ten answered for him and laughed.

"Does that mean?" one of the young men asked.

"Oh I cannot have candidates evaluating prospective candidates," Demetri said. "No no, that would not do. Only troopers and above can do that. I will now call you trooper and you will call me..."

"Sir!!" they all yelled out. This time Demetri joined them in their laugh.

Over the next weeks, their days were the same. They would start at dawn with their morning exercise. Then have breakfast. Then they would ride out to the herds and speak with the children guarding them. Demetri was always at the fore and the others took their cues from him. He would show this child how to tie a better knot, or that one a likely place for a wolf or bear to hide. The proper way to hold a spear when riding down a wolf or a bear. How to use the horses ears and nose to guide them and watch for danger. How to watch for the movements of birds and rabbits to use as warnings of approaching danger. How to signal their mates to danger and for help.

After lunch would find them watching the training of the new warriors. Making mental notes and observations which they would share among themselves that evening. All the while, they were respectful and helpful to all, not only the families that took them in, but the whole community. The next day, they would start again. Each day, more children joined them in their morning ritual and soon, some of their mothers.

Close to the end of the last week, the event that Demetri had been waiting for happened.

The afternoon training session had barely begun, when the big mouth from before came up to Demetri with five of his buddies in tow.

"You, Mr. Bigshot," he said loud enough for all to hear. "You were supposed to come here and teach us. So far all I have seen you do is practice your stupid dance, talk with children and walk around here like you own the place. You and your little wimps."

Demetri said nothing. He just pointed and beckoned.

"Sir!" she said. She was the smallest and youngest of his ten.

"Trooper," Demetri said. "A gnat and his friends are bothering me. Take care of it will you?"

"Sir, my pleasure sir!" she said and Demetri turned his back on the six tough guys and sedately walked away.

"Oh this will be fun," the big mouth said. "Typical. Pussy lets a pussy take the fall for him."

The group fanned out in a semi-circle before her and she turned sideways to them, her knees slightly bent and open handed arms before her elbows bent. With a roar, the big mouth took a run at her followed by his partners and in a blur, she exploded into motion. She caught and twisted the bigmouths punch, twisting him to the ground to trip two of his fellows, then swept her right leg at another's knee, dropping him to the ground, before twisting to deflect another punch and without seeming to hit him, dropped him to the ground. In seconds it was over. She stood straight and straightened out her clothing, brushing at some dust and looking at her nails.

"Sir, I believe the gnat problem has been resolved," she said. "But I think I may have broken a nail."

"That will never do trooper," Demetri said. "Do make sure you take care of that before tomorrows ride."

"Call assembly," he said to the training officer.

"I will take ten and ten only," he said to the young people assembled before him. "You have been told of the test. We leave at dawn tomorrow."

Then he left the field, followed by his troopers.

At dawn, without a word, they left. As before, he lead them outward for two hours, then circled back to the rear of the camp where the targets had been set up. He and his troopers never let the rest get any closer to them than fifty paces. At five hundred paces from the camp, they switched back to their saddled mounts and let the pack and free horses fan out behind them as they formed a line ten abreast and increased speed. At four hundred paces they broke into a gallop, at three hundred they loosed their arrows, then as a group hit their targets with first the lance, then the sword. Then their free horses demolished the targets with teeth and hoof as they passed. The group assembled in a line and watched the prospective candidates arrive and try to do the same.

Of the two hundred that had started, only fifty made it to the end. Of the fifty, only fifteen had all four horses with them. Of the fifteen, only ten had horses good enough and had hit all the targets with arrow, lance and sword. Six female and four male. The big mouth and three of his friends were not among them.

"You ten," Demetri said. "We leave at dawn. Bring your weapons, two quivers of twenty arrows, enough food for a week and whatever else you think you need."

As before, they left at dawn and rode without a break for four hours. Demetri let them settle in and as the water in the pot came to a boil, he bade the candidates to join them. He personally handed them their tea and bread.

"Once you have earned it, I will learn your name," Demetri said. "You will be addressed as candidate. You will call my people trooper and me sir. A candidate does not talk to me or a trooper without being asked to. You will keep one horse close and hobble the others and let them loose to graze. At all times you will have one guard on the horses, one guard on the perimeter and one patrolling the camp. Where we are going there are only bears, wolves and wild men to worry about. They will take or kill us and our animals. You will switch off every four hours. Tomorrow we will ride twice as far as today. Your horses are out of shape, but they will do better than you will. Three of you will leave an hour before the rest of us will. Leave your pack animals with us. We will take care of them for you. You will make up your own rotation. I want different people each day. You will pair up with one of my troopers who will show you what to do."

"Maybe, just maybe, you will survive the next few weeks. Then maybe you will survive the next year. If you do, you will have the right to be called a bear. And maybe, just maybe, the right to be an eagle. For you see, I am not even an eagle. I am only a bear. Maybe I will be an eagle too one day. Time will tell."

"We leave at dawn," and like before, he stood and went to his tent. His troopers followed him to theirs, leaving the candidates to sort it out. Throughout the night, the sentries had surprise visits. This time Demetri slept through the night.

"Candidates, set up camp," Demetri said. "Troopers follow me."

They had ridden hard for four hours. The scouts had found a suitable camp spot and they had just stopped. As the candidates began setting up tents and hobbling horses, Demetri took the ten troopers a hundred passes away and had them sit down facing him.

"Troopers, you are doing well," he said. "Our basic organization shall be ten troopers, just like the Bears use. Each troop will have a sergeant in charge and a corporal for when we break into teams of five. Right now I can handle everything as there are only twenty of you. That will change as we get more numbers. The High Council has determined that we will require more numbers and soon. Word has gotten around about us. You all noticed that there were many more trying out and more finished than with your group. The next bunch will be better prepared. We will be taking twenty from the next camp, thirty from the one after. Not all of them are going to be as well qualified as you or this new group and I will not have the time to give individual attention to them like I have with you and this group. I will need help. We have fought together, we have been together and working as a team for a while now. You know who should be your leaders, decide who your sergeant and corporal will be. Also, I want each of you to team up with one of the new candidates. You have learned a lot and can teach them."

"This is, I am sure you noticed, a bi sexual unit. Right now the numbers are even. I don't expect that to stay that way. For a number of reasons one of which I will get into now. You are all young men and ladies, away from home and parents for the first time and as boys will be boys and girls will be girls, things will happen. We are all human beings after all."

"So, first off. Any male that forces himself on a female without her permission and survives the attempt will be killed by me on the spot."

"Ladies, if you get pregnant, you are out of my unit, no exceptions. The job is far to rigorous and I cannot risk the loss of a female or her child. Our people need both. The father will be gone too. I expect discipline in this as in all other things that we do. That being said, what I don't know, I don't know. Oh, one more thing, any fighting over boys or girls will not be tolerated. Is that clear?"

"Ladies, a moment of your time? The rest of you, see to your camp and I need some tea."

Demetri waited until the men were back in camp before he addressed the women.

"As I am sure you are aware, I am a male," he said and put up with the giggles. "If you haven't noticed, my body is different than yours and functions differently. I am stronger, bigger and have more stamina than you do in most things. In a stand up fight, I have significant advantages over you. Having said that, you have learned to overcome that by using your bodies and smiles to disarm us. You are taught that from an early age. That will not work on me or any of the men we are training here, nor will it work on any trained warrior. We fight the weapon, not the person. But you have other advantages. You are faster and lighter. You have quick minds and adapt to situations faster. You will have to use that to your advantage or you will lose, every time."

"Next, your bodies have certain requirements, that mine does not. So far, the four of you have been able to find solutions for that. I will not pretend to know, nor attempt to make recommendations as I am frankly not qualified to do so. No matter that your mothers have told me what to expect. I am still not qualified. Your new sisters, will also have been told what to expect, as you were, by their mothers and sisters. Only you know what they will be facing. I expect you to help our new sisters to adapt to our situation. Maybe even, they might have some new ideas that you can try. This I leave to you. Now, your commander requires his tea and to rest, so he can oversee and undo the damage you new troopers are going to do to my poor new candidates."

The High Council had determined before the groups had split up, that the groups would come together at a central point once a year. This would give an opportunity for the groups to renew acquaintances with each, conduct trade in animals and goods and for the leadership to get tighter in one place to meet face to face and make decisions. The time had come and Demetri halted his now seventy troopers a day out from where the assembly was to be held.

He held his now usual welcoming ceremony to the new troopers and had all seventy assembled now before him.

"Tomorrow, you will reunite with family and friends once more," Demetri said. "Some of you for the first time in a year. Disperse, have some fun, relax. You deserve it. All of you have worked hard to be here. You are the first. Everyone that comes after will not have that distinction. To be the first, the best of the best. I expect you to act like it. We do not have to lord it over anyone. We know who we are and what we are capable of. We don't have to prove ourselves to anyone. I have worked hard and so have you, to create a certain image of us, no matter the provocation, you will not react to disrespect except to ignore it. You will give respect to any Bear, no matter their status, as you are not yet bears. You will give respect to our elders and be helpful if you can. We will be generous to the young ones. They are our future and look up to us."

"Everyone knows and has seen our selection processes. We will not divulge any of what happens after that. Nothing. Is that clear?"

"Your next year is going to be tougher. Now we will be taught to operate in large formations as we will have more numbers. The new candidates will still have to be taught how to do what you have been taught to do, as that is our primary purpose."

"Tomorrow, we will make a grand entrance. Then I do not want to see you, or hear from you for a week, I need a holiday too. Dismissed."

Chapter Five

They were on the trail a half hour after the sun had broken the horizon. Two hours later Demetri spotted the first scout. A half hour later the next, this one made a signal to some one behind him.

"Trooper," Demetri said to the trooper directly behind him. "Bring in the scouts and flankers."

Before the order could be completed, one from each came pelting back to report patrols of ten mounted and armed horseman converging on them. Demetri acknowledged the reports and told the messengers to bring their companions back to join the main body. Shortly after that, they had an escort of ten riders to each side and ten to the front. Although the escorts tried to engage them in conversation, they were ignored. The escorts were hard pressed to keep up with the seventies pace and soon were falling back as their horses tired. The seventy then switched from bare back to saddled horses on the fly as one unit.

The place chosen for the gathering was in a broad valley and the troopers crested the hill before it in column of two and slowed to a trot. Laid out before them was the large encampment and people were streaming out of it to greet their arrival.

As they crested the hill, the seventy split from a column of two, into two lines abreast. Seven groups of ten separated by five paces to the sides and rear smoothly formed. Pack and spare horses ranged behind them as they had been trained, Demetri alone and five paces in front of the centre. Without command, as one they pulled the lances from the scabbards behind their right legs and jammed them behind the right knees and came to a canter. When the lines were dressed, they came to a gallop and collapsed together until they were knee to knee. Demetri pulled the sword from his back and pointed it in the air, waited a few heat beats and swung it level with his horses head and seventy lances came to an unwavering line of steel pointed at the becoming concerned spectators.

Seventy two mounted and two hundred eleven unmounted horses thundered down the hill at a full gallop making the ground tremble. A hundred paces from the spectators, they started a high pitched scream and more than a few of the spectators began to run. All but the armed, armoured and shielded hundred that the seventy were aiming for. These locked shields, in two ranks, the first going to one knee and bracing steel pointed two pace long spears on the ground, the second rank levelling the spears over the front ranks shoulders. At fifty paces, Demetri raised his sword and swung it level to the right side. The onrushing horses skidded to a stop, five paces from the line of spears they faced, their lances still level with their horses necks. Then Demetri raised his sword point first in the air and in a ripple starting on the left of his line, each lance was raised in turn to point skyward.

Demetri rode sedately up to the line of infantry and swept his sword to his face and then down to point at the ground on his right side.

"Reconnaissance Squadron, reporting as ordered! Sir!" he yelled.

"Company stand down!" the officer commanding the infantry yelled out and he strode forward and returned Demetri's salute with his own sword.

"Welcome to the Reconnaissance Squadron," the officer said. "You may dismiss your squadron Commander."

Demetri once again saluted with his sword and Barney backed up until he was once again five paces in front of the line of troopers, then turned to face them.

"Reconnaissance Squadron!" Demetri yelled. "Dismissed!"

"Hoorah!" the troopers belted out, then broke formation, collected their three horses and in small groups dispersed to greet family and friends.

"Impressive Demetri," Alphonso said sticking out his hand as Demetri dismounted. "I suspected what was coming, but I still almost pissed myself as you guys rode down on us."

"And the myth grows," Demetri said, ignoring the hand and pulling his sisters husband to him in a big hug.

"Ach, finally someone adult I can talk to," Demetri said. "I won't have to be a babysitter or teacher for a while."

"That bad eh?" Alphonso said.

"Oh, they are a good bunch for the most part," Demetri said. "I have the first groups taking over training for the newer ones. That helps a lot. I just never get a chance to let my hair down, you know?"

"Ya, I do," Alphonso said. "At least we here can get together and let off some steam once in a while. Oh, by the way. The council wants to meet with you this afternoon."

"Not going to happen," Demetri said. "I just got here. The plan for the rest of the day is. Unpack and get my horses settled in. Find my quarters. Have a bath, put on some clean clothing.

"Have a dinner cooked by someone who actually knows how to cook and sleep in a real bed. I plan on sleeping in the next morning and checking the horses I left behind. Then meeting friends. The next morning would be good though."

"They won't be happy," Alphonso said. "But I can see your point. Greta has planned a special meal for you tonight, so that is covered. I think those three there will be able to help you out finding your quarters and looking out for your horses. I have to dismiss my troops and become a human being again. I'll catch up with you later Demetri."

The three that Alphonso had mentioned were standing in a line a few paces away. A tall lad of about eighteen, flanked on the right by a blond female of the same age on his left and a young lad of about fifteen on his right. Demetri assumed his usual command blank expression and walked up to them, his four horses following him and spreading out behind him. The girl came forward a pace and came to attention.

"Sir! This candidate has been ordered to take care of your horses sir! With your permission sir!" she said and made a move to gather Barney's reins. Barney laid his ears back, rolled his lips back and snapped his teeth inches away from her face, stomping his right hoof hard just in front of her foot. The startled girl jumped back and tried to regain her composure. Barney relaxed his lips, rolling them slightly and popped his ears back up, assuming the, what, who me? Innocent look all horses have.

"Lesson one," Demetri said. "Our horses are trained to look out for themselves. They will attack any strangers coming near to them. You are lucky Barney is in a good mood young lady. Barney, the young lady has been ordered to look out for you and your team mates. Do you approve? Attention candidate! Do not move a muscle."

Barney stepped up to the girl and looked at her, up and down, twisting his head from side to side and flaring his nostrils as he took in her scent. Then he stepped back and one by one, the other three horses came up and did the same thing. Then they all looked at each other and rumbled, shaking their heads left and right and up and down. Barney walked forward once more and nodded his head several times and laid his head on her shoulder for a second.

"Barney says it is ok," Demetri said. "Barney, go with this young lady. She will unsaddle and groom all of you. Go relax for a few days. Young lady, they will follow you now. Please have my saddle and packs brought to my quarters, which I cannot tell you the location of, because I do not know yet."

"Sir! No problem sir!" she said. "The candidate knows where they are located sir!"

She moved off with Barney and the three mares ranged behind her in pairs. As each horse came by the tall lad, they nudged him in the belly with their heads as they passed.

"Well Alex," Demetri said. "It seems as though you have sprouted some."

"Sir yes Sir!" Alex said. "The candidate would escort the commander to his quarters Sir!"

"Who is the youngster?" Demetri asked.

"Sir! With your approval, this candidate has chosen the young one to be his replacement Sir!" Alex said.

Demetri gave a quick glance at the youngster and nodded his head. He pulled the scabbarded sword off his back and tossed it to the youngster.

"Ok Alex, as of now I am on holidays and not the commander and as far as I know you are not a candidate or perspective candidate, so I will call you Alex," Demetri said. "You will still address me as sir, but not so formally eh? Now I find I have a few minutes to spare in my schedule. You may take me to see my other horses and tell me of their progress eh?"

He found that his herd had grown by six and Alex informed him that his mares were in foal again and that his stallion had bred another eight for him.

"He is in great demand sir," Alex said. "I think that Barney would be even more so sir."

"Good job Alex," Demetri said. "The two year olds have been broken?"

"Yes sir," Alex said. "I have a line of volunteers to use them for herd duty sir."

"Young fellow," Demetri said. "You will begin to train them in formation riding this spring. Not before and not hard. I wanted to take those three mares with me this year but I guess that is out."

A commotion broke out in the middle of the horse herd. Horses were milling about, neighing loudly and two groups quickly formed. Over two hundred horses came together in two lines facing the rest of the herd, with Barney at their head and challenged the rest of the herd. Stomping feet, lifting lips and swinging heads. A large mare from the bigger herd came forward and rubbed her head on Barneys neck.

"Well that went faster than I thought it would," Demetri said as the horses broke off and began to mingle and graze again. "I thought we might have a few major scraps first."

"Ok, I'm going to need some replacement animals. Barney comes with me. Three geldings I think. Put the word out. I and Barney have the final say on which animals and the terms. Now where are my quarters? I can't stand the smell of myself anymore."

After an evening with his sister and Alphonso and an early night, Demetri found that untrue to his stated intentions, he could not sleep in. He found himself outside the temporary corral set up for his families horses gazing at them. Barney strolled up and rubbed his head on Demetri's shoulder and then butted him several times.

"Ya, I guess you're right," Demetri said and he began to look around for the gate. Spotting it, he walked around the perimeter toward it and Barney was waiting for him, pawing at the ground impatiently waiting for him to open it. Demetri opened it up enough to let Barney squeeze through and then rapidly shut and latched it again.

The two of them walked side by side to the river, both taking a drink of the slow moving crisp and clear water before splashing through to the other side. The water only came to below the knee on Demetri and the current was not strong, so wading across was easily accomplished. Once on the other side they continued to walk in the grey predawn light until they were a few hundred paces from the camp. At that point, Demetri removed his boots and shirt, folded up his pant legs and began to slowly perform his dance like movements. Barney, several paces away, also slowly went through his own movements. They had not trained like this together alone, for over a year. After an hour, they stopped and moved closer to each other, Demetri sprang up on Barney's back and together they slowly performed a ballet. Demetri swaying left to right, front to back. Arms going this way, then that. Barney delicately raising front hoof then rear, pivoting this way then that. At no time did they move fast. Everything was in slow motion. Then they both came to a complete stop. Both man and animal wet from sweat and in one blurring motion, redid the same exercise at full speed. Now the movements were fast and very violent. It ended in a series of pirouettes by Barney kicking rear legs and front, Demetri slashing his right arm down and to the side, then Barney reared on his hind legs and slashed the air with his front hooves, spinning in a circle, while Demetri slashed to left and right around him. Barney came back down to the ground and stopped. Demetri slid down from him and put his arms around Barney, man and horse hugging each other, both breathing deeply with sweat poring off of them. Neither of them noticed the group of young herders looking at them with mouths open or the group of ten troopers watering their horses at the rivers edge who had just witnessed something they had never seen before. Man and horse working together as a team. A highly effective and deadly team.

"He hasn't taught us everything," a female trooper said. "But I see now why we practice those movements. He didn't even have a saddle or reins."

"He has been teaching us the basics," a male trooper said. "Any of you have anything to do for the next couple of hours? Come on then. Let's get out of site and start to practice."

"Those three geldings and four foals, or no deal," Demetri said. "I have no shortage of other offers."

The horseman from the Russian group scowled and looked at the ground.

"I have him for the rest of the week?" the man asked. "Ok deal then."

"Good, bring your mares and then leave the geldings," Demetri said. "My people will put them together."

"Alex, I want those three geldings ready to go when I leave here," Demetri said.

After changing into clean clothing, Demetri walked down to the centre of the camp, where the big council tent was set up. He nodded at the troopers he met on the way and greeted fondly friends he had made over the years among the five groups. It was close to midday by the time he was ushered into the council tent.

"So good of you to finally deem to meet your leaders commander," an older man said a frown on his face.

The man sat with his back straight in a large chair in the centre of the group. Demetri looked around at the thirty assembled people in the tent and did not like what he saw. The man clearly dominated the group and he along with four other big men were the only ones armed in the group and stood apart from them all.

"I have just come home from a year in the wild, far from friends and family," Demetri said. "I can just as easily go away."

"I am the leader of this community and you will do as I command!" the man said.

"You serve at the peoples command sir," Demetri said in a quiet voice. "As do we all. If the people no longer have confidence in me, I will gladly leave and let others take over. I did not leave one corrupt regime to serve in another one."

"Who do you think you are?" the man demanded. "I tell you, I am leader of this community and you will do as I say."

"I am Demetri Bekenbaum, a free man and I choose not to follow you or acknowledge you as my leader," Demetri said and he turned sideways to the five men before him and slightly bent his knees.

The big man gestured to his four henchman and they advanced on Demetri.

"Take this unmanly dancer from my site and string him up as an example to the people," he said.

Demetri did not wait for the four men, but exploded toward them. Before they could draw their swords he had two of them gasping for air through throats that were crushed. The third had barely pulled the first inches clear of the scabbard, when his nose was driven into his skull and the fourth had his arm broken and the artery in his neck crushed as the sword came clear. In a flash Demetri cartwheeled and drove both his feet into the large man's chest flinging him backward in his chair. Then he looked into the man's eyes, drew the man's sword, placed it beneath his Adams apple and stopped.

"I do not recognize you as my leader and have pledged to rid my people of tyranny," Demetri said, pushed the sword into the man's neck and watched him die.

He stepped back and looked at the others in the tent.

"After only a year," he said quietly. "You have returned us to this after only a year. I leave in the morning."

"Wait!" came a voice from the tent opening. A group of leather armoured warriors entered the tent. Each had a sword in hand and they fanned out in an arc around Demetri. Demetri pulled the sword from the man's neck and turned to face them.

"I will serve no man as slave," Demetri said. "I am prepared to die a free man. Are you?"

"Yes," Alphonso said and he let his sword drop, the others with him did likewise. "We had no idea Demetri. We came here to stop this."

"I am but one man," Demetri said. "You are thirty."

He pointed to those around him.

"They were only five. Sometimes a few must sacrifice so that many may live. Being a leader of the people demands that sacrifice from us. If you are unwilling, then step aside. The people do not want sheep as leaders."

Demetri threw the sword at the feet of the thirty and elbowing his way through the warriors, left the tent.

Demetri had his saddle across his shoulder, bridal and saddle bags across it. His sword strapped to his back. His bow was in his free hand and two quivers of arrows on the saddle.

"Get all my horses together Alex," he said dumping the saddle on the ground. "Take the three geldings and the mares back to their owner. Do it now!"

In a few minutes, he had Barney saddled and he and his small herd were galloping out of the camp. Headed he knew not where.

"Do you have enough water in that pot for tea for us," Greta said sitting in her saddle. Her face and clothing were caked in dust, as was the female trooper with her. She was the one that had so impressed Demetri with her bow a year earlier.

"Look out for your animals first," Demetri said. He rose and wrapping a rag around the pot handle took it off the fire and filled it in the small stream next to his camp. Placing it back on the rocks around the fire, he sat back down again.

Hearing a nicker and a laugh, he looked up and saw Barney nudging and pushing the female trooper, she gabbing his ears and tugging on them laughing.

"Alphonso his troop and the thirty are behind us," Greta said. "They will be here by nightfall. I came to make sure you stayed. Margarete said you would stop just after midday. She was right."

Demetri grunted and pulled his saddle bags over. Rummaging through them, he pulled out his bag of tea leaves.

"Come on Demetri, think," Greta said. "They are just farmers. As soon as Al found out, he came running to put a stop to it. The man was cunning. Those people are not trained warriors. Not like us. They are herders, mothers and fathers."

"And they will all die because of it," Demetri said. "Do you think the Church will let us live now? Any of us?"

"We know Demi, we know," Greta said. "But the transmissions lately have been conciliatory. All forgiveness and such. Some of the council were beginning to waver. Until this. He and his group were actually Churchmen and they convinced them things would be different."

Demetri looked into the distance and his eyes found themselves straying to the trooper playing in the water with Barney.

"You could do worse you know," Greta said softly. "The children adore her and she them. Look even Barney loves her. You are not getting any younger you know."

"Ah come on Grets, I'm five years her senior," Demetri said. "That and I am her commander. Besides, I have no time for that now."

"If not now when?" Greta said. "God put us here to make better lives for those behind us."

"Ah shit, she don't even think of me like that," Demetri said.

"Just go down and talk to her," Greta said. "There is nobody here but us. Nobody will know."

"It's not right Grets," Demetri said. "People will say I used my influence on her. Besides, if she shoots me down, it might ruin everything I am trying to build here."

"Oh, the mighty Eagle, being shot down by a mere trooper," Greta said. Now she was getting angry. "You charge into a group of Holy Warriors intent on killing you. Defeat a large band of Wild Men and defeat five well trained Holy Warriors with only your bare hands and you are scared of a twenty one year old, hundred pound girl? Just go and talk to her. It's not like she is going to bite you or anything."

Demetri looked at the ground beneath his feet for a moment. Then he sighed and stood. He slowly walked to the steam and stood watching her and Barney for a few minutes. Finally Barney saw him and snorted, lifting his head up and down. The girl turned around and saw Demetri standing there. The blond ponytail had come unpinned from the crown of her head and was across her left shoulder to lay across her breast. She followed his gaze and brushed the hair to fall onto her back. Both of them stood staring at each other. Barney picked that moment to make something happen. He butted the girl hard in the butt with his head knocking her off balance and into Demetri's arms. Then he splashed them both with a front hoof and pranced away, kicking his back heels in the air as he went.

Demetri held her in his arms feeling her supple body against his and looked down into her eyes and felt himself swoon.

"SSssory Sir!" she exclaimed and pushed back from him, falling on her butt in the stream.

The spell broken, Demetri stood and looked at her, trying to keep a stern look on his face. Finally he could help it no more and started to laugh. Thinking something was wrong, she looked about her frantically, looking for something amiss. Demetri still laughing, held out his arm to her.

"Come on Margarete, I'll help you up," he said.

"What did you just say?" she said. "Sir."

"Oh, I am sorry if I offended you trooper," Demetri said, wiping the smile off his face. "That was not my intention I assure you."

She looked up at him with his hand still out stretched to help her up. She grabbed it at the elbow with her right hand and snaked her left leg behind his knees while she pulled, tumbling him into the water head first. As he came spluttering up, it was she who was laughing now at the look on his face. Then he collapsed on his butt beside her and they both laughed.

"I am Demetri," he said. "My friends call me Demi. I am told your name is Margarete Marie."

"Margarete will do Sir, um Demetri," she said, holding her hand out. He took it and marvelled at how soft it was, even with the callouses from sword and bow. He kept hold of it as he stood and helped her up. Demetri looked to where Barney was standing one ear pointed at them and he pointed his finger at him and waged it.

"Bad boy Barney," he said. "You have gotten Margarete all wet with your playing around."

Barney snorted, put that, what, who me look on his face and started grazing.

"Come on to the fire," Demetri said. "The tea should be ready and you should get out of those wet cloths." He had a hard time keeping his eyes off her nipple erect breasts as they walked back, or the tight butt as he let her walk before him.

"If you ladies will excuse me," Demetri said when he came back to the fire. "I am going to get out of these wet cloths. It gets cold out here as soon as the sun starts going down."

"He does have a nice butt does he not Marg?' Greta said as he walked away. "I hadn't noticed Grets," Margarete said.

"That's not what your sister tells me Marg,' Greta said. "Now go get some dry cloths on before the poor boy's eyes pop out of his head."

'The things we have to do,' Greta thought as Margarete moved to the other side of the trees to change. Looking over to the horses, Greta saw Barney looking at her. She smiled and saluted him. He nodded his head up and down and neighed, then turned his back and started grazing again.

"I don't know what got into that fool horse," Demetri said. "That's not like him."

Margarete came back and sat down on the other side of Greta.

"Must be because he got lucky today," Greta said. "Alex said the mares were all but backing up to him. Oh look, doesn't she turn a lovely shade of red Demi? Oh, you too by the way."

A large cloud of dust could be seen just poking over the horizon.

"We have a couple of hours yet I think," Demetri said nodding at the cloud.

"I do hope you will pin that lovely Eagle on your collar," Greta said. "You need to remind people who you are from time to time."

"I know who I am," Demetri said. "They know who I am. There is no need to show off."

"You are an Eagle Sir?" Margarete said. "But you said.."

"Oh let me guess," Greta said. "If you are lucky, you might become Bears instead of troopers. Maybe someday even Eagles. I am not even good enough to be an Eagle, so dream on. Same speech he gave us."

Now Demetri dug in his saddle bags and retrieved a small cloth covered object. Greta took it from his hands and unwrapped it. Then she gently and lovingly pinned it on his left collar. The sun glinted off the highly polished brass.

"He is not just an Eagle Marg," Greta said. "He is THE Eagle."

Then she stood, came to attention and saluted, holding it until Demetri returned it.

"Ah sit down already," Demetri said. "We are just some friends having a tea by the river."

"When they came back from Home World," Greta said. "The six brought back with them knowledge of how it was back in the old days. How it was that our families had come here. How it had been for them back there. How we had been turned away from our original purpose by self serving men and the Church. How we could make simple changes that would vastly improve our lives.

"We all knew that the Church would try and stop us once they found out. We began to look for ways to protect ourselves. We found writings of ancient civilizations, two who had dominated much of Home World in their time. We saw that we could easily adopt their ways and defeat the Church with low tech long forgotten methods. We adopted our infantry tactics from a group called the Romans. Our cavalry from a group called Cossacks. When we were training and developing our tactics. Demetri could always see our attacks coming and was always prepared and would defeat us almost all of the time. Finally someone asked him how.

"He told us, he molded his troop after a group of conquerors called Mongols. A nomadic group of people who had banded together and ruled much of Home World. No one they faced could stop them. Even behind high stone walls. How the Cossacks had copied and modified the tactics to suit themselves, but that the tactics would only be a short term solution for us here.

"We decided to train some of our people in these tactics and chose Demetri to lead them. They would have to be young people, already used to horses and low tech life. It was decided that when the time came to make the break we would start with your age group. You would train to become light cavalry. To be our eyes and ears. To strike hard and fast in our enemies rear to cause panic and fear. We kept searching for an appropriate name for them. Then someone watched Demetri training his peculiar dance moves and said, 'he looks like and eagle with his arms stretched out like that. An Eagle ready to pounce.' The name stuck and here you are."

"But you have not been training us in these matters," Margarete said. "You have been training us how to move fast and light over long distances. How to spot movements from afar and to plan how and where to observe and not be seen."

"Which comes first," Demetri said. "Walking or running? First you must learn to walk, then you learn to run. Our prime function is to spot and identify the enemy. How many they are and the direction of their travel. The habits and formations they use on the move, their fortifications at night. Then we report that back to the infantry and cavalry, so they might plan their attacks. To do that, we must be fast, light and unseen. This I have been teaching you. Next you will be taught, how and when to fight and when to run. That is what we will be doing. Hitting hard and running. Our job will be to wear the enemy down, to make them tired. So that when our main body comes to them, they will be defeated. If we get lured into a main fight we lose and our people lose. That is why only the smartest and the best will be Eagles. We have to be."

"The Cossacks beat a much larger and more power full army like that," Greta said. "It is called death by a thousand cuts. You cut the enemy quick, but make him bleed. Over and over again. He begins to become wary, no longer on the offensive but on the defensive. All the while he is getting weaker and weaker. Soon he has not the capacity to harm you any longer and you strike him hard and for real. He is not expecting it and is defeated."

"We will hit them fast," Demetri said. "From every direction at anytime and anywhere. At night, in the morning, at noon. Appearing out of nowhere and disappearing again."

"Like you have taught us girls how to fight a much bigger and stronger man," Margarete said. "Many short sharp punches to the body and dance away."

At that point, the scouts from the main party came into view and they stopped talking. The main group came behind shortly and started to dismount.

"Trooper Rosenthal," Demetri said. "Show them where to water their animals."

The other nine of the original ten looked at Margarete and then at Demetri.

"What are you looking at trooper Chimilovitch," Demetri said. "Get off that animal and cool him down before he founders."

"Sir! Said Chimilovitch.

"What the hell Mags?" he said to Margarete in a low voice as they walked away.

"Officers," she said, shrugging her shoulders.

The thirty civilian leaders and five military came up to Demetri and Greta. The military ones saluted and had the salutes returned by both of them. The nine troopers looked again at Margarete, who again shrugged her shoulders.

"Ok," Alphonso said. "We realize the error of our way. We apologize. It won't happen again, blah blah blah. We don't have time for this shit Commander. What we predicated would happen is. They are bring more Holy Warriors and Inquisitors in, which in their zeal and arrogance is only creating more unrest, resulting in more troops being sent. The last batch included two battalions of regular army troops. The Emir is working hard to keep things under control, but he has no control of the Church. We are going to have to up the time table Commander."

"Now before you get all hot and bothered," a civilian leader said. "The people had already decided on this matter before the gathering."

"The selection process has already been completed," Alphonso said. "You will have enough candidates to round up your numbers to eight hundred. You already have seventy fully trained. I know your methods. You already have them training in leadership roles. We just knocked off six months from your training schedule. A month, six weeks tops is all they will need. Then start the advanced training. They haven't spotted us yet, but it is only a matter of time. We need to be ready."

"I am going to need more than just troopers," Demetri said.

"Way ahead of you," Alphonso said. "You will have two hundred highly skilled support people. Medical, for both animal and human, armourers, fletchers, bow makers, herders for the pack and spare horses."

"Shit, now I am going to have to train an officer for them," Demetri said.

"You aren't the only Eagle in this group big brother," Greta said. She had put her Eagle on her collar. "The kids are old enough to get by without their mother now. I have already chosen my people. We will go through the first six weeks along with the others. We need to be able to keep up and protect ourselves."

"Well, you've got it all figured out then," Demetri said. "What do you need me for?"

"The battalion needs its Colonel that's why," Alphonso said. "Is he always this dumb Major?"

"He never used to be," Greta said. "Maybe we are just getting smarter?"

"You ten, don't get comfortable over there!" Demetri said. "Rosenthal saddle Barney, Chimilovitch, you and the rest of those reprobates take down my camp and get it packed up. The sooner we get going the sooner we are back to our nice cushy beds. Hood, you and Rosenthal take one of my spare mounts to ride. Let's go, let's go people. I have a lot to do and no time to do it in."

The ten, with Greta exploded into action. Horses were saddled and the camp was swiftly taken apart and packed away. The Civilians all looked at Alphonso. They had not understood a word Demetri had said.

"Don't look at me," he said. "It's a dead language from the Home World. I think it's called Russian."

Within half an hour, they were off at a canter right from the start. Demetri went to the head of the column and stayed ten paces ahead of them and would let them no closer. Soon they stopped trying.

"He has a lot on his mind right now," Greta said. "He is right. We have no time and a lot to do. Things you cannot help him with. We are making this up as we go you know. Book knowledge is fine, in theory, but until one actually does it, one really does not know if it will work. Some of it hasn't. That's what training is for."

"How long have you been an Eagle?" Margarete asked.

"It was me who named us," she said and spurred to ride with her brother. Soon both were in deep conversation.

"Do you know how lucky we were?" Margarete asked her fellows. "He picked us himself. He trained us exclusively himself."

"We are his Ten," Chimilovitch said. "Everything we are and are about to become is because of him. We are the Ten."

They all looked at each other and started to chant Ten, over and over.

"They finally got it," Greta said looking over at her brother. "They got it faster than the five of us did."

"Their teacher got better," Demetri said. "Those ten are like we six. The future of our people."

The group behind them began to sing. The song Demetri had taught them. They all knew the words and the meaning behind them. Demetri looked at his sister and smiled. Then he too started to sing and brother and sister picked up the pace.

'No my brother,' she thought. 'You are the future of our people and all of us would gladly go through the gates of hell after you. None more than Margarete.'

Chapter Six

The sun only had a sliver over the eastern horizon when they crested the hill and started the decent into the valley the grand camp was in. Demetri slowed to a walk and waved the ten to come closer.

"Five of you disperse to the groups," he said. "Find one of the seventy and tell them to tell their brothers and sisters to meet us by the river bank after the sun is up. Then find the highest ranking officer in the group and escort them to my quarters. You ten will meet me half way up the hill at dawn. Your swords on your backs. Chimilovitch, you Rosenthal and Hood will join me in my quarters after you and the others put the horses and tack away. You others wait outside my quarters until I call for you."

Demetri stepped off of Barney, patted him on the neck and then removed his weapons and saddle bags from the saddle. Slinging the saddle bag across one shoulder, the two quivers on the other, he held the lance in his left hand and landed it on his left shoulder. The hand carrying the bow swinging as he walked away. Reaching the tent, he balanced the lance on his shoulder and pulled the tent flaps apart, he laid the lance on the ground in front of his bed, the point facing the rear wall, flung the saddle bags on the bed, hung the quivers and bow on the pegs for them attached to the ridge pole. Pulling the scabbard from his back, he carefully draped it across his one chair's back and crossed to the small stove in the front corner. He got a fire going, then lit the two lamps he had. Going to his foot locker at the foot of the bed, he flung it open and rummaged through it, finding the box he was looking for and threw it on the bed, then closed the footlocker and sat down opening the box. In side were ten small boxes. He arranged them on the foot locker and took two and placed them in a jacket pocket. He had just finished that when Greta announced they were there.

"Come in," Demetri said.

The three removed their caps and the two young people came to attention and tried to salute, catching their hands on the roof as they did so.

"Now you know why we don't salute indoors," Demetri said. He left them standing at attention and pulled the two boxes from his pocket holding one out to Greta. "If the Major would be so kind?"

Greta came forward, clicked her heels and accepted the box and pivoted to face Chimilovitch. Demetri stood even with her and also clicked his heels together. Then they both pulled out the shiny brass eagles from the boxes. Greta pinned on Chimilovitche's, Demetri Margarete's. Then they both took one step back, raised their right knees to belt level and stomped them on the ground. They clicked their heels together and bowed their necks stiffly.

"Welcome to the Eagles, brother and sister" Demetri said. "I had planned a more elaborate ceremony, but time is short. Sit, all of you, please."

"Our ranks are about to be swelled," he said pacing back and forth in front of them. "When we leave here there will be over a thousand of us. Major Bekenbaum will be in charge of two hundred support troops. I will be in overall charge. I will be requesting another fifty from the groups. I will need personal troops and couriers. Major Rosenthal, you and Major Chimolovitch will train the extra fifty. They will not be as good as the rest are."

He smiled at the looks the two had.

"A lot to take in all at once eh?" he said. "Of course, if you don't want it, I could always make you just common troopers."

Both of them shook their heads, dumbfounded.

"Right then, both of you will be in charge of a wing of the battalion. You each will have control of four captains, who will be in charge of one hundred troops each. These will be called squadrons. Each squadron will be made up of ten formations of ten. There will be one lieutenant in charge of five formations and one sub lieutenant in charge of every two. Sergeants will command the other. The eight captains will be made up from our ten. Lieutenants, sub lieutenants and sergeants to be made up from the rest of the seventy. If you run out, make do until you can promote suitable candidates. Ah our visitors have arrived. Come in Commanders, come in."

"Thank you for joining me at such short notice," he said. "I won't keep you long. As you know our time is short and I find I will need ten more candidates from each of your groups. Have them report with the other candidates in two days. Thank you for your time."

The five nodded their heads and left the tent.

"Major Bekenbaum if you would help me with the honours?" Demetri picked up four of the remaining boxes, Greta the other four. He indicated the entry way. "Brother, sister, if you please, call the ten together."

Margarete and Chimilovitch ducked out of the tent calling stand to. He motioned Greta to proceed him and exited the tent to face the ten in a long line in front of him. He beckoned the two new majors to join them. Then he started on the left end accompanied by Margarete and Greta the right with Chimilovitch. They went down the line pinning Eagles on each collar. Once they had finished the last two. The four of them took three paces backward, came to attention and saluted the eight standing in front of them. He then put them at ease. A small crowd had gathered to see what was going on.

"Welcome to the Eagles brothers and sisters," he said. "I handpicked and trained each of you. You are the best of the best, you are my ten. I expect much from my Captains. You will NOT let me down. Vonhoadle, you still have that bottle tucked into your jacket? Hand it over."

Demetri spun the top off of the full bottle and let it fall in the dust at his feet. He raised the bottle high.

"To the Eagles!" he said and took a deep pull. "To my Ten!" He took another pull and handed it to Greta who saluted the ten and the Eagles. The bottle made the rounds and came back to him empty. He turned it upside down to make sure, then tossed it to the corner of his tent.

"Now go," he said. "Celebrate your Eagles and your promotions. If any of you show up tomorrow to drunk or hung over to function, I will kick your asses back to candidate so fast you'll not know what hit you. Now get out of my sight!"

"You too Greta," Demetri said. "Go have some fun, celebrate. It might be our last chance for some time."

"What about you Demi, are you coming?" she asked.

"No dear sister," he said kissing her on both cheeks. "They need to be with each other tonight, not me. Besides.."

"Yes I know," she said. "You have a lot to do and little time to do it in."

He smiled a sad smile, patted her on the shoulder and went back into the tent.

Greta caught up to them as the first of the bottles were being passed around the camp fire they had claimed as their own. Margarete saw her coming and looked over her shoulder to the laneway behind her.

"He's not coming Mags," Greta said. "He has a lot of Colonel things to do. The regiment always comes first. If he does not come to see you tomorrow night, you go to him. Now come on, tell me some juicy stories of your fun and games together nyet?"

Demetri pulled out his old comm unit and after making sure he had enough charge to do what he wanted to do, he turned it on and browsed through all the reports he was interested in. then he shut it down again and packed it away into one of his packs along with the small solar charger for it. Taking the pot of now luke warm water off his stove he poured a cup and dropped some tea leaves into it. After a few minutes of looking into it, he took a sip and stared at the entrance to his tent. He sighed and rose, putting the cup on top of the stove and opened the footlocker. He pulled out the tightly rolled bundle of dark blue clothing he found there, laying them carefully on his bed. Then found the high dark brown boots with laces running up the front. He took off the clothing he was wearing and starting with the dark blue with large red stripe running down the outer edge of each inseam, he donned the uniform. Next was the white shirt, which he tucked into the pants. Sitting on the bed, he put on the boots tying them up to the top, his pants tucked into them. He made sure he rolled the edges neatly around the tops of the boots. Then he removed the Eagle from the collar of his other jacket and carefully pinned it on the dark blue tunic laying on the bed. Now he pulled a dark blue almost black beret out of the footlocker and taking a rag, polished the brass crest on it. A large tree leaf flanked on the left by an eagle and the right a bear. He laid it beside the dark blue jacket on the bed and walked out of the tent.

It was still dark. A hint of gray light poking over the western horizon. He saw the two young people that always seemed to be near by him, rise from the fire they had been sitting beside and came to attention. They rotated, but there were always two. They stayed out of the way, but usually within earshot.

"Saddle Barney and bring him here," Demetri said. "Inform Major Bekenbaum, my Ten and the rest of the troop, they are to assemble in the main square in full uniform a half hour after dawn. Horses saddled and in full uniform. You are to remind Major Bekenbaum I said full uniform."

"Sir!" they both said.

"And candidates," Demetri said. "All candidates are to be in formation on the north side of the river. No later than sunrise. Dismissed."

Both candidates saluted, then sprinted away. One in the direction of the horse lines, the other towards his sister's quarters.

Demetri walked back into his tent and took the box holding the other eagle crests out and put in on the bed. Then he opened another larger box, taking out ten smaller boxes from it. He put five in one jacket pocket and five in the other. Then he buttoned the shirt right up to the top and donned the jacket. It was the same dark, blue almost black that the rest of the uniform was. It had a dark red stripe running down the outside of each arm sleeve, around the bottom, and down the outside where the buttons went. The two closed breast pocket covers were also dark red, held closed by the gleaming brass eagle crested buttons that also held it closed. Once he had buttoned it up fully, he draped his sword across his back and adjusted it so that the hilt was over his left shoulder and that it was held tight to his body. Hearing hoof falls stop by his tent, he took the beret and walked out of the tent, putting the beret on. Square to his head and coming to rest just above his eyebrows. He took the reins from the candidates hands. The candidate was looking at him. Her eyes were wide and moving up and down as she took in the uniform.

"There is a box on the bed," Demetri said. "If you would so kind and carry it for me?"

"Sir!" she said and scurried into the tent, to return with the box in both hands held before her.

"Follow me," Demetri said and started walking.

Greta was waiting for him, dressed as he was, her horse saddled and at her shoulder. She wordlessly walked in step with him. As they walked, they were joined by the Ten, in their dark blue uniforms that matched, almost, Greta and Demetri's.

"Candidate," Demetri said quietly. "Hand the box to Major Chimilovitch if you please. Then join your comrades."

When they reached the centre square, the rest of the troop was waiting for them. In formation. Demetri stopped five paces away from them and the ten formed up in a single line behind he and Greta. The other troopers kept silent but they nodded at each other and pointed with chins at the subtle changes to the uniforms.

"Troop prepare to mount," Demetri said. His voice just slightly louder than normal. "Mount"

Then he swung Barney and with Greta beside him, walked out of the square, the two majors behind them. The other eight captains taking position on the right front files of five of their troops.

The sun was almost fully over the horizon, when in that formation they walked cross the river to the other side.

"Troop to deploy in line!" Demetri ordered without stopping and heard the thunder of hooves as the eighty deployed into two lines behind him. Halfway up the hill he ordered the halt and he and Greta went two paces further before they spun around to face the troopers.

"Dismount!" Demetri said. "Officers! Front and center."

"Majors, hand ten boxes to each Captain," he ordered. "Reform on your troops once you have your boxes Captains."

"Attention!" he called once all the captains had rejoined their troopers. He put his hands on the pommel of Barney's saddle.

"You are the first," Demetri said. "You were picked first. The best of those who tried first. You had no idea what you would be facing, what was expected of you. To be honest, neither did I. All of us and I do mean all of us, including me, surpassed my expectations. We truly are the best of the best. Congratulations Eagles. Captains, if you please?"

While each Captain went down the line pinning Eagles to their troopers left collars, Demetri slipped the five boxes from his right pocket to Greta. She looked inside one and smiled.

"Greta, you stay here," Demetri said. "When I come back, follow my lead. I'm winging this."

He let them congratulate each other for a few minutes then called them to attention.

"Officers, front and Center!" he bellowed.

He waited until they were lined up five paces in front of the other troopers and moved Barney out at a slow walk. He trooped down their line looking each one in the face as he went by them. Then he went behind them and addressed the rest of the troop, riding up and down the lines as he did so. Looking each trooper in the face as he passed them.

"Congratulations, you are now all Eagles," he said. "But that does not mean things will get easier for you. In fact, your learning has just begun. I cannot be every where. Tomorrow we will be joined by almost a thousand wet behind the ears kids. It will be your job to teach them everything you know. Their lives and yours will depend on it very soon. You will teach them to forget they are Americans, British, German, Russian and Cossack. You will turn them into Eagles."

"You have noticed, the Lieutenant Colonel and I have a few more trinkets than you do. We like you have and will, have received these for what we have done. Not for who we are, or who we are related to. They were earned just as you have earned those badges and the buttons that go with them. There is only one way to earn the cap badge. You must have faced and survived combat. These ten standing in front of you have done just that. They defeated twice their number in mortal and deadly combat. With distinction and honour."

Now he rode up to and beside Greta. He nodded at her and they both dismounted and walked in front of their horses. One by one he called each of the ten forward by name asked for their beret and personally pinned the badge on it and placed it back on their heads kissed them on both cheeks and saluted them. All but Margarete. He called her last.

He held her at arms length, his arms on both her shoulders after he was done and looking into her eyes, felt himself drowning.

"Wwwould the Major do me the honour of allowing me to escort her to the officer's party this evening?" he stuttered out softly.

"Who's asking?" she said softly in return. "Demetri or the Colonel?"

"Demetri Margarete," he said.

"Well Dem, you can pick me up at six then," she said. "And Dem? My friends call me Mags."

"Very well then Marg," he said, releasing her and saluting. She returned his salute, about faced and with a little extra swing in her hips joined her comrades in the line.

"She handled that very well," Greta said. "I would have told you to piss off doing that in front of everyone."

"You ain't seen nothing yet," he said smiling. Then he wiped the smile off his face.

"Officers! About Face!" he growled.

"Battalion will salute the Ten! Salute!" he ordered. "Mount up!" He put the smile back on his face.

"Now we show those wet behind the ears, snot nosed candidates how Eagles dance," he drew the sword from his back and spun Barney around to face the in formation candidates ranged along their side of the river bank. On the camp side was a large crowd.

"If any of you dummies embarrass me, I will bust you back down to chicken herders so fast my boot will hardly have time to connect with your ass."

"Just you make sure you can keep up, old man" Greta said right beside him, just as loudly. They both laughed and started to sing as they and their horses, began the slow opening movements of the dance. They began to move forward a step at a time and the song sped up as did the movements. By the last verse, they were at full speed, the ground trembling from eighty sets of hooves striking the ground violently and the air vibrated from the air passing over blades that moved in a blur. All the horses, as one reared on the hind legs and thrashed their fore hooves at the end, no more than ten paces in front of the candidates lines. As fast as it had started it stopped. Not a horse or a trooper moved. Swords laying across right shoulders.

Demetri looked at the candidates ranged before him a blank expression on his face and he slowly rode up and down the line.

"Today, you stand before us as children," he began. "Like all children, you think you know everything, are tougher than nails, that nothing can beat you. Well you won't be able to hide behind mommies skirts anymore. Tomorrow you are mine! Maybe, just maybe, if you can keep up and survive the next while, you might be able to do what we have just done. Maybe. I have been surprised before."

"Enjoy tonight. Tonight will be the last night you enjoy as children. Make sure mommy tucks you in nice and snug tonight and packs you a nice yummy lunch for tomorrow. Because tomorrow at dawn, your asses are mine. God help and protect you all."

He raised his sword over his head and twirled it, bring it sharply down to his right. Then he started walking toward the centre of the formation slowly, his officers forming in rows of five behind him. Seeing he had no intention of stopping, the ranks before him split leaving them room to pass and he came to a trot. He nor his troopers looking at those they passed, they trotted directly to the horse lines and as one dismounted and replaced the swords back into the scabbards at their backs.

"Ok gang," Demetri said. "We have been invited to the regimental officer's party tonight. Make sure those uniforms are perfect. Your parents have been given the right buttons for you. Oh one more thing before you go. Marg come here please."

She came up and stood at attention in front of him.

"Sir!" she said.

"Any of you guys have any thoughts of dancing with my date tonight forget it," he said. Then he put his hands on her shoulders and kissed her. On the lips. He felt a jolt of lightning flow through him.

"That's for saving my ass with your bow that day," he said loud enough for everyone to hear. Then he kissed her again.

"That's for saying yes," he said staring deep into her eyes.

She came close and pulled his head down to her with her left hand and kissed him hard, folding herself into him. Then she pushed him back.

"That's for asking me," she said just as loud as he had earlier. "And if any of you floozies have any ideas, forget them. He's all mine!"

Then she kissed him tenderly this time and slow while the rest of the troopers cheered.

"Ok you two, leave some of that for tonight," Greta said. "My man isn't here yet and your making me all hot and bothered."

"Oh goody," a voice behind them said. "I guess I'm getting laid tonight."

"Al!" Greta yelled out. She spun around and sprinted to him jumping up, straddling her legs around his hips and her arms around him. She kissed him hungrily.

"Shit Al," one of Alphonso's comrades said. "If she's like that after only a couple of days, what's she gonna be like after six months?"

Greta stuck her tongue out at the man over Alphonso's shoulder and jumped back to the ground. She took his hand and started to drag him away.

"Do unsaddle my horse for me brother?" she said over her shoulder. Then with a giggle, she broke away and ran, Alphonso right on her heels.

For the fifth time in an hour Demetri got up from his seat and walked to the door. For the fifth time, he turned around and sat down again, this time on the bed. Looking down at his feet, he fiddled with the blouse of his pants around the boot tops. Ran his hands through his hair, stood up again and this time walked out of the tent. He started to walk to his right, then heard someone clear their throat behind him. Demetri stopped and looked back to see Alex run his hand over his head.

"Shit!" Demetri said and walked back into the tent and grabbed his beret, walked back out and jammed it firmly on his head. Turning left, he started to walk again, only to hear Alex clear his throat again.

"What this time?" Demetri asked, running his hands over his uniform. Alex just pointed the other way.

"Oh, right," Demetri said. "Go, play with your friends. Both of you. Get out of here, that's an order. Oh and Candidates, if you say anything, I'll kick your asses."

He walked along, head down staring at his feet. He almost walked right by, when Alex cleared his throat again.

"Sheeit!" Demetri said under his breath. "Get your head out of your ass Demi."

"Thanks Alex," Demetri said. "Now really, both of you get out of here and have some fun. It is going to be a long hard time for you starting tomorrow. Go on get."

They made no move to leave. Demetri cocked a fist and moved toward them pointing the other hand away from them. This time they left.

Demetri stood in the shadows across from Margaret's family tent. He could not hear what they were saying, but it sounded like they were having a good time, from the amount of laughing he heard coming from it.

"Alright dummy," Demetri said. "If you can face down Holy Warriors and Wild Men, you can do this."

Demetri marched head up, to the tent raised his right hand and paused. Then a look of determination on his face, he slapped the tent entrance twice with the palm of his hand and stepped back. Instantly the tent went quiet.

"Yes?" Margarete's mother said as she came out.

Demetri quickly grabbed the beret off his head and held it in both hands before his belt buckle.

"Demetri Bekenbaum, Mrs. Rosenthal," he said. "I am here to escort your daughter to the reception mam."

"Oh, I am sorry Mr. Bekenbaum," she said sadly. "I am afraid she got tired of waiting and left with her friends."

"Ah," Demetri said. "Well then mam, sorry to trouble you. Good evening to you mam."

"Mama!" Margarete said as she flung the tent flap open and stepped out.

"Oh this one," the mother said. "I thought you meant Evelyn her younger sister. Not this old Tom Boy."

"I love you too mama," Margarete said. "Shall we good sir?"

She grasped Demetri's elbow, placing her arm through it and turned him toward the council tent. She looked back over her shoulder. 'Oh my God' she mouthed. Her mother blew her a kiss, then reached behind her into the tent and dragged her husband out. Kissed him and taking his arm followed behind.

Like the pair of young people they were, Demetri and Margarete spent most of the night dancing. The short breaks they took, were with the original ten, who took every opportunity they could to embarrass Margarete. She gave back as good as she got and the table was always laughing. Demetri smiled and laughed, but only listened.

Then after one break, Alphonso and Greta joined them, his light brown uniform contrasting to their blues. He withstood their jibes and gave a lot of his own and was soon regaling them with hilarious times from school days back on home world.

"What about you Demetri," Margarete asked. "You must have some good stories from there?"

"Not really," he said. The smile gone now. "If you would all excuse me for a moment?"

"He is two years older than I," Greta said as Demetri walked out the tent entrance.

"He saw what they did to our parents. I was hiding in the fields. They were hard on him at first on Home World. He would not bend. Then something came over him. He started studying hard and soon they left him alone. Then we came home and all this started. This is the first time I have seen him have a good time since before they took us off world."

"You'll find him with Barney Mags," Greta said. "Go to him. Please?"

Margarete stopped when she saw him. He had his arms around Barneys neck, his head resting on the big horses jaw. Then she stepped forward and the spell was broken when Barney spotted her and grumbled softly. Demetri pulled up his head quickly and dropped his hands to his side. She came up to him and put her arm around Demetri's back, slapping Barney gently on the neck with her other hand.

"Do you want to talk about it?" she asked softly.

"Not really," Demetri said. "It was what it was. My father used to tell me, 'That which does not kill you makes you strong.' So far he has been right."

"But they took your childhood away from you," Margarete said. "I feel so terrible for you." She turned her head and kissed him on the cheek.

He turned her and looked her in the eyes.

"You have enough joy for the both of us," he said "I will steal some of yours. Did you know you have gold flakes around your irises? It is the most beautiful thing I have ever seen."

She felt herself being drawn into his blue almost grey eyes and felt her knees go weak. She put her arms around his neck and held on as she kissed him, losing herself in his embrace and he in hers. They both began to breathe heavily and she felt herself moving against him and groaned slightly as his hands slid gently over her breast. Then he gently pressed her back.

"Not now, not yet," he said. "You know nothing about me. Tomorrow I am the commander again. I must not, will not, let anything get in the way of what our people must do. But know this Margarete Marie Rosenthal, I will be coming for you."

"You don't get away from me that easy, Demetri Bekenbaum," she said, still with her arms around his neck. "You owe me. I saved your ass remember? I loved you when we were children, before they took you away. I loved you more when you let me show the others how good I was. Not know you? I have watched you my whole life. I see you with the children. So loving so caring. I see you with the old ones, the same way. I see you smiling as you walk away after giving us shit for doing something stupid. I see the concern when we do something that might get us killed. You push us hard and we love you for it."

"Marg," Demetri said. "I think I loved you the first time you and your mother came to train with me. I love the way you laugh, the way you walk, the twinkle in your eye. How you wrinkle your nose when you are concentrating on something. Like now, I feel on top of the world when you are near...But."

"Yes Demi, I know," she said. "The people and the battalion come first. If you can live with that with me, I can live with that with you. If you haven't noticed, I happen to be in command of a wing

of snot nosed, wet behind the ears candidates in this battalion. You
and I will have little time for anything else. Now kiss me and take me
home."

They walked back to her parent's home, arm around each other's
waist, her head on his shoulder. They stopped in front of the tent and
listened to the female voices talking inside.

"Evelyn is excited about tomorrow," Margarete said. "She
finished in the top five during qualifying."

"Almost as good as her older sister," Demetri said giving her a
little squeeze. "I'll make sure she is with Chimilovitches wing. It will
be hard enough on her without you looking over her shoulder all the
time and I don't need you worrying about her all the time."

"Thank you," she said. "I was going to ask about that tomorrow."
She looked into his eyes once more. "I am going to miss you terribly."

"And I you," Demetri said. They kissed slowly and he held her to
him, her head buried in his chest. He took in the scent of her hair
and pulled the hair from her face so he could see her eyes.

"I have to go," he said and kissed her lightly. "Be safe."

"God keep him safe," she whispered as he walked away. "We need
him. So do I."

He was almost out of site when she saw him jump in the air and
click his heels together before he came down and raised his right fist
in the air.

"So how did it go with the big hunk?" Emily said as Margarete
came into the tent.

"I think he loves me," Margarete said. Her two sisters rushed to
her side and gathered her in a group hug, all of them jumping up and
down and squealing.

The next morning at dawn, the Eagles left the camp at the trot
in formation, spare and pack horses at their sides. The candidates
rushing to catch up. The Eagles broke into a gallop before they could
and they never did, until they stopped at midday.

"Tomorrow will be harder than today," Demetri heard Margarete say. "Your horses know what to do and want to, but as out of shape as they are, they are in better shape than you are. Tomorrow we ride twice as far and twice as fast. You will set up a guard. There will be three from each ten on guard at all times. One with the horses, one riding perimeter and one in the camp. Keep one horse close, hobble the others and let them loose to graze. Change up the rotation of your horses each day. Three of each ten, will deploy as scouts tomorrow. You will pair up with an officer for the first rotation, then you will be on your own after. The scouts leave an hour before we do and leave their pack animals with us. We leave at dawn people. Be ready."

"Been a major all of a week and already gunning for my job," he said as he walked by.

"What are you looking at candidate?" he growled. "When you can ride as long as she can and fight at the end of it, then maybe I'll let you look at me. Get back to work. Godamn rookies!"

Alex dropped his eyes and hurried away to look out for his horses and help set up camp. More determined than ever now to be one of Demetri's hundred.

Chapter Seven

Demetri had been pushing hard the three days since he had left the last squadron. He rode until it was dark, unsaddled his horse, spread out his rain coat as a ground sheet, the saddle for a pillow, rolled his blanket around himself and slept until dawn. Then he was back in the saddle again. He had not pushed at the normal pace, but still, he and Barney were both tired and dirty. No matter, he would have a few days to relax when he arrived at the next squadron. He had purposely travelled light and fast to arrive a few days early.

The last eight months had flown by for him. He spent a month with each squadron, observing and helping with the development and training. Not only of the new troopers, but also of the officers. Showing them the tactics they would be using. Not only for the observation role, but the harassment role and basic formation and tactics to operate as a group. He had them practicing, not only as the aggressor, but in defence. How to plan and execute an ambush, or a direct assault. How to infiltrate enemy lines and camps. How to observe without being observed. The competition was fierce. Each troop wanted to be the best and each trooper the best trooper in that troop.

Demetri worked hard to instil that they were all on the same team. There was no dishonour at being bested by comrades. Only things to learn from the defeat. After each exercise, he debriefed the officers and the troopers. Heaping praise on things done right and pointers to fix things that failed. Even how things could have gone better for the victors had they done things differently. Praising good parts of the losing side he had observed. The officers picked up what he was doing quickly and adopted Demetri's command style for themselves. Demetri had even picked up some ideas from them and incorporated the ideas for himself.

He was about an hour from the next camp when he spotted a movement out of the corner of his right eye. It wasn't much. A ground squirrel had risen, briefly looked around, squeaked and sprinted for its hole. But it was enough for Demetri to spot the scouts head as he ducked back down. Demetri smiled as he thought of how the Battalion would run circles around the regular cavalry and infantry troops they would be exercising with and against in the upcoming joint training exercise, scheduled for the month after this one.

The sun was completely gone, by the time he was challenged by the first guard riding perimeter duty. A series of night bird whistles signalled his arrival and he was not challenged further as he rode to the visible camp fires. He was met at the edge of the camp proper by an officer and two troopers.

"Good evening Colonel," the officer said. "We will escort you to your quarters sir. The Colonel and the Major have invited you to dine with them sir."

"Very well Subby," Demetri said. "Lead on my good man."

Demetri took in the camp as he rode down the centre aisle. It was laid out properly. The troopers were gathered around their communal camp fires for their evening meals. Weapons were close to hand and horses nearby. An enemy would have a tough time of it, trying to catch the squadron unawares and attacking.

He was lead to a single tent. Demetri dismounted and took his saddle bags, rain coat, warm coat and blanket from the saddle and handed Barney off to a trooper.

"Colonel, a fire has been started for you and water set to warm for you to clean up," the sub lieutenant said. "If you require anything else, the troopers and myself are at your disposal, sir."

"Thank you subby," Demetri said. "That will be all for now."

Demetri entered the tent and tossed his equipment on the small folding cot inside. He shrugged out of his tunic and shirt and tossed them on the bed as well. Rummaging around in a saddle bag he found a clean shirt and trousers, unrolled them and tossed them on the bed as well. In a short period of time he had sponged off the worst of the dirt and shaved. He would have a decent bath and wash his dirty clothing in the stream he heard just beyond the camp, in the morning. Donning the cleaner clothing, Demetri jammed his feet back into his boots and sat on the cot. Digging into his other saddle bag, he dug out his communicator and turned it on. Expecting the usual, he grabbed his battered broad brimmed hat and was about to turn it off again and leave, when it beeped the reception of a message.

The file it contained was quite large and from the date stamp, had been sent the afternoon before. Demetri hit play and frowned as he saw an overhead shot of a base camp. The shot had been taken at about five hundred feet in the air. It clearly showed the neatly laid out camp, women, children at work or play. The animal herds and even a work party arriving with logs dragging behind them. The text that came after said, the camp had moved that day and had not been spotted again and asked for his recommendation. Looking at the standard time clock on his display, Demetri decided to wait until the next morning to send his reply. Then he shut down the unit and put it back into his saddled bag. He rose and exited the tent, jamming his battered hat back on his head.

"Well gents," he said. "Take me to your leaders. Knowing my sister, she is probably already upset with how late I am."

"Demi!" his sister exclaimed as he entered the tent. "What a pleasant surprise! We hadn't expected you until next week at the earliest."

She hugged him and kissed him on both cheeks.

"Somehow I don't think so," Demetri said. "Your first scout saw me a day and a half ago."

"I told you he would spot them Major," Greta said. "You remember Major Rosenthal Colonel?"

"Had you trained your people a little better they would not have been spotted Colonel," Margarete said. "Mine spotted him the day before."

"But you forgot about ground squirrels Marg," Demetri said. "You do look quite cute with your butt hung out in the air."

"Damn! I knew it!" she said as she flung herself into his arms and kissed him.

"Come on sit down," Greta said. "Mags cooked this herself. She only got in a couple of hours before you did."

They sat and ate. Demetri listened as his sister and Margarete regaled him of all the things that had happened to them in the last eight months since he had been there. How well the troopers were working together and how they would be the best at the upcoming exercises. He was happy they got along so well, almost like blood sisters. Their manner was easy with each other and Greta paid attention when Margarete spoke about new ambush techniques they had tried, what had worked and what had not.

"But enough of us," Greta said. "What has my big brother been up to?"

"Not much," Demetri said. "I just wander around and answer questions. Our people have a good handle on things, much like you have here. Every trooper in every troop thinks they are the best. You will have your work cut out for you Marg. Some of them are very, very good."

"We all are Demi," Margarete said. "How could we be not? We have you as our example. We have all heard how you are everywhere. In the night and the day. No matter how hard we try, we cannot best you. You are always one step ahead of us."

"Not quite," Greta said. "You got him, nyet?"

Both the lovers looked down at the floor and turned red.

"Well," Demetri said. "As much as I hate to disappoint you sister. I will not be able to give you any more ammunition for your gossip tonight. I really am beat. It has been a long eight months and I am afraid I pushed hard the last three days to get here early."

He stood and bent over to kiss Margarete tenderly.

"Thank you for the lovely dinner Marg," he said. "I really appreciate it. One day I hope I can do the same. Now good sister, Marg, I must go before I fall down."

"Something is wrong," Greta said. "He was joking and laughing when he rode in."

"Yes," Margarete said. She pulled a trinket out of her pocket and laid it on the table in front of Greta. It was a thin silver chain with a silver and jade cross on it.

"He put that on my saddle by my head last night," she said. "When I woke up, he was just in earshot already mounted. He waved, laughed and then took off. That is not what I saw here tonight. Even his kiss was different. More tender. Something is wrong."

They both cleaned up and as they shared quarters, they bade each other good night and turned off the lanterns. It was a long time before either of them fell asleep.

Demetri was up starting a fire in his small portable stove well before daybreak. After it was burning nicely, he walked over to the latrine area and did his morning business, then walked over to the small stream and filled his tea pot. Placing it on his stove, he sat on the edge of the bed starring at the tent roof until he heard it come to boil. Pulling his saddle bags on to the bed, he pulled his little tin of tea and his cup out. Pored himself some water and dumped a tea leaf into it. After packing the little tin back in the saddle bag, he brought out the communicator and turned it on. Once it was ready, he took a sip and typed 'Status' and hit send.

'Request for parley and safe conduct agreed on. The five have been selected and twenty five for escort.' Came onto the screen.

'Full mobilization as planned. Meet at discussed coordinates. Time frame?'

'Will order full mobilization at end of transmission.' Came the reply. 'Estimate one month to coordinates. Parley in month plus a week.'

'Very well,' Demetri sent. 'Battalion will rendezvous in one month. Transmission end.'

'See you in a month Demi, transmission end.'

Demetri then consulted his on board map and wrote down a set of coordinates. He cued up the addresses of those who would receive the next transmission and started to compose.

Both women's communicators went off simultaneously. Both of them sprang up from their cots instantly awake. This had never happened before. Never in the last four years had the communicators ever been used. In fact, most of them doubted they even worked anymore.

'Full immediate Battalion mobilization. Rendezvous with Division at following coordinates. Dispatch my twelve troopers immediately. They are to join up enroute. Will be leaving for rendezvous point one day from now. This is not a drill. Time to earn our Eagles. Send acknowledgments, then communication silence. Out.'

"Shit!" Margarete said. She sprinted for the tent entrance, her long unbound hair flying behind her.

"Stand to!" she yelled at the startled guards. "Stand to! Now!"

One of the guards ran to an iron triangle and started banging his knife round the inside edge of it yelling stand to stand to, at the top of his voice. The call was repeated by every guard and sentry in the camp and the camp exploded in a flurry of activity.

Margarete and Greta were fully dressed and armed by the time her Captain and officers were in front of her.

"Captain, the Battalion has been mobilized," she said. "Send riders to each squadron immediately and tell them this is no drill. We leave tomorrow at dawn. Have the commanders twelve report immediately to me. Everything but essentials for today and tonight to be packed away. There will be time for questions later. Officers meeting in two hours."

By the time Demetri reached the command tent, twelve troopers were waiting for him, Margarete and Greta standing with them.

"At ease," Demetri said after he returned the salutes. "Pack food for a month and a half. Be prepared to fight on the way and at the end. Set up camp on the west edge of the main camp, all horses and equipment ready to leave at dawn tomorrow. Figure out your own command structure and let me know before we leave. Oh and have all four of my horses there as well."

"Colonel, I will need four of your people," Demetri said to Greta. "One of each I think. Can they have enough supplies ready?"

"Yes Colonel," Greta said. "Can your people help with the extra pack horses?"

"I forgot about that," Demetri said. "Thank you for reminding me. Yes, the other squadrons will be linking up with us on the way. We will spread them out among us. You have asked for an officers meeting Major?"

"Yes sir," Margarete said. "In two hours Colonel."

"Very well," Demetri said. "I will attend. I will leave you to your duties ladies."

He returned their salutes. Then wandered through the camp seemingly aimlessly for the two hours.

He gave them an extra fifteen minutes before he walked into the command tent. He strode to the front of the tent, turned round and told everyone to sit while he stood with his feet at shoulder width, his arms behind his back.

"Colonel," he said. "Your people will be ready?"

"Yes sir," Greta said. "All supplies and equipment are packed, troopers ready for departure sir. Your four are setting up at your camp sir."

"Very well," Demetri said. "Major?"

"Sir," Margarete said. "Messengers have been sent to all of the squadrons sir. We should hear back from them by midday. All but essential equipment for this squadron has been stored and packed. Horses have been readied sir."

"Very well," Demetri said. "Three days ago a drone acquired a video fix on one of our hunting parties. It followed them back to the main camp. Once it left the area, the camp departed. No further detection of any thing has been observed. Frankly I am surprised it took them this long to find us. This event has been planned for and we are implementing the plan. A conference has been arranged between five of our representatives and the civil authorities and Holy Church. Assurances of safe conduct have been given by both sides to and from the conference have been given. This conference will be held in a month and a half."

"While we all hope and pray that the conference will result in a peaceful resolution, experience tells us it will not. We will be at war people. The reason for your existence, your training is here. They mean to wipe us from the face of the earth. They have all along. They cannot and will never understand that we do not need their interference, that we do not accept their narrow view of God's purpose for us all. They do not want our ideas to spread, no matter that they are better for all people."

He stopped for a moment, his expression grave and looked at the concerned faces of the officers looking at him. Then he smiled.

"We aim to show them the error of their thoughts," he said. "Four years ago a small, hardly trained group wiped out some of their best. We were outnumbered four to one, had inferior weapons and little training, yet we prevailed. We have had four years now to prepare. If we barely trained kids could beat them without a single injury, what do you think will happen when they face us?"

"Excuse me, oh mighty warrior big brother," Greta said. "We did so have an injury. I broke one of my nails."

"Pardon, my mighty warrior sister," Demetri said. "I had forgotten how delicate your nails are. I do hope you have rectified that since?"

The room erupted into laughter as Greta looked at her nails and blew on them.

"Ok, ok settle down," Demetri said. "You are all as well trained as you can be. They have better equipment than we do and are also well trained and skilled. At their type of warfare. Their methods will in most cases not work against us. Their armour, in most cases, will not stand up to our weapons. But, for all that, they are still very brave and will fight and fight hard. You must never forget that. They can and will do us a lot of damage if we get caught and put in a situation where their tactics and weapons will have the advantage."

"Now go. Be with your troopers. Get them ready. This world is about to change. Dismissed."

As the officers filed out of the room, they were buoyed up and in good spirits. Finally, they would have a chance to do what they had trained so long and hard for.

"You two, go spend some time together," Greta said. "I can handle anything that comes along."

Margarete and Demetri spent the rest of the day wandering from troop to troop talking with troopers and looking them over. As they walked, they held hands and even had been seen snatching a kiss when they thought no one was watching.

"Look at them," one trooper said. "Not a care. If they are not worried, why should we be?"

The sun had gone down and the two of them were off away from the camp by the streams edge. They had their arms around each other and she had her head on his shoulder.

"Surely they will see reason?" Margarete said.

"We can hope love," Demetri said. "Follow your training. Your troopers are good. They won't let you down. Use the tactics we have developed and everything will be good."

"How can we loose with you at our head," she said squeezing him."

"I won't be with you," he said. "Not at the beginning. You will do well, I train only the best."

"What do you mean you won't be with us?" she said spinning to face him.

"Oh I expect at some point we will meet up again," Demetri said. "But at the beginning, I aim to make them understand that we own the night. Come on, I'll walk you back. I leave well before you do and need to get some sleep."

She watched him walk away from her tent, her heart low. He walked with his hands in his pockets, seemingly without a care in the world, but his head was down.

"God keep him safe," she said in a whisper. "Let him come back to me."

"If it's God's will," Greta said putting her arm around Margaret's shoulder drawing her close. "We are but God's servants."

Chapter Eight

The cardinal slammed his fist hard on the board room table, several glasses spilt wine on it. All of the churchmen and some of the counsellors sitting around it had very concerned looks on their faces. The Emir, his military commanders and the rest of the councillors did not.

"We had them!" the Cardinal said. "We had them all and your incompetence let them get away! The ayatollah shall hear of this, I assure you!"

"I am sure he will," the Emir said. "We told you it was premature and that you would find nothing. Yet you spent how many millions of the Holy Church's hard earned money on a foolish, ill prepared and even worse lead assault. For what? Some few hours of flight time for your pilots and wearing out your men for nothing? Besides, as you are found of reminding me, this is Church business and no concern of mine."

"For four years we have no trace of them," the Cardinal said. "Then suddenly a flurry of messages that pin point their exact location. If you would have given me more men like I requested we would have had them!"

"No, all that would have happened is that I would have spent a lot of my hard earned money for nothing," the Emir said. "These people are smarter than you give them credit for. I, nor any of my people know why the sudden flurry of messages or the request for a negotiation. The messages are in a code we cannot break, so we have no idea what they say. I can only assume, they consulted on when to start negotiating. Perhaps they are all starving and want to reconsider?"

"Well we shall meet with them," the Cardinal said. He was calmer now. "We must have our people back and examples made so that this never happens again. I am formally requesting representatives from the Civil Authority attend the negotiations and that members of the Civil Defence be in attendance."

"As far as the Civil Authority is concerned, there has been no wrong doing," the Emir said. "These people caused us no trouble and were very profitable. They owed no funds to us. Our investigations concluded they acted in self-defence after your man exceeded his authority. The Holy Church agreed and has agreed to compensate the Civil Authority for costs associated in repopulating the area. I have been told this is a Church affair and that the Church will handle it. Of course, the Civil Authority will attend as you requested, but it is your affair, not ours."

"Let it be so," the Cardinal said and rose to leave. "Have your people ready to depart when the time comes."

The Emir turned to his military commander as they left the board meeting.

"Your people do not interfere," he said. "They do not lift a finger unless they are directly threatened. Do you hear me? I don't care if every single one of those black clad bastards are killed, you do not lift a finger to help. This is a bloody mess that they started and I will have no part of it!"

"Where is my Godamn tunic!" Demetri yelled. It was time to leave, his equipment was packed, horse saddled and his tunic was missing. During the last week, all of his troopers had joined up and they were now just over a hundred strong. They had to go now if they were to reach the negotiating place before the negotiations took place. The scouts had already left and daylight was wasting. He had just decided to forget about the tunic and leave when a trooper came skidding to a stop in front of him with his tunic in hand. All one hundred troopers lined up in formation quietly in front of him.

"Sir! My apologies Sir!" She held the tunic in front of him. "Sir! We put your eagle and leaf on the collar for you sir."

Demetri was about to give her a blast. The brass badges were to bright to be worn for the work they were about to do. Then he saw hers and looking at his tunic saw the same ones on his collar. The eagle and leaf were sewn on a small patch that had been attached to each collar. They were dark, in contrast to the tan uniform and stood out, but not noticeably so.

"All of us will have them sir," she said. "The ladies in our home camps worked day and night to get them ready for us sir. I am sorry I was so slow getting yours on Sir! No excuses sir!"

"My apologies Sergeant," Demetri said. "I was unaware of this."

"Yes Sir," she said. "We wanted it as a surprise sir. I was just a little slow on getting the tunic from you sir."

Demetri turned his back to her and held his arms out. She put the tunic on him and he turned around and buttoned it up. Then brushed some imaginary dust from the eagle.

"Well Senior Sergeant," he said. "Mount up. And Senior Sergeant, the Senior Sergeants place in the formation is beside her Colonel."

He mounted his horse for the day, waved his hand over his head and in a cloud of dust and a thunder of hooves, the squadron was on the move. Demetri had been wondering who to promote to the position and she had given him the out he needed.

It was harder going in the trees than the prairie. There were few open spaces and they had to space the troops out to make room for each other. Seldom could they ride four abreast and many times they were in single file. It took almost an hour for the squadron to pass a point in places. They reached the town on the edge of the boarder a week before the negotiators did.

They made their camp several miles from the town and scouts were out immediately. The town was the same as the one where they had confronted the Holy Warriors four years earlier and had not changed much in that time. The Holy Warriors showed up a few days after. There were many of them. One thousand to be exact. As soon as defensive positions had been prepared, Demetri and his people had mapped them out. The landing zones for the main party were determined, as well as any open spaces that could be used as landing zones for an assault. At night these were especially prepared, just in case. Plans were discussed, torn apart and replanned. They were done. Just in time.

Demetri's five negotiators and their twenty five Cavalry escorts arrived first. They were escorted to quarters that had been arranged for them. They had arrived in the late afternoon the day before the meeting was to take place. So far everything was proceeding peacefully and each side greeted each other cordially and with respect. Demetri hoped it stayed that way and that the negotiations would come to an agreeable end.

First came the camera crews and news media. Then a dramatic entrance by the Bishop who would be conducting the negotiations on the Churches behalf and finally, the Civic leaders and five hundred Civil Defence troops. Demetri was in the tree line observing all this, especially the troop deployments of the troops. These men were professionals and looked it. Where the Holy Warriors strutted round showing off their weapons and power, the professional troops went about their business quietly and without flash. They handled their weapons like they were extensions to their bodies, not something to flash about and intimidate people with. The defensive positions they took were mutually supporting and would cause an attacker a lot of grief. If they were armed and used tactics familiar to them.

All of this was caught on camera and the talking heads were giving a play by play description of what was happening and why.

Demetri turned on his communicator and followed along as he dropped back to his camp.

To the Bishops credit, he let Demetri's people outline their end of the negotiations. That they were willing to forget about all the abuses and were willing to open up trade between the two parties. All they wanted in return was to be left alone and not be interfered with.

Demetri sighed a sigh of relief when the Bishop agreed that things had gotten out of hand and the Church was willing to overlook the transgressions and to start meaning full trade once again. But, there were conditions. First, reparations would have to be paid for costs incurred by the Church and the lives lost. Second, inquisitors and priests supervised by himself would be installed in each group to ensure that Church doctrine was strictly adhered to. Finally, an example had to be made that the Church would not be trifled with and non-adherence to Church doctrine would be severely punished.

Then before anyone could say anything, he had the Holy Warriors in the room arrest the delegates and their escorts and sentenced them to death. All but two, who would carry word back to the people of the Churches decision. The sentence would be carried out by the end of the day.

"Call assembly Senior Sergeant," Demetri said quietly. His officers had been following the proceedings as he had been and word quickly got around as to what had happened as the troopers assembled.

'They are going to hang them,' Demetri typed into his communicator. 'I don't think I can get there in time to stop it, but will try.'

Demetri walked up to his assembled troops and called them to attention.

"The Church has decided not to honour our negotiations or the right of safe passage," Demetri said. "They intend to execute our people by the end of the day. I intend to try and stop it and if I cannot, then to make them pay. This will not be subtle, it will be a full out frontal assault. They don't know we are here and are over confidant of their abilities. If they harm or kill our people, no Church men are to be allowed to leave the field alive. If anyone else takes up arms against us or tries to resist us, they will die. If they do not, they will not."

"Full armour for troops and horses. One last thing. The Bishop is mine. Get moving, time is short."

The Bishop pushed back his plate and drank the last of his wine. Dinner, as horrible as it was. Was finished. He would be glad to get out of this back water and back to his own quarters in the Capital. The Bishop stood and started for the door, the rest of the delegation scrambled to accompany him. He walked outside and with satisfaction, saw the scaffold for the public hangings had been set up properly. The prisoners would be hanged five at a time. He would be home before the sun went down. Waving his hand, he walked to the chair he would be sitting on to witness the executions and sat down. Every movement followed by the ever present video drones.

The first five were marched onto the scaffold, quickly had their arms and legs tied and ropes put round their necks. All of them stood straight. Three men and two women, they said nothing and other than the look of hate in their eyes were expressionless. All of them refused the blindfolds offered them.

"You have been tried and found guilty of the crime of Blasphemy," the Bishop said. "You are to be hung by the neck until dead. Your bodies are to be buried in unconsecrated ground and never to be marked. Have you anything to say?"

An older man on the left side of the scaffold begin to sing. It was a slow mournful song, sung in an unfamiliar language. The others soon joined in. they did not sing loudly, but few gathered in the open town centre could not hear it. The Bishop decided to be merciful and allow them to finish their song and as it came to an end he stood. Waiting for the right moment when the video drones would catch all of the action.

Then the singing started again. First from the other prisoners held below the scaffold. They sang it in Standard and they too sang it low and slow. Then they stopped as the hillside echoed, not with their voices, but many others. Not in a low voice, but in a loud and slightly faster fashion. The prisoners below smiled and the old one on the scaffold smiled, as did the other four.

"Pray to your God bishop," the old one said. "Pray for forgiveness, for those that are coming will have none."

Demetri nodded at the Senior Sergeant and she uncased the large battle flag and swirled it about her. The formation started forward as the bishop raised and lowered his arm.

The ropes had barely gone taught from the bodies hitting the end of them, when cries from sentries calling assemble to arms were heard. The Bishop and others rushed to the edge of town and witnessed a remarkable site. Two rows of fifty mounted people five paces apart were slowly coming down the hill. The people and the horses were encased in some kind of very shinny and very bright substance. They had very long sticks with metal objects attached to the ends jammed against their right knees between knee and horse. A very large banner, blue yellow red with a large black bird on it was in the front row centre. Beside this rider was another. They were slightly ahead of the rest of the group. The other rider had a one pace long, thin, shiny metal stick in his right hand. He and his horse appeared to be doing some kind of a dance, as were all of the other horses. It followed the slow beat of the song.

"Oh shit," said the commander of the Civil Defence Force. "Get ready boys! Remember, we do not fire unless directly threatened!"

The dance stopped as the beat of the song went faster and the horses broke into a trot five hundred paces in front of the Holy Warriors forming up in their lines. They held their batons in their right hands and shields in their left over lapping each other. They formed in a block, one hundred wide and ten deep. Long range lasers were positioned in a line of ten to each side and levelled at the on coming horsemen. Who at four hundred paces broke into a canter and the ground began to tremble from the hoof beats. Five horseman from each line of the side of the formation broke into a gallop and formed a line in front of the main body, who know came knee to knee and spurred to a gallop as well. Lowering their pointed sticks level with their horses bobbing heads and the singing abruptly stopped. The leading twenty horseman pulled little sticks from packets bouncing on the saddles, placed them on strings attached to other oddly shaped sticks, pulled back to their ears and let loose. A whirring sound was heard then sickening thumps as arrows pierced shields and armour and flesh. They did not hit the front ranks, but the ones to the rear. Once, twice, three times they fired, then split and thundered down the front of the lines firing as they went. More than half of the unshielded laser men were down, before the order to fire was given. What few shots got off did nothing but bounce away or shatter into nothingness. Then the real horror arrived.

The first rank of forty horsemen arrived. Lances pierced shields and shattered ceramic body armour to be embedded into flesh. The bodies were flung violently backward into the ranks behind them from the force of the blows and the horses began to lash out with their hooves at anything that was near them. Dropping the lances, swords were drawn from backs and the sick sound of metal cleaving through flesh was heard along with the screams of the wounded and the soon to be dead. The front rank carved a path twenty paces wide into the centre of the formation five rows deep before the speed of the attack was blunted. Then the second rank hit. They split twenty to a side and hit the sides that had escaped the initial onslaught. All the while the archers were riding around the sides and rear, dead men sprouting arrows, followed their wake. The churchmen broke and ran, but there was nowhere to run. Horsemen rode them down, swinging back handed, taking heads off at the throat as they passed by the fleeing men on foot. The twenty five on the ground joined the fray, grabbing whatever was at hand for weapons. Hammers were a favourite.

The Bishop scrambled into the centre of the Civil Defence's formation and stood trembling.

"Attack you fools!" he yelled at the commander.

"This is Church business," the commander said. "Not ours."

The attack was over. Only one Churchman was still alive and Demetri rode up to the front of the professional soldier formation and stopped. His armour was covered in still wet blood. The arm holding the sword was a solid red to the elbow and the sword was dripping. Barney menacingly pawed the ground in front of the front rank, his forelegs covered in blood.

"We have no quarrel with you," Demetri said. Then he pointed his sword at the Bishop.

"I will not attack these men to get at you," he said. "But your life is forfeit. We did not ask for this. We came in peace to negotiate a peaceful agreement that would benefit us all. You broke your word of safe conduct and dishonoured your people. We were willing to share, but now we will take it all. You will learn to fear the sound of a twig snapping in the forest, the sway of the tall grass, the bumps you hear in the night. For we shall be here, there and everywhere."

Demetri let the sword dangle from his saddle from a cord attached to it and pulled out his bow and drawing back an arrow, let loose. The arrow cleanly pierced the Bishops light armour directly in the heart and drove him back off of his feet from the violence of the blow.

"This town and our original settlements are now under our control," Demetri said. "No harm shall come to those that stay and agree to our laws. No harm shall come to those who decide to leave peacefully. Commander, I would leave now were I you, for nothing that flies or moves other than by foot or horseback will be operational in a few moments."

"Right," the commander said. "Get everyone including the delegates into the flyers now!"

His men swiftly broke formation and gathering up the Civil Authority delegates, moved toward the vehicles.

"Remind the Emir that we have no quarrel with him," Demetri said. "But if we are threatened or attacked, we will retaliate."

"Captain!" Demetri called out and he was soon joined by the nearest captain.

"Full perimeter guard," he said. "Get the rest to strip the bodies of anything we can use and to retrieve as many arrows as we can, especially the heads. I want these bodies all collected. We have to bury them as soon as possible. Then in shifts, have the trooper's cleanup and change uniforms. Have the support troops bring up the equipment and horses. Casualty list for me yet?"

"No reports on casualties at this time sir," the captain said. "I believe the Senior Sergeant is working on that sir. I will get on the other things right away sir."

A group of local officials were standing in a gaggle not far away. All of them had worried looks on their faces and from the way they were dressed, they were the elite of the town. Demetri dismounted and letting Barney follow him, he approached the group.

"I am Colonel Demetri Bekenbaum, commander of this unit," he said. Noticing the look of fear some of them had and where their eyes were directed, he put his bow back on Barney's saddle and took his full face helmet off and placed it on the pommel. He ran his hands through his hair to smooth it out some.

"Damn thing gets hot," he said. "I assure you that no harm shall come to you or yours unless we are provoked or attacked. Please inform your people of that?"

"What is to become of us My Lord?" a well dressed woman in her late thirties asked.

"I am not a lord mam," Demetri said. "I am just a poor herder that is in temporary command of this small detachment. Please assemble your town's people and I will inform all of you at the same time what the future holds. Now, if you will excuse me? I have a lot to do and little time to do it."

"Captain Brown," Demetri said, returning the salute of the regular cavalry commander of the escort. "I am truly sorry we could not arrive sooner. Perhaps we could have saved the delegates."

"They would have just gunned us down instead," the Captain said. "The timing was almost perfect. None of us thought we would survive this mission anyway. What can we do to help?"

"Some water for my people and animals to begin with," Demetri said. "Is there some kind of bathing facility here? Once we have all the bodies cleared away and we know it's safe, I want my troops out of this armour. It's heavy and hot."

"There is a recreation facility that has twenty five shower stalls," the Captain said. "I'll have five of my people check it out to make sure it's clear and to stand guard. We are retrieving our weapons now."

"If you have any casualties, my medical people are on their way," Demetri said.

"Just a broken ankle and some cuts and bruises," the Captain said. "With your permission, I will set six of my people on town patrol."

"Very well," Demetri said. "Have your Sergeant report to my Senior Sergeant with the location of the showers. I have asked for a meeting with the townsfolk and I would ask that you attend as well."

"Of course Colonel," Brown said. "If I might suggest sir. A shower before the meeting?"

"My clean uniforms are not here yet," Demetri said. "Besides, a little reminder of what may be is always good, nyet?"

"Always the sly one Demetri," Brown said smiling. "Some vodka after the meeting?"

"If I have time George," Demetri said slapping him on the shoulder. "Now get, I want some sleep tonight."

"Report Senior Sergeant," Demetri said as she came up.

"No casualties sir," she said. "Only minor bruising and a few scrapes on troopers and horses sir. I have arranged to have our dead properly cared for sir."

"Very well," Demetri said. "We will have the ceremony at day break."

Demetri picked the sword up from where it dangled on his saddle and undid the cord that hung it there. Looking around he found a dead Holy Warrior nearby and dragged the tunic off the body and began to clean his sword with it.

"The Bears will be mounting a roving patrol of the town," he said as he worked. "Their Sergeant will be reporting to you the location of the bathing facilities. Rotate our people through it, twenty five at a time. After they have looked after their horses. I have asked for a town meeting. I want you there. After that Janet, I need you to have a shower and I want to call assembly of our people. I think we will let the Bears provide security tonight."

Janet saluted and hurried away to carry out his orders. As the town's people started to assemble, Demetri finished cleaning his sword and placed it in his scabbard across his back. Then he began to take off Barney's armour and stack it beside him. Using the dead warrior's tunic, he wiped down the sweat stained hair as well as he could. Then taking out curry brush and comb, began to work over the tired animals body. Barney softly rumbling his pleasure as he did so. Captain Brown came up just a Demetri finished up. Barney took a few steps away and found a suitable spot in the road, dropped and rolled.

"I don't know why we bother," Demetri said shaking his head. "George, could your people pull guard duty tonight? My people have been up since well before dawn."

"No problem Demetri," George said. "My people had a good night's sleep last night.

By now, the towns people had all arrived and were standing around in small groups. Janet arrived with two troopers who took Barney and his equipment away. Demetri nodded and the three of them, Demetri in the centre walked in step and in line up to the towns people who all became quiet and gathered around.

"I am sorry you had to witness this violence once again," Demetri said. "Our hope had been to have a peaceful conclusion to the negotiations. Negotiations that would have resulted in peace and prosperity for all of us. Unfortunately the church had other ideas. As a result, this town has been annexed by my nation and is no longer a part of the Federation. In a few days more of our people will be arriving. We have no intention of taking over your town, just in it's administration. Those of you who have worked with us before know how we operate. We will be extending our tax and civil codes to this town and it's inhabitants. If any of you do not wish to stay, we will not hold you. We expect you to govern yourselves as much as possible. The only caveat we have is that no representatives of the Holy Church will be tolerated in lands we administer. We don't care what, if any religion you follow."

"Right now we have disabled any means of electronic communication. Shortly we will be destroying any means of artificial transportation. As soon as our people arrive, we will provide you with new and better suited to the environment living accommodations and the ceramic buildings you currently use will be destroyed. Please take some time to discuss this among your families and each other and let us know of your decision. Questions?"

"You would include us in the same level of taxation as you use?" one man, a blacksmith from his dress said. "We would be free to trade with whom we wanted and be free of the Church's taxes?"

"Yes," Demetri said. "As long as you follow our general laws you are free to conduct the towns affairs as you see fit. Just make sure your local laws do not conflict with ours, or make the taxes to heavy to pay for."

"The councillors will retain their positions?" one of the better dressed of the group asked.

"For the time being," Demetri said. "We will not appoint any for you. You will decide by free vote who shall be your leaders, sometime in the future. This will be explained to you once our people arrive."

"Well I for one am staying," the blacksmith said. "I made a lot of profit before you people left. You always traded fair."

"Who owns that backhoe," Demetri asked pointing to the machine.

"I do," a man in the middle of the people said. "Why?"

"I would like to bury all these bodies a soon as possible," Demetri said. "Could you help us out?"

"Ya no problem," the man said. "I've got two more of them. We can be done in a couple of hours."

"That would be very kind of you," Demetri said. "I would like to have a ceremony just after day break."

"Can't be to soon for me," the man said. "I've had enough of that sort to last my life time."

As everyone dispersed to their homes, Demetri turned to his fellow soldiers.

"Ok it looks like our gear has showed up," he said. "George, keep an eye on things for me would you. I really have to get out of this uniform and armour. I've got a really bad itch I can't get at. Come on Janet, let's get cleaned up."

Demetri stood alone. The Sun was up over the horizon on his left shoulder. He stood at ease with both hands tucked into the small of his back and overlooked the two formations of fresh uniformed and showered troopers. They were split into two groups, two almost identical banners were planted in the ground, one in the centre of each group. The one in the centre of the large group had a blue, yellow, red horizontally striped filed with a large black eagle on it. The one in the centre of the smaller formation had a bear in the centre.

Each group was divided into smaller groups of ten, each with its own smaller version of the flags. The smaller groups were divided further into two groups of five standing in two ranks. The larger group had five groups of ten across and two paces behind them were the other five ranks. The bear formation had one rank of five in the front centre and two ranks of ten behind them. The lines were perfectly straight, all the troopers standing as Demetri was. Legs shoulder width apart, both hands tucked into the small of their backs.

Behind Demetri were three rows of long narrow freshly covered trenches. In front of the trenches were five stacks of fire wood, the length and width of a body. On top of each was a wrapped white sheeted bundle.

"Brothers and sisters," Demetri began. "Yesterday we participated in a battle. We experienced, most of us for the first time, the taking of human life. The brutality of it. The finality of it. Make no mistake, those we killed are gone, never to return. They had lives, just as we do. Mothers and fathers, sisters and brothers. Wives and children. We have learned that war is not glory and bloodless. War is messy, bloody and noisy. The cries of the dying, calling for mothers, or sweethearts or God in their anguish."

"Some, like our five brothers and sisters, died with dignity and courage a song on their lips. Others ran, hoping to preserve their lives."

"We, the few, know our lives are short. We know that death awaits us all. That it is not just good enough to die well, but to live well."

"The ones we faced, fought bravely. They were well trained and had quality equipment. They fought for what they believed in. We however, were better trained, had better tactics and were better prepared. We had the backing and power of our people behind us. They were fighting to preserve the right of their leaders to stay in power. The right of the few to live lives of luxury while the many starve and live in poverty. They say their god gives them the right to do this. Their god says the many must serve the few. That the many must conform to a narrow view of what is right and that those who do not conform are to be killed. Our God loves us all. Our God gives us choice to be whatever we choose to be. Our God only demands that we try the best to be whatever we choose to be. Our God expects us to help each other achieve our goals. Our God understands that sometimes we make the wrong choice, that the path to our lives has many twists and turns, not just one strict and narrow path. "Our God has a plan for us all, knows that each of us has a part to play and encourages us to be the best at what we can do to play that part."

"We fight not to preserve the right of the few to live in luxury. We fight so that all people can have the right to provide a better life for themselves and their future generations."

Demetri removed his hat and went to one knee, making the sign of the cross with his right hand, the troopers in their formations did the same.

"Holy Father, I ask that you take the fallen to your home. To welcome them as they did what they thought was best. I ask that You comfort their loved ones in their grief. I ask that you hold my troopers blameless for the taking of Your children's lives. If blame is to laid, lay it on my shoulders, as they followed my training and my orders."

Making the sign of the cross again Demetri stood and replaced his broad brimmed hat back on his head. He called the five Bears standing in front of their group forward. Each had an unlit torch in their hands. Taking a lighter from his pocket, he lit each of the torches. When the last one was lit he nodded and called the formations to attention and saluted holding the salute until all five piles of firewood were burning and the five Bears were back in their formation. Then he began to sing. After the first words, the rest of the troopers joined in. the song was slow and mournful. Then as the flames took hold, the songs beat increased and as the flames roared, so to did the voices. As the song reached its peak in volume and speed, Demetri lowered his arm and reaching into a pocket pushed a button on the remote he had there and the circling video drones came to the ground, ending their transmission as the song started from the beginning and troopers feet and arms began to move and they broke their formations and formed a circle around the fiercely burning piers. Celebrating the lives of the five.

Dancing in celebration of the five. Dancing in celebration that they had survived.

The two forward scouts arrived first, the third had sprinted back to the main column. Now Margarete rode at a trot at the head of the lead troop as they poured into the town. Taking in the fire and the figures dancing around it, she swung the formation in that direction and had them fan out. The rest of the battalion formed up around them and the colour guard came forward to join her. Having heard and felt the horses approaching, Janet called the troopers to order and they formed up facing the rest of the battalion. The two large colours were uncased and Margarete ordered the salute.

Nine hundred swords rasped clear of scabbards and were swept in front of faces and down to the side and the battalion colour dipped.

"Major!" Janet yelled. "Number eleven company present mam!"

"Battalion!" Margarete yelled. "At Ease!"

Then she spun her horse around and faced the battalion.

"Number one company, A wing, provide security!" Margarete ordered.

"Colonel Bekenbaum, have your people set up in a central location. Battalion officers meeting in one hour. Battalion officers set up your camps on the towns perimeters. Color party with Colonel Bekenbaum's people. Move!"

"Senior Sergeant Armstrong," Margarete said. "Dismiss your people and a moment of your time?"

"Where is he Janet?" Margarete asked after Janet came up.

"He was standing right where you are when we started to sing," Janet said. "Then we all kind of got caught up in it all. I'm sorry Mags I just don't know. Shit! I'll send everyone out to look for him."

"Don't bother," Margarete said. "I'll find him. Have your people help mine settle in Janet. You guys did a good job here. The Bears are a day or so behind us. You want me to post a guard around the fires or do you guys want to handle it?"

"I think that's already been handled for us," Janet said nodding to the twenty five Bears who were positioning themselves around the fires. They had their lances held away from their bodies at an angle, the empty hand behind their backs. All of them were facing outward, the fires at their backs.

"Very well Senior Sergeant, carry on," Margarete said.

She swung her horse around and walked out of the town to the south and up the small hill that still showed the massed hoof prints of the charge. She found him sitting with his back against a tree, hat in his hands and his head on his knees. Barney was grazing a short distance away. He looked up as she rode up, snorted once, then resumed grazing.

"Fine thing," Margarete said as she dismounted. "A girl chases her man for over a month and then he hides from her."

He looked up at her, tears running down his cheeks.

"They stood on that scaffold," he said. "Their heads held high with the ropes around their necks and they sang Marg, they sang. I could do nothing about it, nothing! The last sight they had was us singing in return, our swords in salute and our colours dipped. Then we danced for them and they died."

She skidded to his side and pulled him to her as he completely broke down.

"They died because of my idea, because I asked them to," he blurted out finally.

"Yes love, they did," Margarete said stroking his hair. "We all will. All five of them asked for that duty Demi. They knew what would happen. We, you me, all of us, will fight and die if need be. This is our life, our freedom. The freedom of our forefathers, the freedom of our generations to come. Yes Demi, you ask much of us. You are our voice, our face, but it our choice Demi. Our choice, not yours. The whole world saw the sacrifice of the Five and heard your words Demi. The whole world."

Chapter Nine

"So Cardinal," the Emir said. "You have once again botched it. We had the opportunity to stop all this, to come to a peaceful resolution. But in your vanity and the vanity of your Church, you have made it worse!"

"I have already sent word to the other districts," the Cardinal said. "In a week, I will have five thousand Holy Warriors prepared to wipe out these blasphemers!"

"You have already lost two thousand troops and fifty transporters as well," the Emir said. "How are you planning on doing that Cardinal? That town is at the very edge of the transporters range of operations."

"We will deploy from mother ships," the Cardinal said.

"You only have three," the Emir said.

"I have been authorized to second two of yours," the Cardinal said. "Home World has agreed. We will supply the troops and the crews and pay the cost. You and your people are to take no part in this."

The Cardinal and his retinue stood and left the conference.

"How many troops do we have available?" the Emir asked.

"Not enough," his defence minister said. "Only twenty thousand."

"Pull them all in," the Emir said. "Have them set up defences for the capital. Hopefully we can hold them off until help from Home World arrives."

"The people of the town and the five outlying districts have embraced our ideas," the councillor said. "They have organized as we suggested and formed their groups. They have been told of our decision to go off the grid, the reason for it and for how long. They have all agreed to abide by that decision and our people are now deploying to help them learn how to do this. They have enough food right now to see them through the rest of the year and will have more come harvest. They have teams out collecting wood for building and heat and have begun the demolition of the current buildings, salvaging what metal they can. The blacksmiths and metal workers are being shown how to make the materials that will be required until we can establish trade with other districts for our needs."

There were over a hundred people jammed into the small town hall for this meeting. Most of them were senior army officers, but a sprinkling of town leaders were among the group, there to observe how meetings were conducted. They had just heard the last of the civilian councillors give their reports. The whole band, minus those required to hold the herds back on the prairie were here. Close to forty thousand people were now camped in and around the town with their families and herds. Demetri nodded at the senior military officer on the panel.

"We were able to salvage five long range weapons from the transports," the general said. "They have been converted so that we can use them for defence and people trained to operate them. We have two thousand short range and five hundred long range man portable weapons and approximately three thousand power batons. These have been distributed among the locals for short term defensive armament until they can be trained and provided with our weapons. Our smiths are showing the locals how to produce not only replacement weapons and armour for us, but how to manufacture and operate low tech forges. Several craftsman have agreed to manufacture lance and arrow bodies for us. They have been shown how to select the material required for this. A number of tradesmen have come forward and are being trained to manufacture bows and strings, others to fletch arrows and affix lance and arrow heads."

"The locals have been informed of our requirement of five years' service," the next general said. "A number of un married men and women have volunteered to serve already and the first group of eighteen year olds are being processed. Training will commence at once. Our older troopers will stay behind to conduct the training and the new people will be integrated with our new batch. The trainers have been advised of this and the training will be adjusted to accommodate. Training of last year's recruits has been completed and selection of the next group of Eagle Candidates will be conducted shortly. The rest of the recruits will be integrated into Bear battalions. This will bring the number of trained troops to thirty five thousand Bears and one thousand five hundred Eagles."

"Local doctors have been met with," Greta said. "They have all had rudimentary training on how to make medicines from scratch and we are showing them the local varieties. The local pharmacist is on board and has come with an idea that should provide some income for local women and children to hunt for the wild herbs and roots as well as to plant them. The medical Corps have enough supplies to provide the armies needs and a small surplus. New members from the new recruits have already been integrated and as soon as they complete their basic qualification requirements, will begin their specialist medical training."

"Horse herds have increased," the next officer said. "As expected, each years foals are better than the last. Four year olds have completed military training and will be graded as to Bear or Eagle suitability. I know you Eagles prefer your own animals, but we may need replacement animals at some time in numbers you may not be able to supply on your own. Excess, old or injured animals, will be used to herd or provide guard animals for the camps and districts. Any draft, pack or animals that don't meet the grade will be sold to the locals."

"Food supply is covered," the next officer said. "We are self-sufficient at this point. We will pick up what supplies we need through trade or conquest as the need arises."

"Thank you for your reports," Demetri said. "Bear commanders, I want you to deploy to the border with the next district. Begin tomorrow. Leave four battalions behind. The Holy Church will assault this town by the end of the week. You have been briefed. They will come by air. Take out as many as you can before they deploy the troop transports, then take out as many of those as you can. Once they have troops on the ground, hit them and hit them hard."

"Once the battle has been joined, my battalion will commence operations in the next district. This will soften up any resistance for you Bears. We will not be taking any towns or settlements. That will be your job. We will hit and then move on. They won't be expecting us and they won't be expecting the speed at which we move from district to district. Leave two battalions behind to deal with any stubborn towns, and a half battalion behind to help the new people integrate into our system. Conduct your Eagle candidate trials tomorrow. The Eagles move out at dawn the next day."

One hundred and fifty young women were among the five hundred who had come in first in the qualifying run. All of the candidates were grouped, not by their settlement groups, but by lottery. Each of the five squadrons would receive one hundred of the candidates. These one hundred would be placed among the existing troops in the squadron. Each squadron would then furnish Demetri with one hundred suitable troopers for his deep reconnaissance squadron. But that was in the future. Right now, five hundred excited young people stood before Demetri, his one hundred and the Eagles officer core. Their dirt and sweat stained faces beaming in what they had just achieved. Proud parents and family members were grouped to one side, curious towns people and a contingent of Bears were on the other. In front of them ranged in their ten troops were the One Hundred, Battalion colours in the middle flying in the slight breeze. Each trooper and the officers ranged in a line before them was wearing their impeccable dark blue uniforms, with berets now on heads instead of the normal wide brimmed campaign hats they normally wore. Each had a sword hilt poking over left shoulders and all stood stone faced, facing the new candidates.

Demetri reached into the big box held before him and passed smaller boxes to the two Majors, who opened them and passed smaller boxes to Captains and so on. Each group of ten candidates had an officer pinning on each trooper, the Eagles they had just won, then had a hand shake from the officer. Once this was complete. Demetri brought out another box which he handed to the Senior Sergeant. Then with the Senior Sergeant at his side he marched up to the twenty five Bears assembled to the side of the candidates. Starting at the left side of the Bear formation, he took off their campaign hat and reaching into the box, placed a dark blue almost black beret on their heads. In the center of beret was the brass regimental badge. A large leaf in the center, an eagle on the left and a bear on the right. Once the captain had received his, Demetri and Janet stepped back, came to attention and saluted the twenty five.

Now Demetri and Janet marched back to his one hundred. He called them to attention and one by one, he went down the line, removing their berets and pinned the same badge on each one, Janet beside him, her sword in her right hand with the blade resting on her shoulder. After the last beret was placed on the last head. Demetri and Janet marched back to the centre of the gathered officers and they all saluted the One Hundred.

While this had been going on, the rest of the Eagle battalion had quietly gathered in their formations behind the One Hundred and two battalions of Bears behind the candidates. All of them in their dress uniforms. Demetri nodded and the battalion regimental color party marched forward, the regimental colors joining the battalions.

"Officers to your commands," Demetri quietly said. "Candidates to join the formation."

The surprised candidates in their grimy and dust covered uniforms were marched to form behind the One Hundred.

"Regiment!" Demetri yelled. "Regiment prepare to pass in review!"

The order echoed down through the chain of command to each troop by their successive officers.

"Regiment! March!" Demetri said.

The full battalion, regimental, battalion and troop flags flying, in a long column four troopers wide and lead by Demetri and Janet passed in front of the twenty five Bears. Each column snapping their eyes to the right as they reached the twenty five, their officers swept their swords out and to the side and the colors dipped in salute.

The three battalions then formed up facing the twenty five. The new candidates in the centre of it, five paces to the front. Now Demetri mounted a gleaming Barney and rode up and down in front of the candidates formation, making eye contact with each trooper as he passed, saying nothing. He reversed his course once he had come to the end of the line and began to speak. Loud enough so the whole formation could hear.

"Candidates," he said. "You have just completed your training. You have just completed a gruelling competition to be allowed to wear those eagles. A few of us have earned the right to wear the badge on our caps and the leaf on our collars. Only twenty five have earned what they have just received. Only five have received the love and affection of our whole people. All thirty of them volunteered for a hazardous duty, knowing full well, they were unlikely to survive it. Five of them did not. These twenty five standing before you, joined the attack. They were surrounded by their enemies and unarmed, yet they did not hesitate. Just because they do not wear the blue uniform or the Eagle does not mean a trooper does not lack courage or the willingness to fight for his people or his cause. Theirs is a different role than ours that requires different skills and they are very, very good at what they do. As will you be soon.

"Make no doubt, your training has just begun. Tonight is your last night among family and friends. Tomorrow, you join your new family. Tonight have fun, dance, enjoy your selves. I am going to."

Then he smiled and pushed his beret to the back of his head and scabbarded his sword.

"Because," he said. "Tomorrow we may die and it is always a good day to die. Regiment dismissed!"

He spurred Barney away. In seconds the formations broke up and the party was on.

Demetri did not slow until he reached the tree line. Finding a game trail, he put Barney to it. Within minutes all sounds coming from the town were gone. Just the muted thumps of Barney's hoofs, the rustling of branches as they scraped across saddle, Barneys side or Demetri's tunic or boots were heard. Eventually they came to a small clearing, stopping at the tree line, Demetri scanned the clearing and the tree line around it. A small brook gurgled through the middle and other than the movements of small birds and squirrels through the branches, no movement or sense of danger seemed present. Barney's ears twitched in every direction and his nostrils flared as he too sought out any possible dangers. Staying alert, Demetri rode out into the clearing toward the brook and coming to its bank stopped. Barney deciding all was fine, ducked his head and took a long drink. This was enough for Demetri, who dismounted letting the reigns dangle on the ground. He stretched the kinks out of his back and squatted. Cupping his hands, he scooped up the cool clear water and drank a few handfuls. Looking around, he spotted a nice sized log and walked over. Finding it clear of biting, crawling insects, he sat down, removed his beret and after tucking it under an epaulet on his tunic, unbuttoned the tunic and the buttons on his shirt down to mid chest. After of few minutes, he took the scabbard off his back and lay down in the lush grass, his hands behind his head. He gazed up at the clear blue sky and let the sun's rays warm him. The clearing soon came back to life as the small animals decided he was no risk. Soon birds were chirping and squirrels were rummaging for things to eat. Barney was munching happily on flower petals and stems. Demetri closed his eyes and was soon asleep.

Demetri opened his eyes as a commotion broke out in the clearing. The clearing resounded with warning cries from first the small birds and then the squirrels as they bounded deep into the tree interior branches. Demetri slowly put his left hand on the scabbard at his side and the right on the sword hilt, ready to draw. Other than raising his head, sniffing and twirling his ears around for a second, Barney stayed where he was, laying on his side. The sound of air going through wings, followed by wings beating and a large bird came to rest in a tree not far to the left of Demetri in the top branches. It was a fully grown Golden Eagle and it was soon joined by another slightly smaller one. Two more young birds, clumsily came to rest in the same tree, all four looking about the clearing. First the male, then the other three focused on Demetri with their yellow eyes. Demetri rolled slowly to his side and propped his head up with his left hand and stared back. After a few moments, each bird stretched out their wings in the exact pose that was depicted on the emblem on his collar and held it. The male looked over at his mate and blinked his eyes. Then he looked once more at Demetri and bounced his head up and down a few times and screeched. He squatted slightly and followed almost as one, the family of eagles took off once again.

Another rustling of tree branches, this time from the edge of the clearing on the other side of the brook. A brown bear and her two cubs came into site. She too looked at Demetri and then she stood on her hind legs and her cubs did as well. Then she dropped back down and nudging her cubs, they also quietly left the clearing. Barney had not even opened his eyes while all this had gone on.

'Odd' Demetri thought to himself. Then he saw that the sun had gone past the eastern tree tops. It was time to go. He stood and wrapped the scabbard onto his back once more. Dusting some twigs that clung to his uniform off as well as he could, he buttoned up the bottom button of his tunic, placed his beret back on his head and walked over to where Barney was laying down.

"Come on lazy bones," he said.

Barney opened an eye, snorted and as he started to get up, Demetri quickly straddled him as he rose. Leaning down, Demetri grabbed the reins and nudged Barney into motion and they slowly made their way back into the trees and to the camp.

It was full dark by the time they came out of trees and made their way down the hill to the town. The party was in full swing, many blazing camp fires with figures around them could be seen and a lot of singing could be heard. Everyone seemed to be having a good time. Demetri unsaddled Barney, brushed him down lightly and turned him loose with the rest of the company's animals. It did not take him long to find where the One Hundred were having their party. There were about five hundred people grouped together in a rough circle. Some sitting, some standing, all having a good time. The ever present vodka bottles were being passed around and the smell of fresh cooked food was in the air. Most of the men and all of the women were not in uniform. All of the unmarried women had their best dresses on, hair unbound, many with flowers woven into the hair. A number of couples were dancing to a lively tune being played. Demetri found a handy tent pole and leaned up against it, watching his troopers be what they were. Young people at a party having fun. Some were with their families, but most were in small groups of friends, just enjoying the night.

An arm went around his waist and his sister kissed him on the cheek and handed him a glass of vodka.

"Where have you been brother?" she said. "Your uniform is a mess."

She brushed the twigs and grass he had not been able to get at from his back.

"Nowhere special," Demetri said taking a quick sip of the fiery liquid. "Just found a quiet spot to relax. It's good to see them let their hair down. Your better half around?"

"I'll have you know, I am the better half," Greta said, punching him on the arm. "Yes, he just popped away for a minute to make sure the kids are ok with his aunt."

"Oh sure," Al said coming up from the rear. "Leave my wife for five seconds and some young rapscallion tries to steal her from me."

He patted Demetri on the back and then swung Greta to him, swept her up and gave her a big kiss. Putting her back on the ground, he kept his arm around her. Greta snuggled up close to him. Not for the first time, Demetri felt something missing in his life as he looked at the two of them.

The music stopped and seconds later some hands clapping a beat started. A lot of feminine giggling was heard and more than a few protests and Demetri looked over at the circle and saw a group of about twenty young women, some being dragged by others, formed inside the circle.

Margarete was being pulled in by her sister Evelyn. She had a light blue skirt with gold embroidering on it. Above that was a white tunic, the top buttons open, revealing her neck. A red belt held her tunic tight to her waist. Unlike the other girls, her blond hair was braided into a long pony tail that came to lay between her shoulder blades.

She was the most beautiful thing in the world Demetri thought and time seemed to stand still as he watched her. She made to leave, but a small group pulled her back in and the music started. The girls started their moves and Demetri could not take his eyes off of her. She was so graceful. He did not know it, but he started to slowly walk to the edge of the circle of watchers. He did not clap to the beat as the others were, he just stood and watched. She did not seem to notice the on lookers or the other dancers, she was lost in the music. Soon the other girls moved to the side and she was dancing alone in the centre, the other girls making her the attraction. Four young men could hold themselves back no longer and with a hoop, joined in the centre, dancing around her trying to get her attention. She seemed annoyed and moved away from each, her held high and away, she continued her movements.

A pair of hands pushed into Demetri's back and he was shoved into the circle. He turned around and before he could give a smirking Greta a piece of his mind, a mighty cheer went up from the crowd.

'No way out now' he thought.

He put his hands on his hips and slowly looked around at the smiling faces in the outer ring, walking around the circle, his back to the dancers as he did so. As he came to where Greta and Alphonso were standing, both of them clapping to the beat, he took the sword from his back and tossed it to Alphonso. This caused more cheering. Putting his hands back on his hips, he made another circuit of the crowd. As he came back to Greta he slowly undid the buttons from his tunic, took it off and tossed it to Greta. Now as he made another circuit, his feet started to move to the beat and he twisted his hips from the left to the right and when he came back to his sister, he stopped, turned around and looked at the other dancers. Although they were still dancing they were all looking at him. All except Margarete, who eyes, closed still, was lost in the music.

Then Demetri took his hands from his hips and dancing, entered the circle. All of the girls danced their way to him and circled him, all except Margarete, who was still being circled by the other boys.

Demetri danced around the circle of girls, looking each up and down, giving Evelyn a small air kiss as he came by her. Then he went back to the centre and forgot about them all.

One by one each girl came to him trying to catch his eye, running their hands down his back or an outstretched arm. He made no move toward any of them and then he stopped. Raised an arm in the air and looked over at the circle surrounding Margarete. He made a sweeping motion with his arms and the girls opened the circle for him. He walked out of the circle and put his hands on his hips again, stopped and watched the dancing.

Now with long strides, he walked back to Greta undoing all but the bottom two buttons of his shirt as he walked. He tossed his beret to Greta, turned back and walked back into the centre of the circle and raised his right hand high in the air pointing at the sky. He pulled it down and raised both his hands outstretched, his arms level with his shoulders and began to dance, crossing one leg over the other and bringing his hands together he sank to squat and back up. The crowd cheered and the music sped up. Now Demetri danced around the edge of the crowd spinning and jumping. Then he came back to the centre of the circle and squatted again. This time he stayed in place and went up and down a few times, then he sprang high into the air and laid back letting his hands support him off the ground, he started to kick his legs, one after another in the air, then alternated a hand and the opposite foot in the air. He flipped back onto his shoulders and sprang back up right and stopped. The music stopped with him. He began a slow movement and the music followed him.

Now it was he who was lost in the music and Margarete slowly danced his way. She danced her moves around him and he ignored her. She came right up to him and he danced away, keeping his glance from her. She quickly followed, trying in vain to get him to look at her. Finally she stopped and just stood, letting her arms sink to her side and her gaze went to the ground and her shoulders slumped.

'I've lost him,' she thought, her heart breaking and she made to leave before the tears that started could be seen.

The music had stopped and the crowd was silent. They could not understand what was taking place. All of them knew how they felt about each other. What had happened?

"You give up easy," he said quietly behind her. She stopped moving and her heart started to race.

Demetri walked around her, his head going up and down as he circled her, his hands on his hips and a stern look on his face.

"A guy might think the girl he loves doesn't love him anymore," he said so only she could hear. "But maybe he only thought she loved him. She never did tell him."

He stopped in front of her and lifted her chin with his right hand. She thought her heart would break free from her rib cage it was beating so hard. Then he gently kissed the tears from her cheeks and her legs turned to rubber. She wrapped both her arms around his head and pulled him down to her.

"Kiss me now or lose me forever," she whispered.

"Get a room!" Greta yelled over the cheers of the crowd.

The now embarrassed couple broke their long kiss and Demetri bowed to the crowd while Margarete punched him on the shoulder. They walked toward the edge of the crowd who were still applauding them and Demetri collected his beret from Greta and slammed it back on his head, giving her a scowl as he did.

"Hey you wanted to," she said. "You were just to chicken. He was standing over there watching you for about an hour."

"What!" Margarete said and punched him on the shoulder.

"Yes, what was the meaning of that young man," Margarete's mother said. "Embarrassing my daughter like that in front of everyone. I haven't seen her like that since she begged Greta for those horses at her qualification test."

"You gave her those horses?" Demetri said.

"Why yes I did," Greta said. "If it is any business of yours. Margarete's aunt and I are old friends. She had better skills than most of the boys, but her horses would have let her down."

"Ha," Margarete's father said. "She needed a little dressing down. Always playing the big shot army commander. Well played Demetri, well played. Ouch that hurt."

Both the mother and the daughter had punched him in the arm.

Demetri buttoned up his shirt and held out his hand for his tunic. He put it on and buttoned it up as well and looked to Alphonso.

"Sorry Dem," Alphonso said. "I had one of the lads take it back to your quarters."

Demetri nodded his head, pulled the tunic down to get some of the wrinkles out, took off the beret and ran his hands through his short hair and put it carefully and squarely on his head to rest just above his eye brows. Then he took a deep breath, stood straight and marched right up to Margarete's parents.

"Sir, mam," he said. "My name is Demetri Bekenbaum. My parents are dead and left me no inheritance. They were fine people and well respected in our community. I have twenty horses, fifty sheep and have a good job in the Army sir."

"Oh my God!" Greta whispered.

"With your permission," Demetri continued. "I would like to ask your daughter to marry me."

The silence was overpowering.

"Well I am not sure," Margarete's father said. "She is awfully young, she just now finished her first year of service, I'm not sure her commander would approve."

"Poppa!" all four of the Rosenthal women said at once.

"Not me poppa!" Evelyn said.

"Oh the older one," he said. "Well I'm not sure of her either. She seems to be married to the Army. Are you sure about that Demetri? She is a bit old you know."

He was awarded a crack in the ribs from a sharp elbow for that remark.

"Demetri Bekenbaum," he said standing tall. "If my daughter will marry you it would be my honour sir."

Now Demetri moved to stand in front of Margarete.

"Margarete Marie Rosenthal, I Demetri Bekenbaum ask you to be my wife," he said.

She flung herself into his arms and smothered him in kisses.

"Um.." he said. "Does that mean yes?"

"Yes, yes, yes," she said and kissed him again.

Demetri gently pried her away from him and turned her to face the two families hugging each other. He put his hands on her shoulders and waited for them to quiet down.

"I am Demetri Bekenbaum. This is Margarete, my wife, daughter of Ilene, house of Rosenthal. What is mine is hers. What is done to she and hers is done to me. So say I in front of God and man."

Margarete turned around and looked up at him.

"What did you just say?" she said. "Do you know what those words mean?"

"Yes," Demetri said. "It is an ancient oath my people used to say. I just gave to you everything that I have and I promised to protect you and your family as best I can."

Margarete put both her hands on his shoulders and looked him in the eyes.

"I am Margarete, daughter of Ilene, daughter of Marie, house of Rosenthal," she said. "This is Demetri my husband. What is mine is his. What is done to he and his, is done to me. So say I before God and man."

Margarete felt a pair of hands grip her shoulders.

"I am Alphonso house of Hood, husband to Greta sister to Demetri," he said. "This is Margarete my brother's wife. What is done to she and hers is done to me and mine. So say I in front of God and man."

Margarete's father put his hands on Demetri's shoulders.

"I am Michael, house of Rosenthal, this is Demetri my daughter's husband. What is done to he and his is done to me and mine. So say I in front of God and man." He said. "Now if this is all? Where's the damn beer?"

Evelyn rushed up and hugged then kissed Demetri and then her sister. Then she sprinted to the centre of the circle and sticking her fingers in her mouth whistled, once, twice and after the third time everyone quieted down.

"Everyone!" she yelled. "The Major and the Colonel just got married!"

"Oh shit!" Demetri said. "Come on Marg. Barney!"

He grabbed Margarete's hand and pulled her after him as he sprinted for the horse lines.

"Barney get your boney ass over here!" he yelled as he ran. "Can you ride like that?"

"Just you try and stop me," Margarete said. "Cody! I need You!"

They both split up at the corral and the horses were waiting by the tack. In less than a minute, the saddles were on and the couple flung themselves onto the backs and were galloping into the darkness.

"What now, my brave Eagle?" Margarete said.

"Have no fear damsel," Demetri said. "All is in order. Slow to walk now and stay behind. We are going into the trees for a while. The trail is quite wide. But still.."

"Ya I know," Margarete said. "Shit happens."

They rode in silence for about an hour and then broke into a clearing. It was the same one he had come to earlier that day.

"Well good sir," Margarete said. "This is perfect. Even in the moonlight it is lovely."

The wind was rustling slightly through the trees, but not enough to drown out the sound of the brook. The water gurgling over rocks not far away. Demetri dismounted and then helped Margarete down off of Cody. He held her close, pushed the hair from her face so he could see her eyes and kissed her. They kissed softly at first and then it became more heated.

"Hold on bub," Margarete said breathlessly. "I don't want you ruining this dress. I have to have something decent to go home with."

"Well yes," Demetri said. "This way madam."

He took her by the hand and walked her to one side. There a tidy lean to stood, big enough for them both. The floor was carpeted with soft pine bows and a large warm sheepskin blanket lay rolled up in one corner. In front, a small rock fire pit had been set up, kindling arranged ready to be lit.

"If the good wife would be so kind as to start the fire," Demetri said. "The husband will unsaddle the poor horses."

Demetri busied himself at his task and Margarete had a fire going in no time and had spread the sheepskin out over the pine bows. She watched him in the firelight as he worked. When he was done, he effortlessly swung a saddle up on each shoulder and walked to the lean to, tossing them in side and arranging them on one side of it. Without a word, she undid the belt and undoing the buttons on the rear of her skirt stepped out of it, taking the underclothing with it. Then she undid all but the bottom two buttons of her tunic. After that, she bent down and pulled off her boots.

"Umm.. very nice," Demetri said and she quickly stood up.

"I was wondering what those legs and cute butt looked like," he said.

He already had his tunic and shirt off and was just removing the second boot. He stood up and she looked down but had her eyes on him as he approached her. He was thin but not slight and well muscled. The right shoulder and form, slightly larger than the left as was hers. Pulling the bows as they did, made the muscles bigger on the one side.

"You have nothing to be embarrassed of," he said quietly. "There is no need to hide your eyes from me."

"Demi..." she said. "I am not a virgin."

She shuddered as he came close to her and pulled her chin up to look at her.

"I won't mind if you don't," he said and he smiled.

"No," she said. "I don't mind. Are you sure?"

"Only if you keep bringing it up," he said and then he kissed her.

She was hesitant at first and then she forced her tongue into his mouth and they were exploring each other bodies and breathing heavily. She moaned as he cupped one of her breasts and began to frantically fumble with his pants buttons and he effortlessly undid the final two buttons of her tunic and peeled her out of it. He leaned backwards lifting her feet off of the ground and walked her to the lean to, gently laid her down on the sheep skin, then stepped back, his eyes on her the whole time as he stepped out of his trousers and she pulled him down to her.

"Demi, be gentle," she said. "It has been a long time."

He was, until she demanded more from him.

They lay on their sides, both breathing heavily looking into each others eyes.

"Have I told you today how much I love you?" she said.

"Only the once," he said.

"I really thought you had forgotten about me," she said. "I hadn't heard from you for weeks, even when we reached town and set up camp. Unless it had to do with regiment business you stayed away from me. Then after the graduation, you disappeared. I was so lost. My sister dragged me out onto the dance. I didn't want to go and the music started and I just danced. Remembering you and what I had lost."

He let her speak. Her hand was rubbing his stomach and chest as she spoke, her eyes far away.

"Then the music stopped," she said. "I opened my eyes and there you were. But you didn't pay any attention to me. No matter how much I tried, you rejected me."

Then she looked right at him.

"I wasn't acting Demi," she said softly and her eyes started to tear. "I really thought I had lost you."

"Never my love," Demetri said. "I am just not good around women. I don't even really know how to dance. When I saw you dancing, I couldn't keep my eyes off of you. I was standing by my sister and her husband by the tents. I was just waiting to get a free minute with you, but you were the most beautiful thing I had ever seen. You were elegant, so graceful. The next thing I knew I was standing at the edge of the circle, mesmerized. My sister shoved me into the ring. What else could I do then? Everyone was watching me. So, like you, I let the music take me. It was only when the music stopped and I saw you walking away from me so dejected that I realized something was wrong. I thought my heart would break right there."

He pulled her to him then, rubbing his hands on her back.

"I never want to do that to you again," he whispered. "I could never live with the pain."

He felt the tears coming off of her cheeks and onto his chest.

"Oh God I've done it again," he said. "I'm sorry, I love you so much Marg, please don't cry."

She held him so close he thought his ribs would break.

"I love you Demi," she said. "I always will."

They held each other tight for a minute then she pushed back from him. "If you don't feed that fire it's going to go out," she said.

Groaning, Demetri rolled over and started to feed more wood on the fire. He waited until the small pieces caught, then layered bigger ones on top of it and watched to make sure they would burn. As the flames went higher and lit up the area, he heard her gasp and felt her hand trace the scars on his buttocks.

"I have another on my right hip," he said. "I got that one when they killed my parents. Those are from when they civilized me on Home World."

"Greta said they were hard on you," Margarete said. "But she never told us about this."

"Nobody but you knows," he said. "They always took me away to whip me."

He lay back beside her.

"They didn't kill me," he said. "They just made me stronger, more determined to get out of there. I studied harder, read as many books as I could, learned as much as I could. The more I learned, the more they left me alone. The more freedom they gave me. Soon I was their star pupil. I got more freedom and more free time. They let me have a skimmer and I explored further from the school and one day I found it. I found where our ancestors had come from. I found a place deep under an ancient building that had a storage place in it. It was full of books and ancient computers. The books were in a language I could not read. I took vids of one of what turned out to be the earliest of the books. Then I found what looked to be some kind of memory storage device and a very large portable computer. I took the computer and the storage device back to my dorm room and put the vids into my hard drive and stared a decryption program on them."

"I took apart the computer and figured out the voltage needed to run it. I worked on the components and made sure they still worked, replacing the ones that did not and I turned it on. I plugged in the memory device and found that it held data files. I transferred the files to my computer and had it decipher them. They were a family history Marg. My family."

"The decryption of the vids turned out to be a hard copy version of the same material. As I read, a lot of the names were familiar. Not just my family Marg, yours, Alphonso's, Alex's. Almost everyone in our district. Every chance I got, I went back there and brought more of the memory devices out. I saved them and encrypted them further and hid them on my com unit, then I took them all back and replaced them. It was not just a family history Marg. It was a history of a whole people. How they lived, how they farmed, how they built their farms. Their system of laws and government. How they organized their armed forces. Tactics they used. There were even files from even earlier eras. Military organizations, weapons, defences, buildings."

"The last was of how we came here. There was even a copy of the original agreement signed by Home World for us to come here. There were six of us taken there Marg. One by one I showed them all the last part. Then I hacked into the admin section of the schools computer and found out why my parents were killed. They had found out about the original agreement and had filed a complaint with the Emir. He agreed with them, but the Church did not. So, like now, they decided to get rid of the evidence."

"It was working to," Margarete said. "My father said no one had any idea of this until you showed us. But that is not why I love you. Well maybe little and maybe a little of this too."

She started rubbing him between his legs.

"I have always been aware of you, especially when you came back from Home World," she said. "There was something about you. Soon everyone was deferring to you, even the elders. I watched you train your original six, even your sister. Every day you trained and I started to mimic your movements. Soon my mother and sisters were as well. When it was time, my father joined your training group and I watched you and your friends as they trained the men. Your sister asked if any women were interested. I was one of the first to come."

"I saw you train hard, work hard. You were firm in your methods, but not harsh. No task was to menial for you and you showed respect to everyone. Then the attack came."

"I had never seen before such bravery as you showed when you rode up to that bishop and when he lit you up, we all thought you were dead. Theory is one thing, reality another."

"On our trek to the prairie, I asked my father about you, why everyone deferred and respected you so. Why you were so different from the other lords. He told me that respect was earned, that just because somebody demanded to be called a lord and demanded respect, did not mean they deserved it. You demand nothing from us Demi. You ask us. Then I saw you with the children and especially Alex. How gentle you were with them, how patient, how you always took a part of your day to teach those that wanted it. I loved you then, before you stood up for me."

"I would have and still will go through the gates of hell for you if you ask me to."

"And I you," Demetri whispered. "Enough of the past. I am more interested in this." She giggled and then gasped and once again they melded together as one.

"Demi," she whispered. "Demi!"

Now she was shaking his shoulder.

"Demi wake up! Can you reach your bow? I can't reach mine!"

Demetri came wide awake and instinctively grabbed for the sword that was not there. He looked frantically around him and saw where she was pointing and relaxed. The mother bear was back with her cubs. The sun was up and bathing the clearing, both horses were still asleep, laying on their sides. A disturbance in the tree across from them revealed the four eagles standing there. Demetri pointed to them.

"Oh my God," Margarete said as the four of them spread their wings, then they screeched and as one took to the air. The mother bear and her cubs rose on their hind legs and roared, then came back down and walked back into the trees. The horses slept through it all.

"Good," Demetri said. "I thought maybe I was hallucinating yesterday. Now you have seen it too."

"It looked like they were saluting us," she said. "They looked just like our badges."

"God provides the signs," he said. "It is up to us to make of them what we will. Now my love, once more, then we must be off. The Army will not wait for us."

They trotted into camp to the cat calls of friends and companions, giving as good as they got. Ten of the One Hundred were still there. Alex tossed Demetri a bundle of clothing and pointed at a tent.

"Your stuff is already packed up and gone," Alex said. "Your clothing is in the tent Major. You better get a move on, they have a two hour lead on us."

Five minutes later they were dressed in campaign uniforms and cantering out of camp.

Three hours later, they were galloping alongside the column of Eagles to the front and to the astonishment of the new troopers, changed horses at the gallop and pulled away from them.

"You snooze you loose," Demetri yelled over his shoulder. "Get the led out rookies."

"It will take you a week to reach the border," Demetri said. "I want you set up and waiting for the Bears. It will take them a further week to reach you. By that time, I want you to have enough intelligence for them on the outlying area to make a plan of attack. I will take Captain Vonhoadle and the ten that rode in with me tomorrow. I will be training them on the tactics we will be using soon. When we come back, they will train ten more. By the time we reach the big district, I want everyone trained and using these tactics. Remember, just scouting. You will not be seen and you will run, not fight if you are spotted. Is that clear?"

The senior officers and non commissioned officers were all present. No one said anything.

"Excuse me Colonel," Janet said. "But if the Colonel is going so am I. I can't train my sergeants if I don't know how to do it myself."

"Very well Senior Sergeant," Demetri said. "Major Bekenbaum will have command of the One Hundred until I return. Figure out between you which of you two majors is in full charge."

"Captain, have them ready to go in an hour," Demetri said. "Now if there is nothing else?"

The officers made their way to their commands, except for Margarete.

"You can't wait until morning?" she asked, pulling him to her.

"No time love, no time," he said. "We need to train so that we may live. Me, you and especially them. At some point the enemy is going to figure out a way to stop us. We need to be ready or a lot of us are going to die."

She kissed him quickly then buried her head in his chest. "Be safe Demi," she said. "Come back to me please."

"You just make sure you are here when I get back," he said. "And all in one piece."

"Yo Demi," Janet said. "No time for nooky. We have to go."

She was mounted and had Barney, Demetri's two remounts and his pack horse with her. Alex and the nine other troopers were ranged in line abreast behind her.

"God damn Army," Demetri said and kissed Margarete one last time before he mounted.

"If ya couldn't take a joke," Janet said. "Ya shouldn't a joined."

"No Godamnd respect around here," Demetri said but he was smiling.

"See you in a month Marg," he said. "They won't come until then."

They didn't see the five hundred new recruits, Evelyn among them, watching them gallop out of camp. Many of the new troopers had their mouths open and all of them had a hard time believing what they were seeing.

"What, did you think today was hard?" Margarete said riding up to them. "Today was nothing. Tomorrow we leave at dawn and we don't stop until night fall. Get your camps set up. Keep one horse saddled and close by. I want guards out. You will switch off every four hours. One set of guards patrolling the camp. Another set the perimeter and another set guarding the horses. All of you will stand guard. Make your own schedule. Get moving people. I had a long night and an even longer morning. I need a message and my nails repainted. Candidate, close your mouth before it hits the ground! Get at it people! What do you think this is a holiday spa?"

"Holy shit Ev," another female trooper said. "My brother told me it would be rough, but I never dreamed it was this bad. Your sister and the other ten started two hours after us, caught us up, pushed up the pace and now they took off again."

"My sister didn't tell me anything," Evelyn said. "She just smiled when I asked and said I'd see. Alex said that sometimes they will go two days at a time, sleep and eat in the saddle. I don't know about you, but I am volunteering for the first shift. I want as much uninterrupted sleep as I can get."

It didn't help her. The rookie camp as well as the guards were kept awake all night by raids. Hell week had begun.

Chapter Ten

Demetri and the ten troopers had covered forty miles before they stopped for the night. They were still on district lands and he decided there would be little or no danger, so no guards would be posted until they went to bed and then only a horse and fire guard would be needed. All of them had tended to their animals and had eaten and cleaned up the dishes. Now they sat around and chatted about everyday things.

"Ok gang," Demetri said. "School time." He waited until he had their full attention.

"What you are about to learn has been used for thousands of years," Demetri said. "Usually by people, like us, who are facing an opponent with better armament than themselves. But once in a while, a whole people would take on others who had the same weaponry, but larger numbers. The key is speed and being where you are not expected to be. Our primary job is going to be to provide information. Information on troop numbers. Types of weapons and defences. Routes to attack and escape. Suitable ground to fight. Suitable to us, not the enemy."

"Our next job will be to disrupt the enemy as much as we can. Operating in groups of ten. Ten can move fast and remain undetected easily. We go into a town, cause some havoc and leave. We ambush groups of troops or supply columns and disappear. We take out sentries and wreck equipment at night, just like the rookies are having done to them. We make them scared of the night or the rustle in the trees. We make them over cautious, so that they move slower and in large numbers or not at all. We make them spend a lot of man power and resources looking for us."

"We pick our spots. Every time we attack, it must be to our advantage, not theirs. We must pick the time and the place. We need an escape plan. All this must be done in country we are unfamiliar with. In short, we will be ghosts."

Now he began to talk specifics. It was nothing they did not already know, but now they would be doing them in earnest, not just to embarrass another troop or company. If they got caught, they would be killed or worse. They could not afford the weight of the laser defeating armour. They would have to rely on stealth and quickness. Their weapons helped them in this. They were silent for the most part and no telltale beams of light to give them away. Their enemy would be relying on high technology detection devices looking for electronic emissions to find and locate them. Devises they did not use. The enemies weapons were mostly ineffective at the ranges their bows would carry and the enemy were slow on the ground. Their armour was cumbersome and heavy. The lasers only had enough charge for five shots and the batteries were so heavy, they could only carry one spare battery. They had already proven that the armour was ineffectual to the weapons that they used and that the enemy was definitely not as skilled as they were in hand to hand techniques.

Tomorrow night, they would be at the border. The next day, they would start gathering information. Then they would plan their disruptions. The troopers were smiling at the end. The fun was about to begin.

Demetri did not like what he saw. He and Janet had spent all night coming to this location. A small wooded hill overlooking the town that was the district headquarters. In a field adjacent to the town were twenty long range transports. Each transport held one hundred troopers. So far there were no guards anywhere. In fact, no one had come near the transports all day. The troops all seemed to be lazing about their camp on the other side of the town. Playing group sports or make work projects. None of them had armour or weapons on them. No patrols or guards had been set up, but the shear numbers of troops would cause trouble for a day time assault. Troopers were also wandering about the town, shopping or whatever. The building that was the command post was easily spotted. It was the only building that had armed and armoured guards posted. There were only four and they had helmets off and were there mostly for show, but they were still there.

For the most part, the towns people steered clear of the troopers. They only spoke briefly with them in passing and then reluctantly. It was clear the townspeople did not want the troops there. Then a plan began to develop in Demetri's head. He pulled his com unit out of his leg pocket and turned it on. He kept the volume low and tuned to a news channel. Then he shrugged his shoulders and typed in a query. Receiving the information, he quickly shut the unit down.

"Was that wise?" Janet asked.

"By the time they figure out it was us and where we are," Demetri said. "It will be tomorrow morning and we will be long gone. Ok, I've seen enough for now."

They backed down the hill into the trees and back to where the horses were and headed back to camp on the other side of the border. Once they arrived, Demetri dispatched two new scouts to observe the night time activities of the town, but on the other side of the town from where he and Janet had been earlier. He wanted the town under constant surveillance from now on. He went to his tent early that night and making sure he would not transmit out of the com unit, he turned it on and called up the information he had downloaded earlier. Before he turned it off again and went to sleep he had a plan.

The Eagles showed up the next day, toward night fall. Only Demetri and Janet were in camp at the time. The others were on patrol or watching the town. He and Janet were sitting around their campfire, a pot of water sitting on some rocks warming and a cup of tea in hand. A freshly killed yearling pig was on a spit rigged up across the fire and a sheep was hanging upside down and skinned in a nearby tree. Once in a while Demetri or Janet would get up and turn the spit a little to make sure the pig cooked evenly, but for the most part, they just sat and watched the battalion arrive and begin to set up camp. Two by two, his troopers arrived and settled down to also watch. The last to arrive were Alex and the two troopers who had been watching the town. Demetri had decided not to watch it this night. One of his troopers produced some potatoes he had stolen and the whole group got busy peeling them and putting them in a large pot of water to boil. In the week that they had been there, they had fashioned lounging chairs and a dining table and bench from the surrounding forest trees. Their tents had numerous pegs to hang clothing and weapons from and saddle trees had been fashioned to keep them off the ground and under cover.

As the battalion troopers happened to glance at them, they received a fair share of nasty looks, especially from the rookies, who most likely were suffering sleep deprivation as well as pain from muscles they never knew they had.

"Senior Sergeant," Demetri said as one troop of rookies walked by on their way to get water. One of the troopers had mumbled something about over privileged officers. "Was I ever that scruffy looking as a rookie?"

"Why not that I recall sir," Janet said. "You was always dressed to the nines and well kept sir. But then what did I know, you was busting my balls all day long so that I could hardly stand I was so tired."

The whole group of them started laughing then and the stories started about the rookie days.

They were still laughing and regaling each other with their stupidity when they sat down to eat. They were getting a few more nasty looks from the rookies who were camped next to them, just now getting their fire going to eat dried road rations.

"Brother, you better have some of that pig and spuds for me," Greta said.

"Not unless ya brung something for the pot," Janet said. "Trooper Young stole that pig fair and square he did. At much duress to hisself too, dontcha know."

"Ya," Young said. "That poor swineherds father like to have gutted me. I left my heart back there on that farm. She was cute and wanted to come along so bad."

"Ha," Alex said. "Most like he would have cut off your balls for you."

"Ya like you had a hard time of it getting that sheep Alex," Young said.

"Why I will have you know, the young man guarding that sheep was more than happy to give me that sheep after I asked him for it," Alex said. "In fact he wanted to give me the whole herd."

"Ya right," Twofeathers said. "After you scared him shitless coming out of the grass at his feet with your sword pointed at his belly. I thought he was gonna shit himself."

"He did," Alex said.

Greta plunked a bottle on the table while the group was laughing. "Will that pay for my supper?" she said.

"Sure dig in," Janet said. "That will do for after dinner. Young, a mug of beer for our leader's sister if you please."

"Beer!" Margarete said. "I'd kill for a beer! Where did you guys get beer? Fresh pork and potatoes too? Oh, I've died and gone to heaven." She grabbed a plate and filled it, then sat beside Demetri elbowing Janet out of the way.

"What, the sister of the glorious leader and a colonel I might add, has to pay?' Greta said. "But a mere Major gets it for free?"

"Oh," Janet said. "I expect the Major will be paying for it later tonight."

"No bloody way," Margarete said, sticking her tongue out at Janet. "My ass is to godamn sore for that. Why hello Colonel sir, I didn't notice you there."

"Oh did you hear that now?" Greta said. "That's all I've been hearing all day. Oh I can't wait to get at Demi! Oh why is it taking so long? Can't we go faster? Then she couldn't keep her eye off him when we got to camp."

"That was before I found out about the beer and the pork," Margarete said. "A girl has to eat you know."

"Speaking of girls," Demetri said. "I happened to see a cute one that kind of looked like the Major over there. Oh hey Alex, look, there's a couple of other cute ones too. I wonder if they would like to come over for some beer and fun?"

"Oh yas," Janet said. "Are there not some juicy rookies over there and here I am with not a thing to wear and my hair all a mess. Why I am going to complain to the Colonel so I am."

"Come on Janet," Margaret said. "You'd like to break one of those poor boys in half with your thighs."

"Ya, but it would fun while it lasted," Janet said.

"Oh my God," a female trooper said to Evelyn. "Isn't that the Colonel and your sister?"

"Ya and my brother in law," Evelyn said. "How can they possibly be so chipper? I'm so tired I can't even hardly eat."

"Yo candidates," their sergeant said. "You've got first watch tonight."

It didn't help when they dragged themselves up with groans, that the group feasting beside them all turned and laughed at them.

"Oh good news and bad news," Greta said. "The Bears are right behind us. They should be here in a couple of days. You have been promoted to general. The council felt the battalion was to large now to be commanded by a colonel."

"Do I get a raise?" Demetri said. "Ok, you're the colonel now."

"Nope, don't want it," Greta said. "I have enough on my hands with the support group. The young lady beside you is the new colonel. Alex, you are now a major and in charge of the Hundred."

"Ya ok," Demetri said. "But not until after the next operation. I need him and Janet. Sorry Marg, you can't have her yet."

"The coms guys intercepted a signal from the big shots," Margarete said. "They plan on hitting us in three days."

"Ya, I got that already," Demetri said. "It was all over the newscast a couple of days ago. We have a more pressing problem to deal with though. There are twenty troop transports and troops in the next town."

"Oh shit!" Margarete said. "I'll dispatch riders immediately. We hadn't counted on that. That's an extra two thousand troopers."

"No, not necessary," Demetri said. "They won't be a factor. Call an officers meeting for the morning. I will brief them on the lay of the land and what to expect. We have it all mapped out for you guys already."

"Oh, so you have actually been working and not on a holiday then?" Margarete said.

"What, we been working all this time?" Janet said. "I thought we was on holidays. That's it boys. I'm complaining to the general so I am."

Chapter Eleven

I t had been a hectic two days for Demetri and his small troop. First Demetri had to have a briefing with the main regular forces on what was going to happen and how. They would depart in three days' time for the next town. Then a briefing with the officers of the Eagles.

The Eagles would arrive at the next town the afternoon of the third day. One hundred of them would disperse, a troop to each farm community in the district. Then a hurried goodbye with Margarete and Demetri and his ten were off. It had taken a day and half's riding to reach a clearing in the trees half an hours ride from the town. They had set up camp and a two trooper watch of the town had been implemented. After receiving assurances from returning scouts that nothing had changed in the town, Demetri started outlining his plan for them.

The troop transports were powered by an electrical generator which was powered by hydrogen. This hydrogen was contained in a fuel cell interior to the vehicle, which had a maintenance access panel located on the underside exterior of the vehicle. Demetri showed them the schematic and colours of the wires in the compartment. They would disconnect the purple wire in the compartment by cutting it with a knife. Then they would strip back the wire about three inches and wrap it around a specific bolt in the compartment. After that had been done, they were to crack a bleed nut on the hydrogen tank just until they heard a small hiss, close the compartment back up and go to the next transport. Each trooper would have two transports to do in this manner. The operation should take no longer than an hour. Then Demetri had given a micro communications unit to each trooper. These were very valuable as the whole army only had a hundred of them. Demetri had calibrated them to mimic the signatures of the enemy troopers in the town, so that any scans by detection equipment would find nothing wrong. Then he had shown them how to operate them.

As soon as it was dark, they had left the camp on foot. It had taken two hours to silently creep up on the town and another half an hour of scanning to make sure there were no guards on the transports and in fact the whole town seemed asleep. Even the enemy's camp had no guard posted and few lights showing. The ten troopers had crept up to the transports and begun working, while Demetri kept watch with a set of low light binoculars from the top of nearby hill. Within the time frame allotted, all the work was complete and they were headed back to camp for a quick rest.

Before daybreak they were up having a cold breakfast of biscuits and hardtack, making sure bows were strung, arrows in quivers and swords sharp. Then saddling up, they made their way back to the wooded hill overlooking the town. Leaving the horses tethered to trees at the base of the hill, the troop climbed to the top laying so that just their heads were in view to the town before them. Now they waited. Demetri put his long range com unit on standby while he watched the enemy camp come alive and troopers began to done their shiny black ceramic armour and weapons packs. Like armies everywhere, they formed up in their squads and were inspected first by sergeants, then under officers. Then they were formed up in mass and the commander began to address them. After a short speech, the troopers were marching in unit formation to the transports. The show was about to begin.

In the capital city, the Emir accompanied by his military commanders and defence staff, took their places sitting in comfortable seats facing a large wall of monitors. At the moment, only the frontal view of the huge carrier ships was visible as they lost altitude and the rebel controlled town came into view. Each of the carriers held ten troop transports and their troopers. The military had supplied the carriers and crews, but the rest was all under control and command of the Holy Church. Against the advice of the military, the decision had been made to come to a hover four hundred paces above the town and deploy the troop transports from that height. No amount of discussion could sway the commander of the Holy Warriors to come in at a much higher altitude. He wanted speed and massive overwhelming force at the outset. Now the other video screens came alive, as drone video craft were deployed. Other than the odd person walking calmly down a street the town seemed deserted. This came to an end as soon as the large craft came to a stop and hovered.

Six undetected high powered lasers on roof tops opened fire. In pairs, the lasers concentrated their fire on three of the five carriers. The beams were expertly aimed to converge at a single point on the carrier. The fuel tanks. In seconds, the three transports, one of which was the command ship, exploded in massive fireballs. Secondary explosions from the interior of the craft blew them apart as the troop transports exploded inside them. One of the remaining carriers had opened its doors and transports were emerging from it as it was hit by two lasers that had shifted target. They aimed through the open doors and it exploded from the inside as the transports still inside were destroyed. The fifth carrier had immediately started to lift as it deployed its transports. It was hit by two lasers, but the extra height had diminished much of the lasers power, damaging only one drive unit which began to smoke. All ten of its transports got out as it limped out of range.

Of those ten transport, three were destroyed before they hit the ground. At that point, ten thousand heavy infantry in bright armour emerged from buildings and formed up in blocks as archers appeared on rooftops and started to pepper the Holy Warriors as they formed in their blocks. The infantry advanced on the Holy Warriors in a curved line that rapidly swept both flanks as the main formation hit the centre of the Holy Warriors. Laser fire from the enemy having no effect on the infantry as the long pikes pierced shield and armour. The black clad troopers died in droves and were being pushed back onto themselves, then they broke and ran. Right into the formation of heavy cavalry that had formed up behind them. The slaughter was complete and overwhelming. There were no survivors.

"It matters not," The Cardinal said. "We have another four battalions coming in from the ground to the west."

"Really?" the Emir asked and pointed to another bank of monitors.

As the troopers entered their transports, a smoking carrier ship came into view clearly intending to land. As it came to the ground and shut down, the transports closed their ramps and almost as one exploded as they hit engine start buttons and the start wire shorted out on the bare bolts, igniting the accumulated hydrogen gas in the engine compartments. Fire balls and pieces of ceramic armour and bodies flew up to a hundred paces in the air. Debris and the shock waves further damaged the carrier ship and it had pieces of ceramic exterior ripped away or had massive holes ripped into it, making incapable of flight. The Bishop in command and his twenty guards stood open mouthed, watching the destruction of two thousand highly trained and equipped troops disappear into a fire ball.

Then the monitors picked up eleven mounted troopers calmly walking their horses down the hill toward the Bishop and his guard. Ten of the troopers where in a line, with one out front. A small flag of blue, yellow and red with a black bird on it was flying from a lance the trooper in the centre of the line was carrying. The other nine had arrows knocked to bows as they slowly rode down the hill. The body guard quickly formed up around the Bishop lasers drawn.

At one hundred paces, a nervous Holy Warrior took a shot and hit the leading trooper advancing on them. He was immediately hit by nine arrows and fell dead. The trooper hit by the laser stopped as did the other ten troopers. Each of them were dressed in an alternating pattern dark and light green uniform, their faces streaked in patterns of green paint. The trooper who had been hit by the laser shook his arms and head out as if shedding water and a voice that was becoming all to familiar to the emir began to speak.

"You people never learn do you?" Demetri said. "Your weapons have no effect on us. As children of God, I give you this one chance to surrender. You see, unlike what the Holy Church has told you, we too are children of God. We just choose not to serve the corrupt Church and its self- serving officials. Unlike the Churches teachings, we believe that God wants only the best for us. For our families to live and prosper under Gods guidance. That God allows us the freedom to choose and is willing to forgive us when we make wrong choices. Not to be punished with death and destruction like the Holy Church teaches. I guarantee safe passage to the edges of this district if any of you chooses to surrender. If any of you chooses to join us, we will welcome you with open arms. If you choose to fight, we will kill you."

The guards looked to each other and their commander and at a nod from him dropped their weapons. As one, they split ranks leaving a furious bishop in full view.

"The same for you," Demetri said. "I guarantee safe passage for you to the next district, you can join us, or die. Choice is yours."

"I'll take the safe passage," the bishop said slamming his hand laser to the ground. "You have destroyed all of the transports. How are you going to manage getting me to the next district?"

"There are some personal skimmers here that should get you to where you can recharge," Demetri said. "Or you can walk. Your choice."

"Sir," the commander of the guards said. "My troops and I would like to stay, if we can. Perhaps we may be of assistance to you?"

"And who exactly is going to protect me then if you are staying?" the Bishop demanded.

"Do you hear that thunder?" Demetri asked. "That is the rest of my battalion arriving. I assure you they will protect you to the border. After that, you're on your own."

The video panned out as a remote controller took control of it and a shot of riders trailing remounts, came over the hill in a long column, four riders wide with flags flying. Then it cut out, leaving the bank of monitors dead.

"Well so much for that," the Emir said standing. "In one ill planned and lead battle, you have managed to loose me all of my carriers and their crews. All of your transports and all most all of your on world troopers. I only have ten thousand troopers on world. They have at least triple that many and from what I just saw ten of them do, that's all they are going to need."

The Emir and his defence and command staff left the room and hurried away to try and salvage what they could of the day. Troops were dispatched immediately to patrol the streets of the capital to at least give the impression of being in control. The whole debacle had been transmitted live at the insistence of the Cardinal. Somehow they had to keep control. It would be six months until the sixty thousand troops and thirty thousand Holy Warriors arrived from Home World. The Emir hoped that would be enough troops to put an end to this mess he had been handed, but he didn't think so. He also hoped he would still be alive when the troops arrived.

Demetri did not allow a minutes rest for the first troopers to arrive. He dispatched the first ten to escort the bishop. Another ten to escort the guards to somewhere safe for the time being. Another squadron were ordered to pick up weapons and armour. Then he ordered his ten to go back to their camp and bring up their gear and spare horses. The crew of the carrier were found alive, but wounded, some seriously and medical people were giving immediate aide while the medical facilities were being set up. The town was buzzing with Eagle troopers setting up camp, clearing debris, going through the now empty Holy Warriors camp and collecting anything that could be used. Demetri did not even have time to greet Margarete in the fashion he really wanted to. The town's leadership had appeared and had to be dealt with before anything else could be done.

Demetri and his commanders informed the town's leaders what they could expect. Anyone that wanted to leave could. He told them the same offer was being given to the outlying farm settlements. That was the choice they had to make. Join the rebellion, or leave. After hearing the rules, they agreed to have a meeting with their people and to have a vote. By the time that meeting was over, the Bear division was arriving and another meeting was held with all the commanders, Eagle and Bear. This being the main distribution point for the province, it was agreed that this town would be the new temporary headquarters and the rest of the army would come here. While the Bears would consolidate the gain in territory and patrol it, the Eagles would, by the end of the week, start exploring and making contact with the next district.

The Holy Warrior guards were then brought in. Demetri explained what would be expected of them and how they were expected to behave. First as citizens and then as troopers. At the moment, they did not possess the skills to join the army. If they wished, they could join, but as raw recruits, just like any other new recruits. Otherwise, the civilians would determine where their skill sets could be best used. All but two, asked to join the army. The other two wanted to go back to farming. Demetri assigned them to the training officer and the meeting was adjourned.

Demetri walked to the camp, where he was joined by his sister, her husband, Alex and Janet. Alphonso handed him a large glass of beer.

"Looks like you could use some," Alphonso said. "Good job today."

Demetri had just taken a sip of the beer when Margarete burst on the scene and grabbed him in a big hug and began kissing him. Then tried in vain to hold him up as he collapsed.

Greta rushed to his side. She found a barely visible large dark stain on his side with a small burn hole above it. She ripped the tunic and shirt off exposing a burn hole in his side, blood coming out of it. Greta hollered for her medical kit and jammed his rolled up shirt on the hole to stop the bleeding. Demetri had passed out by then.

"What the hell happened?" she asked. "I thought you guys had everything under control."

"One of the guards got nervous and popped him at just over a hundred paces," Alex said. "He just shook it off. We didn't even think it hurt him."

"Shit!" Greta said finding an exit wound on his back. "Two inches to the left or two or three paces closer and he would have been a goner. This wouldn't have been much had he gotten aide right away. He's lost a lot of blood."

Demetri opened his eyes and found he was staring at a ceramic ceiling. He was laying on his back on a real bed, a blanket up to his chin. His right arm was laying on his chest and had a tube stuck in it which was attached to a bag of plasma hanging on a pole. Turning his head to the left, he saw three other people lying in beds. Two of them sat up as they saw him move. He did not know any of them. One had his ribs bandaged up, the other an arm and elbow in a cast. The other had both legs elevated in casts. Other than a burning in his side and being very thirsty and tired, Demetri felt fine.

"What the hell happened to my beer?" he croaked. "I'm dying of thirst over here. What the hell?"

He found he was strapped to the bed and could not move. Two medical people came to his side. One gave him a drink while the other rushed out the door.

"That's not beer," Demetri said. "That's water!"

"Sorry, no beer right now," the medic said. Then she stuck a thermometer in his mouth and wrapping a band around his arm, took his blood pressure and pulse count.

"He'll live Colonel," the medic said to Greta as she came up and saw the readings.

"Damn right I'll live," Demetri said. "Now unshackle me before I get really pissed instead of just slightly annoyed."

"Now brother dear, be good," Greta said. "You took a blast at a hundred yards. You're lucky you're not dead. We had to do that so you would not pull out the IV's. Pull the IV first, then turn him loose."

"Where's Marg?" Demetri asked. "Is she ok? What about the rest of my troopers?"

"Everyone but my blockheaded brother and these carrier fellows are fine," Greta said. "Marg was here all night. I sent her home to get some sleep. Ah speak of the devil."

Margarete came dashing in the room and flung herself onto the bed hugging him fiercely.

"Um dear?" Demetri said. "Not that I am complaining, but can you put your hands someplace else, that kind of hurts."

Marg jumped back upright and turned red, blushing and mumbling that she was sorry.

"Ok mister, you can leave," Greta said. "You make sure he takes it easy for a couple of days and drinks lots of fluids missy. No beer or vodka either, just water and soup. We'll see after a few days. Now get, I'm busy."

Marg and Greta helped him get dressed in a new clean grey uniform. Then Marg and Demetri slowly walked out of the room.

Arms around each other's waists. Marg made sure she didn't have her arm on the burnt side.

"Colonel, did I hear that right," the trooper with the bandage around his ribs asked. "He took a blast from a hundred paces and survived?"

"Yes," Greta said. "The dummy didn't even have any armour on. Then he spent the rest of the day conducting meetings. He damn near bled to death the dummy."

Margarete looked at Demetri laying on his side facing her, arm around her middle. She studied his calm face. Sometimes, not often, he was troubled when he slept, but today was not one of those times. She took her right hand and traced the outline of the wound beneath the bandage wrapped around his waist and thought of how close she had come to losing him. So like him to take the risks himself and then to think of everything and everyone else first. What would she, and more importantly, the rest of them do without him?

She was late and while she had been late before, she had an active life style after all, this time she felt it was different. She would not tell him yet. He would make her stay home and they were at a critical point in the campaign. Both of them were needed. She would tell no one. It was a good thing he had been hit by a laser and by a nervous trooper at long range. The laser had cauterized most of the wound, a sword cut or arrow hit would have been much worse. He would be up and about quickly.

She had to get back to work today. She had spent the last two days in the hospital and all of today with him. Plans had to be made, troopers dispatched. They only had six months until Demetri thought reinforcements would arrive from Home World. They had to be ready for them. She felt his arm rise and brush a stray strand of hair from her face and looked up to see his baby blues focused on her. She felt her blood rise and her breath quicken as she lost herself in his eyes and guiding his hand to her breast, she kissed him hungrily.

Demetri looked at her as she lay on her side in the bed he had just left. Her blond hair lay across her shoulder to mid waist. Soon she would be awake and the beautiful long hair would be put up in braids and curled up around her head. At the height of just a pace and half, the top of her head came to his shoulder, but what she lacked in size, she made up for in passion and speed.

Not for the first time, did he thank the Powers above for her and for allowing her to join with him. When the time came, he knew she would be a great mother. She had a good rapport with the children and was an excellent teacher to the young. He only hoped he could be as well and that their children would have a better life than what he had. But that was in the future, today, back to work. First he must begin to start rebuilding his strength. It would be needed.

He was buttoning the last button on his tunic as he came out of the door. The two guards posted outside came to attention and saluted as he put the beret with its badge on his head. Today he had the good one on. The one with the shiny badge. Trailed by one of the guards, Demetri headed for the horse lines. Barney spotted him as he came up and trotted over to get his ears scratched and sniffed at Demetri's side, before giving him a soft nudge in the chest and laying his head on Demetri's shoulder. Demetri laid his head against Barney's and gave the big beast a hug.

Demetri ducked underneath the rope corral and grabbing a handful of main, jumped up on Barney's back. Walking to the entrance of the corral, Demetri asked the guard there to have Alex and Janet join him and kneeing Barney, left the corral. Coming to the edge of town, Demetri nudged Barney into a trot and rode almost to the top of the hill outside of town and dismounted. Then, taking off his boots, he rolled up his pants legs to mid-calf, took off the tunic and unbuttoned his shirt to make it loose. Rolling up the sleeves of the shirt, he began the slow opening movements of his practice routine, Barney matching him a few paces away. As he worked, his mind began to plan the next moves of the even more increate dance they would be doing with the authorities and Home World. Even taking it easy and moving slow, he was hurting after the hour was up. Barney looked disappointed that they would not be doing more when Demetri stopped.

"Got some coffee in the thermos here boss," Janet said. She pointed to where it was sitting.

Demetri had not even noticed they had come up. Margarete, Alex, Greta, Janet and Alphonso had joined him and were now mounting, to finish the work out. Barney joined the line in the centre as his normal spot. Demetri took one of the thermoses and poured himself a coffee, then sat down and watched. Looking at it from afar, Demetri saw how graceful and exquisite the movements were. Rider and horse working as one, the movements of horse and human melding together in harmony. Someone seeing this for the first time, would see a beautiful dance with horse and rider. One who had seen it for real would know that the arm movements meant the thrusting of sword or lance, ducking blows or shooting arrows. The graceful hoof movements, strikes to head or body of horse or man, the swaying of horse heads, attacks or defensive moves. The melding of horse and human into a powerful fighting machine.

Human and horse were breathing heavily and sweating slightly when they were finished their work out. The riders dismounted and walked to where Demetri was sitting. All of them poured themselves some coffee and sat, making a circle. Barney looked at Demetri and nodded his head up and down, before joining the other horses in their grazing.

"Alex," Demetri said. "I want you to take the hundred and scout out routes for the main body. Marg, you take the Eagles to the next town and secure it. Al, split half your troopers off to secure the mines, the others follow to the next town. I'll stay behind and coordinate here for a bit then dispatch the rest of us to the next town.

We keep leap frogging. I don't expect much or any trouble. Al, set up our relays as designed on the highest hills you can find. That way, we can keep in contact without any electronic signals. It may be slower, but it is way more secure. Janet, pick ten of the hundred for me and ten to replace them for Alex. You stay with me."

"What do we do if they resist us?" Margarete asked.

"If they fight," Demetri said. "Defend yourselves, then bypass them. If they don't fight, blockade them. Nothing in, nothing out. That's Al's people's job. We won't force them to join us, but trading with us will be most difficult."

"If they want to trade?" Alphonso asked.

"No problem," Demetri said. "They pay ten percent tax on the value of the goods out and in. We use the goods or cash to upgrade weapons and animals."

"Alex, find a good route for the main body and good spots for the relay stations and camp spots along the way," Demetri continued. "Keep in contact with Marg. Marg, don't get to far ahead of Al. Al, you don't get to far ahead of the main body. Everyone keep up the training. Once the shit hits the fan we are going to need replacements. Both human and horses. Janet, don't feel left out. You are going to be busy. Your nine are going to be my body guards and runners. Link up with Al's people and find another ten. Once my loving sister clears me to move, we will be moving fast. Now, everybody but the love of my life clear out of here and get the show on the road."

Janet tossed Demetri a length of rope and she and the others mounted and rode off. Demetri quickly fashioned a halter for Barney. Barney was generally good, but there was no sense in courting disaster, as the whole encampment would be buzzing about. Demetri and Margarete walked slowly back to camp hand in hand, their horses trailing behind them.

Demetri still could not believe she had chosen him. She was just under a year younger than him. There were a lot better looking guys she could have chosen, with better jobs and lively hoods than he. Really, he had very little. Eight horses and about a hundred Bison he could call his own. That and his weapons and clothing. The Church had taken and resold his parents land and possessions. Demetri had very little of his own. Before all this started, he had been getting by fixing electronics for barter and trading to upgrade his horse stocks. Then some people had hired him to train their horses. He had been doing alright, but nowhere near as good as the other men his age.

"Have you thought about what we are going to do after this is all over?" Demetri asked.

Margarete slipped her arm around his waist and laid her head on his shoulder as they walked.

"I don't know," she said. "Maybe I'll find myself a hunk of a man with some horses and some Bison, make a nice yurt and have a couple or three kids. Travel around the plains for a bit, find a nice spot and build a house and drive my hunk of a husband nuts."

"You deserve better than that Marg," Demetri said.

"As long as I have you, I have all I need," she whispered and kissed him behind the ear.

They had come to almost the edge of the bustling town and stopped. Soon their alone time would come to an end and Margarete would have to leave. He dropped Barney's lead rope and stood on it just in case. Turning Margarete so she was facing him, he put an arm around her back and took his other hand and rubbed his thumb gently on her cheek. He wanted to say more, but he couldn't, he found himself drawn in by her eyes. She pulled him close and dragged his head down to hers and for a time they were lost in their own world. Both of their hearts beating as one.

"Hey you two. No time for that," Greta said. "Marg, your people are ready to go. Now you kiss my brother one last time and get going."

They kissed one last time, holding the embrace as long as they dared. Then Margarete pulled away, trailing her hand down his arm as she left. Then she faced forward, pulled her head up and walked briskly the rest of the way to her waiting aides, who immediately surrounded her wanting clarification of orders. A groom came with a fresh horse and swiftly switched tack to it. Margarete mounted and with a last quick look back at Demetri, ordered the march and the one thousand Eagles were on the move at a trot, she at the head.

Greta slipped her arm around Demetri's waist as they watched first the Eagles depart, then the Bears with her Alphonso at the head, left at a walk. As the last troops crested the hill, brother and sister broke apart. She to her medical teams, he to his waiting aides and the meetings with the town's officials and the commanders of the rest of the Bears. They only had six months to accomplish what they had set out to do. Then reinforcements from Home World would arrive.

Chapter Twelve

I t had been a very long two weeks, before Greta cleared Demetri for travel. His days had been spent answering questions and giving advice to delegations of farmers and district officials. Then more questions from the command group of the thirty five thousand Bear troopers that would be following along. Supervising training of not only new recruits, but of the ever increasing numbers of what was left of the Holy Warriors who had decided that serving with the Bears was a better option than dying for leaders that did not care if they lived or died.

Finally the day came and Demetri left with his small and fast moving troop. Well smaller anyway. Along with his ten troopers, Greta and her medical staff were along, adding another twenty humans and one hundred horses. Greta had forbade the normal fast pace for two days. Now they were back to the accustomed switching horses on the fly and moving fifty miles a day. The first few days, Demetri's side had been bothersome, but now it was a dull ache he hardly noticed.

They had left the foothills and were now in the mountains proper. The skimmer and transporter trails they followed were well built and maintained. They followed river valleys and natural gaps between the mountains and while the pathways were narrower than the ones in the lowlands and foothills, the grass shoulders were wide enough for the horses to travel without hurting their hooves. Only rarely, while crossing bridges or tunnels, did the travellers have to ride the hard surface roadway itself. There were plenty of areas along the way for grazing and camping areas and the group easily made their fifty miles per day. The settlements they passed were friendly and supportive of the cause offering homes to stay overnight in and food for the journey. These were people who like themselves had suffered under the repressive governance of the Holy Church. At first they were towns that catered to the far flung farms and cattle ranches, then they slowly changed to lumber and mining based towns. The people were used to rough conditions and the change in governance and the methods reverting back to low technology ways of doing things were taken in stride and in fact the towns were progressing faster than the more technological dependant low lands had.

As they climbed, the air became the more familiar thinner and colder air that they were used to. But as they reached the peak, they too began to suffer from the high altitudes. Snow was still in evidence in some of the valleys where the sun did not fully reach yet this time of year and warm coats were needed at night and early in the day. Soon, they were once again descending. This time they entered a much drier area. The trees and plants began to change to dry land country verities once again and in a few days, the group was in the shadow of two mountain ranges. The land opened up to broad plains, pierced here and there by streams and rivers, but mostly dry and cut by ravines and dry stream beds that experience told them to stay out of. High country heavy rains and snow melt would make those low areas death traps for any who dared to camp or travel them. Flashes of light in code from hill tops, told them their progress was being followed and soon scouting parties could be seen following them. It was no surprise to one afternoon come on a large encampment spread out along the inside edge of a curve in the slow moving wide river. They had caught up to the first Bear contingent at last.

As they came nearer, people began to come out of the encampment and watch them approach. Demetri turned to Greta who was riding beside him and smiled.

"A little show?" he said and raised his hand in the air and twirled it.

Immediately and almost in unison, the group switched horses on the fly from the bareback ones they were riding, to the saddled mounts and formed up in a loose column of four. Waiting a few seconds for everyone to get settled in saddles, Demetri reached behind him and grasped the lance residing in its stirrup behind his right leg. Waiting for a second, he pulled it out and jammed it between his right knee and Barney's saddle. The rest of the troop did the same and then tightened the formation so they were knee to knee four abreast. The spare animals and pack animals followed behind, also in columns of four. Someone in the middle of the troop started singing a raunchy version of a popular marching song and it was quickly picked up by everyone.

Demetri looked over his left shoulder and Greta was singing loudly, a large smile on her face. Looking to his right, he nodded at Janet who raised her eagle crested pennant festooned lance high and then to her left. The troop broke into line abreast leaving a gap for the three in front. Then Demetri brought them to a canter and the song changed pace along with it.

Now faces could be seen in the crowd watching them approach and younger children were pointing and excitedly jumping up and down and yelling to their friends and parents. A group of officers and guards formed up and Demetri swerved the troop to approach them, all the while singing. When they reached to within a hundred paces of the group of officers and men, Demetri slowed so he filled in the gap in the line behind him and the troop edged together until the line was knee to knee.

Then anxious mothers gathered up or called to their children as the line spurred to a gallop and after one last verse the line went silent. All that was heard were the thundering of hooves as the line of galloping horses came closer and closer. When they reached twenty paces from the line of standing soldiers, the lances all came down to the horizontal, all pointed at the chests of the now concerned line of officers and soldiers. Soldiers were hurriedly pulling swords from scabbards and looking behind and around them for escape routes. The officer in the centre calmly stood facing the grim faced charging line, crossed his arms across his chest and stood sideways to them. At ten paces the Eagles let out a blood curdling yell and came to a dust spewing and horse sliding halt, five paces in front of the line of Bears.

"What do you think Colonel?" Demetri said. "Should we let them live?"

"Depends," Greta said. "Their commander had better prove to me he is glad to see me first."

She tossed her lance to Janet, slid off her horse and ran up to the still standing with arms crossed commander, grabbed him and kissed him in front of everyone.

"Ok," she said breathlessly after a few seconds. "They can live. Temporarily." Then she grabbed her husband by the waist and dragged him away, to the laughs of the Eagles.

"Somebody show us where to set up camp and put our horses," Demetri said, putting his lance back in its stirrup behind his right leg. "Horses first, then camp. After that, somebody better have some good hooch around here."

"Fall them in Senior Sergeant," Demetri said as he turned his last horse loose from the grooming he had just given him.

He looked at the troopers lined up before him. They were dusty and their grey field uniforms were wrinkled and well used and stained from sweat, both horse and human. He walked down the line and while they were dusty and dirty, their equipment was all in good shaped and they all stood tall, eyes focused above his head as he inspected each of them. Walking back to the centre of the formation, Janet beside him, he began to address them. First in Standard, then effortlessly switching to German and Russian and back to Standard.

"You have done well on this trip, as expected of Eagles," he said. "I am sure all of you have relatives and friends among the Bears. And if not, well I expect you will make some. Take the rest of the day and the next to be with or make them. Other than looking after your animals, you have no other duties for that time. I don't want to see or hear from any of you for the next day and a half. Now get out of here!"

Demetri had just finished digging out his cup and tea pot from his saddle bags in his tent and walked to the fire when Janet came up and poured him a cup from the pot in her hand.

Taking a large sip, he sighed deeply and sank to his butt in front of the fire.

"Thanks," he said. "I needed that. That order means you too Janet. Go find some friends and take some time off."

"No, I mean it," he said as she made to protest. "I am a big boy and can look after myself. Get out of here. Go find your folks or even better yet, go find a hunky guy and have some fun. You and I, for that matter, are not machines. No matter what everyone else thinks around here."

"But sir," she said. "We have much to do..."

"And little time to do it in," Demetri finished for her. "Yes I know. But all work and no play make for a dull boy, or in your case girl. Go on get out of here. Go sow some wild oats or something, I don't care what. I don't want to see or hear from you for the next day and a half or anyone else either. I need some time off too. Get!"

She looked a little shocked and moved away slowly looking behind her at him more than once. Then she reached her tent took up a pail of water and entered. A short while later she remerged wearing a clean uniform and her hair let down to cascade down her back and around her shoulders.

"Holy shit!" one of the new troopers said. "She really is a human after all."

Janet walked up to the five new troopers, all of them young and looked them up and down. She ran her hand down the chest of the mouthy one and looked him in the eyes wetting her lips with her tongue.

"Maybe when you grow one of these," she said, grasping his crotch and rubbing her chest up against his. "You might have a chance at some of this."

"But don't hold your breath honey child," she whispered into his ear. Then she laughed and flaunted away, swinging her hips as she walked.

"Way to much woman for me," Demetri said to the young troopers.

"Now don't you go breaking to many hearts out there Senior Sergeant", he yelled to her back as she walked away. She turned, looked back at him and stuck her tongue out.

Demetri re-entered his tent and quickly donned his normal uniform. The one without rank badges or anything else on it and disappeared into the main camp itself before anyone could find him and want his attention for something. Unless someone was close enough and actually knew him, he knew he looked just like any number of young male troopers that were in camp. In fact, he was remarkable in the fact that he was unremarkable. He disappeared into the crowd. Around supper time, he found a group of young people his own age and they invited him to join them, so he did and spent a pleasant evening talking about girls and horses and listening to their plans for the future.

"What about you Dem?" one of the young fellows said. "What are you going to do after all this?"

"I have a small herd of horses and a few Bison waiting for me," he said. "I am going to find a nice place in the foothills back home for my allotment. With the forest nearby and maybe a small lake to go fish in. I am going to find the most beautiful woman in the tribes, win her over, build her a wonderful house, have a bunch of kids and grow old with her. Nothing fancy my friends. If all this is the most excitement I have in my life that will suit me fine."

The group fell silent for a while staring into the fire and thinking similar thoughts.

"Hey Dem," one of the girls asked as he rose to leave. "You never told us what you do or what unit you belong to."

"Oh, sorry," he said. "I do a little of this and a little of that for the Eagles, nothing serious."

Demetri rose, making an excuse and walked away.

"Oh my, an Eagle," the girl said to her buddy. "Maybe I should make myself the one he's looking for."

"Don't hold your breath," a stunning tall blond with an Eagle and Senior Sergeant badges on her uniform said, with her arm around a handsome Bear officer.

"He's already taken," she continued. "And I am sure his wife would tear your eyes out without blinking. That my young friends was The Demetri. The commander of this whole army."

"Holy Shit!" more than one of the young people said. "He's just like us."

"Yes and no," Janet said. "Yes, he is a human being. Yes, he is young and has dreams and longs for this to be over and to lead a simple life. No, because we will never let him."

After a blissful, non-interrupted night of sleep, Demetri the next morning once again wandered the camp. Staying away from those he knew and striking up conversations all over the camp even helping one young mother out with her chores at one point. Her husband was off doing his duty at one of the signal stations for the next week. In the late afternoon, he found himself at the archery range, where a group of pre-teens were practicing. He soon found himself among them, giving them pointers and supervising them. Listening to them as they progressed, he felt their joy at discovering new strengths and skills and their hopes to be as good as their older siblings or parents or heroes. His and Margarete's names mentioned often. He moved away from them and sat down on the ground watching them and remembering what it had been like for him at that age.

He felt a presence beside him and an arm went around him and a hand went inside his shirt and rubbed his side while soft hair brushed his cheek and soft lips kissed his neck.

"When you weren't in camp or with Barney, I thought I would find you here," she said as she dug her fingers into his arm pit as she was wont to do.

He swung her around and was holding her close kissing her.

"Where did you come from?" he said. "I thought you would be on the other side of the mountains by now."

Margarete pushed him away as they began to heat up letting their passions run.

"Woa up there big fella," she said breathlessly. "Not in front of the children and not while I'm wearing my best uniform."

It was then that Demetri remembered where he was and noticed she was in her dark blue dress uniform, complete with all the badges. One of the girls training had spotted them and nudged her buddy. Soon the whole group had turned around and were looking at them.

"I'll have you know I am on day off," Demetri said standing. Then he reached down and helped Margarete up. She stood, smoothed down her uniform, came to attention and saluted.

"Colonel Bekenbaum, First Squadron, Eagle Division reporting for duty sir!" she barked out.

"At ease," Demetri growled, returning her salute.

"Officers on Deck!" one of the youngsters yelled out and the group of them formed up in line at attention, their bows jammed up against their left sides, right hands to temples in salute.

Demetri marched up to them, returned their salute and trooped the line, looking each trooper up and down as he came to them. He then marched back to the still at attention Margarete and inspected her in return. Tugging her tunic down where it had ridden up on her hips and tucking a stray lock of blond hair back behind her ear.

"Unlike the Colonel here," Demetri said. "You have your people in good order Cadet Corporal."

"Sir! Thank you sir!" the young girl said.

"Colonel," Demetri said to Margarete. "Officers especially senior officers should always strive to provide an example to their troops. What do you have to say for yourself?"

"No excuses General!" Margarete said.

"Very well Colonel," Demetri said. "You will accompany me to my quarters where we will discuss this matter further. Cadet Corporal, keep up the good work, dismiss your troopers."

As the astonished cadets watched the couple walk away, they saw the General of the Army put his arm around his wife and his head on her shoulder as she held him close.

"Nobody is going to believe this," the Cadet Corporal said. "Do you know who just spent the afternoon training with us?"

"Now really," Demetri said a while later. His finger circling one of Margarete's nipples as they lay in each other arms on his bed. "You are supposed to be two days further up."

"As much as that is turning me on," Margarete said taking his hand away from her breast. "I won't be able to answer that if you keep it up. We are having a bit of difficulty with the next town and they want to talk with a senior officer. An Eagle senior officer. So here I am. The rest of the division is where it is supposed to be."

"Anything serious?" Demetri asked. "Perhaps a show of force?"

"No, they are just being obstinate and unwilling to accept the changes," she said taking his hand and putting it back where she had taken it from. Then she slipped her hand between his legs and stroked what she found there.

"Now shut up and make your wife happy," she murmured.

"Yes mine commandant," Dimitri whispered and he did.

"What's this all about then?" Demetri asked the Bear Captain. He and his ten troopers had left at dawn and ridden hard for three hours to get here. He was in no mood for foolishness today.

"Sir, the town's people refuse to join us," the Captain said. "As you ordered, we have kept out of the town and isolated it. The town's leaders are demanding access to other regions and are refusing our terms to do so."

A group of fifteen people were dismounting a transporter and walking toward them. Fifteen of them had hand blasters out and ready for use.

"Ok Captain," Demetri said. "Mount up and accompany me. Senior Sergeant, put the troop at the ready and if any of those idiots there so much as points one of those things in my direction, make him into a pin cushion."

The troopers in their dark blue uniforms spread out in a line, bows with arrows knocked and walked their horses to within the outside edge of the blaster effective range. Demetri motioned to the Captain and dismounted. He walked toward the delegation and stopped about five paces from them. Looking at the young towns men with the blasters he saw one was more belligerent than the others and addressed him.

"If any one of your people even so much as raises one of those weapons the lot of you will be dead before you even get it levelled at me," Demetri said. Then he turned to the unarmed leaders of the group.

"What's all this about then?" he asked.

"We refuse to join your unholy rebellion against the Holy Church," one of them, a priest, spat out. "We refuse to acknowledge your form of governance and refuse to follow your laws and decrees."

Demetri shrugged his shoulders.

"Your choice," he said. "We have no problem with that. As I am sure the good Captain here has told you."

"We demand our God given right to trade for supplies, food and goods," the priest said.

"Again, we have no problem with that," Demetri said.

"Others do not have to pay what you are forcing us to pay," the priest said.

"All the others have chosen to join us," Demetri said. "We should reward you for not joining? We will not prevent you from trading, but you will pay ten percent tax on value of goods you ship out of your territory into ours and ten percent tax on the value of goods shipped into your territory from ours."

"We will not!" the priest spat out. "We will pay no tax at all to people in rebellion!"

"Then starve," Demetri said. "Anyone caught bringing goods into or out of territories controlled by the new order will have their goods confiscated and if they resist, will be killed."

"We will fight you!" the young man with the blaster said. "We are not afraid of you!"

"You should be," Demetri said quietly. "If any person in my army or any of the citizens my army is pledged to protect is harmed in any way, from anyone in this town, I will kill each and every person in this town. Men, women, children, old people. I will raise this town to the ground and leave nothing of value to anyone. This I promise you. You don't want to join us? Fine. You don't want to pay our taxes? Fine. You raise your hands against us, you all die. Is that clear enough for you priest?"

Then Demetri spun on his heels and followed by the Captain walked back and mounted Barney.

"If you people change your mind," he said. "Just let the Captain here know, so that he doesn't have his troopers kill anyone unnecessarily. Starve, freeze to death or not. Choice is yours. Is that coffee I smelt back in your camp captain? I am sure my troopers would enjoy a cup before we return to base camp."

"Big tough guy," the young man with the blaster said.

"Hey," Demetri said pulling his sword from the scabbard at his back. "There are only ten of us and twenty of you. Come on, make my day. I haven't killed any stupid Holy Warriors and their stupid priests for while."

"Shut up you idiot," one of the older unarmed men said "You too priest. If you guarantee us free access to markets, we will pay your taxes."

"See, was that so hard?" Demetri said putting the sword back in its place. "You pay you trade. Very simple. Good day gentlemen."

Demetri had lunch with the Captain and his officers.

"I shouldn't think you will have much trouble anymore," Demetri said. "You will have to keep vigilant especially with that hot head priest and the mouthy one. They will try to pull fast ones on you, but hey, you are officers, your men try that in you all the time."

Demetri let them laugh and comment on that for a minute.

"So this is how it works," he said. "It is really quite simple. It all works on tens. You calculate the value of the good in or out. Then you take ten percent of the goods or the value of the good either way. Then you take ten percent of that for you and your troops. The officers get ten percent of that. The commander ten percent of the officers ten percent. I want everything written down and copies sent back with the ninety percent. You will report any deficiencies and send back for discipline any one and I mean anyone, officers included, who steal from us or take bribes to look the other way. This will be a good deal for all of you and if only one of you is caught by us to be stealing or taking bribes, we will replace the lot of you. Understood?"

"All of you will be a lot better off doing this duty than if you were in garrison or on the line," Demetri said. "Make sure your troops know this. And oh yes. I have and I am sure a number of my troopers have, a number of excess horse flesh and in my case a nice Bison herd I might be willing to trade with, wink wink. Also, we will be setting up a permanent camp and settlements in that valley where the base camp is. Nobody seems to know what to do with the land and the council is negotiating with the Emir on the purchase of it. A group of smart young fellows like yourselves and your troopers could make out pretty good if they wanted to. Especially with firsthand knowledge of the good land like you fellows do and the funds you will have available after this duty is over. Just a thought."

It was well after dark when the troop returned back to camp and Demetri back to the loving arms of his wife.

"We are what, fifteen days from the edge of our lands to here and ten from the capital and the space port?" Demetri asked. Breakfast was over and all the senior officers were seated around the table, smoking or drinking coffee, their aides sitting behind them.

"This is a good spot," Demetri continued. "Al, keep half of your troops behind and start scouting out a place for a permanent settlement. It needs to be on high ground, have ready access to water and supply routes and easy to defend. Once the next division comes up show them where it should be and have them start building it. Then, I want plans of attack and defence made up. We make our stand here."

"Is that wise Dem?" Alphonso said. "That renegade town is a half days ride from here. They will map out everything and report it."

"I'm counting on it," Demetri said. "Let them see what they see. They are town's people and definitely not soldiers of the plains people. All they will see is a settlement going up with obvious defences on flat visible land. We know better. So when the time comes, I want the attacker's funnelled onto the settlements defences and then we hit them where they don't expect us to. The Off Worlders will be in culture shock by that point anyway and will be expecting us to make a stand in front of and in the settlement itself. Anything we can do to help that out is a good thing. We have five months people. Maybe a little longer depending on how long my Eagles can delay them. Make the best of it."

Chapter Thirteen

Five days later, Demetri, his small group of Eagles and Alphonso and his fifteen thousand troopers made contact with the main Eagle group. The Eagles had set up a fortified position and without being told, Alphonso split his group into two and soon his troopers were busy building two similar but much larger fortifications, one on each side of the Eagles. Suitable flat ground was found and staked out, then a three foot wide and deep trench was dug along the perimeter, the dirt piled up on the inside edge of the camp effectively making a six foot high wall. Then three troopers came together and tied one pace long stakes each of them carried, into a tripod and jammed it into the piled up earth embankment, points angling out. Anyone attacking them would have a tough go of it.

Inside the walls, tents were laid out in neat rows, with clear wide streets leading to the two gates, one in the rear and the other to the front, as well as between the rows and leading to the command tent which was in the centre of the camp. Movement, even while under attack would be swift, from one end of the camp to the next. After ensuring their people and animals were looked after, Demetri and Greta made their way to the centre of the camp and the command facility.

"Good to see you General," Alex said. "Everything has gone according to plan so far. Until we arrived here anyway."

"Let me guess," Demetri said. "An obstinate priest is holding us up? This was expected. This is after all the last district before the capital district."

"A priest, yes," Alex said smiling. "Stubborn yes, obstinate no. He refuses to meet with us, or to let us pass. Not just the town, the whole district. We felt it wiser to wait."

"I agree," Demetri said. "Send a messenger to this priest and tell him I am here and wish to speak with him. I will meet him on neutral ground of his choosing."

"The hundred have found a way around them and have scouted all the way to the capital and back," Alex said. "We have found a way around them and can cut them off if we choose."

"Not just yet," Demetri said. "Let's see if we can come to some kind of agreement with these people first. Al, do you think you can get some of your people into the Capital? I am afraid that my Eagles will stand out like sore thumbs in there."

"Ya," Alphonso said. "We are going to need supplies anyway. I have a lot of traders with me. That should do, if we can get around this bunch that is."

"Ok, set it up," Demetri said. "If we can't make a deal with these people, have Alex show the route around them."

They spent the rest of the hour hearing of the condition of the Eagles and the progress they had made in scouting out signal stations and possible attack and defence routes. By that time. Alphonso's defences were complete and the messenger had returned. To everyone but Demetri's surprise, the priest and his governing council had agreed to meet after morning mass. At Demetri's camp.

"Good morning Father," Demetri said. "It is so good to see you again. Come sit, ladies, gentlemen?" Demetri gestured to the large boardroom table that had been set up in the command tent.

"Can I offer you some refreshment?" Demetri said. "Beer, wine? We have a variety of foods on hand should you wish."

"Yes thank you General, most generous," the priest said. "It is good to see you again as well General."

He held out his arms and the two men hugged and kissed each other's cheeks.

"So sit," Demetri said. "Eat drink. Father you here beside me."

"Your parents Father?" Demetri said. "They are well I trust?"

"As well as can be expected under the circumstances General," the priest said. "Fathers business is suffering slightly do to the shortages and they do not eat as well as they used to, but they can stand to lose some weight."

"I trust no one is suffering greatly," Demetri said. "That was not and is not our intention."

"Oh no," the priest said. "Actually father is doing better now than before. Lack of raw materials means he is unable to make as many products as he once did, but that just drives the price of them up. People still want to buy them. No one is starving or getting ill General. It is just the luxury items and food stuffs that are in short supply. In fact our district is doing better than before."

Nodding heads of the priests people around the table confirmed the statement as did the smiles.

"So, I fail to see where the problem is," Desert said. "By coming to an agreement with us, we guarantee you full access to our markets and products. Assuredly, we no longer require nor want a number of items you produce, but we need others that I am sure that you can modify your current factories to produce. Our tax regime is also much lower than the previous regimes is. Which will leave more money in your peoples pockets. Rest assured we have no issue with your people or with the Emir and his people. Our only issue is with the Holy Church and their high handed and draconian methods."

"And that is the root of the problem," the priest said. "We, all of us in this district are followers of the Holy Church, as are many in the Capital region. While we admire your reforms and in fact have already implemented most of them already and working on the rest. We cannot abide by you refusing us to worship our religion."

"Is that all?" Demetri said and he laughed, as did all the other commanders at the table.

"Oh," Demetri said as he saw the looks on the priest and his people. "I am sorry if we have offended you. Our problem is with the Holy Church itself, not religion or God. You are free to worship whichever religion you choose or choose not to worship. We really do not care. No, what we refuse to do, is to bow down to some off world idiot who thinks his is the only way. That God only speaks through him and his followers and that those of us who don't should be punished and persecuted. No you believe in what you want and leave us free to believe in what we want. That is all that we are fighting for. Give to God what is Gods and treat each other with the respect all deserve. That is all we require."

"Well then," the priest said. "I told you my cousin was a reasonable man. I told you he and his people would not care. That your fears were groundless. What you have heard from those bigots to the east was all hogwash. For God's sake, they even think we are blasphemers. So having heard him, do you now agree?"

"Bring the papers," the priest said. "My people have elected me their leader and I will sign on their behalf."

The agreement was brought forward and the priest had them all read it before he signed it, winking at Demetri as he did so. With a flourish he signed it and handed it back to Demetri who also signed it and had Alphonso sign it in behalf of the Bears and the council.

"Well now Dem," the priest said. "Enough of this pissy beer and wine. Where is that famous vodka of yours and introduce me to this wondrous thing of beauty that I have been hearing about. Greta. Come give your cousin John a kiss eh? Al, have you been keeping her out of trouble?"

"The other way more like," Alphonso said giving John a big hug.

"Are uncle and aunty able to come visit?" Greta said breaking away from John.

"Oh yes," he said. "In fact they are in town now at my house waiting for us....My God!"

"Margarete, I would present my cousin, Father John Asminove" Demetri said. "Cousin John, my wife Margarete."

Margarete bowed her head and did a slight curtsy. John took her hands and looked from her to Demetri and back several times. Then he crushed her to his chest, tears streaming down his face.

"Oh thank you, thank you my dear," John said. "We had lost hope. He was so lost."

"Alright cuz, let her loose you letch," Demetri said. "You're just jealous you didn't see her first."

"Your damn right!" John said holding Margarete out once again at arms length and wiping the tears from his eyes.

"A toast!" he yelled out. "To the end of tyranny, a better world for us all and my cousins lovely wife!"

"Really my dear," a very tipsy John said several hours later. "You could have done much much better. For years we thought this lunk only thought about his lofty ideas and his horses."

"That's pretty much all he does think about," Margarete said. "Well, I think I am at the top of the list though. Me, I think just about the same as he does. Ok, you two have fun, I have duty tomorrow. Do make sure he doesn't pass out on the floor will you?"

She kissed him and turned to leave. He held her hand as long as he could before she walked away, their fingertips brushing as she did.

"How you can get anything done around her is beyond me," John said shaking his head.

"It is tough some days," Demetri said. "Sometimes I have to remind her, others she has to remind me. We have other duties and others are relying on us to do our jobs."

"I know that feeling all to well," John said nodding. "Greta looks well."

"Yes she loves what she is doing," Demetri said. "Like us, she and Al have to spend a lot of time apart. She really is quite good at what she does and is probably our best doctor. But don't let her or Marg's good looks and fun domineer fool you. They are both Eagle qualified and will kill you without hesitation."

"Look Dem," John said after taking a quick look around to make sure no one could hear them talk. "The Emir wants to meet with you. He said two days after we signed an agreement, he would come for a visit. Would you agree? It would have to be on the quiet. His son is a very good horseman and is wanting to buy one of mine. That is the pretence he is going to make to come."

"Ya no problem," Demetri said. "You guarantee my safety and I will guarantee his."

"Oh you have nothing to worry about us, but I know you will," John said. "The Emir will be happy to hear of yours though. You and your people scare the shit out of him."

"You just let him know that the riders that will be on both sides of him when he comes in are mine," Demetri said. "My own. They are there to make sure he has no accidents."

"You've got people behind us already?" John said. "I should have known. How many? No don't tell me. What I don't know I don't know."

"Cousin, we could have cut you and your people off completely before you even knew we were here," Demetri said. "Now cousin, why don't you gather up your people and head on home. I am sure your people are starting to worry and I really have a lot to do before I can get to bed."

"Shit," John said as they walked back to town. "They've had us surrounded since they got here and we didn't even know."

"The ones in the blue uniforms," one of the councillors said. "They look like they would eat you as soon as look at you. The ones in the brown uniforms are almost as bad and there are more of them."

"And more of them on the way," John said. "They are taking anyone who wants to join. In fact it is a requirement to serve if you want full citizenship. Home World and the Holy Church should have listened and agreed to their terms. They have just lost this planet and don't even know it yet."

"Is he really your cousin?" the counsellor asked.

"Yes," John said. "His mother and my mother were sisters. He and Greta had been chosen as had I, to be sent to home world for schooling. The local priest was jealous of them and began to impose stiff fines and ever increasing taxes on their people because of it. My uncle stood up to him and the priest trumped up some blasphemy charges against them. The Holy Warriors came, executed Demetri's parents in front of he and Greta, then carted them off to Home World. At first he did well in his studies, they wanted him to be a priest. Then they started to get tough on him and he retreated inwards. Now they have lost him completely and all his people. My people and me. I will fight with him till my last breath and the last drop of blood in my body."

They ran along the road that bordered John's estate property. At the head of the line was Demetri with Margarete to his right. Behind him was Greta with Alphonso on her right. They were followed by Janet and the other nine members of the escort party in pairs. Each side of the estate was one thousand paces long, had a thick hedge of Nanking Cherie trees as a border and had a road on all four sides. The Nanking's were in full bloom, the delicate flowers giving off a pleasant odour.

Inside the hedge, the estate was divided into four equal parts. Three pasture and one apple orchard. In the center was a sprawling complex of horse barns, corrals, machinery and storage buildings for farms equipment and the orchard. A large house with several guest houses was in the very center. John resided in one of the guest houses. The main house was seldom used, but the Emir and his retinue had arrived the day earlier and were occupying it. Demetri and his escort occupied four of the guest houses. Every morning for the last three days, they had run this same route, coming out of the estate and swinging right, running along all four edges of the estate then back to the corrals. It was five thousand paces in all. They ran instep, each foot of the group hitting in unison. The stride was about a pace and a half, the pace was quick, but not fast. They were wearing their grey coloured field uniforms and light weight boots. Once they reached the corral they used for their training they stopped and removed the foot gear, rolling up the pants to mid calf. Shirts sleeves were rolled up to just below the elbow and shirts unbuttoned so as to be loose. Then they formed two lines of six with Demetri and Margarete in the lead and started the slow graceful movements of their daily exercise routine.

The normal quiet routine had changed this morning. The Emir's escort of ten was also training, but on the other side of the corral. There were twelve of them. They used a similar regime, but much faster and louder, in that they punctuated each punch, kick or movement with yells. Then they paired off with two pace long wooden sticks and started flailing away at each other. Demetri and his group, kept up their own regime and appeared not to notice the ever increasing noise and activity level across from them. The other group finished and stood watching Demetri's group and more than one rude and lewd comment was made both at the male and female members of Demetri's party. They were ignored until the very end, when Demetri turned, place his left hand over his right fist, brought the hands to his chest and bowed to the other group. Then Demetri walked out of the coral and the group headed to their guest houses to clean up, have a light breakfast and dress for the next part of their day.

Today, John would be showing his horse to the Emir and his son in the competition ring. There was a small grandstand on one side and Demetri had been asked to come and watch, along with all of his people. So they all put on the dark blue, almost black dress uniforms they had brought along for this reason. The uniforms were identical except for rank badges and in Alphonso's case, the Bear on the collar instead of the Eagles the rest of them wore. The group sat in the far right of the grandstand and soon, the Emir's escort arrived in their dark green dress uniforms and took up the far left. Demetri looked over, established eye contact and nodded. He received a sneer in return and several comments were made that he could not hear but made the other group laugh.

At that point, the Emir's party arrived. Father John was walking beside the Emir, a young lad of about fifteen, a tall man in a dark green senior officer's uniform beside him. Behind them an immaculately dressed woman with another dark green uniformed man beside her and finally two dark green uniformed troopers.

"Attention!" Demetri called out in Standard and all fourteen of them rose and assumed the position of attention and as the Emir reached the first of them, they all brought their right hands to their foreheads in salute and held it. The Emir barely glanced over at them, continuing on his way to the center of the grandstand.

"At Ease," Demetri said quietly after he had passed the last of them and they all dropped the salutes, moved right feet over six inches and put both arms behind their backs, clenching hands in the small of their backs. Once the Emir's party had seated, Demetri let his people also sit. The green uniforms at the other end of the grandstand had not moved and now the snickers were clearly audible.

One of the troopers spoke with Father John and approached Demetri's group.

"Father John would present his cousins to the Emir," the trooper said.

Standing, the two couples followed the trooper. Demetri deferred to Alphonso and Greta allowing them to proceed he and Margarete. The four of them stopped in line abreast in front of the Emir, came to attention and saluted. The Emir looked puzzled looking at them, then John whispered into his ear and the Emir nodded at the group, who then dropped the salutes, staying at ridged attention.

"Emir," John began. "May I present my cousin Greta and her husband Alphonso Hood."

"Sir!" both of them said and clicked their heels and nodded their heads stiffly, before resuming attention.

"My cousin, Demetri Bekenbaum," John said. "And his wife Margarete."

"Majesty!" Demetri said, both he and Margarete clicking their heels and bowing their heads.

"Well met," the Emir said. "We would have you join us. Alphonso, you beside me. Demetri beside my son Jamir. Ladies, if you join my dear wife Fatima?"

"Your Highness," Demetri said addressing Jamir before he sat.

"So, Alphonso," the Emir said. "We were treated on our way here with the site of ten mounted troopers following us here, five on each side, just outside blaster range. They easily kept up with us the whole way. I have heard that riders such as those can ride easily triple that distance by changing horses on the fly. Is that true? Can you do that?"

"I also have heard this Majesty," Alphonso said. "Unfortunately, my mounted infantry and heavy cavalry are not trained in this maneuver and in any case it would be impractical for us to do so."

"Yes it was a nice display of horsemanship," Jamir said to Demetri. "But we were not traveling fast. In any case the horses were not overly impressive. Father John has much better ones."

"I have heard that as well Your Highness," Demetri said. "I have as yet not had the pleasure of seeing any of Cousin John's horses."

"Well feast your eyes and eat your heart out," John said as a pitch black sixteen hands high stallion was brought into the arena. "That cousin is my best stallion. The end product of years of selective breading."

The stallion was prancing beside the handler, who had a tight grip and a short hold on the bridal.

"Would Your Highness care to try him?" John asked. "He has been especially trained for you."

Jamir quickly rose and jumped into the arena. The handler kept control of the animal while he mounted and settled himself in. Then he stepped back and let Jamir have control of the animal. Jamir kept him on a tight rein, keeping the horses head bowed and he ran him around the perimeter of the arena a few times, then he started the graceful movements of the empennage routine.

"I noticed those troopers escorting us were fully armed," the officer said to Demetri.

"Your safe passage was guaranteed sir," Demetri said. "They were there to ensure that. We have run into some people who are not happy with how the Emir is dealing with us."

"You think my people are incapable of defending the Emir?" the officer said.

"I am sure they would have tried their best sir," Demetri said. "Our people were just there as a backup precaution."

"I trust my people have not caused any difficulties with yours?" the officer said.

"It has been my experience sir," Demetri said. "That often young bored elite troops tend to be overly confident of their abilities. Talk is cheap sir. My people have nothing to prove. Your people are not bothering us sir."

"And what are your duties sir?" the officer said.

"I have been given a small command sir," Demetri said. "My cousin felt that perhaps I could be of some use between our two groups and my people agreed. But it appears that Alphonso has things well in hand sir."

"Oh Father!" Jamir exclaimed as he jumped to the ground and ran over to the Emir. "I really must have him! He is magnificent!"

"Well then," the Emir said. "Come then, time to negotiate."

He rose and followed by his retinue exited the arena, once again ignoring Demetri and the rest of the blue uniformed troopers, to the great pleasure of the Green uniformed troopers.

It had been several days since they had exercised their mounts. Alphonso had been summoned to attend the Emir for breakfast, so the thirteen of them saddled their mounts and took the route they had been running at the trot in formation with the horses. Not bothering to dismount, they opened the corral gate and shut it once again as the last trooper entered. Then they spread out in three lines. The officers in front and two lines of five behind. Then they began to put the mounts through their movements. After a few moments, swords were drawn from the scabbards at their backs and they began to practice the slow movements they would use in battle conditions. They kept at it for an hour and horse and human were sweating when they were finished.

"Very pretty," one of the Emirs troopers said. They had been watching the whole time. "Care to try that one on one, on the ground with one of us? You can use one of our practice swords if you don't have any."

"Sir," Janet said quietly.

"Make your day Senior Sergeant," Demetri said.

Janet handed the reins to her horse to one of the other troopers and walked over to where the mouthy one was standing.

"Sure, why not," she said. "One hundred credits to the winner, or I don't play."

"Easy money," the trooper said, tossing her a wooden practice sword.

Janet took the sword and walked away a few paces swinging it around finding the balance. Then she walked back, put both hands on the hilt, raised the sword in front of her face and bowed to her opponent, who just laughed at her and attacked. She easily batted the man's sword aside and walked away from him. He came at her again with a blood curdling yell and slashed at her right leg, she pivoted out of the way and tapped him on the back with her blade, once again walking away from him.

This went on for about a minute, then the man fully attacked her, his sword moving so fast it blurred and the air whooshed as it swung. Janet deflected each of the blows and more than once hit the man on the back swing. Then he lost his cool and really went after her, malice in his eyes. Janet toyed with him for a bit, then whacked him hard in the chest, stuck her right foot behind his left knee and tripped him. He landed hard on the ground. Janet once again brought the sword to her face and bowed.

"You can send the credits to my barracks," she said tossing the practice sword so that it landed beside the man on the ground. "I'll be there until the end of the week."

She started walking back to collect her horse and heard steel clearing leather behind her and spun around. The trooper had grabbed a sword and was coming at her, naked sword held high. In a motion so fast it could hardly be seen, she had the sword from her back and was in full attack mode before the man even got close to her. In seconds he was desperately trying to defend himself from the relentless attacks Janet was doing to him. Finally she had enough and with a quick swipe, broke the man's sword from the hilt and on the backswing sliced across the man's throat, drawing blood, but doing no real damage.

"Next time you draw steel against one of us, make sure it's a real sword not a play toy," she said. "This one has cut heads off for real."

Then she turned her back on the man and examining the edge of her sword, she gathered up the reins, rescabbarded the blade and the whole troop walked out of the corral. Seeing the Emir, John, Jamir and the rest of the officers standing there watching, Demetri flung his reins over Barney's back and walked over to them, Barney docilely walking behind him.

"You should really train your people better sir," Demetri said to the officer. "Your equipment and their training is subpar. Son, what do you think of our mediocre horses now? Like ourselves, we were only exercising right now. Here, I'll show you what those pretty moves you play with are really about."

Without taking the reins, Demetri vaulted into the saddle, drew the sword from his back and Barney exploded into action. The hooves striking out fast and hard pivoting opposite to Demetri's sword swings, man and horse instantly melded into an efficient killing machine. They kept at it for over a minute. Then stopped dead.

"Barney can do that for a long time," Demetri said quietly. "He can also run sixty miles in a day and fight at the end of it. That pretty horse of yours would be dead in under an hour. If Barney let him live that long."

"Enough of this playing around," he said. "If you and Alphonso have not come to an agreement by now, there will be none. Once you people decide to get serious, come find me. Maybe I'll talk with you. Otherwise, we are coming for you next. Be ready."

Still not touching a rein he and Barney swung away leaving the Emir standing there dumbfounded.

"As I said to you on many occasions," Alphonso said. "I am but a heavy cavalry commander. Demetri allowed me to conduct these talks with you because you seemed to defer to me. That man Majesty, is the not only the general of our elite fighters, he is the overall commander of the whole army. I was just here to accompany my wife, who is also a member of that same elite force. All thirteen of them are and you can tell your trooper commander, that the Senior Sergeant is nowhere near as good as a lot of the other troopers we have and that sword has indeed cut off a lot of heads for real. As has mine. We are not pretend warriors sirs. We are the real thing."

Within an hour, they had changed into their field uniforms, packed up their supplies, gathered up their spare horses and were heading out of the estate. On the fly and in front of the gawking Emir and his retinue, all fourteen of them, including Alphonso, switched horses and broke into the regiments song as they accelerated into a canter, bare back, spare horses trailing behind them.

A week later, back at the base camp that was beginning to take shape, Demetri received a relay message that the Emir wanted to meet with him in the Capital city. About half of the Capital District had been cut off at that point. Demetri declined. Three days later, the District was completely cut off and import and export tariffs imposed on all goods.

The next morning came a request to meet back at John's estate. Demetri declined. More and more of the Bear groups had arrived. Work on the central compound was progressing and the groups were fanning out across the broad, dry plains. They established smaller central areas and the herds of bison, sheep and horses began to graze. Demetri, finally bored of the make work projects he was supervising, delegated others to those tasks and decided to visit the outlying encampments. Margarete decided to join him. Her position also mostly administrative at this point.

Under pain of severe repercussion, Demetri was not to be disturbed unless in case of life or death. Unfortunately, they did not travel alone. They had a personal guard of ten each, plus each district they came from and the one they were going to, supplied ten more each. So with officers and runners, the retinue was seldom under fifty people and one hundred and fifty horses, who also required keepers. It generally took a couple of days to get settled into the next encampment. Meeting with the local leaders both military and civilian. Being hosted at functions and things of that nature. Eventually, Demetri would get down to what he was really there for. Evaluating the new candidates. How well their training was progressing. The quality of the horses being brought on line. The grade and quality of the Bison and sheep herds. How much fodder and grain was being produced. The types of local industry being conducted and the supplies that were needed to conduct all of this activity. He well knew that armies travelled on their stomachs. How much food supply they had for animal and beast would in a great way determine the success and longevity of any campaign.

Each budding settlement he came to, were actively engaged in producing bundle after bundle of arrows. Some had close proximity to wooded areas and made shafts. Others had easy access to metal and made arrow and lance heads. Others had an overabundance of birds. Both wild and domestic and made the veins which made the long range accuracy permissible. Then were the bow makers. These traded bows for bison horn, wood and glue to manufacture the bows and bow strings. Others excelled in making leather goods. Saddles, horse tack, scabbards, belts, packs and bags. Still others ropes of many lengths and thicknesses. All of this activity resulted in vigorous trade not only among the scattered groups, but also the established settlement areas who valued the goods highly and traded necessary metals and food stuffs for them. A very few, were skilled enough to make the special swords and pike heads the army needed. These individuals had their apprentices making common knives and farm implements and as more metals like highly malleable silver was traded, they began to make luxury goods like jewelry and belt buckles.

All of this was traded with every one including the Capital Region and the fanatical Central Hub regions, who of course paid heavily to import and export with them. This also generated profit. This profit was used to purchase things they could not make themselves. Like the light weight highly polished silver coated garments the troops and horse would wear in battle.

Everyone seemed happy. The budding settlements were progressing from yurts to permanent housing. Well-fortified and defended. The yurts themselves were becoming better as were the means to transport them. All was progressing as planned.

It was several weeks into the tour now. Demetri and Margarete were relaxed. They were very rarely apart, spending most of each day together and every night. One day fed up with all of the attention, Margarete told everyone to leave them alone, and they were going riding, alone. Of course this would not and could not be allowed, the powers to be thought. Several well placed arrows and the threat of more and deadly ones to follow, finally persuaded most of the well intentioned to leave and the dedicated ten of Demetri's, to keep out of arrow range, which ensured at least a little privacy.

Finally coming to a nice little brook with a not to bush encrusted bank, they both dismounted and left their mounts to graze. Margarete removed her boots and stockings and dangled her feet in the water as Demetri lay back, his arms crossed behind his head and looked up into the clear blue sky. They stayed like that for about ten minutes. Demetri gazing at the clouds and Margarete across the stream. Margarete reached over and took one of Demetri's hands and placed it on her belly.

"What the Hell!" Demetri exclaimed. He felt a rippling coming from her belly.

"That my love is your son or daughter," Margarete said. "I am six months pregnant."

Now she rolled up her tunic and the bulge, though small could be seen.

"I have been altering my clothing so you would not notice," she said. "But now, no, I can no longer hide it."

All the while she would not look at him. She stayed looking into the distance. Demetri sat up, his hand still on her belly, now gently rubbing it. He took his other arm and put it around her shoulder holding her close to him. Now the tears she had been holding at bay began to flow, but still she said nothing, dreading what she would now hear.

"Well that's it then," Demetri whispered into her ear, before he kissed her neck beneath it. "Rules are rules, even for us. I think we have a problem though. How can we go home? We don't have one."

"Whaaa, what do you mean," Margarete stammered. "You are not furious with me?"

"No Marg, quite the opposite," Demetri said. "I could not be happier. I love you so much right now, it hurts."

"I will go home to my parents," Margarete said. "As you said the rules are the rules."

"Then I go with you," Demetri said. "My place is with my family no matter what the rules say and by the way, that is what they say."

"You would give all this up for me?" Margarete said, now the tears were really flowing and she buried her head into his shoulder.

"Give what up?" Demetri said. "A choice between being with my wife and child when they need me or freezing and starving to death out here leading an army that does not really need me. No, family first."

Then she flung both her arms around him and kissed him.

"So missus," Demetri finally said as she let him loose. "I have absolutely no experience in these matters. What now? What can you do or not do?"

"Well, I won't be able to be very active soon," Margarete said. "If we are going to leave, it should be sooner than later. I will consult with Greta, but I think horseback will be out shortly. For my safety and the babies."

"Ok," Demetri said. "I suppose we should head back and inform everyone then."

After one last kiss, they both rose and mounting, rode toward the now scrambling to get out of harms way escort.

"Stay where you are!" Demetri yelled out.

The couple rode up to the now in formation line abreast escort.

"The Colonel has an announcement to make," Demetri said leaning over and putting his arm around Margarete who held her head up and defiantly looked into each troopers eyes, one by one.

"The General and I are expecting a child," she said clearly. "Anyone have a problem with that?"

"Shit Mags," Janet said. "The way you two have been going at it, we were wondering why it was taking so long. Pay up you bums I win the pool."

The formation broke up as the troopers came forward to hug and congratulate the couple.

"When?" Janet asked.

"Three months more, I think," Margarete said. "I'll ask Greta for sure when we get back to the main camp."

"Ha, I knew it," Janet said.

"You win again?" Demetri said.

"No, not that one," Janet said shaking her head. "Greta wins that one."

"Is everyone in on this?" Demetri asked.

"Yup," Janet said. "Except for you two."

"Speak only for Demetri," Margarete said. "I have eleventh of July booked in the pool."

"No fair!" Janet said. "I have the eighth and Greta the fourteenth. No fair, unfair advantage. I am going to complain to the General so I am."

"Sorry, conflict of interest," Demetri said. "I have the tenth booked."

"You bum!!" Margarete said. "You knew?"

"Umm.. well..." Demetri said looking for a way out.

"Hubby would know dummy," Janet said. "Young attractive active girl starts getting a little pudgy. Not to mention sex and every day and not moody for five days a month. He's not your regular dummy male you know Mags."

Margarete punched him on the arm, then kissed it and the happy group rode back to the settlement laughing and joking all the way.

Demetri was almost ready the next morning to head out and watch a group of candidates train, when an aide came up.

"Riders coming in," the aide said. "Large group from the Capital Region. They want a meeting ASAP sir."

"Ok," Demetri sighed. "Gather the gang. Oh Colonel dear, visitors coming. Do be presentable?"

They were twenty in all. All of them on horseback and in the dark green federal uniforms. The Emir, his son and wife included. They spread out in line abreast in front of Demetri and Margarete and saluted. Demetri let them hold it while he looked at each trooper, the Emirs wife and some of her ladies turning red, the son beginning a frown under his scrutiny. Then Demetri came to a stiff attention and returned the salute crisply.

"Welcome to my modest camp Majesty," Demetri said. "Please dismount. Captain, find some accommodation for the party. Senior Sergeant, show them where they can barrack and stable the horses."

"Would you and your aides care for some refreshment Majesty?"

Blue coated aides were bustling around finding chairs and tables after they had seen how many would be staying. Everyone was soon seated and talking pleasantries over slightly cooler than outside temperature beer.

"Well Majesty," Demetri said. "As pleasant as your journey no doubt has been, I am sure you have come for more important things than just a brief holiday."

"That is correct," the Emir said. "First I would apologize for your treatment when we last met. I really did think your brother in law was in charge for one thing. We also did not realize that all of you were in the army. Also, there are many eyes and ears and appearances need to be kept up. For the welfare of us all."

"We will speak no more of it," Demetri said. "Unfortunately, I was not informed of your arrival and have a function I must perform. I am sure you could use some rest after your journey. Colonel Bekenbaum will see to your needs. We will meet later this day."

"Could I and some of my staff join you sir?" the Emir said. "I assure you, we will not get in your way."

"If you wish," Demetri said. "It will most likely be boring. I will be observing some of my young people training is all."

"Ah, that would be a treat for me," the Emir said.

"Suit yourself," Demetri said and lead the way. The Emir, and in fact the whole group came along. Margarete accompanied the Emirs wife and her ladies and soon they were all sitting on the grass hillside watching the group of fifteen year olds going through their drills. To the left of them was a group of preteens at the archery butts launching arrows at targets.

"You start them that young?" the emir asked.

"It takes many years to master the bow," Demetri said. "Not just the eye hand coordination, but the arm strength."

Jamir snorted at that comment.

"You must excuse my impolite son," the Emir said. "He thinks he is somewhat of an expert with the bow and sword."

"The butts are there," Demetri said. "The equipment as well. I am sure Jamir would not mind demonstrating his mastery for us?"

"What with those child's toys?" Jamir said.

"All the more impressive then," Demetri said. "The children will observe a true master at his peak demonstrating a skill they are struggling to master. They will appreciate it. Come."

Demetri stood and looked at Jamir, who finally stood and tugging down his tunic followed Demetri to the archery range.

"Attention on deck!" one of the ten year olds yelled. Immediately, all fifteen of them formed a line at attention, bows grounded in their left hands and saluted with their right.

Demetri came to attention and returned their salute. Then he trooped their line inspecting each of them. He stopped in front of a shorter than normal, blond haired blue eyed girl and asked for her bow. It was old but well cared for. Handing it back to her he asked for an arrow and inspected it.

"You are proficient?" Demetri asked.

"Sir, yes sir!" The young girls said. "I will be qualifying for Eagle Candidate on Friday sir. Then I will be replacing my older sister who will be graduating with her Eagle sir!"

"Demonstrate for us if you please," Demetri said pointing at the targets.

The young girl saluted and marched over to the range, turned sideways and shot five shots, the last three in the air as the first two hit the target. All in the bulls eye.

"Very well," Demetri said as she came back in line. "Your bow and arrows please?"

"All right Your Highness," Demetri said holding them out to Jamir. "Your turn."

Jamir grabbed them out of Demetri's hand and marched over to the firing line. Demetri right behind him. The young man gasped as he pulled on the string not expecting the strength of it. Then he let loose. It took four shots to hit the target. The last one just outside the kill zone.

"Lesson one," Demetri said. "Never underestimate your opponent, or, overestimate your abilities."

Demetri handed the bow and its quiver of arrows back to the young girl.

"Your Aunt and I are expecting you to accompany us young lady," he said. "You had best not disappoint us."

"Sir! Yes sir!," she said beaming.

"Perhaps you would not mind giving a little instruction to the Ensign here on how our bows work?" Demetri asked. "Ensign, I am sure the Emir will not mind if you stay behind. Be sure to have him back at my quarters by supper then?"

Demetri gave one last salute and then joined the others, still watching.

"That will be good for him," the Emir's wife said. "He has so little interaction with kids his own age. But she is a little young for him no?"

Demetri looked back to see the little blond showing Jamir the proper stance and holding position for the much stronger than he was used to bow.

"She is thirteen," Demetri said. "She was held back to coach the youngsters and we have a policy that two members of the same family can't be candidates at the same time. Her older sister should be graduating this year and she can take her place."

"But she is so small," the Emir's wife said.

"So was I," Margarete said. "But a certain young commander saw my potential and helped me. My niece has had an easier time of it. Myself, Greta, Janet and our other sisters have broken the ground for them."

"She is your niece and has to still qualify as a common trooper?" the Emir's wife said.

"Yes," Margarete said. "As did I and Demetri and as we still have to do each year. These Eagles are earned, not given away."

"Demetri? I may call you Demetri? I am Jasmine," the Emir's wife said. "You are not concerned we are all armed with blasters?"

"No Jasmine, not at all," Demetri said. "It takes two seconds to draw the blaster, another second to aim it, another to pull the trigger and then you have to hold the target for two seconds to do damage. At the first sign of any of you moving your hand to a blaster, I and Margarete would be moving. In the six seconds it would take for one of you to shoot at us, we would not be in the same position and would most likely have that person at the least incapacitated or dead. The rest of you would look like pin cushions from all the arrows sticking out of you right after that. It is you that should be concerned, not us."

"Yes dear," the Emir said. "I have seen them train. Our people are no match for them at all. Which is why we are here. That female Senior Sergeant you saw earlier? She was the one who so roundly defeated Rothberg and he is one of our best."

"Well Majesties," Demetri said. "I normally conduct business after breakfast. I will have someone show you your quarters, they will be rough I am afraid. Someone will be along to collect you for dinner."

"Senior sergeant a moment, captain, you as well," Demetri said as he and Margarete returned to their tent. "Captain, you will entertain and keep tabs on the officers. Senior Sergeant, you the enlisted men. They are our guests and shall be treated as such. If I hear of any of our people starting anything, I will not be happy. Captain, have Ensign Walsh join us for dinner."

"Is that wise Dem?" Margarete asked once they were alone. "He was one of their top commanders."

"I need to see their reactions to him," Demetri said. "I also need to see how he reacts. I want to give him a company. I need to know he can handle this type of thing."

The guests arrived enmass and while there were some second glances at Walsh, nothing was said. Jamir and Margarete's niece seemed to be hitting it off.

"She is filling out that uniform nicely," Demetri said. "I seldom see her dressed up. She is always in those loose fatigues."

"We had hoped she would grow a little taller like her sister," Margarete said.

"Oh, I remember another cute little blond that turned out ok," Demetri said. "Perhaps her Aunty should have a little chat with her before she leaves? We don't need her going all boy gaga now."

"Janet will cure her of that in no time," Margarete said and smiled. "I had to tune her in you know."

"You tuned up the Senior Sergeant?" the Emir said as he sat down. "I caught the tail end of that."

"Well, we were much younger then," Margarete began. "We were in the first group of candidates for Eagle training. Janet had the hots for a skinny little big mouthed punk and she was about to blow her chance. There were only four females in the group. We were the test group and she was going to blow it for all of us. So first I kicked his ass, then I kicked hers. She clued in after that."

"What happened to the guy?" Jasmine said.

"I'm not sure," Margarete said.

"He's farming," Demetri said. "He finished his mandatory service as a pike man in a Bear unit, found a girl, has three kids and about a hundred bison back home. It was important that all the girls pass. I had to work hard just to get them included in the program and I was proved right."

"You have no..um.. issues," Jasmine said.

"The first year we had a few," Demetri said. "The girls gave as good as they got. Oh and we have some rules."

"Rules?" the Commander said.

"Young people, will be young people," Demetri said. "First rule. Girl gets pregnant, both girl and boy go home. No exceptions."

"Rule two," Margarete said. "Girl says no, girl means no. Doesn't matter if she said yes before."

"What happens if rule two is broken?" the commander asked. Both Jamir and Margarete's niece were listening now.

"Best case, minor infraction, he gets castrated," Demetri said. "Worst case, death. And if more than one were involved, they all die."

"Now, it is no longer a problem," Margarete said. "They all know how important it is. They all want their Eagles. It has trickled down to the Bears as well. We have few problems and they are handled quickly if they arise. We find, the whole unit will get involved. Nobody wants a degenerate in their unit and with the Bears, the girls still have to serve their full five years, in the field. So the pregnancy time is added on."

"We are fighting for our survival," Demetri said. "As a people, we are all on board. Except for those nut balls next door and you people that is."

"Ah," the Emir said. "As you say. Tonight is for socializing. Tomorrow for business eh?"

"No exceptions?" Jasmine asked looking directly at Demetri.

"Ah," Demetri said. "Word has spread already then. That is correct Majesty, no exceptions. Margarete and I will be leaving as soon as replacements are put in place."

"What do you mean leaving!" the Emir demanded. "You are essential to this matter."

"Majesty," Demetri said. "My wife is pregnant and the rules are the rules. I am but just a poor herder and a young one at that. There are others more qualified than I to conduct negotiations."

The Emir made to protest further, but his wife put her hand on his arm and when he looked over to her, she shook her head.

"My husband," she said. "You are always harping that the law is for all and that none are above it. This is one of their laws. The General and Colonel should be commended for setting an example. Now my dear Margarete, come, let us women go and discuss women things. Like how stubborn our men can be."

She rose, kissed the Emir on the cheek and putting her right arm through Magarete's left and gathering up Margarete's niece as they went, exited the tent.

"She certainly does not look pregnant," the Emir said. "How far along is she?"

"Six months or so," Demetri said

.

"At six months, Jasmine was already very big," the Emir said.

"Captain," the Commander said addressing the Ensign. "I see you have switched sides."

"Sir," the Ensign said. "We were outnumbered and out gunned. Drastically so. We were abandoned by our previous command who knowingly sent us on a suicide mission. The General could have killed us out of hand had he wished. Instead he offered us full membership and entitlements. I took him up on it and have not regretted one second of that decision. Sir."

"And I do not blame you," the Emir said. "You were sent on a suicide mission. How could it not be with those people. But I judged the Generals temperament correctly and it has turned out well for you. I see you are an officer?"

"Yes Majesty," the Ensign said. "I am but a lowly Ensign sir. Barely tolerated by my troop mates, but I am managing."

"A full Captain serving as an Ensign?" the Commander said.

"Yes sir," the Ensign said. "I have barely enough experience for that. I have qualified my minimums and am being fast tracked for an Eagle. Hopefully I can qualify, Sir."

"He is a little deficient with the bow," Demetri said. "That is only to be expected. You people have little experience in that area. Learning our sword and unarmed combat techniques is exceptional. It would appear as though he has ridden somewhat in his past. But still does not have the stamina for us at this point."

"Not for lack of you people trying," the Ensign said and then he smiled. "That which doesn't kill you..."

"Makes you strong," Demetri finished for him and they both laughed.

"I still think my horse is better than anything you people have," Jamir said.

"Ah my son," the Emir said. "Perhaps a small demonstration tomorrow Demetri?"

"The Ensign here has a passable pony," Demetri said. "Perhaps a short ride tomorrow Ensign? Perhaps the Emir would like to put his money where his mouth is? Two hundred credits?"

"Done," the Emir said.

Jasmine, Margarete and Maria sat in a line on the outskirts of the camp away from the sounds and smells of the camp. I was a beautiful night, cloudless and windless, the stars shining brightly overhead. Margarete had brought a jug of beer and the three of them passed it back and forth among themselves. They sat silently, each in their own thoughts, staring at the stars.

"I never see this at home," Jasmine said. "The city lights dim the sky. On our travels here, we have seen how the people prosper under your regime, your ideas. All except that next village over, who still operate under the old rules. Even though your people show great restraint and charge them less than the Holy Church used to in tax, they still do not prosper as the other towns and districts do. We are very impressed with what your own people have accomplished in only five years. Can you tell me how all this was accomplished?"

"Demetri came home from Home World," Margarete said. "At first, he just stayed by himself. He shunned most modern things and reverted back to ancient times in the way he did things. Then people began to notice that his methods with his breeding programs with the cattle and horses, were producing better results than theirs. They began to copy his methods and soon the whole settlement was prospering. We were not the only ones, the whole district was doing it. The class that was with Demetri at Home World all taught these methods to their settlements. My parents and the other elders all thought that this was the new teachings from Home World and we thought nothing of it. Instead of being thankful for the increase in taxes the extra revenue brought in, the local administrator and priest raised the taxes so that even though we were bringing more money in, we had the same or less than we did before. Then the priest noticed that Demetri and the others of his class that went to Home World, did not come to church Saturdays and they fined them for that. Demetri refused to pay the fine. They took him to court and he proved to them that he was doing nothing illegal and that in fact the taxes the Church was imposing were illegal and the taxes the state was charging us were outside the guidelines established by your Majesties."

"Several days later, they came to arrest Demetri, he ran them off. The Elders agreed with him and they had him teach the rest of the settlement on how to resist these bandits. We, the whole settlement drove them off. Then we began to teach the other settlements how to do it and Demetri showed us how to defeat your weapons. The rest you know. I was much younger then, about Maria's age."

"So this was taught to them at Home World?" Jasmine asked. "Perhaps then when word comes back things will not be as bad as we fear."

"Demetri and the others learned these things at Home World," Margarete said. "How I am not sure, but I do know they were not taught them. It had something to do with our ancestors is all I know."

"My people came here the year after yours did," Jasmine said. "The legends say that your people did not want to rule and that they let us instead. It really did not matter, our ways and yours were similar and somebody had to be in charge. For many generations things went smoothly, then the Church began to exert its authority and my people felt they had no choice but to comply and little by little things got beyond our control and the Church took over. So here we are."

Jasmine sat quietly, contemplating for a moment.

"My people and yours, have as far as memory goes, always had similar values," Jasmine said. "My people believe in freedom to worship or not as everyone wishes. Everyone has an equal voice in matters that involve all. Women have an equal share in all."

"In Ancient times, my people, like yours, often had differences in opinion with others not of our persuasion and we had to fight many wars. Unlike your people, we were small in numbers. Where your people had the numbers and the will to fight off the large Empires, my people often had to make compromises to keep our freedom, but the Emperors paid dearly with lives whenever they tried to impose their will on us, so eventually, they came to their senses and left us alone."

"Then came foreigners from a land far away. They had better technology than we did and they defeated the great emperors and they set their eyes on our land. We sent a delegation to meet with them and they agreed to let us live as we were as long as we paid taxes to them and cause them no harm, which we did."

"Then a Muslim insurrection happened. These sprang up every second generation or so. It was no surprise to us when it happened. They were very bad and closed mined people, who believed that only their path to God was the correct one and they killed anyone who disagreed with them. The foreign empire was not in great strength in our area and while we and they tried to hold these bad people at bay, we were steadily losing ground to them. They became stronger and more emboldened as they won victories, while we became weaker as we lost lives. The decision had been made to start negotiations with these invaders when we were sent word that help was on the way."

"When they arrived, we were at first disappointed. They were other foreigners from a different empire. They spoke a language that most of us could not understand and the first group of white men, did not seem to like the second group. But right from the first, this second group proved they were different. The listened when we spoke. They shared with us their medical knowledge. They went out and met with the local settlements and provided good advice. They even had women with them. Soon we began to trust them and then the fighting started. At first small fights, but becoming larger as time went on."

"This second group of white men proved to be mighty warriors and each time that they went into battle, they won great victories and never lost a man. Finally the Muslims decided to get rid of us all and sent a great army to do battle with us. The second group of white men had a great leader and he chose a place to meet this horde of invaders. We only hoped to delay the invaders and cause them some harm before retreating to our defences. Instead, this great leader, placed his men in two lines of five hundred blocking the invaders who were ten thousand strong, all cavalry. They charged in mass formation and the small blocking force stood their ground singing their song and began to kill and kill and kill. Then the leaders second force of support people rose up from behind the hill flanking the invaders and the killing became more intense and our people joined in. Out of the ten thousand that attacked, less than two thousand got away."

"Two generations later, a great war broke out among the great empires of the day and one of the smaller empires decided to take advantage of that and to invade us and take us into their empire. We were holding out, barely, when once again help arrived. From the same white people that had saved us before, led by that great leaders grandson. They had changed their flag a little and were now moved to a different country farther away, but they were the same people."

"Once again, three generations later, the Muslim people were once again threatening us. Killing our people and enslaving us. We were hold up in our last fortress and were down to our last few fighters, when help arrived and the Muslims were defeated and driven away. Once again, by the same foreigners as before and lead by a direct descendant of the first group."

Jasmine stopped speaking then. She fished into a pocket and pulled out a communicator and after fiddling with it for a while, found what she was looking for and showed it to Margarete. It was a very old photograph in grainy black and white. But the two people on horseback in the picture were clear as was the out stretched flag behind them. An Eagle on the left and a Bear on the right. The Caption below read. 'Colonel Andreas Bekenbaum Earl of Katherental and Lieutenant Colonel Elizabeth Bekenbaum, Countess of Katherental, Russian Life Guards Horse Cavalry, 1871.

The next photograph, was of a young man standing on an armoured vehicle of some sort with a large weapon on his hip. The outstretched flag was similar, but now had a large leaf in the centre of the Eagle and the Bear. The caption read, 'General John Bekenbaum, Lord Strathcona Horse, Canadian Expeditionary Force, Afghanistan, 1917.'

The next photo was in colour. A sand coloured armoured vehicle, the front wheels off the ground as it flew across a hill, dust swirling behind it. Two Large flags were flying from the rear of the vehicle. The one on the left a blue yellow and red flag, with a black

eagle on the left a brown bear on the right and a red leaf in the
middle. The flag on the right, with two large vertical red bars on each
edge and a large red leaf in the middle. Flame was coming out of a
large tube at the front of round turret mounted on top of the vehicle.
A helmeted man was half out of the vehicle gripping with two hands
a large device that was also spitting fire out of it, a large amount
of brass cylinders coming out of the top of the device. The caption
read. "Colonel Richard Bekenbaum, Third Earl of Didsbury, Fourth
Battalion Princess Patricia's Canadian Light Infantry, Afghanistan,
2005.'

"So you see Countess Bekenbaum," Jasmine said. "Your people
have always come to our aid when we have needed you the most. Just
as you are now."

Chapter Fourteen

They had started out at the normal cavalry speed and after two days, had increased the distance traveled. Now Demetri thought, the Emirs people were ready for the final trial. He would increase the pace tomorrow and see how the Emir's people and horses handled it.

Subtle changes had begun with Emir's party. The whole party, women included, practiced every morning in their own training regime, which was similar to the Eagles, but heavy on the lance and sword work, where the Eagles trained slow, they trained fast. They had a prayer ritual they conducted each day, chanting in their own language. They, women included, began to wear loose fitting garments, light blue tunics, gold colored sashes around their middles, the Emir and his family wore gold colored turbans wound around their heads, officers had red and troopers light blue. All of them had begun to call Demetri, General Bekenbaum Sahib and the men had stopped shaving. Demetri's ten and the twenty in The Emir's party began to mingle together in the evenings, the Emir and Jasmine spent the evenings with Demetri and Margarete. During the day, Demetri and the Emir talked business, during the evenings, everything but. Tonight would be different.

"We have been on the road together for a week now," Demetri said. "We have made plans and agreed to a strategy. I know you want to train in our methods. I think this is not a good policy. Yes your people, like ours, have a tradition of light cavalry. But your function is not the same as ours. We are trained to operate independently, to wreak havoc behind the lines and scout for the main forces. We are trained to inflict as much damage as we can where we are not expected, using methods not familiar with our foes. My Eagles, like our horses, are bred for this. We were the first to stand up to the Mongols. We learned from them and altered their tactics to suit our needs. As did your people. But where your people had mountains and trees to help you, we had none. You depend on speed and accuracy. We also, but add stealth. We were fighting a foe that came from the steppes like us. What is coming is going to demand the best from all of us. My Eagles and your Singh, we cannot do it alone. We each have our roles. But the real work will be done by the Bears. The Pike and spearmen. The heavy infantry in their shield walls and the heavy cavalry with their brute force. We are only support for them."

At that point voices started to sing in Russian, slow and soulful. Demetri looked toward Maria who rose and walked away, singing as well, he put his hand on Jamir's arm as he rose to follow and shook his head. A few moments later the song picked up its pace, to that of a horse at a slow walk and Demetri followed by Margarete rose and joined the song. Janet and the ten candidates, Maria among them, came into view mounted, with three horses each trailing. Demetri and Margarete came to attention and returned the salutes of the eleven as they rode by. Then without missing a beat, the eleven broke into a trot then a canter and in a swirl of dust, were gone from the camp. The thunder of forty four horses hooves changes to a gallop and the song did as well, only stopping when the hoof beats could no longer be heard.

"By morning they will be in camp," Demetri said. "Get some sleep. Because by midday tomorrow, so will we."

As Demetri had predicted, Jamir's horse was the first to drop out, then one by one the rest of the Emir's group's horses. He had planned for this and the horses were replaced by Cossack mounts and wranglers were left to bring the stragglers in at a slower pace. The main group did not slow from the canter, except to dismount and walk for ten minutes every hour. The Emirs party were becoming better at switching horses on the fly, but were still a long way from the ease of the Eagles in performing the maneuver. They crested the last hill and the defences of the camp came into view. Large groups of people began to form, leaving an empty space between the lines of people.

Demetri raised his right arm, hand clenched into a fist, Barney and the rest of the Eagles war horses came up abreast of them and Demetri lowered his arm and all eleven of them switched mounts, found the stirrups and bows on the saddles. They formed into two columns of five behind Demetri, the remounts fanning out in line beside them and they broke into a gallop, leaving the astonished Emir and his party behind. At two hundred paces, the Eagles rose to stand in the stirrups, knees gripping horses flanks, they drew arrows from the quivers mounted on the saddles and began to shoot, the first arrows hitting targets while two more were still in the air. They kept firing as they passed the targets, then flipped backwards on saddles and kept shooting until they were once again out of range.

They circled around, coming to a walk and rode back to the area where the targets were set up. The Emir and his party were looking at the targets, that now looked like pin cushions, all the arrows in the kill zone on the straw dummies.

"Imagine a thousand, just like us, doing just that," Demetri said. "This is our function in the battles to come. Day after day and we are very, very good at it."

As expected, Demetri and Margarete had been barely dismounted when they were inundated by aides demanding their attention and the rest of the day was spent in handling the various minor details that had been neglected in their absence. At midday the next day, Demetri and Margarete, dressed in their dress uniforms, presented themselves to the command group. All the top generals and civilian leaders along with the Emir and his commanders were seated behind tables arranged in a U shape.

"General and Colonel Bekenbaum reporting sirs," Demetri said. "The Colonel and I are having a baby and as regulations state, we are herby resigning our positions as required. Our replacements have been informed and will take over immediately. Thank you for your time sirs."

They both came to attention and waited to be dismissed.

"At Ease," the Emir said. "Your resignations are not accepted. You will continue on in your administration duties until such time as the medical staff deems that Colonel Bekenbaum is unable to perform her duties. As soon as the medical staff determines that Colonel Bekenbaum is once again capable of performing her duties and passes a qualification test, she will resume her duties in the field. The General shall return to the field as soon as the medical personnel determine that the Colonel and the baby no longer require his presence. Dismissed."

"Sir, I must protest," Demetri said.

"Sir, these regulations were put into place by a committee," Margarete said. "I and the General were part of that committee. It is not good for discipline, for officers to be exempt from these regulations."

"These regulations were implemented to keep hot blooded youngsters from making mistakes that could cause harm to the army and themselves," the Emir said. "Not mature married warriors like your selves. As the regulation states, we will pull you from the field. It is within our discretion, whether to allow you back in the field or not. You both will still have to pass the tests required to hold your positions afterward. One change we have made to the regulation, is that it will be up to the medical people to approve first, the females ability to return to training and eventually the field and that she in fact wishes to do so. We will not compel or punish any female who wishes not to return to the field, but to become a mother and stay back with her child. Other duties will be found for her to compete her mandatory service period. Now once again, dismissed."

Demetri and Margarete came to attention bowed their heads, about faced and marched out of the tent. For once they were not surrounded by people demanding their attention. Until they reached their quarters. No longer housed in a tent, but a wood structure that housed an office complex in the front and a small living quarters behind the offices. Greta and two nurses were waiting for them.

"Colonel," Greta said motioning her with her right arm to the open door to the living quarters. "If you will? We will make our examination now."

Demetri was left to his own devices, in the office and after rummaging around, found a half full bottle of vodka and a glass and poured the glass full. He walked over to his desk, taking off the tunic and laying it across a chair opposite. Loosening the shirt collar and rolling up the sleeves of the shirt to just below his elbows, he sat behind the desk and plunked his feet on the desk taking a deep pull from the glass. Jasmine and one of her ladies breezed into the office and raised her eyebrows. Demetri just waved with the hand holding the glass to the door leading to the living quarters and the two women disappeared behind the door.

Once again, Demetri was left to his own devices. Once in a while female laughter could be heard coming from the other room and Demetri smiled. It was nice to have no responsibilities for once. Then the door banged open and the Emir carrying a tea pot walked in. he plunked the pot on the desk, removed a cup from his tunic pocket and then like Demetri took off the tunic tossing it on top of Demetri's on one chair and then plunking himself down on the other. He poured himself a cup of tea, then he also loosened his shirt collar. He raised his cup as did Demetri his glass and they silently saluted each other before taking a sip. At that point the females in the other room erupted into shrieks and laughter.

"Women," the Emir said. "So many secrets."

"We have a saying in our family," Demetri said. "Women, can't live with them, can't live without them."

"We have something similar," the Emir said. "Our families have long been linked Demetri."

"Yes, I have seen your files," Demetri said. "But this is a different place and a different time."

"Not so different my friend," the Emir said. "I spoke with your commanders on your recommendations and they agree to them. We only have one transport left and there is no way it will be able to transport all of those troops down from the transport ships. That means they will have to land and will leave them well past reserves on their fuel. We only have room to land sixteen. So they will have to refuel then take off and remain in orbit until the other fourteen can land and do the same. Then they will go back to Home Planet. I assume you plan to stop them here?"

"Something like that," Demetri said.

"I of course will be asked to add my troops to the mix," the Emir said. "That will amount to one hundred twenty thousand troops you are going to face. They are also sending their top people to command. You are going to have your work cut out for you. Even with your methods"

Demetri just shrugged his shoulders and poured another glass.

"It's a long way from the Capitol to here," he said. "You have to travel at the pace of the slowest. I do not. If you do not want to lose a lot of your people, I would suggest you find a way for us to distinguish your selves from the rest."

"We have three months to do that," the Emir said. "My commanders will be training our people to the old ways. You will have no problems in that regard. Now, it looks as if the ladies are finished whatever it was they were doing in there and I must get my people ready to leave in the morning."

The door to the living quarters had opened and Jasmine, her two ladies, Greta and her two nurses and Margarete walked out.

"Well brother," Greta said. "Your wife is good and truly pregnant. That's what you get for not keeping it in your pants."

"You see your Majesty, no respect around here," Demetri said. "As if you can keep from dropping yours any time Al smiles the right way."

"Why that is a ladies porogrative, unlike you randy goats," Greta said kissing him on the cheek. "Now, no more horseback for her and no more lifting heavy things. She is also to start slowing down and taking more rest breaks during the day. I will be assigning two clerks to help her out and two senior aides to take over much of her work load. Now everyone out of here and leave these two alone. They have had an eventful few weeks."

The Emir rose, put his tunic back on and then curiously he and the three ladies in his party bowed and left the office. Followed by Greta and her two attendants who came to attention and then left.

"Well I guess we will be left alone for the rest of the day," Demetri said. "Guess I will get caught up on this paperwork."

"I have a better idea," Margarete said, her shirt hitting the floor as she walked back into the living quarters, undoing her skirt as she walked. She almost had it off when Demetri reached her and picked her up, carrying her to the bedroom.

A knock on the office door the next morning heralded Janet as she walked in. She was in dress uniform and came to halt and heel clicking attention in front of Demetri.

"At ease Senior Sergeant," Demetri said. He was dressed in a casual field uniform, no tunic and shirt sleeves rolled up and shirt open. "What's on your mind?"

"Sir, the Singh detachment is awaiting your inspection and review before they depart Sir," Janet said.

"Right then," Demetri said. "Marg, get your butt out here, the Emir and his gang are leaving."

"Good morning Janet," Margarete said as she walked into the office. Her long blond hair was flowing freely across her shoulders and down her back. She was wearing a loose fitting skirt today, with a field uniform shirt unbuttoned like Demetri's. "Best we not keep them waiting then."

Janet held the outside door open for them and the couple walked out arm around each other's waists smiles on their faces. Lined up in two rows before the office, with Jamine and the Emir in the front center were the twenty troopers of the Emirs party. They were dressed in light blue tunics and brown trousers, gold colored sashes around their waists. Each trooper had a lance held at an angle from their bodies and the officers a sword unsheathed on their shoulders.

"Attention!" the Emir bellowed out and swept his sword in front of his face and the lances went from the side to the front.

"First Afgahn Lancers all present and ready for inspection Your Highness," the Emir said.

Demetri and Margarete dropped their arms, came to ridged attention and returned the salute.

"Carry on," Demetri said. He walked to the left end of the line and with the Emir to his left and trailed by Margarete and Jasmine walked down the front line and then the rear, checking each immaculate trooper as he went. Finished the last row he marched back to the centre.

"Very well commander," Demetri said. "Carry on."

"Permission to leave the field Your Highness?' the Emir asked.

"Very well," Demetri said.

The Emir had them mount, then in column of four they passed in front of a saluting Demetri and Margarete and left for the capitol.

"What was all that about?" Margarete asked.

"Beats me," Demetri said, letting her proceed him into the office, he put his hand on Janet's arm and shook his head in the negative. "Probably just a respect thing. Didn't you say you were heading to your sister's to see her?"

"Oh yes," Margarete said. "I am late." She swept out of the office in a swirl of skirt and started toward her sisters.

"Take a load off Janet," Demetri said gesturing to a chair. He took two bottles of beer from a cupboard, uncorked them and handed one to Janet.

"Spill it," Demetri said.

"The Singh's told us, Your Highness," Janet said.

"Told you what Janet?" Demetri asked.

"That you are the direct descendant of a powerful family on Home World," Janet said. "That as a condition of settling this world, Your family was to have complete autonomy and rule of the planet, Your Highness."

"Ok Janet, that's all BS and you know it," Demetri said. "Our people are who we have always been. Farmers and tradesmen, that's all. The Emir's family runs everything. My folks were no different than yours Janet so stop all this Your Majesty crap. They are just trying to drive a wedge among us."

"They said they had proof Dem," Janet said. "Look what they just did. That was not normal, nor how the Emir and his wife kept deferring to you and Margarete on the way back here."

"Again, just trying to drive a wedge between us Janet," Demetri said. "They may have said they are on our side, but watch how that changes when the troopers from Home World get here. They will outnumber us two to one, even with our support troops factored in. Stop that rumour right now Janet."

"Well as far as the Eagles are concerned," Janet said. "You are our lord Demetri and my Attaman as well."

"Be that as it may," Demetri said. "We all have to abide by the rulings of the councils Janet," Demetri said. "Don't forget that."

"As it should be Janet," Greta said from the doorway. "Now I am sure you have some new horror to subject the poor new candidates to. Why don't you leave Demetri to his sister and brother in law, we have some family business to attend to with the new father to be."

"How many others know?" Demetri asked after Janet had left.

"As far as I know just the ten of us," Al said. "I take it you have not told Margaret yet?"

"No," Demetri said. "Damn the man! I am still trying to figure out if he is sincere or just playing an angle. Ok get word to the other seven. Stop the rumours now!"

"Oh come on Dem, everyone is already acknowledging you as leader anyway," Alphonso said.

"War leader is one thing," Demetri said. "What the Emir is suggesting is something else again. We keep this to ourselves got it?"

Life in camp soon settled into a routine. Each day as the sun came over the horizon, Demetri, Margarete, the ten Eagles that were their guards and any other Eagles in camp performed their training ritual for an hour. Then after a quick cleanup, breakfast. Demetri then took reports and had a meetings that he was required to have. Then paperwork until midday. After the midday meal, he toured the training facilities always ending with the preteens, where he was usually joined by Margarete and a few other Eagles.

Most of the Eagles were trickling into camp, their major function of scouting out possible routes, escape and engagement and the planning and placement of semaphore relay stations, now complete. They were now supervising and taking part in the advanced training required for each Eagle candidate. Margarete along with the other Eagle commanders was developing a new training regime for the Eagles and scheduling exercises for joint maneuvers with Bear battalions. Margarete's role was becoming more and more administrative, much to her consternation. But each week saw her physically more challenged as far as mobility was concerned as she grew ever closer to her due date.

Evening meals were spent with friends or family and increasingly, Margarete began to retire earlier, leaving Demetri a lot of time to contemplate what was coming. Intercepts from the incoming transports had confirmed the number of transports and troopers coming. The fuel state they would be in when they arrived and the supplies they would require once on the ground. It was extremely expensive to transport from Home World in terms of fuel, food, water and space requirements, so the transports were always loaded to a bare minimum. They would have just enough fuel to land, as well as the other supplies to keep the troops more or less comfortable. Demetri had determined to make their unloading and stay in planet as uncomfortable as possible right from the beginning. The fuel was the biggest concern. If they could refuel the transports, they could land anywhere after the initial landings and the rebellion could do little about it.

The landing field could accommodate eleven transport ships at once. That would leave four in orbit until the first eleven were refueled. Even if they took out the refueling tanks, the ships in orbit could land and occupy any of the pumping stations and storage facilities in planet. Demetri spent his nights looking at maps and making then rejecting plans. Then one evening, he put a projection of the map of the whole inhabitable region of the planet on a wall and stared at it for most of the night. Going to bed that night still with the problem on his mind.

By morning he had an inkling of a plan and by the time the morning exercises were complete had a firm idea. He sent an aide for the head of the bow manufacturers and the fertilizer manufacturer president. Then Alex requested a meeting and things became clearer for Demetri. Now all he needed was time. Time and assurances that what he was contemplating had a reasonable chance for success.

"Alex," Demetri said sticking out his hand for a shake. "It has been a while."

"Yes sir," Alex said grinning. "I hear congratulations are in order sir."

"Yes well that's what comes from letting a female turn one's head Alex," Demetri said. "And I'm loving every minute of it."

"Maybe I'll find myself a nice little filly too," Alex said. "After this is done anyway. I hope I am as lucky as you were."

"Lots of time for that Alex, you're what 21?" Demetri said. "So far all you know is the military. Me too, mostly, but Marg and I have a plan for after this regrettable nonsense is over. We want our kids to grow up normal. Well as normal as we can anyway."

"Yes, other than the Eagles, I don't know what to do," Alex said. "Well like you said, I have time. Look, if you don't have anything pressing for us, the 100 could sure use some time off Dem. We have been on duty for almost a year now."

"Nothing pressing for them at the moment Alex," Demetri said. "Tell them to take a couple of weeks off. But I can't send them home. We might need them in a hurry. Plus we only have two months left. It would take to long for them to go home and get back here."

"No problem sir," Alex said. "Most of us have family in camp anyway. Besides who wants to be around family when it's party time?"

Demetri laughed along with Alex at that.

"OK, one last thing, then take a couple of days off yourself," Demetri said. "No rest for us commanders you know. How is Ensign Walsh turning out?"

"Good enough to be promoted," Alex said. "He has been leading his own troop the last six months. Actually he is teaching us a lot about being an officer Dem, to be honest."

"Ok, have him and yourself report to me after supper then Alex," Demetri said.

"Have a seat Lieutenant," Demetri said. "Major you too. Some vodka? This batch is fairly decent."

Demetri poured them each a tall glass of the clear liquid then sat across from the two men.

"How are things progressing with you Lieutenant Walsh?" Demetri asked.

"I think fairly well general," Walsh said. "The men seem to be comfortable with me and I have had no serious problems with them. As expected, my bow skills are still not up to theirs, but I make up for it in other areas. You would have to ask the Major sir."

"I already have Walsh," Demetri said tossing a small box at him. "Which is why you are out of uniform at the moment. Congratulations Lieutenant. And that is full Lieutenant by the way."

Walsh opened the box and saw the insignia of a full lieutenant inside, which meant he was now in charge of two troops.

"So now to the point of the meeting," Demetri said. "Can you pilot a deep space transport?"

"Yes sir," Walsh said. "I was scheduled to replace the next inbound transport pilots before all this. It's part of the normal routine. We ship in, spend six months on planet, then rotate out."

"Are there more of you with us?' Demetri asked.

"I think, three Eagles, four Bears and three who chose to be farmers," Walsh said. "One stayed with the Emir."

"Well, I think the three farmers just volunteered to be Bears," Demetri said. "Give their names to Alex after the meeting. Why did the one with the Emir stay?"

"He's one of the Emir's people sir," Walsh said.

"Ok, this stays with us for now," Demetri said and he flashed the map of the landing pad in the Capitol on the wall. "I need those eleven transports not to be there the same night they land. How many qualified planet transport pilots do we have?"

"I think maybe twenty," Walsh said.

"Ok," Demetri said highlighting an area beside the refueling tanks. "There are five refuelling tankers in this area. They need to be gone the same night. Find the best qualified pilots and send them to Alex. They will be part of another contingency that you don't need to know about. So what I need from you Walsh. With what you have learned and experienced of our methods, can we steal those transport ships and take them someplace else secure after they land and are unloaded? Coordinate with Alex and let him know what you would need to make that happen. If it is feasible, you will be in charge of that operation. You have a week to come up with a go or no go operation."

"Yes sir," Walsh said. "I can't guarantee the three farmers or the Emirs man sir."

"Not your concern," Demetri said. "Plan for both contingencies. Them coming or not. Next a question. How thick is the hull around those transports fuel cells? I already know there location."

"About a quarter of a pace sir," Walsh said. "Thick enough to withstand anything, including massed lasers that we have sir."

"Ok Mr. Walsh, thank you." Demetri said. "Dismissed. Have some fun if you can, but keep close. Alex will be asking for updates on this as soon as possible."

"Ok Alex," Demetri said after Walsh had left. "I want those tanks destroyed, the tankers and the transports brought here. I will begin limiting the fuel allowed into the Capital Region and the city itself drastically. I also want all of these refuelling stations, pumping stations and tank farms destroyed as soon as you can."

Demetri beamed the information directly to Alex's scanner.

"The One Hundred will conduct the mission itself," Demetri said. "I will delegate the destruction of the other tank farms and pumping stations to the Bear detachments in place in the districts."

"But you are leaving the main facility intact," Alex said highlighting the facility on the wall.

"Yes I am," Demetri said. "We will be blowing the pumping station just here the day of the landings."

"But they will send the four transports in orbit to take that facility if you leave it," Alex said.

"Oh my yes," Demetri said. "Oh, and look, it is a days march behind us. Oh my, what an over sight. Could be we are over confident in our abilities eh?"

"I'm glad you're on our side sir," Alex said grinning.

Later that afternoon the arrow and fertilizer manufacturing heads were in his office.

"I need a device that can shoot an arrow of sufficient size and velocity to penetrate a flying target at four hundred paces," Demetri said. "It needs to penetrate a quarter of a pace of armoured ceramic. It needs to be portable and as light as possible and be able to track. Possible?"

"Yes I think so," the arrow man said. "The projectile would have to be large though."

"I had thought so," Demetri said. "It will also have to have a device I will be asking our friend here to develop for us as well."

"So, after penetration of the armour," Demetri said to the fertiliser man. "I want a controlled explosion to occur in a confined space. I believe a mixture of nitrates and liquid carbon products could accomplish that?"

"Yes, we have experienced some unpleasant results during experimentation," the fertiliser man said.

"I will assume you can duplicate that result then," Demetri said. "We need an ignition source that will only ignite after penetration. I will leave the details up to you. This all needs to be held as secret as possible. Keep the processes as separate as possible. Only the three of us will know exactly what we are planning until I start to train crews to operate the devices."

"How much time do we have?" the fertiliser man asked.

"I need the first prototypes in three weeks," Demetri said. "Fully trained troops in no less than two months."

"I don't think I will have a problem," the fertiliser man said. "I just need to know the size of the delivery package and figure out how to integrate our package to it and the ignition system."

"We are already working in a similar device for the Bears for defence," The bow manufacturer said. "We can fire a projectile about five hundred paces vertically right now. The projectile is about two paces long and iron. In tests we easily penetrate a land transport. Yes I think I can meet the deadline and we are already training operators."

"Alright gentlemen," Demetri said. "As I said, this is to be kept as secret as possible. This is an Eagle funded operation and so far only the three of us know about it. Is that absolutely clear?"

The next day, the three farmer pilots were in Demetri's office along with Walsh and Alex.

"Gentlemen," Demetri said. "I know that you were given certain privileges when you decided to join us exempting you from military duty. Unfortunately I find myself requiring transport pilots and am three short. I need the three of you to fly a transport each from the Capital to another location. Your only job, will be to gain entry to the transport and to fly it to the location. Security will be provided by others."

He saw the three men look at each other, two of them had concerned looks.

"No," Demetri said. "I cannot guarantee your safety. You are all ex-military men and know that I cannot. I can however, assure you that we will do all we can to keep you from harm."

"Can you tell us why you need those transports?" one of the men asked.

"If we do not secure those vehicles," Demetri said. "It will enable the enemy to land troops anywhere in sufficient numbers that we will be unable to easily repel them. I am sure that given enough time we could defeat them, I am not sure it would be done in time before those same transports returned with more troops from Home World. If we can capture them we do two things. We stop the enemy's ability to use them and we can use them. We could just blow them up like we did with the air transports, but then we would not have use of them ourselves and I think we will need them in the future."

"Count me in," one man said immediately. "Don't get me wrong, I like farming, but I miss flying."

The other two after a minutes thought, also agreed.

"Ok," Demetri said. "Walsh, get them minimal qualified ASAP. Alex, get a hundered Eagles as security for the pilots, I'll clear it with the Colonel. They report to you only and you only to me on this project. Set up your own camp separate from everyone else except the Hundred. Pay scale will be Eagle Officer pay gentlemen. Dismissed. Alex, have an aide ask the Colonel to see me at her convenience please."

Margarete came in and plunked herself on Demetri's knee, kissing him.

"Thank you for getting me out of that conference Dem," she said stroking his cheek. "I know it's important. The General's Lady and Eagle Colonel setting the example and all that, but some of those women are full of themselves Dem."

"I can imagine Love," Demetri said. "Unfortunately this is business Colonel."

"Well to bad," Margarete said. "We are alone and I am not moving. I don't know for how much longer I will be able to sit like this, so there. General Sir. Now what can I do for you general?"

"I need a hundred and ten of your best Colonel," Demetri said. "Ten to replace our guards. I will be needing them. The other hundred will be attached to a secret operation. They will be gone for a minimum of two months. Oh and they are coming out of your budget and troops."

"Thanks a lot," Margarete said. "What secret operation?"

"If I told you it wouldn't be a secret now would it Love?" Demetri said kissing her on the neck. "Seriously, the fewer people that know about it the better. I don't even know all of it. Nor does Alex. That way if any of us is captured, we can only say so much yes?"

"Yes, I understand," Margarete said. "I run some operations like that too. How soon do you need them?"

"Yesterday," Demetri said.

"Ok," Margarete said. "Janet, get your bony ass in here."

"Colonel, General," Janet said. "What can I do for Your Laziness's?"

"Find ten replacements for yourself and the other of the Ten," Demetri said. "Then get your boney asses over to Alex, he will tell you where to go from there. I want a hundred of the Colonel's best troopers as well. Coordinate with her Senior Sergeant with that and I want it done by daybreak tomorrow got it? And no you are not allowed to ask why or for how long."

"Sir!" Janet said, coming to attention and then about facing and marching out.

"Lieutenant!" Demetri hollered to his aide. "The Colonel and I will be taking the rest of the day off. We are not to be disturbed even if the world is coming to an end. Now where were we Love?"

Chapter Fifteen

Not for the first time in the last few days, the general cursed the black uniformed holy warriors and their leaders. When he had been awaken from the deep sleep, he had been informed that all the heavy transports on the planet had been destroyed in a badly planned and executed attack by the planets holy warriors. That had meant, that instead of running his troops and equipment down on the transports, they would have to land the deep space transports on the planet itself. While it was within the design specifications of the craft, it would leave them without enough fuel to obtain orbit again. The space port could only hold eleven of the large craft, which meant that four of the ships loaded with his troops and supplies would have to stay in orbit until four could be refuelled enough to take off and make room for them.

To make matters worse, the rebels had destroyed all but one of the fuel refineries, pumping stations and pipelines that fed the capital and only gave the capital enough fuel for its immediate needs. Knowing this, the emir had rationed everyone in the city and had saved enough fuel to fill the five fuel tankers the planet had. This should give the four interplanetary vessels enough fuel to get into orbit and allow the four still in orbit to come down. The refuelling could not take place until all of the transports had been unloaded. This task had taken most of the day before, finishing well after the sun had gone down and for safety reasons, the refuelling had been put back until this morning.

No matter, the general thought, it will give the troops a couple of days to get their legs beneath them and to acclimatize themselves to this new planet, where the sun came up from the west instead of the east. More for show than anything else, the general had stationed about twenty fully armed and armoured troops around the landing pad. They looked intimidating in their armour, helmet visors down and the dark red form fitting ceramic armour polished so that it shaun brightly in the morning sun. Around a hundred locals mounted on horses stood around the platform looking on. The general had been told that many of the locals now used horses for transportation as fuel for vehicles was scarce. These ones all had ten foot poles mounted to the rear of the saddles, weird, curved stick like objects attached to one side of the saddle under a leg, two containers of smaller stick like objects with feathers at the rear, were mounted to the rear of the saddles, one to each side and another three foot long stick with a leather wrapped handle strapped to their backs, with the handle poking over the left shoulder. They were clothed from head to toe in some sort of material that was very reflective, as were the horses.

What strange habits these people have, the general thought and dismissed them from his mind as simple curiosities to be explored later as he heard the unmistakable sounds of the fuel transport vehicles starting up and taking off from their loading area at the fuel storage tanks across town. Looking that way, he missed two men dressed in flight uniforms entering each of the interstellar transports. As the fuel transports reached a level high enough to clear the tallest buildings, they swung out, throttled up to full throttle and headed out away from the space port and out of town. Just then, the engines on the space transports powered up, drawing his attention to them just in time to see his twenty troopers sprout five sticks in the chest each and topple to the ground. He and his five personal guards pulled out their blasters, the guards the more powerful and larger versions as the space vehicles reached take off velocity and in a roar of dust and noise all eleven of them took off and headed in the same direction as the tankers.

Spinning around, he saw that the riders were replacing the curved sticks back onto their saddles and coming together to form a line four across and ten deep with a blue yellow red flag with an eagle on the left and a bear on the right flanking a red leaf at the head of the formation. One rider pulled away from the formation as they headed out of the space port at a walk and headed their way pulling the one pace long sharp steel stick from his back as he came. One of his guards fired a blast at the man. He kept coming and another took a shot. The next one shot at the horse. None of the shots seemed to have any affect on rider or horse as they kept coming. Three paces away from them he stopped. The other riders started to sing a song in an unfamiliar language as they rode away and the rider smiled. He was under thirty years old and was three paces tall. He sat on the horse smiling at them, the metal stick in his right hand came up before his face and he slashed it down and to his right side keeping there.

"Well general," Demetri said. "If you want your space craft back and some fuel for them, the emir knows how to get a hold of me."

Then he once again saluted with the sword, placed it back in the scabbard at his back, spun his horse around and galloped after his troopers. Just as he exited the space port gate, a series of explosions and flames came from the fuel storage area as the tanks blew up. Just that fast, the general had lost most of his advantage over the rebels and twenty of his troopers.

The plan was unfolding exactly as he had drawn up. The general, his staff, the new bishop and his staff and the emir and his were all seated in the large conference room watching the large monitors located all around the room. All five of the space craft that had been in orbit were coming down at the one remaining functioning refinery on the planet. One craft for each side and one to land in the centre. Drones had been dispatched from the craft and were beaming back pictures of the sight. The only activity seemed to be centred around a number of oddly shaped devices similar in design to those the riders at the space port had carried on their saddles but much bigger. These had five troops each that were maneuvering the devices to keep track of the space craft as they descended. The craft came to a hover and began to lose altitude, the doors at the rear and on every side opened, revealing massed troops ready to exit and take control once they were on the ground. The general would not only have control of the refinery, but would have fifty thousand troopers to the rear of the enemy. Once the craft were refuelled, fifty thousand troopers at a time, he would surround the enemy camp. This insurrection would be over in a matter of days.

The craft reached a height of one hundred paces from the ground and without a signal, each of the strange devices launched a large stick at high velocity at each of the five space craft. Each stick hit the craft in the body and the fuel tanks and penetrated fully. Then to his horror, the general saw each of the space craft erupt in internal explosions, pieces of ceramic exploding outwards, troopers bodies along with them. Then the vapours in the fuel tanks exploded, the craft completely destroyed, pieces of craft, fire and troopers falling the long distance to the ground. Then the screens all changed to a single picture. That of the same young man who had been at the space port, this time dressed in leather form fitting armour.

"General, I regret the loss of life you have forced me to make," Demetri said. "We are all Gods children. I told you I was willing to talk. I am still. There is no need for further loss of life. To your people or mine."

"Do you think you can defeat me as you did the holy warriors?" the general said. "I am not some half trained want to be soldier. I am the real thing. I have beaten better trained and equipped rebels than you before. With half the troopers I still have left. I'll see you rotting in hell before I negotiate with you!"

"So be it," Demetri said with a sad smile on his face. "May God be with us all."

All the screens in the room went blank and the general looked around the room and saw the look of shock on everyones faces. Everyone except the emir and his staff.

"I warned you," the emir said. "But you did not listen. What do I know you said. I am but a back water fool. Well, I am not the fool who just lost a third of his army and a third of home worlds space craft. This is all on your head."

Chapter Sixteen

Margarete and her staff and hoovering nurses, had observed the attack. Pieces of smouldering wreckage and shattered ceramic from the transports were everywhere. As were the bodies and pieces of bodies. There were no survivors. The height of the transports when they had blown apart, had been to great for any possibility of survival.

She could waddle around, barely and made many stops, but she briefly toured the area. The crews of the large cross bows had been assembled and she had congratulated them all. As she turned to leave and head back to the carriage that she had arrived in, a great spasm of pain gripped her and fluid began to pore down her legs, as she gripped her belly.

The nurses were on her in seconds.

"We need a building!" The head nurse yelled out. "Now! That one will do." She pointed to one of the refineries office buildings.

"One of you idiots run to the carriage and grab my bag. The big black leather one and bring it to me.

"You two!" She yelled at two of the bigger of Magaretes guards. "Carry My Lady over there! Now!"

The two men scooped Magarete up. One arm from each man under her knees and carried her like she would be sitting in a chair. Following the fast moving head nurse into the building. The trooper with the bag came charging in right after. Then every male was rudely banished from the building.

Greta's horse came flying into the refinery and she was directed to the building. The horse was still sliding to a stop, when Greta piled off of it and pelted into the office building. Soldiers, Bears and

Eagles, began to converge on the building, standing in loose groups in front of it. Looks of concern on each soldiers face. If they spoke, it was in hushed tones. More and more troops arrived. Then the sound of horses at the gallop as Margaretes family arrived. The women entering the building, the men pacing outside.

"When I find Demetri, I am going to cut his balls off!" The front row of gathered troopers barely heard Margarete scream.

A few minutes later, a large war cry belted out. This one was heard ten rows back. The office complex yard was deadly quiet now. Then the front two rows heard a babies cry. Followed by another war cry, then another babies cry.

Minutes later, Greta, her arms and the front of her tunic stained in blood, her hair akimbo, walked out of the office and saw the thousands of troops standing quietly in front of the office. Not a sound to be heard.

She took one breath then another, then thrust her head up high.

"Twins!" She belted out as loud as she could. "Boy and Girl! Mother and babies are fine!"

A great yell rang out, loud enough to make the ground tremble. Loud enough to be heard in the town a mile away. Then they began to sing their regimental song loud enough to be heard in the town.

A rider galloped into the town and yelled out the news. The town also began to sing. The telegraphs spread the signal. Within the hour, the farthest reaches of the army knew. Parties broke out everywhere.

Just before nightfall, the Hundred, Demetri at their head rode into town. They and their horses were tired and dusty. They rode into an encampment in the middle of a great celebration and rode to the corals unnoticed by the partiers. For the most part.

"I take it we won," Demetri said to Alphonso as he and a large group came up to them.

"Oh ya," Alphonso said. "Spectacular. Transports blowing up, troops falling all over the ground. No survivors."

"One more thing, also spectacular," Alphonso continued, pulling an unopened bottle from behind his back. The One Hundred were now all gathered around to hear the news.

"Our great and glorious leader just became a father!" He belted out. "And like a true hero, he can't just have one kid. Two! A boy and a girl!" He spun the top off of the bottle and thrust it at Demetri.

"What? When?" Demetri stuttered as everyone began to shout around him and pound him on the back.

"About an hour after the battle," Alphonso said. "Greta says Margarete and the kids are fine Dem."

"Twins," Alphonso barely heard Demetri say. "A boy and girl."

Demetri stood, head down looking at the bottle. He took an absent minded sip of it and looked at it some more. Then he punched the bottle in the air as high as he could reach.

"I'm a fucking father!" He yelled out, brought the bottle to his lips and this time took a deep pull from it. "Twins!" Another deep pull. "God damn!" A final deep pull and he tossed the bottle to Alphonso, grabbed the nearest trooper and hugged him.

"God damn I'm a father!"

Then he started to dance and hug everyone he came up to. Bottles were flourishing everywhere now. All cohesion lost, the One Hundred began to dance around, hugging Demetri and each other, jumping up and down. The oh so prim and proper One Hundred let their hair down and became what they were. For a time they could forget what they did and just be young kids again.

Part Two

Chapter Seventeen

IT HAD TAKEN A WEEK to come up with a plan. Another week to acquire the vehicles required. Now, almost a month after the disaster at the refinery complex, the Home World troops were ready to march. In areas all over Capital City, vehicles of every size and description were mustered. Everything that had a motor and wheels had been requisitioned in the city and crammed full of food, water, anything that would be needed on the trip.

All available fuel from the barely functioning refinery in Capital City had been taken. In other areas of the city, 40 thousand Home World troops, 20 thousand Holy Warriors were going through final inspections. In and around the palace, 10 thousand of the Emirs troops were gathered with their supply wagons and spare mounts. Another 15 thousand manned the hastily erected defences around the Capital City.

Ninety percent of the off world troops would be walking. The rest were either high ranking officers in lavish vehicles or hastily modified armed skimmers which would patrol up and down the flanks of the column and scout ahead of it.

The Emir had volunteered to provide his troops as the vanguard and scouts. He had been laughed at and told to keep his untrained and useless horse troops in the rear.

With a final prayer and speech from the Cardinal, the column set off. Soon, Capital City was echoing from the sound of marching feet.

It was mid day before the first troops left the city. The Emir dismissed his troops to their barracks. There being no sense in standing around until it was to dark to leave. They would leave in the morning.

The massive column only made ten miles that day and even at that, the last units arrived well after dark. The Home World Commander had his troops moving out at day break. By mid day, they had passed the next town and the Holy Warriors were just leaving the previous nights camp.

The Emirs troops arrived at the camp at that time and in no hurry, found a suitable spot and made their camp for the night. It had only taken them 3 hours to cover the short distance at a walk. Unlike the other commanders, the Emir knew when things would become interesting and was in no hurry right now.

The main column made 15 miles that day. A respectable distance on foot. The camps were all in place and soldiers all bedded down well before dark this night. They were still in high spirits. The food was plentiful and good. The march, while long, had not been strenuous. There were a few men with blisters or tight legs, but not many. The doctors were not busy.

The Holy Warriors came in 4hrs later, the last of them after dark.

As the day earlier, the main body of soldiers was on the road at daybreak. Just as the Command column in the centre began to march off, the Emir and his cavalry arrived. Once again setting up camp for the night. The overall commander was about to head over to them and reprimand them, when he looked over at the Holy Warriors camp. They were just now beginning to stir.

The Emir and his retinue approached the Commander and stopped.

"I was just going to come over and give you shit," The Commander said. "But you might as well stay here tonight. By the time those people hit the road, it will be afternoon already."

"As you wish Commander," the Emir said. Then turned and joined his troops.

As his last column left the camp, the Commander took one last look at the Holy Warriors, shook his head and entered his command vehicle. Then surround by skimmers, one before, after and to each side of his vehicle. They sped out of camp.

It was almost dark when one of the soldiers in the rear Holy Warrior battalion rotated his head around to get the kinks out of it. They had finally been allowed to remove the heavy helmets and place them on the packs at their back, but his neck was still sore. To go along with the sore feet and legs. He was not used to walking at all, let alone for this long.

As he swung his head around, he gazed at the hill to the right of the column.

"Oh Shit!" He exclaimed and reached for the helmet at his back. "Alarm! Alarm!"

The men around him looked at him and looked where he was looking. Then swore and they too grabbed helmets and weapons. More and more men became aware and finally a weary officer looked at the hill and swore.

"Form UP! Form Up! Enemy to the right!" He yelled out.

At the crest of the hill, barely visible with the sun behind them, stood five hundred horses in a line. As the battalion lined up in their 100 man wide and ten deep formation. The horses started down the hill at walk. As the first three lines of soldiers locked their shields together to form a wall, the supply vehicles gathered at the rear of the formation. Then the horses began to trot. Halfway down the hill, they came to a gallop and the ground began to shake.

Just as they could see that the horses on the wings of the formation had no riders, the 100 riders in the centre rose to stand in the stirrups at 200 paces the first arrows were in the air. At 50 paces the last arrows were shot, bows dropped to hang off of cords and swords drawn, just as the first flight of arrows hit the front line. The arrows easily penetrated the ceramic armour of the soldiers and passed straight through the shields to the man behind. Then the next flight of arrows hit and just as the third flight hit, the horses hit the wall.

The men in the rear ranks were packed to tightly to use their blasters, the ones in front were dead or being cut down by flashing swords. The riderless horses were also fighting. Hooves and teeth slashing and smashing the useless armour. The men in the rear ranks broke and ran for their lives. They were not pursued. The 100 riders headed for the supply vehicles whose drivers jumped out and ran.

The riders found the refuelling vents, stuffed rags in them and set them on fire. Then turned and unhurriedly rode away, spare horses trailing behind them. Leaving the moans and cries of the wounded and soon to be dead behind them.

The Emirs troops came up just as the Commander and the Cardinal arrived on the scene early the next morning. Where the main battle and been fought was easy to see. Men were piled on top of each other. Some missing heads, others arms, many with arrows in them. Others had caved in skulls, but other wise unharmed. A small group of less wounded were trying to help the more severely wounded soldiers. These had pieces of uniforms tied tightly around ribs and mid sections.

All of the supply trucks and the contents were completely destroyed. Some still smouldering. Less than a hundred of the battalion had escaped unharmed, over eight hundred had been killed.

The Emirs troops kept moving forward. They all looked at the devastation and carried on. The Emir and his aides stopped beside the Commander and the Cardinal. He said nothing, just stared at them.

"Tell your people to get their heads out of their asses Cardinal," the Commander said. "You people keep up, or this will not be the last massacre." The Commander turned and with his aides began to walk toward his vehicle.

"Where are you going?" The Cardinal asked. "We must have a mass and bury the dead."

"Do what ever the hell you want Cardinal," was the reply. "Your people don't keep up, we don't support them."

The Cardinal looked to the Emir for support. The Emir shrugged his shoulders, turned his horse and trotted after his troops disappearing down the road.

That night, once again the weary Holy Warriors had set up camp in the dark. Now they were out of touch of the main column who once again had made 15 miles that day. The men were beginning to grumble about their commanders. Many had seen the wounded from the desolated battalion arrive. Those that had not, had heard about it. Rumours were flying about what had happened and the more the stories were told, the more they were exaggerated.

The men had just fallen to an anxious unsettled sleep, when at first singly then in increasing number, the supply vehicles for five battalions began to explode. Soldiers piled out of tents, arming themselves and setting up defensive formations all over the camp. The area all around lit up by the fires of the supply vehicles.

The next morning they were up early and all on the road as the sun came up. That was also when they found all the guards of the five battalions laying with their throats slashed open.

Not once during the next week was there an out right attack like the first one. But almost every night something happened. The supply vehicles were the favourite targets. The Holy Warriors only had ten left. These were guarded by fifty men at night now. Then the attacks shifted to the camps themselves.

In the morning, whole tents of soldiers would be found with their throats cut or heads smashed in. One night, horsemen had run through the camp, setting fire to tents, slashing and killing anyone who came near them, only to disappear into the darkness.

Demetri had left three days after the news of the birth of his twins. The two days after, he had been in no shape to do much of anything. It was almost non stop partying. To the amazement of everyone, Demetri had staggered out of his command tent at daybreak of the third day and stumbled his way to the stream bordering the camp. Then, fully clothed had flopped face first down into it. After a few seconds, Demetri had stood up, growled and started walking back to his tent shaking the water out of his hair as he came, like a large dog would.

"Right," he said to his guards outside the tent. "Officers meeting in ten minutes."

The officers came in, all of them on time, to find Demetri fully clothed, his hair still wet and rolling up his bed roll.

"As regulations state," he said continuing tho gather his things. "I have to report to the main camp and be with my family. I will need an escort of ten troopers for that. Send out a rider and get replacements for them as they will be staying with me. Alex is in charge for now. Keep doing what you are doing. We are hurting them.

"Ok, get going. Alex, you stay please."

Demetri had his sword draped across his back by the time the officers had left the tent. Now he grabbed his bedroll and heavy jacket in one arm and his ever ready and packed saddle bags in the other.

"Hit them tomorrow Alex," Demetri said. "Nibble, nibble, nibble. Make sure to take time off once in a while to rest the men. You should be linking up with the rest of the Eagles soon. That's when you hit the main column. Watch out for those armed skimmers. Any Questions?"

"We'll be alright My Lord," Alex replied. "Safe trip My Lord."

"Not to safe I hope," Demetri said smiling. "I would just love to cross paths with their scouts."

His four horses were ready to go and waiting for him as he left the tent. Barney was saddled, which was the proper thing. They both needed the exercise today. Demetri tied his bed roll and saddle bags to the cantal and the heavy coat to the horn, then grabbed a lance at random from the rack of them outside the tent.

At that point, ten riders with remounts in tow, appeared, Janet in the lead. They were all the youngest and newest of the 100. Demetri just nodded at them, swung into the saddle, placed the lance in its scabbard behind his right leg, settled himself into the saddle and abruptly took off at a trot The ten were right behind him.

Alex watched them disappear into the distance then turned to a waiting aide.

"Send a rider to the main column," he ordered. "Tell them His Lordship is headed back to the main camp and said to send us ten replacement troops. Everybody else has the day off. Tomorrow we go back to work."

The lead column of black armoured Holy Warriors came into view. As normal, they had no troopers out front or to the sides to warn of an impending ambush. The road was flat at this point and the trees had been cut back fifty paces on both sides of the forrest, leaving a nice grassy area.

Alex and the 89 remaining troopers were just inside the tree line out of easy view of the road and the troops removed their bows from the saddle sides, put one arrow in their mouth and another held loose on the bow string ready to draw.

The thousand man column was broken into ten columns of 100 spaced ten paces apart. The men marched four abreast, with

Captains and two aides marching in front and lieutenants and sergeants to the outside leading edge of each platoon.

Alex waited until the centre companies of the battalion came abreast of them, then nodded and came out of the tress. He stopped, looked left and right to see all his troops in a line, pulled the arrow back to his right ear and let it fly kicking the horse into a gallop as he did. He pulled the one out of his mouth and shot again, then let the bow dangle on the cord attached to the saddle, drew his sword and made ready for the impact.

The first warning of the attack was the brief thrumming of the arrows before they thunked into the ceramic armour and the bodies behind it, then the thundering hooves. The impact of horses crashing into men and then the slaughter began. Swords were rising and falling. Severed heads, limbs and blood flying in the air. The screams of terrified or wounded men.

The Eagles rode right threw the company and out the other side, leaving ninety dead and dying men behind them. In less time than it took to tell the tale, the raid was finished.

That night, the weary and manpower depleted Holy Warrior Division reached the main column at night fall. None of them was complaining about the rapid pace of the march now.

Alex moved the camp 30 miles that night and the scouts were out looking for ambush sites the next morning. his ten new troopers had arrived, the next morning, their remounts loaded with supplies. All of them feasted that night on fresh meat and fruit for the first time in weeks

The ambush site was perfect. Again, the road was treed but for a fifty pace grass green space on both sides. Half a mile on the other side of the road was an old trail that they could travel on. Both sides of the road, the trees were to thick for the armed skimmers to follow.

The only difference between this raid and the last, was that they hit the rear column of the Home World troops. They used lances instead of swords and he had ten more troopers. The result was almost the same. On the other side of the road, the attackers quickly reached the trail and in single file trotted toward the front of the main column.

They had a two hour wait. The main column had stopped. Soldiers had been scouring both sides of the road looking for them. The wounded and dead had to be cared for. Then the column required reorganizing, before finally proceeding once again.

This time, the Eagles used the sword, having discarded the broken or cracked lances after the last attack. Again the attack was fast and devastating. Now the Home World soldiers knew what to expect. They thought.

The next day, the armed skimmers were moving up and down the column constantly. Always looking, always vigilant. But they didn't see the 100 laying down in the tall grass just outside the tree line. Guessing from the sound of the tramping feet, Alex stood up. He had an arrow already knocked and five more with the points stuck in the ground beside his right foot. The other troopers rose as Alex did. They knocked and shot five times. The primary targets were the skimmer operators, then anything that moved. Arrows gone, they casually walked into the trees, then started to run. The horses were tethered twenty paces in the trees and as hastily deployed soldiers entered the trees to look for them. They found nothing once again.

So far, all of the attacks had started or come from the right side of the column. Basically because that's where the Eagles had their camp. Now they crossed the road after the column had passed and went to the other side. Just as the last trooper was entering the trees on the left side, Alex bringing up the rear, started into motion, he spotted the lead scouts of the Emir's troops. He smiled and waved and had the smile and wave returned, then he was off to join his people.

"Commander sir" the Emir said. "Once again, I offer my troops to help chase after these traitors."

"You and your pointed sticks and horses are going to do any better than my armed skimmers and troopers?" the Commander said. "I don't think so. You stay right where you are. The only reason you people are here is because I was ordered to take you along. Dismissed."

A few days later the column was hit again by archers on foot, but from the left. Another change, was that the two platoons sent to see where they had gone, were ambushed by the Eagles and their swords. After an hour and an half of hearing nothing from his missing two platoons, the captain sent two more, who discovered the bodies.

Now everyday they were being attacked. This time, by small groups of no more than ten. All day long. At times, men who stopped to relieve themselves were attacked by aberrations, covered in branches, leaves and dirt. By the time anyone could react, the aberration had melted into the trees.

Now at night, arrows, sometimes fire arrows, but most times not, hit the tents, guards and anything else in sight. Day and night, the army was loosing men. It was beginning to fray every ones nerves.

Once they reached the plains and were out of the trees, the daytime raids stopped, but the night ones did not. One days attack had been spotted well before any damage could be done to the column itself. The armed skimmers had massed on the point and attacked the attackers, who turned and fled. Three miles away, but still in full view of the main column, the skimmers had almost caught up to the fleeing horsemen, when the horsemen accelerated away and over a small hill.

Over the hill at a full gallop had come a column of 1000 mounted troopers who made short work of the armed skimmers. Then destroyed them. Just that fast, the Home World army had lost two thirds of its armed skimmers and heavy lasers.

"OK if we have a few days off Colonel," Alex asked Greta. "Our horses and equipment could use some rest and repair."

"Take tomorrow off Alex," Greta answered. "You guys have done a good job out there. Day after tomorrow, head to the main staging area. We will take over here for you. They should be hitting that defiant town in a couple of days anyway."

This was all part of the plan anyway. The plan was to have the 100 relieved at this point and Greta had arrived with a whole battalion of Eagles to take over for them. The 100 had been on the go for almost a month now and they looked it.

Their uniforms were now more dull brown than light grey, especially on the right arms and chests and arcs across their backs. Horses and troopers were shaggy. A lot of the males had beards and all of their clothing had been patched over in many places. Their arrows were almost all gone. They had used up the last of their lances long ago.

Even walking in camp, they walked and talked softly, heads in constant motion, eyes flicking everywhere searching for hidden danger.

'Yes' Greta thought. 'They need time off. They are near burn out.'

THE DAY BEFORE THEY were scheduled to reach the final friendly town, the leading battalion of the main column saw the road before them blocked by five hundred horses. As the battalion started to form their lines, the horse men came to a gallop and attacked. They hit the column hard, causing much damage and after no more than five minutes, turned and galloped away as the first of the armed skimmers arrived. The skimmers chased after them and over the hill.

On the other side of the hill, they were hit by massed arrows from the fifty horseman on each side of the road. A few were able to turn around and escape the carnage.

Once the column reached the town they breathed a sigh of relief. The two days they spent there had been quiet. No attacks at night or by day. The day they left, they left the town priest and the mayor hanging on a hastily erected gallows. Then men who had protested a little to much about all the vehicles, fuel and food the town had, being taken by the Holy Warriors.

That day and every day after, the column was hit. The tactics this time were different. Now a full battalion of horseman would attack them approaching in a long line. As the column came into range of the archers, they would shoot three arrows and ride off. Just as that battalion rode off, another would hit from the other side. Sometimes both sides would be hit at the same time.

The armed skimmers tried, but they were no match for the horsemen. Shooting on the move was iffy at best and as soon as the skimmers stopped to shoot, they were hit by massed arrows. The horses were faster than the skimmers and fuel was running short, so they were told not to pursue anymore.

At last, the Commander called the Emir to a meeting.

"I want you to send some of your people out as scouts every morning," he told the Emir. "The rest of your people I want in formation in the centre of the column. You will repel and chase after the rebels from now on."

The Emir nodded, turned around and left the Commanders quarters.

The next morning, the cavalry had disappeared.

That day there were no attacks. The Commander assumed the Emirs cavalry was driving the raiders away. Just after midday the column crested a hill. Before them, behind a large plain and behind a stream was the enemy camp. Now he could do the job he came here to do. Kill all the rebels.

Chapter Eighteen

"Margerete!" Jasmin exclaimed as she entered the small house. "Where are they? I must see them!"

She hurried over to where two women were sitting holding a closely wrapped bundle each.

"Oh they are so beautiful," Jasmin said. "And you? You are well?"

"Well enough to join my troops tomorrow," Margarete replied.

Jasmin looked at her for a second then nodded her head.

"On the defences," she said. "That is good."

"No," Margarete said. "I will be joining the assault. I command two battalions."

"Hush Jasmin now," the Emir said. "You should not judge. You will be beside me tomorrow as well. Where is he?"

"With the little ones like usual this time of day," Margarete answered.

At that point, one of the babies started to fuss and the Emir was ignored as all the women began to fuss over the babies.

The Emir caught his two aides eyes and motioned them to follow. Unnoticed by the women in the room, they left. Once outside the Emir looked around and then asked one of the guards posted outside where he could find Demetri and the way was pointed out for him.

As the Emir walked to the practice area, he looked around. The streets were well laid out in a grid pattern and straight. All the smaller streets lead to a single north south wider street, which was mostly paved and still being worked on.

Crews were out sweeping and removing debris and the ever present horse manure from the streets. Large oxen drawn barrel shaped wagons were stopping at each house and delivering water that was pumped into large cisterns located beside each of the homes. Other oxen drawn tall sided wagons were collecting refuse from the homes.

While many of the dwellings, especially on the outskirts of the settlement, were still felt covered or canvas tents, large numbers of them, especially on the main street, were sturdy permanent houses and buildings. These all appeared to be well built and sturdy. The dwellings with large green spaces in the front and large gardens in the rear, growing vegetables and fruits.

The only men the Emir saw, unless in uniform, were over fifty or under sixteen. There were also fewer than to be expected females of that age group that should be present in a town this size. Everywhere he looked, people were sharpening weapons, testing bows and working on shinny metal armour. All of this work being done under awnings.

As the Emir came out of the rear of the camp, he saw figures ranged in a long line on an elevated platform, one pace off the ground. The sight and sounds of flight after flight of arrows flying and the thunks as they hit targets, filled the air. Youthful shouts for more arrows were being yelled everywhere and small figures with large baskets full of bundles of arrows, raced up the platform and handed the bundles off to other youngsters who undid the bundles and placed them point down beside the right leg of an archer.

All this time, the archers drew and shot, drew and shot. The air constantly full of arrows. This went on for ten minutes, then a whistle sounded and the shooting stopped. All of the archers congregated around a tall man, while the ones supplying the arrows came down to the ground and circled a smaller one.

After a short while, the archers left the platform and moved off. Then a mighty yell rang out from the younger kids who had been supplying the arrows and they too began to leave, joking around and dancing away from their commander who was grabbing any that came near and tickled them.

A group of older people took their places on the platform. The archers had five bundles of arrows with them. The others were a mixture of people with long poles with wicked spiked axes on top, spear men and others armed with spiked hammers or large hand axes. These were spread out equally. One halberd, one spearman, one axe man. Behind them were the archers.

A short whistle was blown and the archers made ready. Another short one and they drew. Then a long one and they let loose and kept firing. The spear men all had large square shields, which they brought up. Then the halberdmen began to thrust downward in simulated attacks, followed by the axmen and spearmen. It all looked like an intricate ballet. All the footman motions were in slow controlled dance like movements.

Once the arrows were depleted, the archers drew pace long swords from their belts and joined the dance.

Once again, the tall man blew a long blow on his whistle and the soldiers stopped and stepped back forming lines along the platform in their different formations. The Emir was now close enough to hear.

"Good job people," Demetri said. "No more training. Our guests have arrived and we all want to give them a good time yes?" There were many laughs at that comment.

"Archers," Demetri continued. "Rest those arms. When our guests arrive, there will be many of them and they will come more than once. Now off you go. Have some fun tonight."

"Gee sir," one of the men with the long halberd said. "Do you think I will have time to get my best suit pressed and a haircut? I want to look good for the guests when they arrive."

The Emir smiled when he heard that. 'There is always one smart ass with these people.' He thought. His smile grew bigger as the older troops rough housed with the young man who had been training the kids came close.

"Yes Your Highness," Demetri said as he came up and saluted. "Your son has learned much and grown up a lot.

"Sublieutenant Jamir! Front and centre!"

Jamir rushed up and saluted to a foot stomping halt in front of them. The Emir, the highest ranking in the group returned the salute. Then with a large smile on his face opened his arms and approached his now embarrassed son.

"Oh, looky, looky," one female spearman said to her team mate as they walked by. "Isn't that cute. The sublieutenant is hugging his poppa."

As the rest of the soldiers started to laugh, Jamir took an arm from his fathers back, raised the middle finger on the hand to them. Which only caused them to laugh harder.

"I get no respect from you people!" He yelled back after them.

"No respect at all!" They all yelled back in unison.

The Emir and his son were now facing the laughing and joking soldiers as they walked away, each with an arm around the others waist. Then with a final squeeze, the Emir broke free and turned to Demetri motioning him to follow. He mounted the platform. Like he had noticed, it was a pace off of the ground and two paces wide, made of thick planking.

The area in front, from two hundred paces to ten, was full of arrows sticking out of the ground. So thick, it would be impossible to walk without stepping on them. Grandmothers and grandchildren under ten years old, were picking the arrows out of the ground. Each arrow was briefly inspected, then placed in one of two bins each person had. In one bin a healthy arrow would be placed, in the other, a broken one.

"God in Heaven!" The Emir muttered. "I'm glad I won't be on the receiving end of all that."

"The good arrows will be reinspected, repaired, then placed back into replenishment bundles," Demetri said. "The broken ones, we will remove the fletching and the arrow heads and put them on new shafts."

"That makes sense," the Emir said. "How many arrows do you expect to use?"

"Depending on the size and duration of the attack," Demetri said. "Between ten and twenty thousand."

"Holy Shit," one of the Emirs aides muttered.

The Emir nodded his head. "Holy shit indeed."

"If you have time," Demetri said. "I will show you the main battlements."

"Lead on My Lord," the Emir said. "Jamir, you can come with us or go visit your mother if My Lord agrees."

"Why not," Demetri said. "He would just be chasing after Olga anyway." Then he laughed.

"Oh, is that so?" The Emir said as he walked away with Demetri side by side.

"Oh yes," Demetri said. "Why just the other day I had to stop one of Olga's older cousins from perforating him, he has been hanging around so much."

"Ha, as if," Jamir mumbled. "More like the other way around. She is becoming a pest. Her and all the other girls left here. It's a real pain. Girls!"

"Can't live with them," Demetri started. "Can't live without them." All four of the older men finished. Then laughed. The aides pounding Jamir on the back.

True enough, as they walked, many of the young women they crossed paths with called out to Jamir and all of the young kids.

"Well, don't get used to it," Demetri said. "You will be rejoining your fathers troops when he leaves."

"Ah shit!" Jamir said. "If anything it will be worse there. Can't I just be attached to one of your formations as a subby?"

"No son," the Emir said. "You need to be with your own people. They need to see their heir fighting alongside them."

"I only go, if you put me in with a line troop," Jamir said. He had a determined look on his face. "As a normal sublieutenant. Not held back in your command troop."

"His trainers say he is almost as good as one of us," Demetri said when the Emir looked at him and raised his eyebrows. "He has learned and learned well, that in order to lead well, you must follow well."

"Very well then," the Emir said. "His people need to see that he will be like them, do whatever is needed to be done. Make it so."

"One more thing," Jamir said. "I bring my own horses."

"He has four of ours," Demetri said. "Fully trained. Your son has a good eye for horse flesh, once we properly taught him what to look for."

"Your division is ready?" Demetri asked.

"Yes," the Emir answered. "Bored, but ready. Your stopping of the raids on their column has been very helpful. The Commander most likely thinks we are scaring you away, or that you have killed us all. Either way he will be happy.

"If anything, your little pin prick raids were more harmful than the full out raids. They are almost out of fuel for the few vehicles they have left and they were down to short half rations only once a day when they hit that town.

"The Commander is counting on wiping you out fast, then attacking the fuel depot."

They had reached the front defensive works by the main gate now and Demetri led them up the short wall to the top. As in any defence, the gates were the weak point. To approach these ones, attackers would first have to navigate a two pace wide ditch placed four paces in front and parallel to the main defensive wall. This small wall, was like the main wall, lined with sharpened stakes all along its length. A three pace long wooden bridge designed to be easily pulled away was across the ditch. Heavy thick wooden gates would be shut to seal that entrance. Then a ten pace long, four pace long lane way led to the main ditch and wall. Another plank bridge and another set of heavy thick gates. Four tall and wide towers were placed behind and along the wall behind the laneway. Anyone entering the laneway would be hard pressed as arrows, rocks and any other thing that was heavy and could be tossed down would be coming hard on the attackers.

The ditch in front of the dirt walls had been widened to six paces and the dirt from it added to the wall to thicken it from three to six paces. Sharp one pace long stakes were placed in thick interlocking rows all along the bottom of it. The walls were placed two hundred paces from the stream and the land cleared so only grass was left. The grass was kept cut short so not to provide any cover.

An attacker would first have to cross the stream forming up on the other side. At one hundred fifty paces, the first flight of arrows would be launched. The attackers would have to march through this storm of arrows until they reached the ditch. Then descend into the ditch, still under fire, make their way through the stakes at the bottom, then clamber up the now two pace high wall to be met with more sharpened stakes protruding from the walls, then the halberds, the spears and finally the swords, axes and deadly hammers.

This was not going to be easy for them.

The commander of the Home World Army, looked around him in disgust. The clouds of thick dark smoke coming from the town had caused him to dispatch a battalion back to the town. Now he and his sub commanders looked at the carnage.

Once his troops had left, the Holy Warriors had stayed behind. The happy people who had greeted them and treated them with fresh food, and banquets, were now gone. Most of the buildings were gutted and ruined. Those that were left had been ransacked. The towns leaders and the priest were hanging from hastily constructed gallows. Long lines of Holy Warriors were in front of open air brothels where the local women were being abused. Women not of child bearing age and young boys, were dragging bodies to large open pits and dumping them in.

"What the hell did you do!" The Commander demanded of the Bishop. "These were people who were on our side!"

"They did not resist the heretics" The Bishop relied. "A lesson had to be taught. It was videoed and the video sent out to deter any other would be Heretics throughout the system. Those that escaped us here, will spread the word on how other hold out towns will be treated if they do not comply with the Holy Churches orders."

"You fool!" The Commander blurted out. "For every person you killed or abused here, you have just made 100 rebels!"

"Get your damned warriors gathered together," he continued motioning his sub commanders to follow him. "If your troops are not linked up with us by the end of tomorrow, I will kill you all."

A family of five from the defiant town had arrived that morning and begged to be given sanctuary. At a meeting of the elders, the family had told of the horrors that had been inflicted upon them, how they had barely escaped with their lives and the clothing they were wearing. All of them were very distraught.

"Was this abomination done by all of the soldiers?" One of the Elders asked.

"No sir," the father replied. "The Home World soldiers were all very polite. They even helped repair some of our equipment that was not working. It was after they left. The Bishop arrested all of our leaders and our priest. Then let his troops loose on the town. We ran, we were lucky, we got away."

Putting their heads together for a hushed conversation, the elders agreed to take the family in and to have them escorted to the medical facility to be examined and treated if necessary.

"This has all been confirmed by our scouts," Demetri said after the family had been ushered away.

"Now you know what our fate will be if the invaders win," he continued. "Give that family a place to stay and supplies. Let them mingle with our people and spread their story. But never let them out of your sight, or out of the fort."

He dismissed the elders.

"It is time," Demetri said. "Emir, return to your troops, as will I. Margarete will be in command of the defences here. Remember the plan. If we execute it well, this will be all over."

Margarete and Demetri bade farewell to the Emir and his family. Jasmine had tears in her eyes as she gave a last hug to Margarete and mounted her horse. Jamir a determined look on his face. Then, they rode out.

"One more night love," Margarete whispered into Demetir's ear. "One more night. Please?"

They did not sleep at all that night. Both worried about what was coming and sharing their anguish with each other. For unlike the others staying behind in the fort, they knew exactly what was coming.

Next morning, in front of the gathered garrison staying behind, Margarete and Demetri acted like the soldiers they were. It was not until Demetri and his escort of ten had ridden out of sight into the trees and she had softly closed the door to her office, that she began to cry.

The Commander took the high power binoculars down from his eyes. He was standing on his command vehicles roof and glassing the fortifications. The other command vehicles were ranged about his. He pointed at the ten riders galloping into the trees.

"We have them!" He said into his communicator. "They are sending for reinforcements. Set up camp and get that Bishop and his commander to me right away."

As his aide rushed away to deliver his message, the Commander stayed. He continued to look over the fort and the defences. It was doable, he thought. We out number them substantially, just with the Holy Warriors.

As his troops came over the hill, they began to disperse and set up their camp on the side facing the fort. His command tent was the first to be erected and he called a meeting of all his officers. It would be later in the afternoon, when the Holy Warriors would arrive.

"Gentlemen," The Commander began. "The enemy have constructed their defences in a good location. It is on a small plateau with hills to the front and both sides. An attack unseen is impossible. The area for five hundred paces on all three sides is clear of trees. A heavy bog and marsh area extends from the bottom of the hill to the tree line on both sides. The trees are thick at those points, so getting large numbers of troops around to the rear will be very difficult and I fear from what we have faced from these people already, would lead to disaster."

The Bishop and his command group arrived at that point and took places in the tent.

"That leaves us with one option," the Commandr continued. "A frontal attack. We are two thousand paces away and it is wide open, so we cannot disguise the fact we are coming. The stream running at the bottom of the hill looks to be shallow at that point as the road leads to and continues on the other side of it. Yes the bridge has been removed, but they have still been crossing the stream without it.

"It is five hundred paces from the stream to the walls. That will allow us to cross the stream and form up. Then it is a dry approach to the wall and the hill is not steep. It looks to me, that there are only five thousand or so enemy in the fort. We outnumber them by a large margin."

"I demand that the Holy Warriors be the first to attack!" The Bishop blurted out.

"Very well," the Commander said after a moment of thought. "When can you be ready?"

"We attack in the morning!" The Bishop answered. "The sooner we eliminate this rabble the better."

Then gathering his entourage around him, they left the tent.

"I want every officer watching that attack tomorrow," The Commander ordered.

"Will we support," one of his subcommands asked.

"No," the Commander replied. "We observe only."

Demetri and his officers were just behind the tree line observing the enemy. The horses were several paces back in the trees. If this was the main attack, an aide would gallop back to the camp and the signal fire would be lit calling all of the troops to arms. For right now, everyone was just watching.

In the Home World part of the camp, there was no sense of urgency. The men were having their breakfast and going about daily camp routines. Officers were stationed all along the hillside, but nothing appeared to be happening other than that.

In the Holy Warriors camp, officers were rushing around. Soldiers were gathering up equipment and donning their black ceramic armour. The troops were gathering in their companies and battalions and priests began their services.

Once that was done, the soldiers formed up in battalion strength and began marching down the hill.

"Orders My Lord?" Greta asked. Demetri had come out of the trees and sat down where he could see the attack form up.

"This is an unsupported attack," Demetri said. "The Home World troops will not be involved. Were I that Commander I would do the same thing. Let the Holy Warriors make the first attack and observe how the defenders defend. It serves two purposes. Can you tell me what they would be?"

After a few moments of no replies, the Senior Sergeant did.

"First," she began. "He will find out our plan of defence, how many we are and the types of weapons we have. If what he expects from what he has faced from us before is true. The Holy Warriors will be decimated, or they will win if not. He is victorious both ways."

"How so?" Demetri asked.

"If the Holy Warriors lose, they are out of his hair," she answered. "If they win, he looses no men."

"Give yourself a cookie," Demetri said after he laughed. "I am going to lose my job if you people keep this up."

The whole group of them came out of the trees and sat down now to watch the show.

MARGARETE AND HER OFFICERS were on the wall watching the enemy form up. Then she looked over to where Demetri and his officers were. They were sitting down passing bottles and food around and watching.

"I guess this will be our show," she said jerking her chin over at where Demetri was. "He doesn't seem concerned. Neither do I. See what the Home World troops are doing? They are watching as well. It will only be the Holy Warriors this time."

They watched the Holy Warriors form up and being marching down the hill.

"Call the archers up," Margarete ordered. "Have the infantry form up behind the walls ready to deploy. But I don't think we will need them."

Chapter Nineteen

The Bishop was marching, surrounded by his ten priests. They marched in a small clear space in the centre of his one hundred man body guard. He was in high spirits. His Holy warriors out numbered the defenders five to one. Yes they would take loses, but unlike on the road, now he had the advantage. In numbers and tactics. this would only end one way, in victory!

Once his men were in blaster range, he would stop and observe.

They splashed across the stream, the water was only knee deep. His troops formed up their assault squares and began to march toward the fort. He placed himself at the rear of the formation and followed. As they came nearer, his confidence rose. The defences were crude, he would overwhelm them easily.

The front battalion was now in blaster range, but had no targets as yet. Then figures rose to the top of the wall. Instead of the short bows the horseman had, these bows were almost two paces long.

A command was given and one thousand arrows took flight. The thrumbing of the arrows loud. Then another and another. Now the thrumbing of arrows in flight was joined by the sounds of armour shattering, the wet smack of arrows hitting flesh and the screams of men.

His men were dropping, row by row, before they could get a shot off. Flight after flight of the deadly missiles came pouring down. Each one targeting a row further back in his formations. A few of his men managed to fire, but only a few of those shots hit an archer. Closer and closer to him came the arrows.

"Retreat! Retreat!" He yelled out.

To late. Now the arrows shifted to the rear of the formation from the front. Arrows were falling all around him. At first the troops fell back in order, then they began to run. All the while, the arrows fell and men died.

"TWO HUNDRED PACES MAXIMUM range," the Commander said as the remnants of the Holy Warriors pelted in panic back across the stream and the defenders stopped shooting the arrows.

The battle field was littered with the dead and wounded, most in the rows they had been marching in. Some of the less severely wounded were staggering their way back to camp. Others were trying to crawl.

Now, under cover of the archers and some infantry with long spears along side, hundreds of old women and children came out and began collecting arrows. They showed no mercy to any wounded they came across. Dispatching them quickly with a thrust with a long knife through an eye or cutting a throat.

Less than a thousand uninjured Holy Warrors returned, none with weapons. The Bishop had an arrow protruding from the back of his left shoulder.

"Take some transport trucks back to that town," the Commander ordered. "Collect as much tin roofing material as you can load up and come back."

"Why didn't you help us?" The Bishop screamed at the Commander as he went by.

"But Bishop," the Comander said. "You insisted we do not. I was just following your orders."

It took several hours to remove the arrows. Even the broken ones were recovered. If any arrows were left, the Commander could not see them and he smiled.

"We have them," he said. "They are low on arrows. That is why they are recovering them. We have them."

"REPORT," MARGARETE ordered.

"Two dead, ten wounded," her aide said. "We used twenty thousand arrows, most have been recovered and are being inspected. The wounded are being treated and will be ready for duty mam. The nearest they came was 80 paces mam. A delegation of the enemy has requested a truce to remove their dead, mam."

"Denied," Margarete said. "They stay where they lay. Have the troops eat and rest up. They may hit us in the morning."

There was a lot of activity in the enemy camp the rest of that day and all of the next. Most of it centred around fifty large transport vehicles. It was to far away to see clearly, but some kind of structures were being mounted on the vehicles.

Meanwhile in camp, youngsters were removing arrow heads from damaged arrows, then passing them on to old men. The heads were then inspected and repaired, or sent to the blacksmiths to be reforged if to damaged. The heads were then sent to older women, who attached them to new shafts, while still others attached fletching to new arrow shafts that were being made by the wood workers.

The archers were inspecting their bows. Some had to be replaced and all had new bow strings attached.

Of course, all of this was observed by the enemies high flying drones. This had been anticipated. All of the infantry had been concealed during the attack except for a few hundred, to make it look good. They were ready in case they had been needed, but, as had been proven, the officers had felt the Holy Warriors did not have the training do drive home an attack.

Other than the activity centred around the vehicles, the enemy camp was quiet. They had small patrols out but other than observation, nothing else was going on. They were not trying to find a way to the rear or sides. No probing raids or attacks were being conducted.

The next day, things were different. Protected by all of the remaining armed skimmers and two thousand infantry, plus three armed vehicles, fifty men with poles entered the stream and began probing the bottom. They began in the centre, then moved out both up and down stream, checking how deep it was and what the bottom was like.

The two infantry battalions moved across the stream to a point just out of bow range with a vehicle in front of each. The third, as if daring an attack moved ten paces in side bow range, turned sideways and waited.

Margetete was on one of the guard towers with her command staff. She had a high power spotting scope and was looking at the vehicle. Every bit of exterior surface now was covered in metal roofing material. She gestured to one of her archers.

"See if you can hit that vehicle," Margarete said.

The archer smiled, quickly notched an arrow, brought it back to her ear and let loose. The arrow arched in the air, then came down to impact on the hood of the vehicle, bounced off and slid down to the ground. Next, Margarete nodded at a crossbowman. There were only five hundred crossbows and they had not been used in the first attack. They were slow to reload.

The man wound up the powerful weapon, placed a bolt on it, aimed and let it fly. The bolt penetrated the turret. But only half way. The turret spun and the heavy laser was pointed in their direction.

"Down! Down!" Margarete yelled. Everyone ducked down behind the heavy logs that covered the lower half of the tower. A full second of sizzling, accompanied by wood burning smell hit just after.

Margarete stood. A man had opened a hatch on the top of the turret and was watching them. She looked down to observe the damage the laser hit had done, then looked back over at the vehicle. The man stood up tall and saluted her, so she returned it. Then he waved, laughed and dropped back down inside, clanging the hatch shut behind him.

"Have the armourer meet me in my quarters," she told one aide. "The rest of you keep an eye on them and report back to me."

The armorer was just walking up as she arrived. They both entered and Margarete went to the ice box, pulled out two bottles of beer and tossed him one.

"They have put metal armour on their vehicles," she said. "Long bow arrows just bounce off, but crossbow bolts will penetrate. What can we do about it?"

"The Onagers should destroy them," the man replied. "But as you know, we only have six and they take about a minute to reload."

He thought for a moment and the said, "After the attack on the transport ships, I wanted to experiment. I have a crossbow bolt that has a small explosive charge in the head. It has the same contact fuse installed in the tip. If, the bolt can penetrate, it will explode inside and at least cause them some discomfort.

"Its worked not bad in tests...But..."

"It's all we have," Margarete said. "Like you said, at least it will distract them. how many of these exploding bolts do you have?"

"Five hundred, " he said.

"Ok, one per crossbow man," Margarete said. "I will send them over to you and you can explain how they work.

"Helmut, have the crossbow Captain report to me."

The sun was just a hint of grey the next morning when she was roused from her sleep.

"They are forming up mam," her aide said, "and it looks like a full out assault."

"Spread the word," she said, as she threw off the covers and began donning her uniform. "Have the jamming of the drones start now. I'll be on the tower."

It was a little cool as she made her way and clambered up the ladder leading to the platform at the top of the tower. It was also a little crowded with the guards and her entourage. The other four towers were the same, as other officers, like her, were gazing out at the enemy camp with binoculars and spotting scopes.

The enemy cook fires were burning brightly and the men gathering in small groups, while others were donning armour and gathering weapons. There was not much hurry, but each movement had purpose and men were pouring over the now armoured vehicles inspecting them.

"Make sure all of our people have something to eat and send some hot food up for the guards," Margarete said. "Have everyone ready to deploy. This man and his people are professional soldiers. It will not be like the last attack. We wait to see how they deploy, then we react to it. Keep the infantry behind the wall. They don't deploy until the last minute."

There was much more room in the tower after all but two of her aides left. Margaret stayed in place watching and waiting. As the enemy finished their preparations and began to form up, she saw the reason for their stream probing the day before.

Three columns began to form. One on the right, one on the left. These had fifteen thousand men each. Another column of ten thousand was in the centre. There were fifty armoured trucks in front of the left and right columns spread across the front and five across the front of the centre column with one in the very centre of it.

Plates of hot food were brought up to the tower. Margarete took hers and wolfed it down, while still looking at the deploying columns. They began to move toward the stream bed now. The two large columns in the lead. It was now clear what the plan was. The two outside columns would hit on both sides of the main gate, forcing her to split her command. The centre column would exploit which ever column was successful. This was not going to be easy.

"Mam! Mam!" An aide on the ground yelled up to her. "It's time mam." Two aides had her armour with them.

"OK! OK!" She yelled back. "Split the archers between the two main columns. Have the infantry do the same. Nobody but the guards are on the wall until they cross the river. Have the Onagers brought up. Half to one side, half to the other. As soon as the enemy starts the main advance, have the Onagers take out the three vehicles in the centre, then shift to the three on the outside edges and work their way inward."

She climbed down and out stretched her arms. The two aides began draping her plate armour around her and helping her adjust it, then handed her her sword which she draped across her back. Another aide quickly braided her hair and wound it up around the crown of her head. Then handed her her shinny helmet. It was a risk, but a tall red plumb was attached to the top of the helmet. All of the officers had something similar. The sound of many boots hitting the ground in unison could be heard as well as thumping, as batons were thumped on shields as each left foot hit the ground.

Margarete looked around. Bundles and bundles of forty arrows to the bundle were stacked within easy reach of the wall. The young kids whose job it was to make sure the archers always had arrows ready beside them. Archers, two quivers, one on each hip full of ten arrows each, where stringing bows and testing them.

The infantry was making final adjustments to armour and testing their axes, swords and halberds. All of them knew what was coming and that everything depended on them holding. Holding long enough for help to arrive.

DEMETRI AND HIS COMMAND staff were also watching. They were twenty paces in front of the trees sitting cross-legged in the tall grass. Once he saw how the enemy was deployed and had begun the advance he stood and made his way back to the tree line.

"Everyone up to the front," he said. "Horses and men armour up. Light the signal fire."

Officers pelted back to the loose lines of troopers one hundred paces behind to relay the order. The one hundred had their armour on the ground beside the waiting and tethered horses. The horses were armoured first, then the men. The horses took on the excitement their riders were showing. There was much stamping of feet and swinging of heads in anticipation of what was to come.

As their preparations were just completed, large bangs followed by muted explosions could be heard. Then the thumbing of arrows and the thumps of impacts. Over and over again.

"It's time," Demetri said quietly. Mounted Barney, settled himself into the saddle and looked around him. Once he saw everyone mounted, he rode toward the battle.

Chapter Twenty

The first surprise came just after his men had formed their columns and began the advance to the walls. Six large arrows came flying across the wall, three to a side. The arrows were three paces long, the heads half a pace wide. They targeted the centre three vehicles of each column, penetrated the armour easily, then exploded. Sending pieces of vehicle in a red tinged cloud of broken pieces everywhere.

Next archers rose to the top of the wall. These archers were sporting bows that were sideways instead of up and down. There were two hundred fifty to each side and they raised the bows and he saw they had stocks on them much the same as his laser rifles. At a command they all put the bows to shoulders and loosed. Five hundred short fast arrows sped across the distance. These shot more flat and faster than the other bows and he had seen what one could do already. All of the arrows were headed for the vehicles, five towards his.

"Out! Out!" He yelled as he flung the hatch open, "Everyone out of the Vehicle!" He pulled himself out of the turret and just let himself fall down the side.

Only three of his ten troopers got out as the arrows penetrated the vehicle and exploded inside. The explosions were not as massive as the larger arrows had done, but they were enough to kill or injure anyone trapped inside and basically destroy the vehicles.

"Shit!" He said as he looked around. Only two of the vehicles were still moving and they were obviously not under control, as they came to a stop after short meandering drives.

Another five hundred arrows came speeding out from the wall. They were still outside the known range of the normal archers.

"Turtle! Turtle!" He yelled out.

He lost five hundred troopers to those arrows before the shields were put overhead and locked together. The next flight of arrows thunked into the thick plank shields they had constructed and while a few were penetrated, no damage was done to the men under them.

"Ha!" The Comander said. "You are not the only one that has read history books Demetri."

Now six more of the large arrows came flying over the wall. This time aimed for the outside edges of his formations. These were not armed with explosives, but tore huge gaps in his lines as they penetrated at least five rows of soldiers.

Every thirty seconds, the crossbows would fire. They were concentrating on his front lines. Soon many had at least three of the deadly missiles embedded in their shields. The formations reached the range of the long bows and the bow men rose to the wall. Wave after wave of arrows began to hit his formations. Once in a while a soldier would go down as an arrow somehow made its way through the locked shields. Soon the shields were bristling with arrows and the inside edges of his formations became a little ragged as they began to clamber over the rotting bodies of the Holy Warriors of the failed attack two days earlier.

Now his centre column began to advance so as to stay in contact with the other two columns. He was one hundred paces behind and would support which ever column looked to be ready to breach the wall. Just as the shields of his soldiers were beginning to come apart from all of the arrow hits, the front line hit the ditch in front of the wall and found the next surprise the enemy had for them.

As his men dropped down into the ditch, they penetrated the light sand coloured tarps across the bottom and impaled themselves on short sharp stakes planted point up on the bottom. The first two rows of his soldiers were stuck on them, but pressing from behind others climbed onto of them and began to navigate up the walls which also had sharp stakes embedded in the sides.

Just when the Commander was about to order his centre column to join the right side another change in the defenders plan came. The archers moved off of the walls and were replaced by soldiers wielding long spears with axe heads on them. Other soldiers with long axes and hammers along side. The long spears came down and pushed or outright killed the men coming up the walls. Soon the ditch outside the walls was full of his wounded or dead soldiers. But that didn't help much. A few of his men made it to the top of the wall but were soon killed and thrown off again.

All the while, the arrows kept coming and coming. Now hitting the centre and rear of his formations and taking their toll as the shields were all but unless now.

The first hint he had that something else was about to happen was when a line of horses galloped along each side of his column. Each horse had a rider that was on the side of the horse, only one leg showing. Then the deadly arrows began to come from under the horses bouncing heads hitting his unprepared soldiers from the sides. The horsemen kept going, heading for the sides of his two formations engaged at the wall.

"Contact right!" The Commander heard from one of his officers.

"Contact left!" Another yelled from the other side.

On the left side, the commander saw what had become of the Emir's missing troops. They were wearing shinny metal light blue coloured armour with orange coloured metal helmets. They were arranged in five lines of one thousand, fifty paces between each line. They each had the long steel tipped lances braced behind right legs and they were just standing on the side of the hill. Waiting.

Another line of one thousand joined them. These were on much larger and more powerful horses. The horses, like the men, were covered in bright brown metal armour. Each man had a four pace long, thick heavy lance. In addition to the swords on their backs, they had devices that had a long wooden handle with a short chain attached. At the end of the chain was a metal ball with spikes on it. These cavalry moved in front of the Emir's formation. They also waited.

Looking to his right he saw ten thousand cavalry in bright shiny armour. The horses were not as big as the ones in front of the Emir's troops, but all were armoured. All but the front row of one thousand were armed with light lances and swords. The front thousand had bows instead of lances. They also just stood and waited.

The unarmored archers were now galloping back to the rear. This time up right and the commander followed him with his eyes and as they reached the rear he saw his doom.

Three lines of twenty thousand infantry were approaching, with a thousand archers in front of each formation. They were also accompanied by two thousand of the cavalry mounted on the heavy horses. The first three rows of the infantry had two light spears clutched in the hands holding the shields and one in the other hand. Behind them came two lines of the deadly halberds followed by swordsmen with each line of swords men having a soldier with a long axe in hand for each ten troopers.

These soldiers were well trained and marched in unison. Each of them armoured in the bright shiny armour and each with a rectangular shield.

"Face the rear! Face the rear!"the Commander yelled to his nearest officers. He keyed his throat mounted micro phone.

"All formations break contact! Break Contact!" He yelled. "Form squares! Form squares! Prepare to repeal cavalry!"

His centre column, mostly with intact shields, turned around to face the rear and saw what was coming. The first two lines locked shields together, the three behind locked theirs over head, just as the first arrows began to hit. He deployed his men into a square leaving the middle open. So far the shields were holding. Looking to the sides, he saw the horsemen begin to move and he had just enough time to watch as the lines of horseman hit the rear of his redeploying columns.

On the left, the heavy horse blowed five rows deep into his column before they were halted. Then began laying about them with their wicked balls and swords. Then the lighter lancers hit. The lines of his men falling apart.

On the right. The archers shot three arrows before peeling to the side and two more as they rode away. Then the lancers hit bowling over men or impaling them with the lances. Out came the swords and the intricate ballets of horse and riders began as horses kicked anything around them and swords were falling on anything.

Then it was his turn. First came the arrows. Then in perfect timing, the men with the javelins ran three steps forward and threw them. Then the next line and the next.

"Face the rear! Face the Rear!" The commander yelled out as the heavy horse hit his rear lines and smashed through them. "Form on me! Form on me!"

The horsemen were not having it their own way. Horses were going down as they were hamstrung by the cycles and axes his men had with them. Many riders were being pulled off of horses and fell with on the ground, forcing the cavalry to withdraw.

The archers could no longer fire as their own men were in close contact. His men met the oncoming infantry and the Commanders world shrank to what was right in front of him. His men were fighting hard and holding their own. Many were going down, but they were hurting the enemy.

His lines were compacting as his men went down. His arm was growing tired from repeated axe blows from the axe he had in hand. Shields were now discarded as they had been shattered and were useless. But none of his men ran. None of his men broke ranks. They knew any hope they had was to stay together.

Then a single whistle blew. It was the type of whistle heard at football games. It blew again and again. Soon other whistles all around him were blowing and the attackers pulled back and out of range of his men.

The Commander looked around him. Already the men he had left were going to their knees or placing hands on hips and gulping huge gasps of air. He was as well. All of his men were tired, covered in blood, most of it not their own. His tight formation was down to around five thousand now and they were completely surrounded by the enemy. The ones that had just been in the front lines, being replaced by fresher, but still blood coated troops.

It was at that point, that six riders came forward. One of them tossed his red covered sword to another, removed his helmet and tossed it to a rider on the other side. Then motioning for the other five to stay in place he slowly rode forward, his hands on the saddle pommel. His and his horses armour were covered in blood and gore. His face was streaked with it and his hair was plastered to his head. Sweat was running down his forehead and as he removed his steel clad gloves, the Commander saw the right hand was stained red.

He was a young man, maybe in his early thirties and looked well fed. He came to a stop five paces in front of the lines and looked them over. The men on their knees rose and like the others hefted their weapons and closed ranks. The man nodded his head.

"Enough" he said, just loud enough to be heard over the cries and moans of the wounded. "Enough. You men have fought bravely and with honour. Enough good men have died this day."

The young man looked around and at many of the surrounded soldiers right in the eye.

"I have no wish to kill more of you," he continued. "Lay down your arms and I guarantee your safety. We will take you in, treat your wounds, give you food. If you wish, we will arrange transport for you back to Home World. Or you may stay here with us. We can always use good men like you. Take your time. Nobody is going anywhere soon."

Then he rode back to his five troopers and they rejoined the other troops. Now dismounting and tending to their horses. They removed the armour and began brushing the animals down applying ointment to the many cuts and scrapes the horses had accumulated.

The Commanders men began talking to each other, then their officers.

"I agree," the Commander said loud enough for his men to hear. "You men have fought bravely today and enough of you have died. And for what? If you men agree, I will accept this offer. If you want to stay and fight. I will die alongside you."

He walked to the centre of the formation, the men gave him a clear space and he waited.

His senior remaining officer, a young lieutenant and a grizzled old sergeant came up to him.

"Sir," the sergeant said. "You done the best you could for us sir. We are all that is left sir. You held us together and that is why we have survived. All of us will die for you sir. But for you, not the God forsaken Holy Church. Just say the word sir."

The Commander looked around at his men. All of them with grim determination in the eyes. Then he looked around him. Twenty thousand archers were surrounding them, each with full quivers.

"No, enough is enough," he said. "You two come with me. Have the men form up please."

Trailed by the sergeant and the lieutenant, the Commander made his way through his men as they formed up in neat lines, all at attention. He kept walking once outside his lines and saw a trooper touch the young man who had spoken earlier on the shoulder and say something to him. He had just finished cleaning his sword and placed it into the scabbard at his back, before turning and walking toward the Commander.

The Commander stopped one pace in front of the young man, put his axe in his left hand jammed it alongside his left leg, came to attention and saluted. The young man also came to attention and returned the salute.

"I am Commander Erlickman," the Commander said. "On behalf of my men, I surrender sir."

He took the axe in both hands and preferred it to Demetri. Who took it from him.

"I am Demtri Bekenbaum, General of these troops and I accept your surrender," then he handed the axe back to the commander. "Please have your men stack their arms commander and we will see about getting your people medical attention and food and water."

"Very well," Erlickman said. "By your leave sir?"

"Carry on," Demetri said. Both men saluted, then moved back to their troops.

Demetri heard the weapons hitting the ground.

"Stand Down!" He yelled and the command was yelled out all around. "Get some food and water to those men and have some medics have a look."

Then he went to one knee and bowed his head. There was much rattling as all the others around him did the same thing. He made the sign of the cross and began to speak, loudly.

"Lord, we ask you to take the fallen, all of the fallen to your bosom. We ask you to give relief to their families in their sorrow. We ask you to help ease the pain of our wounded brothers and sisters. Finally, we ask you to give wisdom to those who attack us. To stop and think before they commit more of your children to harm in the future."

Then he made the sign of the cross once more and stood. He saw that the Commander and his soldiers had also taken a knee and bowed their heads. Then as he turned to address his officers he came face to face with the black robbed and slightly wounded bishop.

"Blasphemer!" Was the only word the enraged bishop got out before Demetri swept the sword from his back and took the man's head off with it.

"Alright!" Demtri said as he bent down and cleaned his sword on the still twitching bishops robes. "Get at it. Get treating the wounded and collecting the dead. Send a transport back to the Capital and get as many backhoes as you can into it. Chop-chop people! Field grade officers meeting in two hours."

"These guys fought hard," Janet said as they walked back to the fort, horses trailing behind. Like Demetri, she was covered in blood and had some minor nicks showing. "We lost four Dem. I know that for a fact. I have bruises in places I don't want to talk about."

"Me too," he answered and they both laughed.

All over the field, weary troops were heading to the fort. Others were rushing out to tend to the less severe wounded, or putting down hopeless cases. They had been hurt, but no where near as badly as the enemy had been. They made their way to a side gate. The area in front of the main gate was piled high with the dead. In some places they were chest high. Tents were being erected outside the walls, long lines of wounded being taken to them. Other long lines, mostly of children, were ferrying buckets full of water to the tents. Others, instead of rushing bundles of arrows to the lines, were rushing bundles of bandages.

Other tents in formations, were being erected for each of the separate commands, with the units flags being displayed in the centre of them. Soldiers were congregating at these and removing armour. The more exhausted falling down, almost immediately asleep.

As Demetri and his six remaining bodyguard headed to their area of the fort, he spotted the Home World soldiers being escorted to their barracks.

"Commander!" He yelled out. "A moment of your time please?" Demetri walked over to him.

"It would be an honour, if you would attend our officers meeting sir," Demetri said. "Some one will escort you sir."

The Commander nodded and rejoined his men.

Chapter Twenty-one

The fight had started two hours after day break and while it felt they had fought all day, it was over before mid day. the rest of the day had seen tired troops heading in sweaty, dented and bloody armour to their camps. The exhausted soldiers gathering together in their groups of ten. Mostly sitting and staring off into the distance. while kegs of beer were everywhere, most were just drinking water, if they drank at all. Mostly, they just held onto the mugs with two hands gripped around it.

Some times somebody would attempt to say something, look around and go back to staring at nothing.

Some groups had members missing. In front of one tent was only one soldier. A big burly man, his badly dented and smashed armour, what was left of it, still dangling on his body. He had both arms draped around his knees, his head laying down on his heaving chest as he openly let his tears flow, making clear tracks through the blood that stained his face and arms. The only survivor of his shield team.

This theme was repeated through out the strong hold.

All through this, carts of wounded and less severely walking wounded made their way to the overwhelmed medical area. Anyone with any kind of medical knowledge was doing what they could. Doctors, medics, nurses, veterinarians, dentists, even mid wives were scrambling to save who they could and making it as comfortable as they could for those they could not.

Officers and under officers were going through their commands, checking their troops.

Janet, her scabbarded sword still across her blood stained once shiny plate armoured back, had just taken an inventory of her section of the one hundred and was making her way back to her area of the barracks. She was tired and needed to get out of the now becoming stifling armour badly. She ignored her surroundings as she walked down the streets, until she came to the single trooper sitting in front of his squad tent. He was no longer sobbing, just sitting alone, his head still down on arms wrapped around knees.

Finally, it dawned on him that someone was standing in front of him. He looked up. Even in her armour she was not big. Standing just under two paces high. Her blood stained and dented helmet attached by it's strap dropped over left shoulder. Her dark blond hair plastered to her head, cut short in the front to keep out of her blue eyes. Her expensive plate armour was even more dented, if possible, than his was.

"Come on then," she said. Her voice was horse, almost gruff and quiet. "Time for some grub and beer."

Then with surprising strength, she gently gripped him under the arms and lifted him onto his feet.

"I think we can handle even a big galoot Bear like you." She said then, turned and started walking. After a few steps she noticed he had not moved.

"Get your fucking ass moving trooper!" She was using her command voice now and was drawing attention from the other tents as she marched right up to him.

"Stand at attention when a Senior Sergeant is addressing you trooper!"

His training kicked in and he snapped to a clattering attention.

"You will follow me trooper! Is that clear trooper!" She had her face right up to him and was basically yelling at him now. "Understood?"

"Ye...yes mam," the big man stammered out.

"Do I look like a godamnd officer trooper? I work for a fucking living not sit behind a godamned fucking desk!"

Now he reverted back to his basic trading.

"Yes Sergeant! Right away Sergeant!"

"Fucking bone head ground pounders," Janet muttered. Then turned and once again started walking to her area of the camp. This time the big trooper followed her.

"What the fuck are you assholes looking at?" Janet yelled at the other troop tents that had witness all this. "Stand to!"

She waited until all forty of them were lined up in front of her and the lonely big man.

"None of you assholes even noticed he was sitting all by himself!" She continued. "He just lost his whole team! Fuck you and Fuck your asshole organization. If I wasn't so fucking wore out, I'd kick all of your asses! You left one of your own to suffer by himself! Look at him! That is what a REAL hero looks like. None of you deserve to even be in the same camp as him!"

She had been pacing up in down of the in line and at attention troopers as she used her battle voice to address them. Anyone in listening distance had heard her and they were all standing in front of their tents now, watching.

"This is not how we treat one of our own!" She yelled. "This man held his position even after his whole troop died around him! Can any of you say the same?"

She was in a fine furry now.

"If not for him, my Eagles and I would never have been able to do what we did. Never! All of us need to work as one. Eagles NEVER leave one of theirs alone. NEVER!"

Now the steam was out of her. She looked behind her and the big man was standing tall. His battered and tattered armour dangling everywhere.

"Come on Brother," she said. "Come to where you will be treated properly."

The now crowded street broke open as the absurd sight of a big burly man followed behind a smaller and slenderer women. Both in tattered dented and blood soaked armour.

Now that the spell had been broken, team mates started searching each other out, making sure no one was alone.

"Hey shit heads!" Janet called out as she wandered in, the big guy trailing behind her. "If somebody doesn't give me a beer right now I'm gonna be major pissed!"

The big guy just looked opened mouthed at the people around him. These were not just eagles. These were the 100!

A multitude of beer glasses were thrust before her. She took two, passing one to her big companion.

"Oh god love a duck!" She blurted out after downing the large glass in one go. Then gave a massive belch.

"Alex, you're about the same size as this guy. Get him outta that shit he's wearing and into a shower before he stinks up the place."

"Yes My Lady. Any thing you say MY Lady," Alex said coming to a foot stomping attention and bobbing his head. Then he started smelling in her direction.

"Ya, ya, I know," she said. "I'm off."

When she came back, the room was buzzing. The beer was flowing and the jokes were flying.

"What's his story?" Alex asked her, gesturing at the now cleaned up big trooper.

"Remember when we hit the line?" Janet said. "One guy was holding his part of the line, right in the centre all by himself?"

"Ya, his whole team was on the ground," Alex said. "He was swinging that pole axe around him so fast you could only see a blur."

"That's him," Janet said. "He was sitting all alone in front of his squad tent."

"Shit!" Was all that came out of Alex.

He filled his glass full and walked to a centre table and stood on top of it. He dug his beret out of his pocket and placed it dead centre, then stomped on the table, hard.

Now everyone in the room gathered around, the big man hanging at the back. He didn't notice Janet beside him.

"What's up Major?" Someone blurted out.

"Today was a tough one," Alex said after a moment of thought. "Ten of our brothers and sisters are in medical. Two are not likely ever to ride again, let alone fight with us. Two are dead."

"We were facing well trained and professional soldiers today people. As tough as we are, as well trained as we are. Had they had equal weapons, things would have been much different. Maybe.

"But we didn't do it all by ourselves people."

"Hell no," one trooper yelled out. "If those Bears up front would have folded, we'd have been screwed."

"Ya," a small girl in front said. "Any of you guys see that one guy holding off about a hundred of the bad guys all by himself?"

"No shit!" Another said. "That guy had some major balls. The whole line was about to break and there he was. All alone swinging that big pole axe around like it was a toy baton. Put the life back into the whole line he did."

"So," Alex said. "All of you know how you feel about loosing our brothers and sisters. How do you think he feels. He lost his whole squad."

"No shit," somebody finally said. "We gotta go find that guy!"

The room started buzzing and people started breaking for the door.

"Hold Fast!" Janet belted out, her voice filling the room. "Once again your loving Senior Sergeant has come to your lazy asses rescue."

She gently grasped the big mans shoulders from behind and pushed forward toward the table that Alex was standing on. He reached his hand down to the man and pulled him up, Janet springing up to stand beside him.

Alex took his beret off and held it high.

"What is the only way to get the badge on this cap?" He asked the now quiet crowd.

"You have to have fought with us right? And what is the only way to get this cap without taking the test?"

Alex made a circle around the table as he was talking ending up behind the big man.

"I think this trooper proved today he deserves both." He gently placed the beret in the right position on the big mans head. Then walked in front of him grabbed him in a hug, then put him at arms length.

"I will serve with you anytime any where Brother. Welcome to the One Hundred."

After a few seconds of stunned silence, the room erupted into load cheers. The big man was plucked off of the table like he was a feather. He was mobbed from every direction, getting hugs and kisses, and not just from the women. As he looked at their faces, he saw all of them with tears running down cheeks, but they were all boisterous and laughing. He felt his spirits start to rise. Then a load bang on the table in the centre drew everyones attention once again.

Janet was standing in the centre of the table a bottle of clear fire in each hand.

"Not so fast!" She yelled out. "The only way you keep that cap Bubu is if can down one of these in one go."

Then she demonstrated by spinning the cap off the one in her right hand, tilting it up and draining it.

"Argh" she belted out.

"Ok, Buba," she said wiping an arm across her chin. "Now I know you Bears can't handle this shit as well as we can. So we'll let you swig a beer after to cool down your throat."

The big man trapped the full bottle off her left hand, deftly spun the cap off and swilled it down. Then he turned around and looked at Janet.

"My name ain't Bubba," he growled. "My name is Charles and fuck you, Senior Sergeant, mam."

"Ut oh" someone in the crowd stage whispered and every one cleared room around the table waiting for the expected fire works.

"What did you just say Bubba?" Janet said.

"I said my name is Charles and Fuck you Senior Sergeant, mam." Charles said.

Janet came slowly down off of the table and stood in front of Charles with her hands on her hips and the space around the table widened as people scrambled to get out of harms way.

"Well Charles," Janet said. "I never fuck on a first date, but rules can be bent no?"

Then she dragged his head down to hers and gave him a kiss, before pushing the now stunned Charles back from her.

"Who the hell stole my beer?" She belted out, headed for the bar.

Charles felt an arm go around his shoulder as he stared after her.

"Quite something isn't she?" Alex said. "I'm Alex, Charles"

"Hey Alex," Charles said still following Janet with his eyes.

"You weren't the only one fighting by yourself today brother," Alex said. "She fought her way up to you and broke the pressure on you."

"That was her? All I remember was a big assed horse flaying anything around it with a rider swinging a sword around it like mad. Both killing or maiming everything in striking distance. I was about done when she showed up."

"That's what we do trooper," a small blond in an impeccable uniform said coming up with a group of officers behind her. "Pull Bears asses out the fire for them."

"Hey Marg," Alex said. "Slumming it?"

"Well someone has to come and keep all the riff raff in line," Margarete said then laughed. "Been getting all kinds of nasty complaints about the ruckus in here."

"Good job out there today Charles," Margarete said. "You need anything, or if these idiots get out of line with you, tell Alex to tell me and I'll come and kick some asses for you."

"She would too" Greta said. "My big brother around here someplace. He missed officers call. So did you by the way."

"Sent my senior captain," Alex said. "Had to much shit to handle here. No, he hasn't been around Colonel. I saw him once. He was surrounded by aides and such. I don't know how he handles it all. Can't anyone think for themselves around here? Nobody ever leaves the poor guy alone."

"Ya well," Greta said. "If you couldn't take a joke..."

"You shouldn't have joined," Alex finished for her.

And with that the officers breezed out as fast as they had come in.

"Can I ask a question?" Charles said. Alex nodded.

"How can all of you be so happy? Like me you lost people today and you guys are way tighter than we were. I don't get it."

Alex gestured to an empty table and poured each of them a glass of beer and motioned Charles to join him as he sat down. He looked down at his glass of beer for a few seconds then looked back up and right into Charle's eyes. Tears were riming them.

"I grew up with three of the injured and one of the dead," Alex said, his voice quivering. "So ya, it bothers me. But you know what? The day I put on this uniform, I was a dead man walking. Every day I'm still walking is a good day. That's how we all think. We live life to the fullest because tomorrow we may die."

He looked back down at his beer for a moment then looked back up. The tears were gone.

"Before every evening meal and before every gathering, we have a fast ceremony." Alex said. "It is fast and simple."

He raised his glass high.

"Absent comrades," he said and drained the beer. Then he filled it back up again. Now a smile on his face.

"Something else you will hear a lot around here," Alex continued. "Today is a great day to die."

"Was that your first fight?"

"Ya,' Charles answered. 'I knew it was going to be hard. but..."

"No shit," Janet said, sitting across from them with a full jug of beer. "We've been in more than our fair share of scraps, but that one was down right nasty. I can only imagine how it was for you guys. At least we knew what we were facing. The shit we did before? That was nothing compared to this deal today."

"Ya right," Alex said. "Just a few minor scraps. Ten green as grass rookies not even out of boot camp, killed four times their number if I recall."

"Are you kidding me?" Janet said. "Not the same deal at all. Shit, Marg killed five with that bow of hers before they even got close. Then Demi started laying about him with that big assed sword of his. All I did was stand there and shit my pants. Ok boys, I am totally wiped. I gotts to go before I fall on the floor."

"What was that all about?" Charles asked.

"She was one of the first ten," Alex said. "Like I said, green as grass. Even Demetri didn't really know how anything would work. One night they were attacked by at least forty bad guys, there may have been more. They formed a circle and took them on. Janet killed five herself.

"Something like you today Bubba."

"I told you, my name is not Bubba."

"If you say so Bubba," Alex said and laughed. "When you have had enough tonight, you're bunking in with me. I have an early morning so be quiet when you come in."

Chapter Twenty-two

Four troop transports from the stolen interstellar ships, had been brought in from the refinery, loaded with as many critically wounded as possible and sent to the capital. The four refuelling ships had been sent as well, loaded with fuel.

The first load of troop transports had returned with three ships loaded with medical supplies, the fourth with five back hoes. The back hoes were immediately pressed into duty digging trenches for the mass graves that were required for the many thousands of enemy dead and the over one thousand defender dead.

The pumping station had been turned on and fuel was flowing to the capital. Even running at over capacity, the refinery only supplied a third of what the capital required, let alone the rest of the planet.

Civil and military meetings were being conducted full time. District leaders were arriving daily to join the meetings and as fuel was being restored, flyers were arriving from other areas of the planet. The discussions were sometimes very vocal, at times threatening to become more than vocal. The emir had to step in more than once to keep order.

Through it all, the inhabitants of the fortress kept doing what they did, paying no attention to the goings on, nor taking part in, all the discussions. Not to say that meetings were not being held, just not with the other groups.

Also, through it all, Demetri was missing. As was Barney and ten other horses. Nobody was to worried. He would be back for the memorial. Except he wasn't.

All the speeches were done. The civilians had already started to disperse and the troops, who had been standing for hours, were about to be dismissed. One of the by now bored troops, had looked up at the hill opposite to the grave site. A single armoured rider, astride an armoured horse, stood at the crest of the hill. The riders lance was beside his right leg. The soldier called out to his officer pointing out this fact and the word quickly spread up the chains of command. Soon all of the assembled troops were looking at the lone figure up on the hill crest.

"Well," Greta said, "Now we know where Demetri is."

An unintelligible from that distance, order was shouted out and the horse began to slowly walk down the hill. A double file of ten armoured horses followed. Once the formation was a hundred paces down from the crest and two hundred from the massed troops the rider stopped.

"Troopers, form line!" was barely heard from the distant rider. Both files of horses broke their lines and formed up, five on each side of the rider.

The rider looked at both lines, then straight ahead.

"Troopers, at the walk. Advance to contact!" he yelled.

The rider and all ten horses, in a perfect line and in step, advanced down the hill at a walk. After a few steps, the walk turned into a trot. Then the rider tucked his lance under his arm, the horses crowded together until they were almost touching and they changed to a gallop. The air began to thunder and the earth to tremble, from hooves hitting the ground at the gallop. At 150 paces the rider began to scream his war cry, his lance perfectly straight and level beside his horses armoured right shoulder. At fifty paces, all the horses squatted on their rear legs and skidded to a stop. Then they spread out to five paces apart. The rider jammed his lance point first into the ground. Then he drew his sword from the scabbard at his back and raised it high in his right hand.

Then began the dance that all the Eagles knew and that many other people had heard about but never seen. The slow intricate moves of horse and rider, hooves and arms in sink. Then the tempo began to pick up and pick up again and dust began to rise from horses hooves and they were now at high speed. Hooves lashing out violently, necks flinging menacingly, teeth bared, ears laid back and they began to pivot in place while the rider slashed his sword violently on alternate sides. Then as one, facing the crowd, all the horses reared up on hind legs and flashed fore hooves violently in the air.

Then it was over. All eleven horses standing motionless. The rider flashed his sword, point upward in front of his visored face in salute and effortlessly, without looking, placed the sword back in its scabbard across his back, the hilt protruding above his left shoulder.

"Troop, at ease," the rider quietly said, and the horses relaxed, taking the weight off of one front and rear leg.

"We are here today to honour our dead," the rider said in a voice that was used to addressing troops in large formations so that all could hear. Those who knew that voice, knew it was Demetri.

"All the dead, our enemies included, fought bravely," Demetri continued. Now he and Barney were walking slowly across the formation. The Eagles noticing that not only had a red and dark blue, almost black, border had been added to Barney's armour, but that he had their cap badge on his head armour between his eyes. As did the other horses.

"Many of us are mourning the loss of relatives, friends and brothers and sisters in arms. Some of us are morning the loss of our horses. We had over five thousand horse casualties, three thousand of which are dead. Our horses are extensions of our selves. We are a team, we operate as one. The loss of your horse is as bad, or worse, than loosing your lover. The bond is so strong."

"Like ourselves, our horses fought bravely, none more so than these ten behind me. They continued to fight even when their riders went down. Fighting beside their brothers and sisters to try and keep them safe.

"Like ourselves, they mourn their brothers and sisters. The riders that will no longer be there as part of their lives."

While he had been addressing the troops, Demetri had been to both ends of the lines and was now back in the centre of the formation.

"Once the Eagles had crashed into the edges of the enemy formation, we began our dance toward the centre. At that point, one Eagle noticed the centre of our infantry lines was about to collapse and on her own, shifted to attack the rear of the enemy in a hope to relieve the pressure on the infantry.

"Senior Sergeant Janet Olynick, front and centre!"

Janet broke from her position in the troop line and marched in front of Demetri, coming to a foot stomping halt.

"About face!" Demetri ordered. "At ease," he quietly said after she had. She shifted her feet to shoulder width apart and placed both her hands into the small of her back.

Her uniform was perfect. Each decoration and brass button was gleaming, the creases of her trousers were perfectly straight and bloused perfectly around her shiny brown high boots. Her beret was level on her head just above her eyebrows with the gleaming cap badge centred above her right eye. Her face was expressionless.

"Senior Sergeant Olynick and her mount Morning Star, without thought of their own safety, left their lines and assaulted the rear of the enemy doing heavy damage to our infantry in the centre. Their assault was so violent and so effective, the enemy had no choice but to turn and address the threat she presented, allowing the infantry to begin their assault of the enemy lines.

"The actions of this single rider and her horse, saved thousands of wounds and deaths and was fundamental in the cessation of fighting.

"Senior Sergeant Olynick, you have my never ending gratitude and appreciation."

Demetri's voice was wavering at that point and he stopped speaking for a few seconds.

"There are only two ways you can earn the uniform and the eagle that the Senior Sergeant are wearing. The first is the same way all of the Eagles have done. Pass the qualification tests, successfully complete the training and the probationary period. The only way anyone in our army can obtain the crossed swords on the Senior Sergeants other collar, is to have been in combat. Many of you here now, have just received those crossed swords. The only way you can get the cap badge on her head is to be an Eagle.

"There is another way to obtain the uniform, beret and eagle.

"Trooper Charles Green, front and centre!"

Charles marched up to Demetri and saluted, then was ordered to face the lines and come to at ease. Other than the rank badges and the head gear, his uniform was identical to Janets. His beret was brown not dark blue and his cap badge was that of a Bear regiment.

"During the main defence, the regiment that trooper Green was attached to, were placed in the centre of the line, his company in the centre of the regiment. Their task was to hold the enemy and fully engage them, until the cavalry could hit the enemy from the sides and rear.

"Trooper Green had just recently joined the regiment from basic training and had never faced battle before. As such, he and his squad, all rookies, were placed in the rear of the formation. The enemy attack was so fierce and so effective, Trooper Green and his squad soon found themselves at the front of the fighting lines. In short order, trooper Green found himself alone. The companies to both sides were beginning to falter under the pressure. The reserve regiment had been ordered to fill the gap in the line, but it was doubtful they would arrive in time. Orders to pull back were being prepared.

"With skill, tenacity and pure ferocity, trooper Green, by himself, with just his pole axe, alone, held the enemy line at bay until Senior Sergeant Olyinick was able to come to his aide and relieve the pressure he was facing.

"Let there be no mistake. It was trooper Green that was the deciding factor in that battle and no other."

Then Demetri rode beside Charles, leaned over and removed his brown beret, then reaching under his left leg, removed a dark blue one and gently placed it on Charles' head.

"Trooper Green," Demetri continued, "I have been told you have no suitable horses. These horses behind me have no suitable riders. Would you accept the obligation to be these horses rider and care giver?"

"Yes sir!" Charles replied.

"And that is the other way to become and Eagle and wear our cap badge," Demetri said. "Janet, if you could grab a couple of troopers and assist Charles with getting his horses to our lines?"

Then without another word, Demetri turned Barney and rode off the field.

Chapter Twenty Three

The sun was beginning to go down and it was the end of a very long day for Margarete. She had been up before dawn, seeing to her children, then getting her uniform and her self in order. Then had come the inspection of the troops. Waiting for the time to assemble. Marching to the grave site and standing for hours while the memorial dragged on. Marching back to assembly area, supervising the dismissal of troops. Then, while her troopers and lower officer corps were able to return to barracks to relax, she and her senior officers had to endure more boring meetings that had little to do with them.

Finally, her duties for the day complete, she headed for the yurt that served as their home, dismissed her escort and entered. Demetri was out of his uniform sitting on a chair beside their small stove a baby in each arm. The tea pot and a large cooking pot were on the stove, a wisp of steam coming from the tea pot and the mouth watering smell of fresh bread and stew filling the yurt.

"Good," Margrete said. "My wayward husband has returned and even made supper."

She came over and kissed him, then started to remove the uniform and donned much more comfortable clothing.

"Thanks for holding down the fort," Demetri said. "You OK?"

"It has been more boring than anything else," Margarete said. "Our people don't really need instruction. They know what needs to be done and do it. Are they asleep and been fed?"

"Yes to both," Demetri said.

She held out her hands and took her daughter from Demetri and they both placed the babies into the single rocking crib. Demetri grabbed a plate from the small cupboard and filled it with stew, giving it to Margarete, then doing the same for himself.

They both sat down and began to eat.

"Are you OK Dem?" Margarete asked. "When you didn't show this morning, I began to get worried."

"I needed time to prepare the horses armour," Demetri said. "I didn't calculate the time it would take to armour them up, so was a little later than I had planned. But it worked out ok. I really did see what Janet and Charles were doing, but was to heavily engaged myself to help."

"When Janet was returning to our part of the camp, she found him sitting, all by himself in front of his squad tent," Margarete said. "So she chewed him out, then the rest of the tents around him and brought him to us. We had already made him an Eagle, you just made it official. Nice touch with the horses though."

"No brainer," Demetri said. "He needs trained horses, the horses need a rider. They will make his training easier."

"If they don't kill him," Margarete said and they both laughed. Mostly because it was true. Their horses were tough and not very forgiving.

"Hey! Tell these bums to let us in!" Greta yelled out from outside.

"Let her in John," Margarete called out to the head of the guard guarding the tent. The flap covering the yurts opening parted and Greta followed by Al and a tall man entered. All of them were in civilian clothing.

"Oh, so my lazy ass brother finally showed up eh?" Greta said, coming over and hugging Demetri.

"Not only that, but he cooked supper and put the kids to sleep," Margarete replied.

"You hear that Al? He cooked supper and looked after the kids."

"Only because he's in the shit house for disappearing for three days," Al replied. Everyone but the new man laughed.

"Demetri, Margarete, this is Gregory, the former commander of the Home Guard troops." Greta said.

Demetri stood and extended his hand to Gregory, who came to attention and bowed his head instead.

"Your Highness," Gregory said.

"What kind of BS did you tell this guy?" Demetri said. He had a frown on his face.

"I didn't say shit," Greta said. "All I said was that we were going to meet my sister in law, because I didn't know my lazy brother was here."

"That is true Your Highness," Gregory quickly interjected. "Her Highness, your sister only said we were coming to meet Your Highness Margarete."

"Cut the crap," Demetri said. "If you want to be formal, you can address me as general and Margarete Colonel. This Your Highness crap is inappropriate."

"But in my research, I found that you and your family are the actual rulers of this planet," Gregory said.

"Technically correct," Demetri said. "but even in the beginning, it was only as figure heads. The people rule themselves and we are only a very small part of the people."

"Oh," Gregory said.

"Have you had a chance to observe how all this operates?" Demetri asked.

"Yes," was the reply. "It would seem that some people are more reactive than others. For instance, your people seem not to be involved at all."

"That is not at all the case," Greta said. Now she was serious and the aw shucks attitude was gone. "Our people have been meeting every night. They will let Demetri know their wishes in the morning before the heads of the clans and ourselves attend tomorrows meeting."

"We have been operating under this system for more than five years," Demetri said. "We are organized in groups of thirty families who elect a representative to a local council who nominates one of their members to a clan council who nominates one of their own to represent the clan in the general council who brings their concerns to the over all leader of the people, who temporarily at this point, seems to be me.

"As I said, my families position has always been to have the people govern themselves, with us as the final say only if necessary."

"This system worked well for many generations, until the Holy Church involved itself into non secular business," Al said. "Until that time, we had a clear separation of church and state. The Church could express their concerns, but they could not intervene in the actual governing of the state. When they did, is when all the trouble began. The Church's clear intention to subvert first, then eliminate the Bekenbaum family if they did not go along."

"Hence the reason you and your comrades are here Gregory," Demetri said. "Home Worlds government has been completely circumvented by the Holy Church. The result of which was the deaths of many good brave men. The fact that the battle was telecast and sent not only to Home Planet, but other satellite planets as well.

"As far as this planet is concerned. Home Planet no longer has any say in our affairs."

"Enough of this talk," Demetri said and he pulled a bottle and five glasses down from the cup board poured each glass full and handed them to all.

"Absent comrades," Demetri said, raising his glass before draining it. Then he refilled his glass, placed the bottle on the table and sat down, motioning for the others to sit as well.

"How are your people Gregory?" Demetri asked.

"Better than can be expected Your... excuse me Demetri?" Gregory said and he received a nod and smile in return.

"Better than we expected Demetri," he continued. "Many of our relatively minor wounded are returning to us. The others are being treated well and there are many. Greta assures me everything that can be done is being done and that many will return to full health in due time. My men and I cannot express our thanks enough Demetri."

He then went on to say the food, contrary to everyone expressing their regrets as to the low quality and amount they were receiving, was actually better in quality and quality than what they received even on Home World. While living in tents was not normal for them in base, the tents were spacious and comfortable. Their guards were courteous, even helpful. The people they met were friendly, if perhaps slightly guarded, which they could understand.

"You do understand, that if you choose to stay you are welcome to do so," Demetri said. "Unfortunately, at this point we do not have the capability to send you back to Home World. But we will do our best to send those back who wish to do so."

"I would be lying if I told you everyone wants to stay," Gregory said. "I myself do as do many others. But many of the men are dubious and wary. You spent time on Home World, you know what it is like there. It may take some time, but I believe all of my remaining men will stay."

They talked about those and other topics for over an hour. Then Demetri stood.

"Look everyone," he said. "I have not been home for two weeks. Tomorrow morning I have to attend my peoples meeting and hear their decision. Then I have to attend the grand meeting of all the delegates. Later on, I have to address my military concerns at yet another meeting. So, if you don't mind, I would like to spend some time with Marg and the kids and get to bed early."

The three visitors rose and made their goodbyes, then left the tent to return to their own area of the military camp.

"He is so young," Gregory said. "So young, so much pressure on him."

"And so very much depends on him," Greta said.

Chapter Twenty Four

It was just after eight in the morning, when Demetri and Margarete walked out of their yurt. It had long ago been decided by the matrons of the clans, that it was unseemly for a high status woman to be looking after her own children, despite all of Margarete's protests, nurses had been found for the babies and that was that.

Although the first of the 3 meetings of the day were with the 5 clans representatives, which were normally low key affairs, the other 2 meetings were not. As a result, both Demetri and Margarete were dressed in the dark blue almost black, with blood red stripes down the seams of the pant legs and the tunics borders and seams, dress uniforms.

On route, they were joined by Greta and Al. Greta in her Eagles uniform, and Al wearing the scarlet tunic and blue trousers with large yellow stripe down the outside trouser seam, the Bears wore as dress uniform.

They entered the large walled tent that was the community tent and were ushered to a long table and shown where to sit along one side of it, while the five clan representatives sat opposite. Standing quietly at the back by the doorway and to one side, were Gregory, the young lieutenant who was his sole remaining officer and the grizzled veteran senior sergeant.

"My Lord," began one of the councillors. "We have agreed to the boundaries of our territories with respect to the Planetary Councils recommendations. They will run from the river twenty kilometres west of the military encampment and extend eastward across the Great Plains region to the mountain range in the east. Many of the tradesman and crafts men, merchants etc, have decided to stay here in the encampment and to make it a permanent settlement. Enough of them, that they make up their own clan."

"It has also been agreed to Award Senior Sergeant Olyinick and trooper Green baronies for their great deeds. In addition, we will be making the clans capital in the centre of our lands.

"We will be voting to keep the Emir as the Prime Minister, with your approval My Lord and to keep the Federal Government in the current Capital City.

"We are also recommending the original five who returned home from Home World with you, be given lands and be your representatives in the other provinces on Oaken My Lord. Again, with your approval."

"Very well, I agree," Demetri said. "Please address these with the main council for their approval this afternoon. Also, please ask the five if they wish this responsibility. I believe my sister Greta should be my representative for the clans lands. This will place me one step removed from my overall responsibilities to the planet.

"The Monarchy will require an official residence and small governmental building. I suggest on where ever the Clans Capital is made. I would also recommend the Clans military barracks and training centre be incorporated in the Clan Capital, as well as the barracks for the Monarchies personal troops.

"The Monarchy shall fund their personal troops themselves. As veteran citizens, the Queen and Myself, will be combining our land grants for our personal properties and herds. The Monarchy will also establish a residence in the Main Capital City, in order to attend official Planetary business. This residence, staff and maintenance, will also be funded by the Monarchy directly.

"All this has been written down and submitted to the Planetary Parliament for their and your, approval."

"Very well," the councillor who had spoken before said. "We will discuss the land grants among our own council My Lord, it is Clan business, not Planetary.

"Will Your Highnesses be attending the main council meeting?"

"Only for the official opening," Demetri said. "It would appear as though I am attempting to influence the proceedings other wise."

And, so it transpired. After a gruelling three months of meetings and parliamentary proceedings, Demetri and Margrete were finally allowed to travel to their own lands.

Of course, it was not permitted for them to be alone. The One Hundred accompanied them. As did almost a full battalion of administration troops, consisting of communications technicians, aides to parliament and such like.

A perfect spot to place the residence was found and construction began on first, horse corrals and barns, then the main residence, followed by barracks and offices for troops.

After a year of living in yurts, everyone was at last living in permanent buildings.

Margarete and Demetri could at last begin the task of being somewhat normal farmers and parents.

Also by R.P. Wollbaum

Baren und Adler
Baren und Adler

Bears and Eagles
Bears and Eagles
Eagles Claw
Eagle's Talon
As Eagles Swarm
Bears Maul
Desert Eagle
Eagle's Nest
Bears Maul and Eagles Claw

Oaken
Rebellion

Wind Riders
Oaken

Wind Riders Zebra
White Ghost
Wind Riders Mitchel

Standalone
Cal's Quest Part 1
Joss Lynn

About the Author

R.P. Wollbaum lives in the shadow of the Rocky Mountains in Southern Alberta Canada.

When not busy composing a new novel, he can be found exploring North America in 'Da Buss'.

Read more at www.bearsandeagles.com.